AT ANY PRICE

A GAMING THE SYSTEM NOVEL

Brenna Aubrey

Silver Griffon Associates
Orange, CA

Silver Griffon Associates
P.O. Box 7383
Orange, CA 92863

Publisher's Note: This is a work of fiction. Names, characters, places, and incidents are a product of the author's imagination. Locales and public names are sometimes used for atmospheric purposes. Any resemblance to actual people, living or dead, or to businesses, companies, events, institutions, or locales is completely coincidental.

Trademarked names appear throughout this book. Rather than use a trademark symbol with every occurrence of a trademarked name, names are used in an editorial fashion, with no intention of infringement of the respective owner's trademark.

Book Layout ©2013 BookDesignTemplates.com

Cover Art ©2013 Sarah Hansen, Okay Creations

Ordering Information:
Quantity sales. Special discounts are available on quantity purchases by corporations, associations, and others. For details, contact the "Special Sales Department" at the address above.

At Any Price/ Brenna Aubrey. – 2nd ed.
First Printing 2013
Printed in the USA
ISBN 978-1-940951-02-7

For Jeff

Acknowledgements

I am very grateful to a multitude of friends and family without whom this book would never have come into being: To Tessa Dare, Kate McKinley, Sabrina Darby , Leanna S. , Courtney Milan, Carey Baldwin, Martha Trachtenberg, and Sarah Hansen.

Still more thank yous go out to Courtney Miller-Callihan, Tammy Falkner, H.M. Ward, Monica Murphy, Leigh Lavalle, Marie Hall, Abby Zidle, members of the OCC-RWA chapter of Romance Writers of America, the Romance Divas, and the NAAU Facebook group.

Lastly but most importantly, a huge thank you to my family. Thank you, Mom for always encouraging me to develop my talent and never give up on my dreams. To my siblings, just 'cause. To my wonderful husband, who sacrifices daily for the sake of my art. And to my two little guys who understand (mostly) that when Mommy's upstairs with the door closed, they should tread lightly. xoxox

The Manifesto

A Virgin's Manifesto... Posted on the blog of Girl Geek on March 14, 2013

I WILL SHOCK MOST OF YOU, I THINK, BY STATING THAT AT THE NEARLY *unthinkable age of twenty-two, my hymen remains intact. No, I won't answer any questions about why this is. Yes, I am heterosexual. No, I won't go out on a date with you.*

Throughout history there has been a global truth established that a woman has higher personal value if she has kept herself "pure" until she reaches the married state. It is ubiquitous across all cultures.

In certain countries, that value is more than moral or philosophical; it's monetary. In India, for example, a husband expects to pay a bride-wealth to his bride's family in exchange for her purity.

In old Europe, a bride's family put up the money, called a dowry, that helped her make a favorable match. Money and property changed hands between the patriarchs of powerful families. And for all this, a woman was de-virginized on her wedding night, whether she loved her new husband or not—usually not.

1

Sex with a virgin was so valued in Japan that a wealthy man could "sponsor" a young apprentice geisha, called a maiko. *All of her upbringing and training with a mentor geisha was paid for, her living expenses and many luxuries provided by his hand. And in return for this enormous expenditure? The man gained the right of* mizuage, *the ritual in which he was given the privilege of taking her virginity. It was expected, that he would never see her again. So this expense was for that one night only.*

Virgins weren't just bartered to powerful and wealthy men, however, but were of value to the gods of the ancients across all cultures as well. Virgin sacrifices to the gods represented the ultimate offering in exchange for something needed, most usually by men. In legendary ancient Greece, the offended goddess Artemis demanded a virgin sacrifice in payment for the insult rendered against her by Agamemnon. The Greeks desperately needed the wind to sail for Troy in order to wage war, but the goddess had prevented it. Agamemnon's daughter, Iphigenia, and her mother, Clytemnestra, were tricked into appearing at the altar of sacrifice by talk of her impending wedding to the hero Achilles. Instead, Iphigenia was slain and the winds promptly blew. Off the previously becalmed heroes sailed, hardly fazed.

The ultimate prize in all of these examples was the woman's virginity and in most cases the woman in question hardly profited from keeping herself pure.

So I ask, in our day and age, can a woman change this pattern and profit from her own purity? I find myself in the unusual position of being able to find out.

I've decided to decry the crimes and impositions put upon my sisters since the beginning of time until now. And I offer, therefore, a new paradigm. One where a woman can sell her purity and enjoy the fruits thereof.

The right to my virginity will be ceded to the highest bidder.

1

I'D REFRESHED THE WEB PAGE AT LEAST TWENTY TIMES during that last hour, endless minutes slipping in between each click of the button. The Manifesto was reality now, and it was about to affect my future in a very big way.

In the end, I sat back in disbelief, the wind knocked from me. It was final. A complete stranger had just pledged to pay three quarters of a million dollars in exchange for my virginity.

I blinked a few times, looking at the figure, with all the zeros following, barely able to breathe. My mouth was as parched as the Mojave but I doubted I had the strength in my legs to get up and grab a glass of ice water.

As I leaned back in my chair staring up at the ceiling, my phone rang. Without even looking at the caller ID, I knew who it was.

"Hey Heath," I breathed.

"Welp, your crackball auction is now closed and it looks like someone wants to pay a freaking fortune to get in your pants. Are you ready to give up this redonkulous scheme yet?"

I took a deep breath and expelled it slowly, wishing my heart wasn't thumping like I'd just run a three-minute mile. "Of course not."

He sighed. "Yeah, I figured. But I'm not going to stop trying, Mia, you know that."

I grimaced. "And you almost never change my mind on anything, *you* know *that*."

He cursed under his breath. "This has been the longest and most expensive game of chicken that I've ever played," he said.

"I told you, I'm not backing out. My heels are dug in nice and deep."

He laughed. "That's not the only thing that's going in deep."

I gasped, sitting up. "Shut up. You promised you weren't going to taunt me about this."

"Fine. But we do this on my terms or we don't do it at all, just like we agreed. I'm not shitting you—I'll pull my support."

I sighed. "Yeah, yeah. You don't have to keep saying that. I get it."

"Stop rolling your big brown eyes. I'm not thrilled about having to sift through all the bullshit and find out what lech has been ogling your pictures on your website."

My stomach squeezed at his words and I didn't say anything for a long moment. This really was lunacy and every time I talked myself down from the panic that hovered at the edge of my consciousness, something else would trigger it to summit levels once again.

"You're not helping," I said, fighting to keep the irritation from my voice.

"Who the hell set up the damn thing? I'm a conscientious objector to your crazy 'new paradigm'—yes—but I'm still not going to leave you hanging."

Relieved, I coughed, wanting desperately to change the subject before he lapsed into another lecture about the self-destructive potential of my actions. "Okay so... Next steps?"

He cleared his throat. "I evaluate the top three bidders based on your all-important criteria. If they're losers, I move down to the next batch and so on until I find someone who isn't a dirty old creep, if indeed there *is* someone who isn't a dirty old creep."

"Okay, you have that list somewhere, right?" I grimaced, picturing the mountainous heap of papers and crap on his desk. He probably hadn't seen it in weeks.

"Christ, Mia. I don't need the damn list. I remember it all. He can't be married. Needs to provide a complete lab workup to rule out STDs. Umm..."

"See? You can't remember half of it." I paused. "Find the list and clean your damn desk once in a while."

He was riffling through paperwork on the other end. "It's right here under the pile of—"

"Shit?"

"I remember another one—criminal history?"

"Uh huh...And what else?"

"Ahh. Here it is, see I told you I'd find it right under my stack of Minecraft notes. Let's see—lab workups, marital status, yadda yadda, okay—proof of money set aside in an offshore holding account."

"And last but not least...?"

"A *really* big one?"

My eyes shot to the ceiling. Typical for him to jump to something like size mattering. "We don't all think like you do."

"Well yeah, that *would* be one of my criteria—what of it? The last one is that you both make an agreement that there will be no future contact between the two parties after the terms of the contract have been fulfilled."

I sat back. "Great. I'm in good hands, then."

"It's my job to make sure you *will* be."

That tight feeling in my gut wrenched again. "That's the plan."

"I've already got e-mails in to the top bidders."

My brows shot up. That was quick. It wasn't really like him to be so Johnny-on-the-spot like this. Heath—my best friend since the eighth grade and a surrogate older brother even if only by six months—was always this protective. When I'd showed him the Virgin Manifesto post about to go up on my blog, he'd freaked.

Fortunately, he calmed down and demanded to have control over the result. It was the compromise I had to put up with in exchange for his help and I knew I could trust him. Heath was the only man on this planet whom I did trust, actually.

We said good-bye and I closed my browser with a decisive click. I was sure my blog readers would demand a recap of the auction results tomorrow. This whole thing had gone semi-viral within the online community of gamers, and even beyond—*Huffington Post*, Jezebel, even Twitter. I squeezed my eyes closed, dreading the thought of writing that post. The readers would want answers and I didn't have any. Not yet, anyway.

Regardless, there'd been complaints for the past few weeks that the auction had interfered with my regular posts. After all, it was a gaming blog, for God's sake!

During the auction hoopla, most of my male readers had apparently come to the consensus that I rated an eight or higher. My opinion was probably closer to a solid six. But gamer dudes weren't usually too picky when it came to women in our community. The main requirements were that a woman was breathing and had reasonably-sized breasts. As a girl gamer, if you stuck your nametag across your cleavage at Comic-Con, you were likely to never have them meet your gaze.

With shaky hands, I went about the next few hours in a haze. I made some tea from the small box of expensive Orange Pekoe—my favorite. I allowed myself the treat because it was a special occasion and I vowed to reuse the bag for breakfast in the morning. Nowadays, I had to enact cost measures like that. My scholarship money had dwindled and expenses were barely being covered by the ads on my blog and my part-time orderly job at the hospital.

The auction idea had spawned from that necessity, despite the "high ideals" of the Virginity Manifesto. I honestly had posted it to open the conversation on reclaiming the age-old tradition of profiting from a woman's purity. And yes, I'd wanted to make a statement about the value of my virginity being used for my own gain. I firmly believed in those ideals but my number one motivation was money, security. After using most of my loan money to help Mom with her medical bills, I had nothing saved up for medical school.

My only option was to hock my future completely by weighing it down under the burden of impossibly huge student loans. Did I really want to graduate medical school and go into three years of residency and throw in an oncology fellowship on top of that?

I slipped an ice cube into the piping hot cup of tea and sipped at it while I broke out my study guides for the Medical College Admission Test (MCAT) with that same sinking feeling that accompanied my study sessions of late. I'd started out this year so hopeful that, with a retake, I could improve my abysmal score of the previous year. But as time had passed, it grew harder and harder to be optimistic.

The test was a little over three months away and there was still so much to review. With a deep breath I dug in and went over the topics for this week: hydrocarbons and oxygen-containing compounds. I checked the clock. I was due to meet Jon at the library for still more studying this evening. The group study would be the next day and, as always, I wanted to be ahead. If I didn't walk in to that session extra-prepared, I always felt as if I was making a fool out of myself.

So I got to work.

***

That night, I met Jon at the university library at our usual study carrel. And truthfully, I was grateful for the distraction from my mind's unswerving preoccupation with the auction.

"So?" Jon said as I settled into my usual chair.

I scrunched my brows at him. "What?"

"Can you come?" He looked at me with his pleading baby blues.

Jon and I had met during the previous year of premed at Chapman University. He'd transferred from one of the high-and-mighty Ivy Leagues. I never did get the full story on what happened there. It wasn't like he was saving money by going to Chapman, a private university with a steep price tag.

My undergraduate tuition had been covered by my academic scholarship and I had worked extra hard to finish the requirements for graduation in three and a half years instead of the usual four, so this last semester was dedicated to work and study. If I didn't improve my MCAT score, this would all be for naught and I'd be looking for something else to do with my BS in biology.

Because of the low score on the test, I was forced to work in a gap year I hadn't planned on because no medical school would have looked at my application with a score of under 20—even though my GPA was 4.0. I would have to wait for a higher score in order to apply to medical school. So, I was using this time to look on the bright side of things. There was no denying that I needed the time to gather funds. My gaze flitted across the table to my study partner with more than a little envy. Jon had no financial concerns and was headed straight to medical school after he graduated next year.

Seeing my continued blank stare, he heaved a great sigh. "Did you forget to charge your phone again?"

I reached into my bag and pulled it out. Dead as a doornail. I sent him a crooked smile and a shrug. "I don't do the texting thing much. I already told you."

He ran a hand through his curly blond hair. "Mia, you need to enter the twenty-first century. First of all, only old people have phones like that," he said with a disgusted wave of his hand.

I pulled my phone back, a protective wave of misplaced affection rising in my breast. What was wrong with a prepaid plan? And dare I tell him that the reason I hadn't received the text was not because I had forgotten to charge the phone but because I was out of minutes and had no money to make my monthly payment?

He knew I was a typical struggling student. He just didn't know quite how much because I never ever invited him to my place. One look around my dive studio and he'd know my financial circumstances in an instant.

I'd never had guys at my place, aside from Heath, but even he usually sniffed down his nose at my converted studio. We had been roommates until the year before when he and his steady boyfriend had decided to move in together. Due to my financial constraints, I'd had to trade down, way down, to my studio that rested above the detached garage on one of those cute vintage craftsman homes. Unfortunately, it was hotter than hell in the summer and a deep freeze—if that was possible in Southern California—in the winter.

"So what were you asking me?" My chest clenched in dreaded anticipation. *Please don't ask me out again. Please don't ask me out again.* I was getting tired of telling him no. He was more persistent than most guys. I tucked a strand of long dark hair behind my ear and looked at him expectantly.

"There's this dinner…" He stopped when I took a deep breath and shot him a look. When I didn't say anything, he continued. "It's a charity event. My parents participate every year and asked me if I'd attend since they can't make it down."

"When?"

"Next week."

"Dress?"

"Formal."

"I don't do those types of events." To say nothing of the fact that I didn't have anything to wear that could even remotely be classified as "formal."

"C'mon, Mia," he breathed, with a groan. "It's not like I'm asking you to marry me."

My back straightened and a tense ball tightened between my shoulder blades. I tried to feel flattered by his obvious attraction, but

I truly found it more of a hindrance to our quality study time. "I'm sorry. Please don't take it personally. I just don't date."

He shook his head, blowing out a breath. "And you are never going to end up with anyone if the only guy you ever hang out with is gay."

I breathed in through my nose and out through my mouth. I knew he didn't mean any harm. He got along well with Heath, actually, had mentioned that Heath could take him easily (kind of a stupid comment because Heath could take out most guys—I was glad to have him on my side).

"What makes you think I'm interested in getting together with anyone?"

Jon sat back, frowning. He was a good study partner and a nice person or I really wouldn't bother. But this was getting tiresome and I knew I needed to get him to drop his delusion or else start looking for a new study partner.

His face fell and I couldn't suppress a twinge of regret. I'd never sought to hurt his feelings, so I figured I'd throw him a bone. "How about we go out for a celebratory drink after the test?"

His eyes lit up. He really was a good-looking guy. A guy I could see myself dating, if I dated. But I'd just about made it through all of undergrad without ever dating a single guy. We went out in groups and I'd been asked out here and there before word got out that I wasn't here for social reasons.

Besides, spending almost all of my spare time playing online computer games and tinkering on my blog tended to kill a social life. And mine had died years ago.

"Okay." He smiled and took up one of his computer-generated note cards. "Name all oxygen-containing compounds that are also acid derivatives."

I took a deep breath, hoping that little concession to softness wouldn't ultimately bite me in the ass. Then I answered the question.

***

The first ring of the phone was included in my dream. I was about to cut into a cadaver during my first year of Gross Anatomy in some nondescript medical school class. I'd placed my scalpel against the skin, ready to cut away the subcutaneous tissues, like I'd read in my books on cadaver dissection, and the corpse began to ring like a telephone.

On the second ring, I was ripped from my dream and so groggy I could hardly place where I was.

I checked the caller ID and fumbled for the receiver.

"Mom," I breathed, reaching for the clock. Seven thirty a.m. Why did she always insist on calling so early?

"Were you sleeping?"

I cleared my throat. "No."

"Liar," she said. "You need to start training yourself to get early. Doctors don't keep late hours."

"Aspiring doctors keep late hours when they have been up half the night studying."

She sighed. "Well, that's no good, either. If you end up exhausting yourself by the time that test rolls around, you won't be worth a single question."

I rolled my eyes as my head fell back onto the bed. *Yeah, that made me feel so much better, Mom. Thanks.* I settled my head against my warm pillow. "Why did you call me this fine morning?"

"I want to know if you need any money," she said lightly.

I gritted my teeth, feeling my jaw bulge just under my cheeks. In my best, light voice I said, "No. I'm just fine..."

"Last night when you weren't home, I tried calling your cell phone." *Shit.* She'd got the recording that said the phone was no longer in service.

"Oh, I must have forgotten to pay the bill."

"Emilia Kimberly Strong."

"I'm fine, Mom. I get paid this Friday."

Irritation crawled up my spine like a swarm of ants in search of a picnic. Like she had the right to get upset with me for lying to her when she was lying to me in the first place! I'd seen the notice of mortgage default the last time I was at home. Second warning, third. Late fees.

She was barely afloat with the ranch. The entire time I'd grown up she'd never had a mortgage. She'd bought the ranch outright when I was just a baby with the money that the Biological Sperm Donor—my not-so-affectionate term for the male who had fathered me—had paid her to go away and have her baby somewhere else.

"Mia, you'd tell me if you needed anything, wouldn't you?" *Mom, you'd tell me if you were about to be turned out by the bank, wouldn't you?* I longed to reply with those words but as usual, lacked the courage to even bring it up.

The ranch—a sort of cross between a guest "dude" ranch and a western-themed B and B—was Mom's livelihood. But she hadn't been able to run it properly since the cancer diagnosis and treatment. So she'd had to take out a mortgage to help cover her medical bills.

I managed my fake-bright voice again. "Of course, of course. Love ya!"

"We haven't even talked—what—"

And damned if the call waiting didn't click through at that moment. I checked the ID Thank you, Heath! If I could reach through the phone wire and kiss him, I would. I loved that guy.

"Mom, Heath is calling through and I think it's pretty important. Can I call you back?"

"I'll call you. It's long distance."

"Okay. Maybe tomorrow?"

"Tell him I said 'hi' and I'm still waiting for him to come up with you next time so I can see him."

"Sure, sure. Love you, Mom." And I clicked off to take the waiting call, took a deep breath and sat up.

"Dude."

"Dollface."

"What's up?"

"I got it narrowed down to two guys. I'm going to meet with both of them within the next few days."

"They're in the area?"

"One of them doesn't live too far away, actually. The other one is back east but he's flying out on business this Thursday. I can meet him then."

My heart kicked up to high-speed velocity. "Okay. What—what are they like?"

"The younger guy is only sixty-two—"

I tensed. *"What?"*

"Kidding."

I sat back in relief. Shoulda known. "Asshole."

"The third guy was kinda up there. Almost fifty. He was a 'no' based on other criteria, too. The younger guy is only a few years older than me. The other one is in his thirties. Pretty yummy. *I'd* do him, but you know I like blonds."

So the younger guy wasn't blond. "What else can you tell me?"

"Rich as hell, of course. Both keenly interested, especially after I sent them the face shots."

I rolled my eyes. Aside from his many other technical achievements—Heath designed and built websites for his day job—his beloved pastime was digital photography. And he was very gifted at it. He was the one who'd insisted, when I'd cooked up this crazy scheme in the first place, on dressing me up in a bikini (one I bought at Anthropologie and ended up returning because it was way beyond my price range). He took snapshots of me on the rocks of the jetty at Corona Del Mar beach.

The pictures he'd posted on the auction website were from the neck down. I guess I had a nice figure even if my breasts were pretty small. But I was on the taller side, which gave me the side effect of long legs. Nevertheless, I'd been pretty sure that my lack of surgical enhancement or fake bake tan would affect the results of the auction. But apparently that wasn't the case.

Despite how much I knew it was time to get it over with and just lose it, it wasn't just a matter of surrendering my virginity to the guy willing to pay the most. I had a carefully laid-out plan in place. First he'd have to submit to a thorough screening by my "bouncer."

"Yes, I'm going to have to find a way to appropriate the one who doesn't win you."

I laughed. "Let me know how that works out for you. Then again, maybe not. I'd rather not know."

"I'm meeting the Californian guy tomorrow for lunch in Irvine. After I meet the New Yorker, I'll be in touch. I asked them both for medical records and I'm having some background checks run."

"It all sounds good."

"Mia, I need to tell you this again, it's not too late to back out of this. Once money is exchanged and plans are made, it's a done deal. But you still have that freedom to walk away and be completely anonymous. I mean, this is not an easy thing to ask of yourself. You've never had sex before and planning to do it with a complete stranger—"

"Heath—"

"I mean, I did make sure to put into the language of the auction that you might require a 'get to know you' period. Maybe a few dates first so it's not just so—sudden?"

I shook my head, trying to suppress a rising mound of frustration. We'd been over this before—several times. "I already told you I'd rather not know him. I just want to get it over with as quickly as possible. It's not a romantic act for me—just a bit of skin. I have no emotional attachment to it. It's high time I lost it. This way, I can move on with my life with a nice fat bank account."

There was a long silence on the other end of the line. I sat up and squeezed my eyes shut and thought of my mom. She'd need another melanoma therapy vaccination soon and those came dear, especially with no medical insurance. She'd probably refuse to get it and choose to pay the mortgage instead. Anger at our helplessness burned at the edge of my awareness. "I told you I'm not backing out."

"Okay. I just felt obligated to say it again."

"And again. And again."

"Right. Now I'm going to ask you another question that will annoy you."

I braced myself but didn't say anything.

"What do you think your shrink would say about this?"

I arched an eyebrow. "I haven't seen Dr. Marbrow for years." I couldn't afford *her* anymore, either. "She released me to my own recognizance. Declared me all healed."

"Riiight."

"You think I'm crazy?"

He sighed. "I think that the shit you were dealing with takes a long time to get over."

I swallowed. Six years wasn't long enough? If not, then how much would it take? A decade? Fifteen years?

"I'm a tough woman," I breathed.

"Hell yeah, you are. I'm just saying—"

"Okay, that's all the preach you get today. No more. Talk to you at the end of the week. I gotta start getting ready for work."

"Are you logging in tonight?" he asked.

"It's our regular game night. You know I'm always there."

"Any word from Fallen?" Heath referred to a regular member of our group by his game name—FallenOne—as we all did, since he'd never given us his real name. We'd all been gaming together for over a year, along with another good friend from Canada, and Fallen hadn't been making our regular group nights for nearly two months.

"I'm not sure what's going on in his personal life right now."

"He hasn't told you? You two talk about everything."

"Not anymore," I said with a twinge of regret. I knew that Fallen read my blog. He'd vehemently opposed the Manifesto. We'd been up half the night in game text chat arguing about it. Was he upset with me because of the auction? The thought of losing friends over this thing didn't please me, so I hoped this wasn't the case.

After we ended our call, I hopped out of bed and into the shower, then pulled on my scrubs and headed to the hospital. And I tried to keep my mind on what I was doing and not the issues that Heath had dug up—nor the end results of the auction. With any luck, things would be all taken care of before I had to retake the MCAT. I could only hope, anyway.

2

I PASSED THROUGH THE NEXT WEEK LIKE AN AUTOMATON, GOING through the motions at work, on my blog, getting various things done. I felt poised on the brink of something—something big. But I wouldn't let myself entertain that idea. This had to be smaller than me. This had to be an insignificant moment in my overall timeline. Soon it would be over and I'd move on with the rest of my life.

But I couldn't help wondering what person I would end up with. If I was lucky, I'd find him attractive, at least. Maybe he'd be good, gentle. He didn't have to be amazing as I was hardly in a position to judge, given my lack of experience.

Ideas like these flickered through my mind and a couple times I caught myself fantasizing about this mystery guy and jumping every time the phone rang as I waited to hear back from Heath. Thus, when the phone finally did ring, it was no surprise that I was, again, in bed—this time for a quick nap after an overnight shift working in the ER.

"What?" I mumbled into the receiver, still mostly asleep.

"Were you sleeping?" Heath's amused voice came over the line.

"Mm. Late shift last night, this morning."

"Ah, okay. Well...get up and brew yourself a pot of coffee because I have your winner and he wants to meet you this afternoon."

I groaned. "He can wait. I'm half dead, Heath. Can't we do this tomorrow? It's my day off and I need some warning—I haven't done laundry for—"

"No can do, doll. He has to fly to the east coast on business first thing tomorrow. He won't be back until the end of the week."

"Heath..."

"Come on. I've reserved a private conference room at the Westin South Coast Plaza."

I remembered my one serious skirt—a crisp business pencil skirt—was at the bottom of the clean laundry basket, wrinkled beyond recognition. And my iron was broken.

"I have to iron my skirt."

"I'll bring my iron when I pick you up."

"I don't have a board, either."

"Then use the table, for chrissakes. Listen, I'm not here to solve your first-world, heterosexual female problems. Get up, get your makeup on and get with the program."

I sighed and hung up, my heart racing. It occurred to me that he didn't tell me whom he'd selected.

I followed his instructions, got up, showered, styled my hair and, surrendering to the inevitable, pulled it back into a ponytail because it wasn't cooperating. My makeup went on satisfactorily and I was in my blouse—white, tailored button-down—and skivvies when Heath showed up. He didn't have his iron.

"What the hell, Heath?"

"I couldn't find it. I think that stupid little twerp swiped it when he packed his crap and left." He referred to the recent demise of his two-year relationship. It had not been a good breakup and Heath was still nursing the broken heart from it.

I shot him a puzzled look. "Who steals an iron?"

"Spoiled little brats like Brian, that's who."

I sighed and glanced at my pathetic excuse for a skirt.

"Why don't you hang it up in the shower and run the hot water?" he asked.

"Give my skirt a shower?"

"The steam will take some of the wrinkles out. A dryer works, too."

"Well I don't have a dryer, so I guess steam is going to have to do. Do you think it will work?"

"Hell no, but might as well try."

I ran the shower until the hot water ran cold—which didn't take long in my little studio. Since living here, I'd become the queen of the snappy shower. When I pulled the skirt off the hanger and tried to smooth out the damp cloth, it failed to cooperate.

Once dressed, I left the bathroom. Heath made a face and twirled his finger, signaling that I should turn around.

I complied. "That bad?"

He shrugged. "It doesn't take a fashion expert to see that that thing is a hot mess—literally."

I blew out a breath. "How much time do we have? Maybe swing by the mall to pick up a loaner?"

He pulled out his cell phone, glanced at it and shook his head. "You're going like that. Besides, he's not paying the big bucks to sleep with your skirt, fortunately for you."

I glared at him. "Sometimes you annoy the shit out of me."

"I know." He shrugged and jerked his shoulder toward the door and walked out. I followed him into a gorgeous spring afternoon.

Once in his blue Jeep Wrangler, Heath maneuvered his way to the nearest freeway entrance down sleepy residential streets cloaked in bright purple jacaranda and whispering pepper trees. Out on the wider boulevard, towering palms—ubiquitous in Southern California—shivered in the cool ocean breeze.

"So who is this guy?" I asked him as we zipped down the 55 freeway.

"You'll find out soon enough. Name's Drake." He shot me a glance like I should know who that was. "Adam Drake."

"And which rich dude is he?"

"The one from out here. Lives in Newport Beach, of course. Don't they all?"

I snorted. "And you said he's young?"

"A bit older than we are. Twenty-six."

"So how'd he get so rich? Trust fund? Daddy's company?"

"Nope, he's completely self-made, actually."

That bit of info blew me away. "How is that possible at his age?"

"He's a software architect—video games."

My mouth opened in surprise. Heath's sense of irony was not lost on me. "I can see why you picked him. He develop anything that I know?"

Heath shrugged. "Maybe."

I shot him a pointed glance. "Just how thorough was your background check?"

"Oh God. I think I know him like a brother by now. We spoke on Monday for three hours. Then had another long chat on

Wednesday on the phone. I was already half in love with him before I even met Mr. New York."

I snorted again.

"Yeah, don't do that when you are in there. He might back out of the whole thing if he hears you laughing like a piglet."

I slapped his shoulder with the back of my hand and he grinned.

Not half an hour later, we sat at a glass and chrome conference table in black leather chairs, sleek granite décor ensconcing us in all that was modern and exuding wealth. I'd driven by this hotel many times but never been inside—and never hoped to have the chance to stay in a place so nice.

My hands drummed on my lap, slapping against my bare knees. Heath stopped me once by placing his large hand across mine but I only resumed the minute he removed it.

"You're driving me up a tree with that."

I shot him a look. He'd just have to deal with my nerves. "Are we really that early?"

"No, he's late."

"If he was that anxious to meet me today, shouldn't he be here on time?"

"He's coming up the 405. After three, it's an instant parking lot. He's probably stuck in traffic."

I huffed. "Can't he take the filthy rich limo lane or something?"

Before I could even finish my sentence, two men approached the frosted glass door into the conference room. One of them leaned forward to snap open the door. He was the taller of the two and wore his dark hair in a close-cropped style. The other man—well, I hardly noticed him when I locked eyes with the first man's obsidian stare.

Heath and I jerked to our feet. My pulse ratcheted up to a near-fatal rate, threatening acute hypertension. The first guy with the dark eyes was the software mogul—I would have bet my every measly belonging on it. He hesitated at the doorway once he'd caught a full glimpse of me and my breath caught when I looked into his stunningly handsome face.

He was about six feet tall and wearing an expensive suit—the kind with a vest under the jacket that looked like it had been tailored for him, hugging his tapered waist and slim hips. The suit looked so good on him that I knew it had to be designer, even though I was the first one to confess that I knew nothing about designer anything.

He was finely built but not imposing. His slacks clung to muscular thighs, his jacket stretched across solid but not broad shoulders. His suit was a crisp, steel gray with a slightly darker shirt and tie. The silver tie clip caught the light and my eyes flicked to it and then back to his face. He had the chiseled masculinity of a marble god. All angles and strong, clean lines.

My heart felt like it might fibrillate or—as a nonmedical student would say—flutter. I'd never been so strongly affected by a man. Especially one I'd only just laid eyes on. His dark eyes met mine and my chest felt like it was about to explode. He stopped, his eyes narrowing. While he gave me the once-over, I sucked in a lungful of air because I'd almost forgotten to breathe during this initial lightning strike.

Shit. It was at that precise moment that I realized I was in trouble.

Drake never took his eyes off of mine, not until he came to a stop just opposite the conference table. He moved like a cat—a sleek predator.

Heath leaned forward, offering his hand and Drake finally looked away to shake hands with him, an arrogant smile on his lips. "Good to see you again, Bowman," he said with a clear, deep voice that only made my heart race faster.

His voice was a caress—a gentle but firm hand that skimmed down my bared spine to settle in a tight fist just at the base. Every sense came alive and my awareness of everything around me heightened. Elevated respiration. Increased perceived body heat. Speedy pulse. Classic signs of sexual arousal.

I almost fell off my heels in shock over the strength of it. Was this *me?* Me? Who'd wondered for at least a year if I might be a lesbian because I didn't find any men I met attractive?

His gaze flicked back to me as Heath laid a hand on my shoulder. "This is our semi-famous blogger, Girl Geek."

Drake's chin tilted in a fetching way as he seemed to be studying me. I bit my lip, every nerve pulling taut. It was amazing how the body's response to arousal and fear were so very similar. And at that point, I'd have been hard put to discern the difference.

Drake waved a hand to my seat while he took his. I sank slowly into mine, the leather sticking to the backs of my sweaty knees. I looked at the man flanking him for the very first time, suddenly realizing I hadn't even spared a thought or a glance for him before this. He was older, balding, with a middle paunch and appeared in his midfifties. He carried a briefcase and appeared to be a lawyer. When I looked back at Drake, I almost jumped at the intensity of his gaze. His eyes shot points right through me, like icy darts. My eyes held his but I swallowed what felt like a watermelon in my throat and tried to ignore the pulse bumping at my temple.

Heath began riffling through a stack of papers on the table before him and Drake looked away from me to follow what Heath was doing. By coincidence, I'm sure, I finally remembered to take a breath at that exact same moment.

Heath pulled out the paper he was looking for and Drake turned back to me. "So do I call you Girl Geek or do I get to know your name?"

I cleared my throat and refolded my hands in my lap. "My name is Mia."

His eyebrows rose. "Mia?"

I fought the urge to fidget, tightening my hands on top of my bare knees. He looked down, as if watching my hands through the glass table. "Emilia. But everyone calls me Mia."

A small smile danced on his lips when he looked up again and met my gaze. "I'm not everyone." His eyes traveled down to my conservative neckline—but no lower, to his credit—and back. *"Emilia."*

My fists clenched. Was he deliberately trying to provoke me with this arrogant attitude? Because if it was unintentional, then this was a *really* bad sign.

Drake cleared his throat and looked pointedly at Heath's stack of papers. "So let's go over the particulars of the contract. Is this just about the penetration of one organ by another or are there specifics laid out? What about touching, kissing? How many times? What about kink?"

My jaw dropped. I couldn't help it. I scrutinized him and he seemed to detect my study even though he was looking at Heath. His sensual mouth tugged up at the corners. That's when I realized that this *was* deliberate. Was it an act?

I turned to Heath, who appeared to be barely able to contain his laughter. He looked at Drake with a strange expression. "That's a lot to cover. And this is a strange venue to do it."

Drake shrugged and his eyes flicked back to me. "How about we just start with deal breakers, then?"

I exchanged a glance with Heath, who nodded and turned back to Drake. "I know of one that we can discuss right now. There will be no fellatio."

Drake leaned forward. "Excuse me?"

I folded my arms tightly against my chest, already burning with resentment. "You heard him correctly. No cocksucking." Yeah, I said it. If *he* could be deliberately provocative, then why couldn't I?

His black eyes darted to mine, mildly amused, still insufferably brash. "Are you on birth control?" he asked abruptly. I blinked. He was definitely one-upping me in the obnoxious department.

Drake's lawyer jerked a surprised look at him, frowning, clearly surprised by the abrupt behavior. Well, at least that was a sign that this sort of thing was unusual from Drake. Still didn't excuse him, though. "All of that is delineated in the paperwork for the terms of the auction, Mr. Drake. Yes, I'll be using birth control but there will also be condoms—"

I stopped as his handsome face split into a patronizing grin. "If I'm going to lay down a fortune for the privilege of experiencing your quivering virgin flesh, I think it goes without saying that I expect to do it without a barrier."

I sat back, clenching my teeth so hard that my head started to ache. My gaze was held fast by the challenge in his ebony eyes. He might have been the most gorgeous creature I'd ever laid my eyes on, but he was also an asshat.

He tilted his head at me, puzzled. "Why is that a problem? If we are both cleared by a physician—"

I unclenched my jaw just long enough to reply. "Recent medical clearance is not sufficient for me. I'd require celibacy for at least the previous six months, so—"

"Then there isn't a problem."

I highly doubted that. I opened my mouth to call him a liar when Heath leaned forward and put his hand on the table in front of me.

Drake's lawyer cleared his throat, throwing a bland look at me and turning to Drake. "We can work all these details out later in mediation. Mr. Drake does have a plane to catch later today."

Drake's eyes darted to Heath and back to me. I could tell he was trying to gauge our relationship. It wasn't the first time a person had looked at the two of us in that unsure, questioning way. Heath was not obviously gay in any way. He wasn't "fabulous" or flamboyant. He was very masculine in his behavior and mannerisms, so he rarely set off people's gaydar.

My gaze turned back to Drake, drawn to him like a flame pulled into a hot, dry wind. I resented the heat on my cheeks. I was not a habitual blusher. Hardly ever, actually. But this man was bringing my Irish up, as my mother liked to say. And what was worse, the more annoyed I grew with him, the more amused he seemed to be.

Drake flicked a glance at Heath and then his lawyer. "Gentlemen, could you excuse us for a moment? You're free to wait just outside the door." Then, almost as an afterthought, he glanced at me. "*If*, of course, that is okay with the lady?"

My face flamed hotter and I folded my hands on my lap. "Fine," I said, wondering if the thirty-something New Yorker was still interested in the deal. There was no way he could be more offensive than this jerk.

Heath looked at me for confirmation and I nodded. He patted me on the shoulder and the two men exited, leaving the two of us across the table from one another, staring.

Finally he cleared his throat and laid his hands on the table before him, lacing his fingers together and dropping his gaze. "I'm sorry if my bluntness has offended you. I assumed that a woman who has placed herself on the block like you have would be comfortable with straight talk."

I laughed. "Oh, is that what that was? I just thought you were being an asshat."

When he smiled, the arrogance was gone and the most delicious dimple appeared at the side of his mouth. I wanted to lick that dimple, to know every nuance of its taste. I shifted in my seat, furious with myself. Why couldn't I control these crazy, darting thoughts?

"Mr. Drake. You are not leaving me with the best impression of yourself—"

I cut off at his dry chuckle. "Do I need to? I thought my bank account did that for me."

Anger sizzled hot and my muscles tensed. I breathed in one long draught and then released it. "I am not a prostitute and I'll thank you not to treat me like one."

"You've sold yourself. You may not see yourself as one, but clearly..." His eyes traveled down my body again.

I shook my head. I couldn't understand his motivation for provoking me like this. As beautiful as he was, each time that he opened his mouth I was finding it harder and harder to picture myself in bed with him. "One night in my life and a bit of broken skin does not constitute prostitution."

His dark gaze intensified, as if with one long, determined gaze he could break through my defenses. I drew back.

"Sex for money is prostitution."

I shrugged, determined not to let him see that he was getting under my skin. "I prefer not to put a label on it. One night of my life does not define me."

Those generous, sexy lips turned up in a knowing smile. "A lot can happen in one night."

I couldn't look away no matter how much I wanted to. My heart pounded, pulse screaming through my veins in concerted throbs, but my head kept telling me to kick this asshole to the curb. There were many things I would do for almost a million dollars. Submitting to this overinflated jerk might not be one of them.

He looked at me with an analytical expression that I might wear while studying platelets under a microscope. "It takes a curious type of morality to save one's self for so long only to sell off that asset to the highest bidder."

My jaw tightened. It was getting harder and harder to cloak my irritation with him. "You didn't pay to get inside my *head*, Mr. Drake."

To cover my discomfort, I pushed Heath's stack of papers across the table to him. "Here's the fine print—everything that I could think of."

He flicked a glance at them and then away, almost bored. "I'm not going to read through that now, obviously. And, of course, I'll have addendums of my own. Along with a nondisclosure agreement."

I frowned. No one had said anything about an NDA to me. "You do know that I'm a blogger, right?"

"Of course. But, aside from your Manifesto, you blog exclusively about gaming, not your sex life. The document is pretty standard, with a little extra wording about our special situation"

He pushed a single sheet of paper across the desk to me. I looked it over. It did, indeed, seem standard, and it specifically mentioned the fact that I could not blog about our night together. I'd never planned to go into any details. I don't write that kind of blog. But I did plan to mention that it had happened. I did have credibility to maintain, after all.

With a bored sniff, I asked for a pen, surprised that he handed me a two-dollar plastic thing instead of a platinum- and gold-plated ostentatious rich guy's pen that shouted, "Look at me, I'm disgustingly wealthy." I hurriedly scratched out my signature on the form.

As I pushed it over to him, I said, "I'm going to need a copy of that."

He bent and signed the paper as well and I had a chance to admire him unnoticed for a few seconds. He really was unbelievably handsome. My heart hadn't stopped drumming its silly ska tempo since he'd walked in the door.

"Of course," he murmured, taking out a shiny chrome-plated smart phone from his breast pocket to photograph the document. After a moment, he typed some commands into it and looked up at me. "Heath Bowman now has a copy in his e-mail. He can forward it to you. I'll have a physical copy mailed to you as soon as possible if you put your address on the back of the form." I bent and complied, hurriedly scratching down my address.

I straightened, ready to give his attitude back to him, now. "It's too bad, really, that I won't be able to write about it. I could have made it sound so mind-blowing—I might even have thrown in a few 'earth-shatterings' for good measure."

A smile played about his sexy mouth as he tucked his pen back into his jacket. "Oh, our encounters will be all that and more."

I shook my head, hiding, yet again, the shock at his words. "It's one night, Mr. Drake. That 'encounters' should have a parentheses around the s."

His look could only be interpreted as smug. "*Encounters...no* parentheses necessary."

My heartbeat slammed against my ribs. Why was his arrogance turning me on? I wanted nothing more than to slap that smug look off his handsome face.

His gaze brazenly lowered to my cleavage and breasts, lingering there. My nipples tightened in automatic response and without looking down I knew he could see. I cursed the fact that I had opted to wear a thin, white blouse.

His eyes returned to mine and this time his face split into a boyish grin. "This is going to be *fun.*"

Self-consciously I folded my arms tightly across my chest, covering my traitorous breasts. I fumbled for something smartass to say in return but failed.

"I'm sorry to make this brief, but I'm on the way to a business meeting. We can work out all the details so that we're both satisfied. I'll be reachable by e-mail, however. Or you can text me."

I almost fell over in relief at the news that he was leaving. I wasn't sure I could take ten more minutes alone in a room with him.

Which didn't bode well for our night. Alone together. Naked. In a bed.

A bead of sweat trickled down the side of my temple. How did he manage to look so cool and crisp in his umpteen-thousand-dollar suit? And how did he manage to look so young and yet act like a thirty-something businessman at the same time?

I cleared my throat. "My cell phone isn't working."

His forehead creased for a moment and he opened his mouth, shook his head and then closed it as if he'd changed his mind about what he was going to say. "I have nothing but your best interests, health and safety in mind, Emilia. Both physically and legally."

Nothing else? Again, I highly doubted that. My skepticism must have been apparent because he settled back, dark brows rising just a little. "Well, I do have my own expectations of how this should go, of course."

I smirked, hoping this time to get some kind of reaction from him. "Of course you do."

But his eyes only narrowed as he stood. I mirrored his actions and he waited for me to come around the table before walking toward the door alongside me. He stood so close that his jacket brushed my shoulder once and I thought my heart would go into arrest from the electric shock that zinged through me. I waited while he reached out to pull the door open. I could see no one beyond the frosted glass of the conference room door.

But he didn't open the door. Instead he turned to me, pinned me down with that dark gaze.

"Was there something else?" I hated how breathy my voice sounded. I took a step back to put some space between us, but it didn't seem to matter. The intensity did not let up.

Then that willful smile again. "No. I'd better not ask," he muttered, almost to himself and I wondered what he'd had in mind. But he still didn't move. His hand on the chrome door handle tightened, the skin around his knuckles paling. This close I could see every feature, his glossy black hair, his dark eyes, his long straight nose and strong jaw. I swallowed and glanced to the side.

"Mr. Drake—"

"Adam," he said, his voice quiet, firm. Then he did something I could hardly believe. He put his free hand to my chin, tilting my head up so he could look into my face. His thumb ran along my jawline and I forced myself not to jump back. I didn't hate the touch— quite the opposite. Even as my nervousness grew, I had to remind myself that he'd be touching a lot more than that very soon. I met his gaze, managing not to flinch.

"Call me Adam," he said, brushing his thumb over my jaw again. "It's only fitting, given that we'll be seeing each other naked soon."

My mouth dropped, cheeks flushing. The reaction seemed to amuse him. I knew this must be some kind of test to gauge my response. I didn't care. Things were finally starting to get real. I stepped back from his grip and lifted my chin. "This isn't a done deal. I could always change my mind." I said, hating how my voice trembled.

He nodded. "You could. And if you can't bring yourself to hear it talked about, you probably *shouldn't* go through with it."

It wasn't that he was talking about it. It was the *way* he was talking about it. But I stayed silent, strongly wishing myself out of this room and miles away.

He leaned toward me so that our faces were only inches from each other. I caught a whiff of his clean scent. My senses reeled, my heart hammered. "In the end, after all the legal talk, after all of the technical Latin terms we've been throwing around, this is going to be about two people. In bed—and probably other places. Fucking."

The guy had the social skills of a caveman. Any minute I expected him to grab me by the hair and drag me out of the place with a club resting on his shoulder. Maybe he had to pay regularly to get his sex. He was a computer geek, after all. A hot computer geek, I'd admit, but still. Those guys planted their butts in front of the computer for hours, crunching code. When did they have the time to go out and pick up a girlfriend?

I decided to give him a little of his own medicine, giving him the once-over, resting my eyes on his chest, his crotch. Unfortunately, that didn't bring about the desired effect.

He had that boyish grin again. "Yes, this is definitely going to be fun," he said.

"You'll be paying enough for it."

The amusement evaporated from his eyes and they hardened so suddenly that I almost gasped to see the change in them. "We'll be in touch, Emilia." He stepped back and jerked open the door, waving me to pass through before him. The gentlemanly gesture came too late to impress me.

I straightened and managed not to wobble on my heels, remembering to keep my shoulders back. My mother's voice about my poor posture rang in my head. Maybe it came from all the time I spent hunched over my keyboard playing video games.

It occurred to me that I still had no idea who this guy was. Video game designer? Multimillionaire? How does a designer get so rich? What was his story? He was really young. I would have pegged him for younger than twenty-six, yet still so arrogant, so in command and sure of himself.

Well, there was always the Internet, where no question need go unanswered. At least I had been able to cover my bill for the month. I didn't really care about the cell phone, but I'd go without water and gas before I'd give up my Internet. It helped me put food on the table, at the very least.

I'd go home and Google him, of course. He was bound to come up, even if he was, as he claimed, a "very private person." He couldn't make the whole damn world sign an NDA.

When I caught Heath's eye, he turned from his discussion with Drake's lawyer. The tight ball between my shoulder blades had migrated to my stomach, twisting and knotting as we made it to them. Drake and Heath shook hands again and we went our separate ways. I made sure he was out of sight before I balled up my fists and spoke to Heath through clenched teeth.

"Are you fucking kidding me?"

"What?"

"Seriously, *that's* the guy you picked? How in the hell did you think I would tolerate him?"

Heath shot me a puzzled look. "I actually thought he had a lot in common with you."

"What, because he makes video games and I like to play them— *too* much, yes, I know—and review them on my blog?"

"Look at it this way, doll. If you don't like your time together, you can give every product he's made a shitty review."

"Hilarious. Did you tell number two to go away yet or is he still an option?"

Heath's mouth thinned. "Simmer down, now. Give it a day or two, okay? He said he'd e-mail you. Maybe he'll be more polite."

"He's not paying to send me e-mails. I'm going to have to be alone with him all night..."

Heath shook his head and sent me a look that said, "I told you so." I sighed and looked away.

"That's the nature of the beast, Mia. It's what you signed up for when you decided to go through with all this—'Virgin Manifesto' ideals or no. You claimed you were taking back the power that had been robbed from women for centuries. Find a way to take back the power from him. Don't let him go all alpha wolf on you and start peeing on every tree. You're stronger than that."

"What about the other guy, is he an alpha wolf, too?"

"Sweetie, they're millionaires. They're *all* alpha wolves. For what it's worth, his behavior with you was very different from what I saw with him when we spoke both times. Maybe it's just a façade he uses around women. It would explain why he's participating in this— what did you call it again?—'new paradigm' in the first place."

The knot in my stomach twisted again. "It's a bad sign if he can't behave himself around a woman. How do I know I'll be safe? What if he's into some sadomasochist shit?"

"Yeah, that's all in the paperwork. No fetish. No bondage. Nothing unusual. You're a virgin for chrissakes, it's not like you would be into any of that. He knows. He was the one who wanted it put into the language of the agreement, kept saying it was important to protect you."

I remembered what he said when we were alone. That it was his sole interest to ensure my safety, physically and legally. Was this some sort of sting? Was he an undercover cop, in reality? Could Heath have been able to find that out?

We had arranged for this entire transaction to take place overseas, in countries where sex in exchange for money was legal. The web server had been stationed in Brazil, the auction run by proxy by Heath's contact there. The actual act would take place in a legally friendly country.

Money would not actually change hands. Overseas bank accounts would effect the transfer. Heath'd had a gay banker friend set up an account in the Cayman Islands for me. It made me feel so clandestine and mysterious. Drake had one too (probably long before this transaction). And the money would soon be resting in a holding account before the transfer was made.

The only thing that was marginally illegal was our meeting on US soil to iron out the details of the deal. However my pride at the neatness of this deal was beginning to fade in the face of Drake and his alpha wolf asshat personality. As Heath and I got into the car to return home, I shot him a veiled look but was quiet the remainder of the way.

I had a decision to mull over. I had to learn more about who Adam Drake really was. But further than that, the reality of my ideals had just slammed me in the face and I had to see if I had the courage to continue with this plan. The way my nerves were tied up in knots, I doubted if I could.

3

I GOOGLED HIM THE MINUTE I GOT HOME AND TURNED ON MY computer. Read a brief Wikipedia entry on him and spent the next hour with my mouth open in shock as I read article after article. I knew a whole lot more about him but I also had tons more questions.

Somewhere in the back of my mind I'd thought the name Adam Drake rang a bell. A distant bell, but a bell nonetheless. Adam Drake was founder and CEO of Draco Multimedia Entertainment, the parent company of one of the most successful and popular Massive Multi-Player Online Role-Playing Games (MMORPG), Dragon Epoch. I played it regularly and wrote about it in a regular column on my blog. In fact, I was due for a new DE update sometime this week.

Something prickly formed in my throat. I saw pictures, press releases, reviews, interviews, write-ups. Pictures of him on panels at the San Diego Comic-Con. He was some kind of prodigy with programming and had developed a unique artificial intelligence engine within a game called Mission Accomplished before he'd graduated high school. He'd sold the program to Sony at the age of seventeen. For 3.2 million dollars.

A millionaire at seventeen years old by his own doing.

From there it just got worse. He'd attended the California Institute of Technology but had dropped out after a year and founded his own company, Draco Multimedia, out of a warehouse in Irvine. Eventually that company built its own multi-complex campus in the same city. They produced several games—the culmination of which was currently Dragon Epoch, a subscription-based fantasy environment that millions of players worldwide paid for the privilege of playing. Including me.

Now I knew exactly what Heath had meant when he'd said that Drake and I had things in common. Or maybe it was his own starry-eyed gamer worship that had gotten in the way. If I was a hardcore gamer, Heath was worse. He was the one who'd gotten me into the whole thing in the first place.

Now I was growing skeptical about Heath's judgment. No doubt he was fan-geeking during those "multiple interviews" where he and Drake had spoken for hours both in person and on the phone.

I brewed myself a pot of tea and glanced at the clock. I had hours yet before work, no desire to study and tons of blog posts to write— at least three reviews, one interview and a couple of spotlights.

And yes, my weekly report on Dragon Epoch. But I wondered how I could keep that completely neutral—as if I didn't know he was watching.

Then again, while my blog was quite popular in the gaming community, I doubted a child prodigy genius CEO had time to regularly read the tripe I wrote. His game was far larger than the trivial comments I made on it. He'd probably been alerted to the auction by one of his underlings. Maybe he'd even glanced over the blog once he'd won.

I'd criticized his game all over my blog. I loved playing it and found it a deeply immersive and fun experience but, as with practically every fantasy-based role-playing game in the industry, it was ripe with misogyny. After all, the companies knew who their main customers were: young, horny guys in their late teens and twenties, suffering through college and all types of social awkwardness. Why not create female avatars and nonplayer characters that were all lithe, sexual and scantily clad? Anything to sell game subscriptions...

My objections were mostly mild and sarcastic. I'd make scathing comments like, "Come on boys, can you imagine your local half-elf healer jaunting down to the pond to collect herbs in her chainmail bikini? Hope she got her Brazilian wax before she donned that thing or else, ouch."

Sometimes I got hate mail, but usually my snark amused the male readers and got a lot of "hear, hear!" from my female readers.

I wondered if Drake had ever seen the column. I wondered if Drake, himself, was a misogynist. His behavior this afternoon had not led me to believe otherwise.

Flustered and distracted, I had the choice of engaging in one of my two favorite activities when I had things on my mind: running or playing on the game. With a sigh and a flick of the computer switch, I picked the easier one—once I'd changed out of that dreadful skirt and into my forgiving yoga pants. I needed to get my mind off of that afternoon's weird encounter and logging into Dragon Epoch was the best way to do it.

I was all set to go slaughter a horde of monsters when my notification list lit up.

*Your friend **FallenOne** is online.*

I was shocked, pleasantly so. He hadn't been on in weeks. A pang of some feeling I couldn't describe resonated in my chest—longing, excitement.

Before I could start the chat, my screen flashed.

*FallenOne tells you, "Hey."

*You tell FallenOne, "Hey, stranger! Where have you been?"

*FallenOne tells you, "Haven't logged on in forever. School is kicking my ass."

*You tell FallenOne, "Should be over soon, no? So glad I don't have classes this semester."

*FallenOne tells you, "Lucky. Had to get on the game to blow off some steam. Wanna go kill stuff?"

*You tell FallenOne, "Always. You going to be on for our regular game night? Fragged misses you, too."

Fragged was the name of Heath's Barbarian Mercenary. I waited. Fallen didn't reply for a few minutes and I wondered what was going on.

Fallen and I had had a friendship, as with Heath and our other friend from Canada, who used the character name of Persephone, for over a year. Fallen had never wanted to join our guild but he played with us regularly even though he never used in-game voice chat and only texted in game. He seemed shy and unwilling to come out of his shell. Still we'd joked around and spent hours LOLing and giggling at the stupidest things. For a while, there, I really thought I had a bit of a crush on him. Sometimes I still felt the pangs of it even though my logical thoughts ruled that as being ridiculous. I hardly knew anything about his real life except that he was on the east coast somewhere and in college. I wasn't in danger. You couldn't fall for someone over an online game and long IM chats, could you?

But then I'd posted the auction. We had argued about it and he'd all but disappeared. And even now he was still distant, hesitant. I had no idea what university he attended or what his real name was—he was that shy. I could have ruled these two instances—my auction and his disappearance—as coincidental if it hadn't been for what came next in our conversation.

FallenOne tells you, "You still going through with that auction?"

I grimaced.

You tell FallenOne, "Yeah."

FallenOne tells you, "I know it's none of my business, but is it really a good idea? You've been through a lot of shit this past year with your mom being sick and that big test. Maybe now isn't the time for you to do something drastic like this?"

I sighed. Why didn't guys understand that for a woman of my age, being a virgin was a burden more than anything else? I just wanted to dump it already. Why not profit from it?

You tell FallenOne, "Everyone's gotta lose it sometime. Why not go out with a bang?"

FallenOne tells you, "Pun intended, I hope?"

I laughed. That "sounded" more like the Fallen I knew. We chatted for a few more minutes before we traveled to the same game zone—the place where our characters were located, the Misty Caverns, in order to go hunt bad guys together. Little more was said about the auction or our personal lives after that. Fallen didn't promise to log in again on our regular game night and with no small amount of sadness I realized that this might be the end of our regular gaming relationship.

Our mutual friend, Persephone, would be sad. She'd been trying to play matchmaker for Fallen and me for months and she hadn't been subtle about it. And me, well, I wasn't sure how I felt. More confused than ever, I guess.

After a few hours, a few hundred oozing undead and several quest rewards, Fallen decided to log off. I kept going—a form of procrastination and avoidance of the things I should be doing and thinking about. The question of Drake, Mr. CEO of the game I so loved, and his arrogance was still on my mind. Killing monsters didn't help so I resolved to go for a run later that evening.

But I never got there because less than a half hour after Fallen logged off, my door was nearly pounded off its hinges. I'd have recognized that knock at midnight in the middle of cyclone. With a smile I got up and jerked open the door.

My two besties—besides, Heath, of course—stood in the door, shoulder to shoulder. I grinned at Alex, the daughter of my landlady, who had her long dark hair pulled back in a ponytail. She had beautiful olive skin and was wearing a tight T-shirt with a printed-on bowtie and the motto *Bowties Are Cool* across her ample chest.

Jenna, her best friend and roommate, with the brightest blond hair I'd ever seen on a person out of childhood—complete with a shock of brilliant purple—fidgeted beside her.

"Password?" I demanded.

The two girls glanced at each other and in unison they chanted, "I aim to misbehave." I grinned at our favorite quote from Captain Mal Reynolds of *Firefly*.

Jenna sidled into the room, squeezing ahead of Alex. She held a Tupperware container that rattled and said, "Can we come in?"

As she was already mostly in the apartment anyway, I stepped aside with an exaggerated sigh. Alex grabbed my arm and gave me a dramatic shake, her dark brown eyes widening. "We are doing a *Doctor Who* marathon at our place tomorrow night. You gotta come. There'll be a drinking game. We shoot tequila every time the Doctor uses his sonic screwdriver. We do a beer bong when he says 'I'm the Doctor.'"

I laughed. I loved *Doctor Who* but I knew I wasn't up for that. Not this week. "I've got my study group—"

Alex stomped her foot and the sound of it echoed on the floor below, which was the ceiling of her mother's garage. "Come on, Mia! There will be cute boys there. Cute boys who love *Doctor Who*."

I snorted. "Yeah, and they'll be even cuter after the beer goggles are on."

Jenna shook her box again and it rattled as she plopped down on my half broken-down couch—the fabric was shredded and patched with duct tape. "Okay, so you don't like to party. We get it. We've been asking you for months. But at least tell me you are going to come to my Dungeons and Dragons game next Saturday."

I groaned inwardly. Not this again. "I'm sorry, Jen, I have to work a double shift on Saturday."

She raised her pale—almost invisible—brows at me and popped off the cover of her plastic container. "You think you're a gamer, punching around on your keyboard, hunched over your monitor? You haven't *truly* gamed until you've used *these*," she said, holding her palm open to display some tiny three-dimensional plastic pieces of all sizes and colors. Some were shaped like pyramids, others were multifaceted spheres. Some gleamed like gems in the late afternoon sunlight. All of them were covered with plain, white numbers.

"That little tiny pyramid looks cool," I conceded.

Her face fell. I'd somehow displeased her. "This is a d-four—a four-sided die. It is perfectly balanced to give me the perfect chance for a completely random one-in-four roll every time."

"Um. Okay."

Jenna pulled out an oilcloth and began polishing the shapes. "You don't get to use cool stuff like this for computer games."

I sighed. "I'm sorry. I promise I'll come soon. But this test has me so stressed out I can hardly think of anything else but studying and working so I can eat in order to keep myself alive so I can continue to stress about this damn test."

Because I'd failed it last year. I'd bombed so abysmally that that failure hung over my future like an executioner's axe. It froze me with fear so that the thought of taking it—and failing it—again made me physically ill inside. Instead, I studied and studied and put off the retakes. The test was offered every month and everything— *everything*—I'd planned for my future rested on that godforsaken test. I hadn't yet found my confidence, or the courage, to try it again.

But if I didn't do it, I'd never be a doctor.

Since school and testing usually came pretty easily to me, I'd thought that the MCAT would be the same. How terribly wrong I'd been. I swallowed an icy pebble of fear, willing myself not to think about it.

Alex plopped down beside Jenna and fingered some of the dice in the box, avoiding my eyes. "We get it," she said, but it was easy to hear the hurt in her voice.

I sighed, sinking down onto the metal folding chair opposite them—I had such fashionable furniture. It was bad, even for a college pad.

"I'm sorry. Really."

Alex looked up, her eyes hard. "I said we get it."

Jenna placed a hand on her arm. "Alejandra, calm down please. I'm sure she'll hang with us again when the test is over."

I shook my head. "Don't you two have finals coming up or something? Why aren't *you* studying?"

They attended nearby California State University in Fullerton, which was on a slightly different schedule than my school, Chapman University. Alex cleared her throat. "Because I'm a communications major and she has such good grades that she opted out of most of her finals, because she's a fucking brainiac," she said, jerking her thumb toward Jenna.

Jenna looked up and despite the crap she'd just given me, I could read real empathy in her pale blue eyes. She was stunning, really— like the love child of a Norse goddess and Alexander Skarsgård. "It's okay, Mia, really. If you ever need help studying or anything, let me know. I could quiz you. I don't know much about bio, but I know there are some physics-related questions on the test and since that's my major..."

I sighed, running my hands through my hair and resting my forehead in my palms. "I'm the worst friend ever."

"No. You're just stressed out and if you keep this up, you'll fail just because you'll be too keyed up to even focus."

I rubbed my forehead with my thumbs, feeling the beginnings of a stress headache. This day! It felt endless, between the lack of sleep after my late shift, the rushed preparations, the unexpected meeting with a pompous but very hot asshole, the weird gaming session with Fallen and now *this*.

Alex got up from the couch and came over to crouch beside my chair. *"Pobrecita,"* she murmured in Spanish, meaning "you poor thing." She slipped an arm around my shoulders. "I'm sorry."

I sighed again and leaned my head on her shoulder. Then she invited me to eat downstairs with her mom and we pigged out on her awesome enchiladas.

"You leave it to me and Jen," Alex said. "We'll find you a hot nerd and then you won't be able to say 'no' to our parties."

I grinned and swallowed, my throat suddenly tight. I'd met a hot nerd earlier that day and found I didn't like him much.

4

AS THE NEXT FEW DAYS ROLLED ON, MY MIND constantly dwelled on the question of whether it was the right decision to proceed as planned. I was finding it awkward to even force myself to do my weekly DE report. This week's had been a bland, neutral commentary on some of the lamer quests in the game. But what about next week and the week after? What about after Drake and I slept together? Would I always be worried that he'd be stalking my blog?

I could opt to cut my regular DE report from the blog. Readers would protest that. I received lots of hits, re-blogs and comments on that feature. My blog was my livelihood. It brought in more money through advertisements than my hospital job currently did. Hopefully it would keep paying the rent throughout med school as well.

So, after days of mulling it over, I came to a decision. And while procrastinating making the call to Heath, I happened to log on and find him on the game

You tell Fragged, "Hey dude, whatcha doing?"

*Fragged tells you, "Killing trolls in the Golden Mountains. This new hidden quest chain is driving me up a tree. Come help me, I need your enchantress. They keep stunning me."

With a sigh, I complied, running my character over to the nearest magic portal chamber to take her to the location where Heath was tirelessly hacking his way through troll parts to find some small clue to the game's latest mystery.

*You tell Fragged, "You and everyone else who plays the game. You didn't try to weasel the secret out of Drake, did you?"

*Fragged tells you, "No. I doubt he'd tell me anything anyway."

*You tell Fragged, "You sure? You definitely chatted with him for a long time."

My character was almost to Fragged's location in the game, at the base of the Golden Mountains, when I got jumped by an aggressive mountain goblin.

*Fragged tells you, "Where are you? I'm up to my asshole in troll guts."

*You tell Fragged, "I have aggro. Goblin jumped me. I'll be there in a minute. Oh and by the way, I need you to get in touch with the number two guy in the auction. It's not going to work with Drake."

I was just finishing off the mountain goblin, my character at half her full life, when he replied.

*Fragged tells you, "Um. What?"

You tell Fragged, "Just do it. I'm almost there—shit! Another goblin! Come help me. He has friends and I'm only at half my life."

I watched as my red health bar—the indicator of my character's life—started to dwindle. I punched buttons left and right waiting for his Mercenary to show up with his mighty sword so he could stand between me and the bad guys. We spell-casters referred to the big brawny warrior-types as "meat shields" because they stood between us and the monsters while we shot them with magic spells.

Fragged tells you, "I'm on my way. I strongly disagree, by the way. If you're going to go through with this, then D. is your best bet. And we probably shouldn't be texting each other about it in his own fucking game."

Fragged arrived to save my bacon when I had only a sliver of health left. I backed up, drank a healing potion and punched my highest-level spell, "Bedazzle," to stun the goblin and his friends. They swayed back and forth with stars in front of their eyes while Heath's Barbarian Mercenary beat them down one at a time.

"Take that, sucker!" I muttered aloud.

I turned back to my keyboard, quickly typing in my next message to Heath.

You tell Fragged, "So why do you disagree about calling it off with him and going to the other guy?"

I finished off the second goblin with a lightning bolt and then sent a healing spell to Fragged, who was down to a third of his life.

Fragged tells you, "Because D. is the best prospect, hands down."

I gritted my teeth, frustrated.

You tell Fragged, "Are you saying that because it is in my best interest or because you have DE stars in your eyes? You are hooked on this game and I know that's what you spent your hours talking to him about— wheedling game secrets out of him."
Fragged tells you, "WTF."

His character, turned to mine and made a rude gesture. In response, I flipped off the screen, though I knew he wouldn't see it.

You tell Fragged, "Real mature."
Fragged tells you, "I'm not very mature when I'm pissed. If you think, for one minute, that I was putting my own interest ahead of yours, then how can you even call me a friend, Mia?"
You tell Fragged, "I don't believe that. I'm sorry. I was mad. Drake pissed me off and it's not going to work."
Fragged tells you, "Stop using his name, goddamn it. Either abbreviate or call me on the phone, and don't effing insult me."

With a heavy sigh, I grabbed the phone and called him. He picked up the phone and without a greeting, he said, "Okay, I get it. He came across about as aggressive as a mustang stallion. I have no idea what that was all about but I'm assuring you right now that he's the far better choice than New York and I'm putting my foot down on this. Now get your ass over to my spot. These trolls are going to take me forever to kill without your help."

"Heath—"

"No, Mia. If you want to back out with Drake, you are going to have to tell him yourself. I'll send you his e-mail address. You let him know what you've decided."

I stiffened. "Fine. I will. I can't blog about his company and his products if I've had a personal relationship with him. It just wouldn't be right."

Heath snorted on the other end. "No, at least be honest with yourself. He scared the shit out of you because you have never been that into a guy you've just met before."

"Whaaaaat?" And in spite of the fact that I was alone, my cheeks heated, my entire body grew hot and I started to sweat.

It was a good thing I had to focus on killing trolls and saving his Barbarian Mercenary's smelly loinclothed ass or I would have died of embarrassment.

"We've been best friends since eighth grade. Back when you were still interested in guys, before that fucker screwed you up, I could always tell who you were into. It's been six years since you dated that little prick and you've never so much as looked at a guy since. In our little meeting, you were flushed and breathing like you'd just run a marathon. Drake turned you on and that scares the shit out of you."

My fist closed on the table and my T-shirt was starting to stick to my ribs. His character was running low on life. I prepared my gate spell to take me away from the area and out of harm's way. I'd tell him I accidentally hit the wrong button instead of healing him.

"You have no idea what's going on inside my head, so stop trying to figure it out."

"Doll, when you asked for my help in this auction, you gave me the right to voice my opinion. My work is all over this venture. Quit squawking because you're losing control."

I wasted the second to the last troll with a killing enchantment. He could fight the last one by himself—with only a sliver of life left. "I am *not* losing control."

"Then admit that you want Drake."

I took a deep breath. "He'd be a conflict of interest."

"Heal, please? And that's not what I asked you."

My finger hovered over the heal button, but I didn't press it. "Are you bound and determined to humiliate me? Yes, I think he's hot. Okay? But that was never a requirement. Now if I e-mail him and tell him he's lost his chance, will you set things up with the New Yorker?"

There was a long silence at the end of the line. "I'll consider it. A heal any century now would be *great*."

"Drink a potion," I snarled. Then I wussed out and shot him a small heal...just enough to let him think he might make it out before I gated out on him.

"Mia, I really think you should think long and hard about Drake." And then he laughed his typical juvenile boy laugh. "Huh. See what I did there? I said 'long and hard.'"

"Can you hear me dying of laughter over here?" I hit my gate spell and disappeared.

Ten seconds later, Fragged showed up next to me in ghost form. The troll had finished him off.

"Now who's laughing, sucker?" I giggled.

"I forgot how bitchy you get when I'm right and you're wrong. Go write your e-mail then. I'm not playing with you when you're in one of your moods. But for the record, I think you're making a big mistake."

I swallowed my frustration, at last relieved that I apparently had won him over. "Yes, yes. It's noted."

So after I hung up, I sat down and wrote it.

Dear Mr. Drake,

I appreciate your interest in my auction and your willingness to lay down a considerable sum to see things come to pass. But since our meeting I've had some time to reflect on the matter and I feel that we would not be compatible in this venture. It was clear to me at our meeting that you lack the desire to put me at ease. This was never a requirement and I know you will point that out in your reply, but as the plans for this have solidified, I've decided that I need someone who is willing to make those extra efforts. As well, I do not think we would work well together and though it is only for a brief time, I still think it would be in my best interests to go with one of the runners-up in the bidding. I wish you well and thank you again for the opportunity to have met you.

> *Regards,*
> *Mia Strong*

Holding my breath, I pressed "send" and sat back, staring at the blinking cursor on a blank screen. After a few tense moments, I released it, realizing that I was a coward. Heath was right. I hadn't been this affected by a man in—well—never. And I had no idea why that was the case, but at the very core of this cold feeling inside me was an icy kernel of fear or thrill. It dried my throat, made my palms clammy. I wiped them on my jeans and stood, unwilling to let myself dwell on it.

Then I went about my day, tidying up the apartment in between writing blog posts and making still more tea. When I got back from vacuuming—a short break because I only have one room in my studio—I saw the "new e-mail" indicator flashing for my attention.

I clicked on it and noted the return address. Not the address I had sent it to, which was a generic Google mail account. adrake@dracomultimedia.com.

I opened it up and it was very short.

Hi Mia,
I'd like to talk with you again. As soon as possible.
Adam

I sent off my reply immediately.

Mr. Drake—
My decision is made.
Mia Strong

Next I did the windows—actually a bit astonished at my burst of desire to clean. I hadn't cleaned like this in months. I hated to clean, but I'd found that, since sending that first e-mail, sitting around and doing nothing, or even just writing blog posts, was driving me crazy.

After finishing the windows, I pulled on my shorts and running shoes, tucked my long hair up into a ponytail and decided to burn off my excess energy with a 5k run.

I was almost out the door when someone knocked. I pulled it open and started in shock.

Filling up my doorway with all of his masculine beauty was Adam Drake. In the very solid flesh. He wore jeans, a casual short-sleeved black button-down shirt and designer aviator sunglasses. He was leaning against the doorframe on one hand and I couldn't tear my eyes away from his firm bicep. He looked even more delicious than he had the day I'd met him at the hotel.

"Um," was all I said. How the hell did he know where I lived? Something tickled at the back of my memory—a hurriedly scrawled address on the back of the nondisclosure agreement that I'd signed. My heart started its furious staccato. I could feel it in my throat, my wrists.

I couldn't see his eyes, but he smiled—a genuine smile this time, not that sarcastic bullshit. "Hi. May I come in?"

I hesitated. My apartment was clean but very humble. This guy probably had a mansion on the harbor somewhere—I was guessing Balboa Island. Worth at least five or six million, probably more. He probably had his own boat in a slip and he lived just down the street from the legendary home of the late John Wayne. His master bathroom was likely bigger than my entire studio.

"It's okay, Mia. I just want to talk."

This was a far cry from the caveman I'd met the previous week. I held his gaze through the shades and then he reached up and pulled them off, folding them and putting them in his shirt pocket. The gold watch on his strong wrist flashed in the sunlight. I blinked and, not believing what I was doing, I stepped back and let him in, folding my arms over my chest.

"You caught me at a bad time," I murmured.

"Yeah, I can see you are about to go running."

I frowned. How had he known that? Sure I was dressed in exercise clothes but how did he know I wasn't headed for the gym instead? Then I remembered that I'd mentioned that I was a runner on my blog. Maybe he'd read it there?

He entered slowly, moving as if he was afraid he might frighten me away. He glanced around the room, his face expressionless, but I couldn't help feeling embarrassed when his gaze settled on my old rattletrap computer. At least I'd been able to swap out that old blocky CRT monitor for a newer flat screen when Heath had upgraded his system and given me his hand-me-down. But it was still a source of shame, especially for a techie gaming addict like me.

My fingers dug into my arms where I held them across my chest. I shifted uneasily. "What are you doing here, Mr. Drake?"

His gaze met mine, that studious look in his eyes again. "I'd like to know why you've changed your mind."

My lips thinned. I squared my shoulders, preparing for his hard sell. "I don't believe I'm required to supply that answer, but out of the goodness of my heart I will say that Heath is the one who chose you, not me. I'm changing Heath's decision, not mine. *I'm* still going through with this. Just with a different person."

His expression remained completely neutral but there was a speculative look in his eyes. "Because of our conversation last Thursday?"

I blinked. "No. I wasn't terribly impressed by that conversation, but that's not the reason."

His eyes narrowed. "Don't I deserve to know why, then?"

I shifted my weight from one leg to the other and looked down. "Because of who you are."

He nodded as if expecting that answer. "Yes, I wondered when that would come up. I was surprised there was no discussion of it at the meeting and didn't surmise that Bowman hadn't told you until after it was over. It wasn't by my choice that you didn't know."

I cleared my throat, suddenly uncomfortable. "Heath Bowman is my closest friend. I don't believe he meant any harm. He just thinks of this gaming thing as something that you and I have in common. But it's a conflict of interest."

He nodded but didn't say anything and for a long moment there was silence. My stomach growled loudly, reminding me that I hadn't eaten yet.

He smiled. "Can we grab something to eat? I'm feeling pretty hungry myself."

We walked to the sandwich shop at the end of the street. It was a little diner with tables on the front patio under a slatted wooden cover. On a breezy spring day in early May, it was the perfect place to sit. Drake and I ordered our sandwiches and sat while waiting for them to be brought out.

My heart was doing its weird offbeat fibrillation again and when I swallowed, there was a cold excitement in my throat. Christ...just from sitting at a table with him? This guy was pure danger to my senses. What was it about him that set me on edge like this?

I cleared my throat and began. "I don't think you're aware of this, but my blog is my livelihood."

"I'm aware of your blog, Emilia. I have been for quite some time."

This caused me to sit back against the chair. The cold of the metal back seeped through my T-shirt. "Is that so?"

He smiled. "Why does that surprise you? Considering the industry I'm in and yours is one of the best blogs out there reviewing gaming material."

I glanced at him skeptically. "Thank you for the compliment, but that's just not true. GameShopper. GeekWorld. All of those other multiauthor platforms far outproduce me in content and hits."

"But they reference you often enough."

I shook my head. "I can't wrap my head around the idea that you even read the blogs."

He laughed. "I'm a normal person, just like everyone else."

"But you're busy CEOing and designing and stuff."

"I was an architect on the game once and take an active interest in my product. I'm always looking for ways to make it better. What's been on my mind a lot lately is appealing to a certain demographic that we seem to have trouble with."

I knew how he'd answer before I asked the question, but I had to ask it anyway. "What demographic?"

"Female, sixteen to twenty-four."

It was my turn to crack that sarcastic smile. "Ah, I get it. So I'm *research* for you, am I?"

He laughed. "No, but your blog is."

I nodded. "It's comforting to know that all my snarking is being noticed by those who count. Maybe someday you might take a comment or two of mine to heart."

His tilted his head, studying me. "I think you have a lot of valuable insights to provide to the gaming community from a young woman's point of view. We need more female gamers speaking out about what they want."

"Great. So then you understand why I'm stopping this."

He shook his head. "It's an unfounded worry."

"But if I'm reviewing your game and you and I are—how could you not see that as a conflict?"

"Because there are ways you can handle it that you haven't thought of."

I clenched my jaw. "Oh, is that so? Like what?"

He looked to the side, considering. "You could temporarily go on hiatus with the DE column and find something else to take its place for a few months. Or you could get a guest blogger to handle it for you."

I laughed. "Are you actually suggesting I drop the free publicity of your game? I can't believe my ears."

But he'd planted the seed of an idea in my mind. One of my closest gaming friends, Katya, who played as Persephone, had been wanting to guest post for some time. I'd never met her in person but, as with FallenOne, Heath and I played regularly with her. I could probably set her onto the task. She was a diehard DE fan.

Still, I hesitated. And at that moment, our sandwiches were delivered to the table. I dug into mine—turkey and avocado on a wheat roll—with gusto. I hadn't had breakfast and was running low on groceries, as usual, and I was still a few days out from the next paycheck.

"I'm still not convinced it's a good idea."

"Then let me to resolve your other concerns," he said, taking a bite of his spicy chicken po'boy and commenting on how good it was.

"I don't think you can." I said in between my next bites.

"Try me."

"I don't think we're compatible."

"How compatible would we have to be for one night?"

I shrugged. It wasn't what I'd really wanted to say. It wasn't compatibility that concerned me. It was this scorching sexual tension that crackled through the air whenever we were near each other. Or at least that's how it was for me. I had no idea what he was feeling. He seemed as calm, cool and collected as on the day we met.

I cleared my throat and leaned forward, my elbows on the table in front of me. "Mr. Drake, it's very important to me that you understand that *I* am in control of this entire situation. It was *my* auction, *my* drive, *my* desire to see an end to an archaic value system that for centuries worked against women and to turn it on its ear."

When he looked at me, his eyes sliced right through me, lanced me to the core. "It all sounds very noble and revolutionary when you put it that way. And here I'd been convinced this entire time that you were doing it for the money."

I sat back, watching him. So the Manifesto hadn't fooled him in the least. I affected a shrug that I didn't feel. "I won't lie. I could use the money. I want to go to medical school and I don't want to be in debt. Some women waitress at topless bars to put themselves through college. Some dance at strip clubs or sell phone sex over the Internet. My decision was to use one night in my life to change the course of things, if possible."

He didn't have to know about my mother's hospital bills and her cancer treatments or even the threat to the mortgage on the ranch property. He didn't have to know about the way I felt like vomiting whenever I thought of any of those things, of the panic that laced the edges of every thought that concerned money. I'd let him think I was just doing this for me. I never claimed to be a selfless saint.

His forehead creased and he got that strange, cold look he did when he'd dismissed me at the end of our first interview. "But ultimately, no matter who it is you choose to submit to, you will end up ceding control. You won't be in control of the entire situation for the entire night."

I looked away but hesitated from biting into my sandwich. "I'd like to feel like I'm in control *now*."

"And my coming here to change your mind threatens that?"

I tilted my head to the side, considering. "It depends on what you'll do if you fail to convince me."

He hesitated a moment, then set his jaw. "I'll step aside."

We watched each other over our empty plates—or at least his, for he had finished his sandwich and half of mine remained. I was still hungry, but that other half was earmarked as my dinner. It was another cost-saving measure I regularly employed. Any time I ate out, I saved exactly half my meal to have later. That way one meal became two.

He stared at my plate. "You didn't eat much. Didn't you like your sandwich?"

"It was great," I said in a cheerful voice as I asked our server to bring me a take-home box.

He scowled. "Eat the rest of your sandwich, Emilia."

"I'm saving it for later." I blushed, refusing to admit that I was so destitute that this half sandwich, a box of cereal and half a carton of milk were about all I had to eat until payday.

When the waitress returned, he took the box from her before she could hand it to me. He ordered two more sandwiches—one of which, I'd told him, was my second favorite here when I'd been suggesting things for him to order. "Can you bring those boxed to go? She's decided to finish this one."

Then he turned and looked at me. "*Now* will you finish that?"

It didn't take more convincing. Though I was embarrassed, I mumbled my thanks around my last bites. His perceptiveness impressed me. Most guys wouldn't have picked up on the fact that I was still hungry. Even Heath probably wouldn't have. He'd never commented on my boxing up my leftovers.

Drake carried the sandwiches back to my apartment as we walked the three blocks in silence. I crunched noisily on the peppermint candy the waitress had left with the check.

"Do you always chew your hard candies like that?"

I darted a glance at him and raised my eyebrows. "I don't suck, remember?"

And to my astonishment, he laughed. "How could I forget?"

He came in again, but only to lay the sandwiches on the kitchen counter; then he headed for the doorway.

I followed closely to see him out. Before he opened the door, however, he turned back to me. Given the narrow entryway, we were in close quarters. My heart started hammering at my throat again.

He looked at me for a long moment. "Emilia, I'm asking you to reconsider. The choice—the control— is in your hands, of course, but don't eliminate the possibility just because of some fears that can be dispensed with."

Despite the strong physical reaction to him, my ire rose to his challenge. "You think I'm afraid?"

He paused, studying my face. "I think there are some things you don't understand. Like this effect we have on each other..." My throat tightened. So he *was* feeling it too. My heart rate kicked up a few notches as if I was already in the middle of my run.

Breathing was difficult, too. "I'm quite aware of it."

He watched me, eyes boring into mine. "But do you understand it?"

"I'm quite capable of understanding sexual attraction, Mr. Drake."

"Adam," he said quietly, his eyes lowering to focus on my mouth. My heart skipped a beat in its frenetic pace.

"Adam."

"Why does it make you uncomfortable to call me by my first name?"

I locked gazes with him, suddenly intensely aware of how close we were standing. I could smell him—a subtle scent, masculine, clean, like the ocean and the hint of peppermint candy on his breath. I could almost feel the heat and power oozing off of him in waves. I swallowed in a suddenly dry throat.

"I don't know."

"I want to give you one more thing to think about."

"And what is that?"

He leaned closer, his head approaching mine. I didn't have the time to step back nor, I think, the willpower to do it even if it had occurred to me. His mouth met mine in a firm, sure kiss.

It wasn't overpowering. That was the first thing that surprised me. It was a subtle give and take—gentle, at first, a warm pressure of his lips on mine. Then he took a step closer and slid a hand around my waist, the other going to my back.

He retreated, just slightly, just enough to allow me to pursue him. His mouth moved against mine, teasing, pressing it open. Now his body pressed against mine, his head angled down to reach me, for I was at least five inches shorter than him.

I opened my mouth to him then and his tongue slid in easily. Nothing tentative in this kiss. He knew exactly what he was doing. He was telling me I had the control, declaring the decision mine and then swooping in and taking no prisoners.

His hands stayed put. I was glad of that though I wanted his touch everywhere—my aching breasts, the throbbing between my legs. Goose bumps prickled up and down my arms. His tongue explored my mouth with surety, easy possession. And—to my utter humiliation—I let loose a small whimper at the back of my throat.

The arm around my waist tightened when he heard it, responding immediately, almost instinctively. He pulled his tongue back, as if inviting me to follow him with my tongue. And tentatively, I did.

I'd been kissed before—back in high school when I was normal and I actually dated. But it had been years, now, and I'd never, ever been kissed like this. My tongue entered his mouth and he made a noise at the back of his throat, not quite a growl, kind of more like a huff. It emboldened me. Empowered me. I thrust my tongue, lacing my hands around the back of his neck. Our heads moved together for long minutes and I felt like I hadn't breathed in a lifetime.

Everything was spinning around me and I—I was spinning too, delirious with want. Like a woman drowning in the middle of stormy sea, in desperate need of a life raft. That sea was Adam Drake and he was pulling me adrift, stranding me in some strange and forgotten land.

When finally he ended it, he pulled away so slowly that I could hardly tell our lips had parted until cool air passed between us. It was then that I saw that he was as affected as I was—flushed cheeks, his breath coming fast, his eyes dark and drunk with desire.

I licked my lips and took a step back, but I didn't remove my gaze from his. He stared at me for a long moment and then fished his sunglasses out of his pocket.

Before speaking, he coughed into a fist, as if consciously trying to affect that previous cool demeanor and knowing he was failing. "It was...That was just something else to consider. I hope you make the right decision."

And with that, without even waiting for me to say good-bye or reply in any way, he was gone.

I fell back against the wall, aware of my aching, awakened senses. Every time I thought about his smell or the feel of his mouth on mine, a new shard of arousal cut me to the bone.

Thank goodness I was already decked out to run. I had planned on 5k but I ended up running twice that before I could even begin to feel the sexual energy burn off. This man had fired me up, intoxicated me. And why? Because of his gorgeous face? His solid, masculine body?

Because of his confident manner? He possessed maturity beyond his years. He seemed much more experienced than other twenty-something men I knew in college. Could life have changed him so much since his college days or had he always been that way?

I found questions like this sliding through my mind constantly for the rest of that day—all through the night as I worked. They harangued me on my day off, too. I couldn't stop thinking about him and wanted to call and ask him to come over and give me a good night kiss like the one he'd given me the day before.

I laughed at the thought. How silly. But I surprised myself with the realization of how much I really wanted it. On day three after

The Kiss, I called Heath and told him to throw away the New Yorker's contact information. We would proceed as planned.

Still, my feelings were mixed. I had a hard time reconciling the behavior of Adam Drake at the hotel conference room the day we met and the man who'd come to my place and bought me lunch *and*, thanks to his perceptiveness, dinner, too. I'd told Heath, but I waited a few more days to tell Adam that I'd decided to go through with it. I didn't want to appear as eager as I was beginning to feel, after all. I didn't *want* to be eager at all.

This was business. And every time I relived the fire of that kiss in my memory, I had to remind myself of that. Business. *Business, Mia. Just business.* Nothing meaningful would ever result from this encounter between us. I'd designed it expressly to be that way. One night of anonymous abandon from which I'd emerge a new woman—or maybe just the same old me without my virginity but with a lot of money in my bank account.

But now, this man was stirring a whole different pot. A bubbling, roiling cauldron of thrilling need. This night might be too dangerous, like staring into the sun or flying too close to the fire or...

Mr. Drake,

I've decided to go through with the agreement as it stands. Please proceed with the business arrangements as outlined in the packet of papers provided to you by Mr. Bowman.

If you prefer, you can speak with him if you have any questions. You'll need to set a date at least two weeks from now but no more than three months. We can discuss locations, choosing from the list I provided.

Regards,

Mia Strong

My heart thumped in my throat when I hit "send." I sat and stared at the screen for almost twenty minutes, numbly paging through my regular gaming news sites and clipping things for my blog. I stared at that e-mail icon until it drove me crazy that he wasn't replying. Did I think he'd change his mind? Was I afraid he would? Or was I just dying to see what he'd say in reaction to this?

Maybe he was in a meeting or on a business trip or unable to get reception. Maybe he was screaming through the atmosphere on his private jet with a pretty hostess in his lap and a martini in his hand. I scrunched up my face at that picture, like he was some kind of young, American James Bond and laughed at my own silliness.

After I got home from that afternoon's run, I checked again. Nothing. Then I made dinner and sat down to watch an old *Friends* rerun while I ate. I'm proud to say I only interrupted my meal once to check my computer and make sure the alerts were working properly.

Maybe he *had* changed his mind? Maybe he'd decided it was too much trouble. After all, I had to question why he'd be interested in this deal anyway. He was young, rich and gorgeous. Weren't there women beating a path to his door? Why would he bid so much money on a woman he'd never met—before he'd ever seen a picture of my face—for one night? Why did he care? Why did it mean so much to him to remove the virginity of a stranger?

After dinner, I dug into my study books for a couple of hours before finally dozing off around ten. Yes, I was living the high life. When I woke up, *Gray's Anatomy* was digging a sharp corner into the small of my back. I pushed the huge book to the floor and the computer chirped.

I don't think I've ever jumped awake faster in my life. I opened up my e-mail and saw his address flashing with the "unread" tag on it. I plunked into my chair and, with a shaky hand on my mouse, opened it.

Ms. Strong,

May 18th. Amstel Amsterdam. 15:00 local time. Check in at the desk, reservation under my name. Pack light. Bowman will make the flight arrangements per my instructions.

See you in two weeks.

Drake

My heartbeat thrummed on every inch of my skin. My forehead broke out in beads of sweat. He'd thought everything through. Amsterdam had been on the list, of course, because of the legality issues of what we were doing. And I'd secretly hoped he'd agree to it, as I'd always wanted to go there, even if it was just for a night. Maybe I could do some sightseeing. I'd always dreamt of seeing Europe. Holland was an excellent start.

I immediately opened up another window and did a search for the hotel and gasped at the pictures I hit. Easily five stars, over a thousand Euros a night. I was getting my cherry popped in style.

But...he had made all the arrangements without consulting me. And while they were splendid arrangements, I was still irked by his assumption of command—again. He'd promised me he'd let me drive this, let *me* be in control. It was likely that he didn't even think about things like that. That they were so easy for him to arrange that it didn't even occur to him that he was wresting anything from my grasp that I didn't want to cede.

After minutes of staring at the blinking cursor in the reply screen, I picked up the phone and dialed Heath. There was no answer.

With a huff and a sigh, I closed the program and shuffled off to bed. Despite being exhausted and having to report for an early shift in the morning—as in 5 AM sort of early—I couldn't sleep.

I kept wondering if I should be irked or not. I kept wondering if I should be reading so much into his gestures. Were there ulterior motives or was this just second nature to him?

My mind wandered over everything and ultimately, kept returning to that feeling I got when he watched me with that intense stare. My skin flushed all over in response. And that kiss. I could remember the tiniest detail of it. Would sex with him be like that—only more?

His mouth had felt so good I couldn't help but wonder what his lips, his tongue would feel like on my body. My nipples immediately tightened at the thought of that hot tongue sliding over them. I imagined the pressure of his hard, heavy body on top of mine, pressing me into the mattress.

My hand moved between my legs, stroking faster and faster against that knotted ache that had stirred into being when we'd kissed.

My eyes screwed tight as the pleasant anticipation built. His hands on my body, his body between my legs. His back under my stroking hands. *Yes.*

I gasped as I tumbled down that precipice, my body convulsing with the orgasm.

At two a.m. I finally drifted off, but not before becoming aware of an unease at the edge of my fatigued awareness. I was captain of my own ship, yes. But I still had to answer to the sea, the weather, the storm on the horizon. And Adam could be any one—or all—of those things. And in my sleep-induced haze, I couldn't help but fear that he was.

5

To Save a Distressed Damsel...Posted on the blog of Girl Geek on May 15, 2013

*H*AVE YOU EVER NOTICED THAT ONE OF THE GREATEST motivators for champions embarking on an epic fantasy quest almost always involves a woman?

Either the knight-errant departs on crusade to prove his love to his lady fair or, more commonly, the lady has been captured and dragged off by big baddies and awaits her hero while locked in a tower or (shudder) a dank dungeon.

Take, for example, the latest in a series of mysterious quests in our oft-bemoaned but much-loved game Dragon Epoch. Players have been summoned to action by the capture of innocent elf princess Alloreah'ala by the race of evil Stone Trolls, who live far under the Golden Mountains.

Every quest, every motivation has something to do with our princess. Every illustration referring to the new expansion of the game has her scantily-clad likeness splayed across it—just to reinforce why it's important to save her. Because she's PRETTY and innocent. And helpless.

Oh and because the King has issued the edict to save his beloved daughter.

Okay, that bag of gold and laundry list of magical equipment might be pretty important, too.

My question is this...why can't these games assume that the women can fend for themselves? My Spiritual Enchantress has a pretty mean Bedazzle spell in her arsenal and she's capable of holding her own.

But why is this nonplayer female character so pathetic—one of a long line of pathetic females? Why can't she defend herself? Why can't she pull some kickass moves, steal the jailer's weapon and keys, bash in some bad-guy heads and save herself? Why must she sit and wait, imprisoned, and in the process become just an object to save?

It's time for the pretty princesses of Yondareth to rebel! Fight your own fight and stop waiting for some dudes to do it for you.

A few days before I was set to leave on a red-eye from LAX to Amsterdam, I went to Heath's house to go over the details of the trip. He printed out my ticket and whistled, waving it under my nose. I snatched it out of his hand and stuffed it into my bag.

Heath's green eyes sparkled as he laughed at me. He had unruly dark blond hair and his cheeks were roughened with a few days' growth of golden whiskers.

"British Airways, first class. *So* high class, Mia. LAX to Heathrow for a layover and then on to Amsterdam."

I sat on his plush couch shaking my head while he tapped away at the computer. I'd only flown a few times before—all domestic flights. The farthest was a trip to Washington, DC with my eighth-grade class. I'd never flown out of the country and in fact had only just received my first passport the month before in anticipation of the auction.

He hit a few more keys. Heath typed fast but always with only two fingers at a time—his pointer fingers. I often teased him about his hunt-and-peck approach, but he never bothered to learn how to use the home keys. "He e-mailed me a signed PDF of the contract which I printed. So, you need to sign a copy, too. Not that this thing would be legally enforceable, mind you. It's an illegal agreement in our country, but it's couched in all kinds of verbiage. Either one of you could weasel out of it. He doesn't pay any money until you put out and you won't put out until you see that the money is safely set aside for that purpose. Strange little situation, with these holding accounts."

I sighed. "I'm so glad I have you and your bestie Joe to work this stuff out for me. There's a reason law school never interested me."

"I had a nice long talk with Drake when I got the contract. He's pretty easy to get to know. He's not a bad guy—for someone who'd pay almost a million dollars to pluck a virgin flower, that is."

My mouth quirked at the irony. What type of person was I, for selling it in the first place? I took a deep breath. A practical person, I decided.

"I made sure to emphasize certain stipulations—once the contract has been 'fulfilled,' there is to be no further contact between you. No phone, no e-mails. Essentially like a restraining order, though we won't have to go that far unless one of you loses it."

I looked away, ignoring a weird twinge at the thought of one of us possibly getting obsessed over this. "Uh-huh."

He tilted his head at me, the glow of his computer monitor reflecting on his stern features. "So, you think you can do this? You were pretty annoyed with him after that first meeting. I knew you were into him in other ways, but you were so determined to go with someone else until something changed your mind. What was it?"

He kissed me and it blew my mind, I thought. How ridiculous. A woman my age being reduced to a blithering moron by one kiss from a desirable—albeit *insanely* desirable—male.

"I just...did a lot of thinking. He's young. He's attractive. It could be a lot worse."

Heath gave a dry chuckle. "Attractive. Huh. I'd say he's smoking hot, but maybe that's just me. He's not even my type, either, but I'd do him."

I smothered a giggle at that mental image.

"So I thought Amsterdam was a good choice, given their open policy and legal support of prostitution."

I rolled my eyes. "Can we stop using that word?"

Heath smirked at me. "Doll, you can call it a freaking clown rodeo if you want. Still won't change the fact that you are going to have sex with a man and he is going to pay you for that privilege."

I looked away but my cheeks heated. I fiddled idly with a hole in my jeans—fraying it so that it grew. I shook my head. I was *not* a prostitute and I wouldn't *be* a prostitute after this whole thing was finished. It was one night of my life. Just one. I was empowering myself—

And I was going to have sex with a man. *That* man. His hands would be on my body, that lush, hot mouth on me. I stayed silent and didn't meet Heath's gaze.

"We also went over what he can and can't do. I wanted to be *very* clear on that. No kink. No bondage of any kind. Straight vanilla all the way for my girl."

"Vanilla is a very tasty flavor, in my opinion."

He sighed and shook his head. "You haven't lived, my dear. But just wait, once you get a taste, I have a feeling you'll be wanting all sorts of flavors after this."

I blew out a breath. I highly doubted it. This was a business deal and I was benefiting from something that not only mattered little to me but had only served as a burden up until this point. I wanted to be rid of the stigma of being the twenty-two-year-old virgin without having to deal with any messy entanglements. I hadn't wanted a relationship for quite some time and didn't see that changing at all in the foreseeable future.

"And no oral, right?" Heath asked.

I looked at him like he was an idiot. As if he had to ask *that*. "That hasn't changed and it's not going to."

He sat back against his computer chair, which squeaked in protest. His gaze grew intent. "The man might want to get his money's worth after all..." Heath said. He tried to give it that jokey air that he gave most of his words, but these held a dark edge.

A cold pulse thumped at the base of my throat. "Don't go there, Heath."

His stared at me. "I don't think you're ready for this. You can't even talk about it."

"I can talk about it. I *have* talked about it. You know everything."

But despite his words, I still couldn't get the picture out of my mind...that dark summer night, dry winds coming out of the foothills. Out on the edge of town, watching the lights and I was sobbing, on my knees. Hands wound into my hair so tightly, pulling so hard that my scalp would ache for days afterward.

I shook my head, my hands crunching into balls. "Stop it. I'm fine."

He shrugged, that nonchalance returning. "Okay. If you say so. Let's see...what else did we talk about? Oh yes, one night straight vanilla sex. Positions of your choice and comfort."

My eyes bugged. "*Positions?* It's just one night."

Heath seemed to be stifling laughter. "Yeah—one night, who knows how many times that means? He's young, very fit, he's probably good for at least two, probably three. More if it's been as long as he says it's been. Eight months. Christ."

"*What?*" I screeched, horrified.

"Doll, you act like you're getting your legs waxed or something—well, admittedly it's your first time so it will hurt a little, but I can guarantee you're going to be having too much fun to notice. Just hope that he's not really big—"

I clapped my hands over my ears as if to block off the rest of his diatribe.

"Mia," he said and waited until I dropped my hands. "Mia, I'm not shitting now. If you can't even talk about it like this, how in the hell are you going to go through with it?"

I watched him for a moment. My best friend since the eighth grade. We were each other's only comfort during some of the worst years of our lives—growing up in a small high desert community as awkward misfits, the both of us. When he came out in the ninth grade, I was the first person he told. When my boyfriend sexually assaulted me in the tenth grade, he was the first person I told.

I shook my head. "I thought it would be just as simple as me drinking a bottle of wine and then lying back and thinking of medical school."

He gave me a sad smile. "It's never even occurred to you that you might enjoy it, has it?"

I shrugged. "You've screened the guy. You say he's trustworthy. He won't hurt me?"

Heath shook his head. "There are no guarantees. You've got to trust that he won't. I tried my hardest. Had him investigated. No criminal record, no dirty rumors of deviant behavior."

I ran a hand through my hair and began to twirl the dark brown end of it nervously around my forefinger.

Heath cleared his throat. "I gotta ask and I know it's a really personal question but... did you start taking your pills from Planned Parenthood?"

I nodded. I'd started my period four weeks before and started the Pill at the prescribed time.

"He's cleared, medically. I saw the report with my own eyes."

I fidgeted. I wanted to back out. But I'd never in a million years admit that to Heath because he'd jump on that hesitation like a Golden Eagle swooping down on a rattlesnake.

"He's in the UK rolling out the European launch of the latest game expansion. But it's not too late to back out of this."

I squeezed my eyes shut. "Please, Heath! Don't keep saying that. I need your support right now. I don't need you to talk me out of this."

"I wouldn't be your best friend if I didn't try to talk you out of this."

And then he approached, plopped himself down on the sofa beside me and wrapped me in his big arms. I planted my face against his broad chest. He smoothed my hair and the panic melted away.

When I left an hour later, I was calm. Reserved. Resigned.

***

I took the entire week off before I left so that I could write, plan and schedule my blogs to be published during my absence. I hoped this would throw readers off the track about what was going on in my personal life. I planted seeds of diversion by mentioning how busy I was getting with my day job. How I'd have to work double shifts for the next little while. White lies to throw the gossips off the trail.

The gossips were already out discussing on other sites when and if the transaction would take place. I had mentioned, briefly, that I would not be able to discuss the results of the auction for many reasons. I'm not sure how many were really interested. My site was about gaming, after all. Most of those guys would rather go on epic raids for their elite gear than get laid—or hear about me getting laid. I understood that. I was one of them.

I also took care of one last thread of unfinished business by telling my mom I was going to be hitting the books heavy for the next few days so I'd be unplugging my phone. It's true that I was bringing study materials on the plane, but the less I told her, the better.

"You sound tired, Mia. Are you sure you haven't been studying too much?"

"There's no such thing as studying too much, Mom. People in my study group have private tutors and one went to a special test prep retreat." I sighed inwardly, wondering how I would be able to compete with the myriad of hopeful medical students who went to these measures to succeed on their exams. Especially when I'd already proven myself a failure. My chest tightened thinking about how, if I had scored well last year, I'd have my acceptance letter to begin med school in the fall already in my hand.

"I worry that between all you've got on your plate with your jobs and studying that you are burning the candle at both ends."

"I have no classes this semester. Believe me, if I could do all this while I was going to school, I can do it now. Don't worry, Mom. Now I get to ask *you* how you're doing."

"Oh," she said lightly. "I'm just great. Things are looking up for me."

I frowned. Looking up? Had she gotten to be a better liar when I wasn't noticing or were things actually improving for her? "What's going on? Has something happened?"

"I'm—I'm not really ready to talk about it."

I sat back, bewildered. Was Mom finally dating again? I blew out a breath. She'd never had any relationships the entire time I was growing up. She had male friends in the community and I know some of them may have wanted a romantic relationship, but my mom had never been interested. When I was a teen, I asked her why she never dated and she shrugged and said she was waiting for me to grow up. Well, I was grown up now. Had she finally decided to get on with her life?

"If it was something serious, you'd tell me...right?"

"Of course," she said evasively.

We hung up a few minutes later and I stared at my phone for long moments. That was one of the weirdest phone calls I'd had with my mom in a long time. She was always an open book with me.

But who was I to talk, really? I was keeping one hell of a secret from her. One that, if she ever discovered it, would hurt her. I had no right to go digging in her business if I wasn't prepared to open up about mine. But still, I was worried. I was protective of my mom and given her experience with the Biological Sperm Donor, she hadn't chosen well in the past.

But Mom was smart and I had to trust that she'd learned from her mistakes. So to take my mind off of my worries and given the fact that I didn't have much to pack, I spent most of the day before my departure wasting monsters on Dragon Epoch. I kept checking the player list for FallenOne but I was not in luck. My notifications list said that he hadn't logged in since that day we had played together weeks before.

***

The next day I was on a flight to Amsterdam with a small overnight bag. I had packed light, per Adam's instructions. He'd clarified in later e-mails that he'd gotten my dress size from Heath and would have some clothes waiting for me. I'm sure he guessed, after spending five minutes in my little dive, that I wouldn't have clothing fit to be seen at a place like Amstel Amsterdam.

I traveled in my most comfortable pair of jeans, a T-shirt and walking shoes, with a small bag of toiletries and unmentionables tucked under the enormous recliner in first class.

I'd gone through every short line at the airport and not a single person blinked an eye at my scruffy clothing and threadbare backpack. Everything was full service and everybody catered to my whim.

I'd had a glass of chilled white wine at the first-class lounge. It took the edge off of traveling alone and the uncertainty of what I'd be facing in the Netherlands. I snacked on smoked salmon and crème fraiche to go with the wine. The jitters only dulled instead of dissipating.

But the plane ride was something else entirely. I'd have fifteen hours of travel, yet, before I would touch down in Amsterdam. So I enjoyed myself in the top floor front of the immense 747. Shortly after takeoff for a direct flight to London, I was served more wine and handed a full menu. Dinner came on a white tablecloth with china and full silverware. I unabashedly enjoyed the pampering and lovely, lilting British accents spoken all around me.

I didn't sleep a wink on the plane—living true to the term "redeye" flight as my eyes were scratchy and gritty by the time I'd deplaned.

Upon our arrival in London, an airline employee greeted me, holding up a card with my name on it. She showed me down to the Heathrow First Class lounge and spa, giving me a list of all the appointments she'd made on my behalf. Then I was treated to a manicure, pedicure and facial before being handed a towel and a shiny green and gold shopping bag. Then she led me into a private bathroom with shower.

After the long plane ride, it felt like heaven. And I still had a few hours before the flight to Amsterdam. The bag contained new clothes—the tags still on them from Harrods department store. A smart dark green and black sundress and even new underthings—silk panties and a matching, lacy bra. I blushed to look at them, but felt so pretty when I wore them that I could hardly be upset at the presumption.

I'd never been spoiled before. And I could definitely see the appeal. I applied my makeup and dried and styled my hair and felt like a fresh, new person. I'd stepped into a whole new world, like a modern-day fairy tale. It was just a short, one-hour hop from here to Amsterdam, and Adam, who was waiting for me.

In Amsterdam, a driver met me and whisked me off to the hotel, speaking cheerfully in almost perfect British-accented English, though he was clearly Dutch. He had the white-blond hair and pale blue eyes of his Viking ancestors.

I arrived at the hotel just around noon and checked in, per Adam's instructions. The clerk handed me an envelope and inside was a smart phone. I asked the clerk if it would work in Amsterdam and he gave me a puzzled look and nodded. I glanced at it and noticed a waiting text message from Adam. It told me to order myself some lunch in the suite and he would see me at 3 p.m. for a day of sightseeing.

The bellhop guided me through a palatial lobby carved out of white marble and up an elegant Y-shaped, carpet-covered staircase to the elevators. I'd learned online that the majestic building dated from the nineteenth century and featured all the exquisite architectural details an earlier era. The bellhop loaded me into a small elevator—the type that had been fitted in as a nod to modern conveniences and seemed alien in this elegant, old-fashioned building.

On the top floor, he directed me to the penthouse suite. And inside I found a space that could have fit my studio four times over. It was appointed in antique furnishings, had a bedroom and bathroom on the lower floor as well as a sitting room with couch and bar. A dark wood staircase led up to the unknown and I stared at it for a moment, determined to go exploring the minute I was alone. I wasn't set to meet Adam for another hour, so I had no idea where he was or if he had checked in yet.

"Mr. Drake..." I said to the bellhop.

"I'm sorry, Miss. I do not know. You can call down to the lobby and ask."

I smiled. "That's okay. I can text him."

The bellhop, who had insisted on carrying my ratty backpack for me, didn't even hesitate or wait for a tip. Instead, he bowed himself out.

A tingle of anticipation started at the base of my spine. I punched in a message on my phone.

Am here. Waiting patiently.

I hadn't seen him in three weeks and in my mind he'd steadily grown more attractive and delicious. Hell, he'd reached almost god-like proportions by now, in my imagination. I was anxious to see him again. This would be the next and the last day that I would.

There was no reply to my text. Likely he was still in meetings or maybe still in the air. I blew out a breath and fidgeted nervously, determined to satisfy my curiosity.

I walked around downstairs, and briefly glanced at the room service menu before deciding I was too nervous to eat. I looked in every corner around the bar and the single bedroom, where I'd dumped my stuff. I wondered—if the bedroom was downstairs, then what was upstairs? A terrace?

I galloped quickly up the stairs to find out. I landed in an even grander bedroom. It was elegantly decorated with a giant four-poster bed and accompanied by similar period furniture in dark woods. The curtains on the sidewall had been pulled aside and the windows looked out over the canals of Amsterdam.

A fresh set of clothes—which I assumed were Adam's—had been laid across the bed, but there was no one in the room. I entered and walked to the bed—a king size, decorated in blues, silvers and light gray French toile fabric. My eyes skimmed over the bed, wondering if this would be the place where things would happen tonight. My heart thrummed again and I swallowed, but there was no way I could tell if that was from fear or excitement.

He was here, already. I heard a noise at the same moment a doorknob—presumably to the bathroom—rattled. I jumped back but before I could skitter out of the room, it opened and Adam stood in the doorway, frozen in mid-step. He'd just exited the shower.

Our eyes locked and my breathing froze. He had one snowy towel slung low around his hips, another draped around his neck. He'd obviously just toweled his hair dry. The short cut was frizzed in every direction as if it had been artfully arranged that way.

And his chest—every creased valley, firm muscular angle chiseled in perfect flesh—gleamed with steam. I sucked in a quick breath.

"H-hi," I finally said, tearing my eyes from his bare chest with reluctance.

"Emilia." He smiled openly with no apparent self-consciousness. "You made it!"

"I'm—I'm sorry for—I didn't know you were even here yet. I was just exploring."

"No worries. My meeting let out earlier than expected so I beat you here. Did you have lunch?"

I fought to keep my eyes from drifting downward again, from fixing on those perfect abs, lightly dusted with dark hair, that seemed to have been sculpted by Michelangelo himself. "I—I wasn't that hungry."

"Order room service. I could use a roast beef sandwich and theirs is delicious. We can catch up over lunch."

"Um," I stammered and looked away and then back to him. "Sure. I'll—just go do that then."

He laughed and pulled the towel from around his neck, throwing it back into the bathroom behind him. And that's when I saw the tattoo.

Scrawled in elegant jade-green script just under his left collarbone, it was easy to read and very simply designed. Just one word. A woman's name. *Sabrina.*

I couldn't look away, my eyes zeroing in on that interesting detail. He glanced down to follow my gaze and then looked up again.

"If you'd just give me a moment...unless you want to stay and do this now?" he said with laughter in his eyes.

My mouth dropped. "I'll go order lunch, then," I repeated lamely before fumbling my way out, nearly tripping down the stairs.

I ordered his roast beef sandwich with the works—he hadn't told me what he wanted on it, after all, and for myself, a grilled cheese with smoked brie and Gruyère.

By the time I was done with the order, he had entered the room, now fully dressed, thank God. Even in jeans and a button-down shirt, he was the epitome of handsome elegance. And even in my breezy sundress I felt awkward next to him. I wondered if that mega-suit he'd worn at the hotel during our first meeting was a fluke. Computer geeks typically didn't suit up. Most of the coders I knew liked to brag about the casual dress their jobs allowed. But he didn't seem like a typical computer geek.

Then again, how would I know? I knew so little about him.

That was the way I'd wanted it, right? Wham, bam, here's your cash, ma'am? And suddenly it occurred to me—with no small amount of fear—something I'd never worried about until this moment. What if I didn't please him? What if he found me wanting in the bedroom? I was completely inexperienced, after all. Would he feel cheated? Like he hadn't gotten his money's worth? I shook my head, ridding it of the odd thought. What was happening to me?

"Cold?" he said, misinterpreting my headshake.

"No. I'm fine. Thank you for the dress." I said, smoothing my skirt.

"Thank Heath, actually. He had to talk me out of ordering a chainmail bikini." When I shot him a weird look, he laughed. "Kidding. I asked him to pick out some pretty things for you on the Harrod's website and have them delivered to the airport lounge. Seems everything went off well."

I snorted. "*Heath* picked this out?"

He looked puzzled. "Yeah. Why's that surprising?"

"He has the fashion sense of a barnacle."

"He *is* gay, right?"

"He's gay. But he's not that kind of gay. He'd wear a burlap sack to work if they'd let him—or if burlap sacks were comfortable."

Adam's eye traveled down my form appreciatively, but not lasciviously. "He knows colors, that's for sure. That color suits your dark hair and eyes perfectly. You look radiant. And more importantly, you don't look like you've just spent fifteen hours in transit."

I spread my arms out in front of me. "Good thing."

"Are you tired?"

"I chugged a Dr. Pepper on the flight from London and bought another one when I landed here."

"Good. Let's eat and then we can see some sights. I was thinking maybe the Royal Palace and a trip down the canals?"

I brightened and he smiled at my obvious excitement. "That sounds wonderful. I'd love to!"

Room service arrived then, and the waiter set it out on the table as if he was a maitre d' at a Michelin star restaurant. And we weren't just eating some sandwiches.

My croissant and melted cheese was to die for. Adam laughed at my obvious pleasure in the food, but I could tell he was having a similar reaction to his roast beef. "If I could get away with flying these in for lunch every day from Amsterdam to Irvine, I'd do it in a heartbeat."

"Oh, that's probably pocket change for you."

"Nope. I could never bring myself to do it. An ostentatious waste. I already feel enough guilt over my carbon footprint and I pay to offset it. But when I do get a chance to stay here, I make sure to have one. I also took one to space with me."

"Shut up!" I said, my eyeballs almost falling out of my head. "You've been to space?"

He nodded, finishing up his next bite. "I spent ten days at the International Space Station last year. Biggest high of my life."

Every minute I spent with this man, he managed to surprise me even more. "Are you an astronaut, too?"

"A space tourist, more like. The Russians sell slots on their launches to the highest bidder. I got lucky. It happens often," he said, shooting me a meaningful look.

But he hardly got a reaction from me. I was still reeling from the news that he'd been to space. "What was it like?"

His eyes drifted off to the side and had a sparkling quality about them, liked polished onyx. "It was...indescribable."

I blew out a breath of disbelief. "Give me something to work with. Come on, just a few adjectives?"

He paused. "Unforgettable. Unbelievable. Like...the entire world had gone silent. The whitest of white points against the blackest black and huge, blue world below my feet."

I took another bite of my delish sandwich, contemplating his words. "That's very poetic for a geek. It's fortunate that I can never quote you because you might have to have your geek card revoked if it gets out."

He grinned. "I'm a geek for life. Not only am I president of the geek club but I'm also a member."

I snickered and bit into my sandwich. "If your geek card isn't revoked because of the poetry it should definitely be revoked for having all those muscles." I said and then blushed scarlet, realizing I was still remembering that vision of him with his shirt off. The firm pecs, the clearly defined abs and biceps, like he'd been chiseled from marble. "Geeks don't have muscles," I said, lamely covering my embarrassment.

It was true. What kind of computer programmer had a body like that? He smirked. "The geeks who didn't like getting picked on in school and decided to bulk up as a deterrent do."

I studied him as I finished up my sandwich, hard-pressed to imagine any idiot picking on Adam. But I had no idea what he'd been like as a youth, so how could I know? Whatever the incentive, it had worked. It, along with his brilliant mind, handsome face and dark good looks completed a whole dreamy package. One that, I'd bet, many women tried to get their hands on. I pondered that in silence over the rest of my sandwich. I'd found no information about any previous relationships online. Maybe he'd made those women sign NDAs too.

We spent the afternoon at the Royal Palace and then on a guided tour down the canal. The city was vibrant, clean, a stunning fusion of old world and new. I'd now stepped into an even stranger world than the one I'd entered in that first-class line at LAX. This world included only one other person and I was sharing every experience, all the conversation—for we were rarely without something to talk about—with him. To use his words, it was like the entire world had gone silent and we were the only two in it.

I couldn't help but wonder what it would be like the next day when it was time for me to get back on the plane for the return trip home. How would it feel to go back to the real world after dancing at midnight like Cinderella at the ball?

At least I knew better than to expect my Prince Charming to show up at my doorstep the next day, ready to jam a glass slipper onto my foot.

We returned to the hotel at around six p.m. and Adam said we should change for dinner. He told me that everything I'd need was in the wardrobe of my bedroom. So I threw it open. There were three gowns—one red, one black and one in filmy crème, all with matching shoes. I chose the black and wondered if Heath had picked these out, too. There was no way. They were all so gorgeous.

I quickly showered, redid my makeup and arranged my dark brown hair in a simple straight style that brushed past my shoulders to the middle of my back.

The black dress was beaded at the waist and at the scoop of the bodice, catching the light with glamorous sparkles. It hung on thin straps and was backless to the waist, gathering in loose folds there.

Because of the design, I'd have to go braless to wear it, but it seemed to support me perfectly, regardless. I picked out a new pair from a handful of pretty underthings—this one a sheer and lacy pair of panties that made me feel naughty just wearing them. I felt like a princess. Or an actress about to take the stage at the Oscars.

I slipped into the matching heels—I wasn't accustomed to wearing them, but these strappy sandals were works of art, glittering with rhinestones. Every step I took sent a flare of brilliant light in every direction.

When I entered the living room, it was to a wolf whistle. Adam stood near the ice bucket with an open bottle of champagne in his hands, about to pour. I turned—carefully, so as not to trip all over myself—and he shook his head. "You're going to be the toast of Amsterdam tonight, Emilia."

My cheer faded, suddenly. I was only going to be the toast of this room. Of his bed. And for far less than a whole night. I'd stepped into a dream and now, in the middle of it, was all too aware that it would be over before I even realized it.

"We'll be dining at Ciel Bleu and, if you are so inclined, there will be dancing nearby in the hotel afterward."

I gaped. "Dancing? What sort of dancing? You mean like waltzing and stuff?"

He shot me a strange look. He looked adorable when he screwed up his face like that. Like a little boy, almost. Almost.

He looked stunning in just about everything he dressed in, whether it was jeans and a casual shirt, a designer business suit or this scrumptious black evening suit and crisp white dress shirt. I couldn't forget what lay under that polished suit. That perfect body, those hard, defined muscles. That tattoo with a woman's name just above his heart.

Who was she? And why wasn't she in his life anymore? I wondered if I'd find the courage to ask before the night was through.

He held a bubbling flute out to me. "Come, have a sip. Then let's be off."

I should have told him that I didn't date. I should have told him that this would be so much easier if we didn't go out. If we just took our clothes off and did this now. But I didn't want to. I didn't want the magic to go away so soon and somehow I knew that the moment the act was finished, it would be.

***

"Not even one little hint? Come on…" I whined over my glass of iced mineral water.

His dark eyes flickered with amusement. "The secrets are not mine to reveal."

Players of Dragon Epoch had been searching for clues to start the secret chain of quests that lay in the Golden Mountains region for months. It was one of the most notorious Easter eggs ever hidden in an online game and here, I had the CEO and chief designer of the game as my captive audience. Hell yeah, I was going to take advantage and try to weasel some clues out of him.

"It's *your* company. Your game! And players have been working on that quest chain for months. There are entire wikis and databases full of clues."

He grinned, looking off to the side, as if remembering something funny. "Yeah. Half of that stuff is pure bullshit. Some of it was planted by our own developers."

I sat back and groaned. "Pretty please?"

"Emilia, you can bat those gorgeous brown eyes at me all night and I won't tell you. I am sworn to secrecy."

I sighed, surprised at the heated flush crawling up my cheeks. I'd been told before that I had pretty eyes. They were large, round, dark and my lashes were thick. I suppose people found them attractive and I usually accepted the compliment with a self-deprecating smile. No one ever told me that I had a gorgeous butt or lovely breasts. Thank God for that because it probably would have made me die of embarrassment. But it was something about the *way* Adam complimented my eyes that made me react so strongly. It was so nonchalant. He didn't throw out the compliment as a way to score points with me or butter me up. He stated that I had gorgeous eyes as if it were a well-known fact—and that no amount of batting them (and for the record, I *never* bat my eyes!) would get me what I wanted.

I wanted his secrets. The game secrets would be great to start with but as I had come to spend more time with this man throughout our day in Amsterdam I found myself wanting to know *all* of his secrets. What drove him to be so successful in his business, to enjoy the trappings of his money without being so ostentatious as to fly in a sandwich for his lunch? What was his family life like? Why hadn't he slept with anyone in eight months and why wasn't he with someone now?

And who was Sabrina? Why did he have her name tattooed over his heart—a man who seemed the very antithesis of making such a sentimental gesture? Perhaps he'd had it done when he was very young or drunk. She was the lost childhood love who broke his heart by moving on to someone else once college came along. Or maybe she was a college sweetheart.

I remembered reading that he'd dropped out of college. He'd already made his first couple million by then. Still, I couldn't help but wonder why he hadn't finished what he'd started—especially when he seemed to be such a driven person.

As I was musing over this, he asked me about my own college plans. "So Heath mentioned that you had finished your BS in biology early and are taking the semester off."

I took a sip of wine from my other glass. I shot him a look. "Yes. I'm calling it a 'gap year' without the Europe experience, but this might well count for that, even if it's only for two days." I sipped again. There was no reason to tell him I was an utter failure and waiting to retake the damn test that was the bane of my existence. I affected a nonchalant shrug. "I'm taking next year off and then on to med school."

He nodded. He already knew that, obviously. "What kind of doctor do you want to be?"

I hesitated, as I often had since I'd done so horribly on the MCAT the previous year. Since that afternoon when I'd stared at those results, slowly watching my dream twist down the drain in a whirlpool of suck. I took a deep breath and squared my shoulders. "An oncologist."

He tilted his head towards me, focusing his attention. "Really. Hard stuff. That would take a special kind of strength to deal with cancer patients all day."

"Cancer is a bitch that needs to get the crap smacked out of it. I intend to stand on the front lines with a big-ass bat."

He watched my fist clench on the tabletop. "Sounds like it's very personal to you."

I took another sip of wine, studied his strong hand resting on the table next to his dinner plate. "It is. My mom had it."

"She's okay now?"

I nodded. For the moment. But as close as I came to losing her, there was always the specter of recurrence hovering near. Were it not for her regular inoculation therapy, that specter would be more than just a wispy ghost. But she'd been telling me for months that she didn't have the money to keep going in and getting treatments. The possibility that she might consider forgoing them entirely almost paralyzed me with fear.

I lifted my eyes to his. They penetrated like arrows.

"That must have been rough on all of you."

"It's just us. Me and her. I'm an only child and I have no idea who my father is, nor do I care."

His expression didn't change. He didn't even move. "So Strong is your mother's name?"

Another sip. "Yep. She's both my mom and my dad. And she's done a pretty good job of it, I'd say."

"I agree."

"You don't even know anything about me."

"I've read your blog." He looked away with a shrug.

I gazed at him with suspicion. "So just how regular of a reader are you?"

An enigmatic smile hovered on his mouth.

"C'mon. Spill it, Drake. How long have you been reading?"

He shrugged. "I don't know, a year or so."

"A *year?*"

He nodded while gazing at the ceiling. "Yeah. Something like that."

"Why didn't you tell me that before?"

"Because you were already freaked out enough when you found out who I was. I wasn't going to add fuel to that fire."

"Shit. Then you know a whole lot more about me than I know about you. You asked me questions like you didn't."

"How else was I going to get you to open up?"

"And here I thought you were just interested in opening me up in *another* way."

At that precise moment, the sommelier appeared to pour us more wine. I blushed crimson, horrified, knowing he'd heard what I said. Adam laced his hands together in front of his face, suppressing his laughter behind them. I shot him a dirty look, which only served to increase his amusement. My eyes narrowed.

"Very funny." I said, once he left.

He pulled his hands away from his mouth. "Yes, it was, actually. I couldn't care less about his reaction, but the mortification on your face was hilarious."

"It's your turn now. Cough it all up."

His brows knit. "Cough what up?"

"The goods. Come on. I signed the NDA. It's not going on the front page."

He took a deep draught of his wine—the same glass he'd been nursing all night. "What do you want to know?"

I asked him what I'd been wondering earlier. "Why'd you quit college?"

He seemed surprised that I knew that. It was on his Wikipedia page, after all. He'd dropped out after his first year at Caltech. "I wasn't learning anything new."

Well, well. He was a boy genius after all. Had I expected any other kind of answer? He cleared his throat and continued. "Sony offered me a lot of money to work for them."

"They couldn't wait a few years?"

"Apparently not. I didn't work for them long, anyway. I quickly learned that the only boss I cared to answer to was me."

I studied him. So he had issues with authority—professors, bosses. But he'd been a model citizen, no records of arrests or juvenile delinquency. He'd likely had a strong family to guide him.

"Where were you born? Where did you grow up? Did you have a big family?"

He grinned. "That's a lot of questions."

I shot him a sweet smile. "We don't have a lot of time."

"True enough. I was born in Pasadena. I lived in Washington State until my early teens, then came back to California to live with my uncle in OC."

The article on him in Wikipedia had provided scant information about his childhood. He'd already divulged way more than I'd learned by scouring Google. And it was not lost on me that he hadn't answered the question about his family. Fair enough, I really didn't want to talk about mine, either. All two of us.

I tried another tack. "What does your dad do?"

"He died when I was four. He was a professor at Caltech."

"Oh, I'm sorry."

He shrugged. "I don't remember him at all."

Another thing we had in common, then. We never knew our fathers. But at least his father had wanted him. Hadn't handed a wad of cash to his mother with the curt order to "get rid of the problem."

I cleared my throat and coughed. "Okay, so more speed-dating questions...What's your favorite color? What is your astrological sign? Where does the Golden Mountain quest chain start? What's your favorite book?"

His eyes narrowed with suspicion but he could not mask the smile curving at the corner of his mouth. "Blue. Aries. Not gonna tell you in a million years. *The Art of War.*"

"Crap," I grumped and then we both burst into laughter.

Dinner continued like that. I learned that he loved Mexican and Chinese. Didn't care much for Thai. I told him about my absolute obsession with the perfect pizza—New York-style Zito's in Old Towne Orange. He told me he'd had the authentic stuff and refused to eat New York-style anywhere outside of New York.

He was astonished to discover that I actually preferred the Special Edition version of the original *Star Wars* trilogy.

He shook his head, eyes widened in mock horror. "I can't even—"

"Oh c'mon. Three words: better special effects."

His expression grew dead serious. "Three words: Greedo shoots first."

I grimaced. "Okay, you have a point there, but I'm not going to change my mind just because of that one little thing—"

"One *little* thing?!" His mouth dropped. "That one moment changed the entire characterization of Han Solo."

I tilted my head to the side. "You know, I think I've only seen the original version once before?"

He blinked. "Your education is seriously lacking."

"Hey, last time I checked I was the one with a soon-to-be con-ferred degree and you weren't."

His eyes glowed over his deepening smile. "Touché." He jerked his chin toward me. "Now it's your turn. Where'd you grow up? OC?"

I shook my head. "I didn't move there until college. Heath and I come from the tiniest backwater community in the high desert hills in California called Anza. Our only claim to fame is that the Pacific Crest Trail goes practically through the center of town. Only freaks and geeks come from Anza."

We talked for a long time, until after dessert. We'd shared a cherries jubilee flambé that had threatened to set the room on fire. At one point, we ended up using our spoons to fence for the last bite. He won, scooping up the last morsel in his spoon and then gal-lantly holding it out for me to eat.

And just next door, for I had been listening to the strains of the orchestra for most of the night, was the dancing. He offered me an arm, like a gentleman out of a nineteenth-century period miniseries. Awkwardly, I took his arm and let him lead me toward the dance floor.

"I don't dance like this at all. Just sayin' that I hope your shoes have metal tips for toe protection."

"Just follow my lead. It's the foxtrot. The steps are easy. Slow. Slow. Quick, quick. I'll lead you."

I frowned. "And how do *you* know how to dance like this? Did you time warp out of *Downton Abbey?*"

He smiled. "My cousin danced ballroom dance for competition. She forced me to be her practice partner."

"Ah." Though I had a very tough time picturing him being forced into anything by anyone.

"Come," he said. "Just follow my cues. I'll guide you with the hand on your back."

And after a few minutes of fumbling, I eventually got the hang of it, though I was quite sure no one would ever mistake us for Johnny and Baby from *Dirty Dancing*.

In this dress, with these glittery heels, in the arms of this man, the sensation of being outside of myself—of living in a waking dream—continued.

After we'd danced a few dances in silence, he spoke softly. "You cold?"

"Nah."

"You're shaking."

Well, yes. Yes, I was. His smell was fantastic and doing indescribable things to me. And he was so close. One large hand clasped mine, the other rested just below my shoulder blade. On my bare back. The heat of him threatened to burn a hole right through me.

I was having trouble remembering to breathe and he wanted to know why I was shaking.

"You nervous about tonight?" he finally asked after a long pause.

I looked up and met his scrutinizing gaze. "Perhaps."

But that wasn't the truth. I wasn't nervous. I was already dreading the drop into reality. The return to normalcy afterward. And the fact that I'd never see him again. How insane. I didn't even know if this was something I'd enjoy yet. For all I knew, I'd hate every second of it. But that's not what was on my mind at that moment. Instead, all I could think of was how much I enjoyed being in his company, trading banter, smelling his smell.

And I already knew that my plan to guzzle wine and lie back and think of medical school had gone up in smoke. I doubted this man would allow me to lie back and think of anything else but him.

We danced only two more before he collected my wrap and the car came to take us back to the hotel.

After all the joking and laughter earlier, the air between us had grown somber, tense. Weighted with the expectation of what was to come. My insides clenched, just below my navel. I was becoming aware of some new, inner fire. It felt like a candle inside a lantern, glowing bright and hot. It was as if my body was already preparing me.

The entire ride back—less than ten minutes, actually—Adam did not touch me or speak to me. He stared out the window, one hand resting on his knee. He was distant, tense and definitely not present in that limo.

When we entered our suite, he placed a hand on the small of my back, guiding me inside. Every nerve in my body instantly jumped at the contact, as if he'd shocked me. The muscles beneath his touch tightened and my breathing rate jumped.

The lights had been turned on and then down, to an ambient glow. A bottle of wine rested in the place of the champagne of earlier that evening. He pulled his hand away and went to it.

"Wine?"

I cleared my throat. "Anything stronger?" I joked. I actually rarely drank hard liquor, but his reaction to my light joke startled me more than anything else. He wore a dark scowl before his features went blank again.

"They don't stock anything hard when I'm here, I'm afraid," he said in a neutral voice.

So he didn't approve of drinking. "But you drink wine and champagne."

"Yes. Sometimes. On special occasions. Or a glass with dinner when it's called for."

I took the glass of deep plum Cabernet Sauvignon that he'd poured. "Sounds like it's very personal to you," I said, echoing his own words back to him.

He took a small sip and settled the glass on the bar, leaning on the hand braced there. "It is. My mother is an alcoholic."

I nodded, instantly regretting the question. That would explain why he'd come to live with his cousins at such a young age. "I'm sorry to hear that."

He shrugged. "I haven't seen in her in years. She lives her life and I live mine."

"Are you afraid that if you drink the hard stuff, it would happen to you, too?"

He looked up. "It's a disease and addiction has a genetic component to it."

Like cancer. I nodded. Suddenly understanding him a whole lot more from the last few minutes than I had in the entire day we had just spent in one another's presence.

He picked up the glass and reached out a hand. I hesitantly placed mine in his. "Come. There's something I want to show you."

I snorted. "Isn't that someone's cheesy line to get a girl into the bedroom?"

He laughed. "Not mine."

He led me up the staircase and to a closed door just before the bedroom. I hadn't noticed it before, when I'd come up this afternoon. He opened it and we were immediately on a rooftop terrace, looking out over one of the canals. Here on the top floor, we could see the roofs of Amsterdam and twinkling lights stretched out before us. The tiny cars in the distant square jockeyed for position around a complex traffic circle, their headlights glowing bright yellow and white.

A chilly spring breeze danced about our hair and shoulders. I went to the rail and he moved behind me, adjusting my wrap over my shoulders. His hands lingered there long moments before slowly slipping down my arms. I suddenly forgot about the gorgeous view in front of me.

He was touching me. Like he meant it. Like he wanted it. I gasped for breath and his hands fell away.

"I remember the first time I saw this city," he murmured, still behind me, gazing out at the view over my head. "I had just sold my first code. Took the summer to travel across Europe and started here. Still had about a year until college. I wasted a lot of time that year, but it was the most memorable of my life."

The display before us seemed otherworldly—all gold, silver and red, like Christmas in fairyland. I remembered the glass of wine in my hand and shakily downed the rest of it. Adam took the glass from me and set it down on a nearby table. When he returned, he stood behind me again, so close he almost touched his chest to my back.

After a few more moments of awkward silence, I leaned backward into him, craving the contact. He exhaled in surprise but said nothing. I shook, feeling every nerve ending where my body touched his. And suddenly I was aching to have his arms around me. "I wanted to do study abroad when I was an undergrad, but the scholarship didn't cover it. I've only been in Europe less than a day and already I'm falling in love with it."

"It's easy to do. And you haven't even seen France yet."

Paris. God, I'd love to see Paris. I closed my eyes and let my head fall back against him. No gasp of surprise this time. My shoulder blades pressed into his hard pecs. His head tipped down, his mouth pressing to my crown. Energy crackled right through me like a live electric tower. Fear was there, too, lurking in the background like a clammy mist.

Then he reached up and tangled his fingers through my hair, pressing along my scalp. I tensed and jumped, instantly reminded of another man's hands wound tightly there, pulling with all his strength, forcing my head down.

Icy terror sliced through me. I gasped, my heart beating its way out of my throat in cold fear. I struggled, pushing away from him, my breath not coming fast enough.

"Get away! Don't—" The world twisted around me and I hit against the railing, holding my hands up to protect myself from him. He'd hit me—so many times—grabbed my long hair and wrapped it around his hands like rope, pulling so hard—so hard. I couldn't breathe. I had to get away.

"Emilia—Mia!" Adam's voice cut through the fuzzy haze of panic that clouded my thoughts. He approached me slowly, eyes wide with concern. Spots formed at the edge of my vision and I felt like I might faint. Breathe! Breathe! I couldn't draw the air in fast enough.

"Mia—My God, are you okay? What is it?"

I put my face in my hands, shaking so fiercely I didn't think I'd be able to talk. "Emilia...do you hear me?"

I turned away from him and closed my eyes. I was safe, a distant voice tried to tell me. I wasn't up on the Ridge, alone and begging

Zack not to hit me again. I was with Adam. I was safe. I couldn't stop shaking.

"Mia," he said again, quietly. He stood closer now.

"I'm... fine..."

"Like hell, you are."

"Please," I said, putting an icy hand to my cheek. My heartbeat danced in my throat and I could hardly catch my next breath. I reached up and smoothed my hair. It was all still there. There was no blood. I was safe. There's no way Adam could have known—hell, there was no way *I* would have known that him putting his hands in my hair would do this to me.

"Emilia. Slow down. If you keep breathing like that you're going to pass out." He took my arm gently and turned me toward him. "Gently. Hold your breath. Close your mouth. Look at me. Look in my eyes." The panic receded as I stared into his dark eyes. He held both my shoulders now. "You're safe, Emilia. There, breathe in through your nose. Keep your mouth closed."

I shook my head, my eyes squeezed tight. "Just..." My voice faded, the cold fear dissipating slowly but leaving an oily trace in its wake. I took a deep breath and continued when I could. "It was just a bad memory. That's all."

"You're white as a sheet. What did I do wrong?"

I shook again and he moved closer, quieting me while I shook in his arms. He pulled me to him and I pressed my face to his shoulder. "I'm sorry—so sorry."

"There is absolutely nothing to apologize for," he murmured.

"I just...I don't like my hair pulled."

There was a long silence. "Okay. I'm sorry."

I shrugged my quivering shoulders. "You didn't know."

He cleared his throat. "We shouldn't do this."

"No," I pulled back from him and stared into his eyes again. "I'm fine. I'm just fine." But doubt clouded his handsome features.

"But if that happens again—"

"It won't. I took care of what I could think of in the paperwork. Except I didn't think about fingers in my hair." I shuddered at the memory of it.

He paused. "Did someone hurt you? Do you want to talk about it?"

I shook my head. I didn't want to talk about it. I hoped he took the shake of my head to mean that someone hadn't hurt me—hadn't wound his hands into my hair, tearing chunks from my scalp as he forced his erection down my throat. I shivered again.

He gently pulled me toward him again, as if expecting me to bolt over the rail at any moment. "Whoever did it deserves to have the shit beat out of him."

I leaned into him and his strong arms came around me, pulling me tightly to him. I was instantly soothed, but my heart was beating an even harsher staccato, pressed up against his sternum. His body felt so hard and powerful next to mine. The smooth material of his jacket caressed my cheek. I closed my eyes.

"Are you all right?"

"I'm fine now. Thanks," I said, my voice sounding as if it came from a far-off place. From that dreamland I'd drifted to all throughout the previous day. Then I lifted my head and looked into his face and I asked him for the one thing I'd wanted all evening. "Will you kiss me?" I asked in a tiny voice.

Without hesitation, his mouth descended slowly on mine, our lips meeting half the distance between us, both heads pressing in for an urgent taste of the other. His touch was gentle, at first, lips firm but closed. But I wanted more—I wanted a kiss like the one he'd left me with that day in my apartment.

My tongue darted out to outline his lips. He expelled a sudden breath and lowered an arm to the small of my back, hooking my waist closer to him. He opened his mouth to my tongue. I deepened the exploration until he met me with his. Another tight gasp from deep within his chest and I was cinched so tightly to him that I detected every contour and ridge of the muscles beneath his shirt. I tilted my head back, eager for more. I locked my hands atop his shoulders, holding him to me.

And suddenly the control was no longer mine. One hand settled at the back of my neck, careful not to twine in my hair while he laid me open with nothing more than his tongue and lips. His tongue delved into my mouth and I couldn't breathe, dizzy with desire. I wanted to whisper his name but I couldn't say anything with the contact so intimate, so deep. And this night it would be deeper still. Fear trembled in my belly. I was actually going to go to bed with a man. This beautiful man.

His mouth left mine, traveling along my jaw to take my earlobe between his lips. His caresses were white-hot and ice-cold at once. Everything in the center of me curled into a tangled tension, crying for release.

His teeth grazed my earlobe and I whispered his name. His mouth and tongue blazed a trail across my neck, my throat. Each touch made my body jump. I arched my breasts into his chest. A deep groan emanated from the bottom of his chest, the first vocal acknowledgement of his arousal.

"Let's go inside," I said, emboldened, my center feeling as if it was on fire and he the only one in the vicinity holding an extinguisher. The boldness was an act. Inside I was shaky and not a little terrified of what this night would be like.

Adam stepped back and took my hand to lead me inside. A rush of warm air surrounded me as we stepped into the bedroom. I thought he would pull me toward the bed, but he stopped beside the couch against the wall. He removed my wrap from my shoulders, slinging it over the back. Then he unbuttoned his coat and did the same. But his eyes never left mine and mine never left his, which glowed like coals under a bonfire.

I was in no doubt now, if I ever had been, really, that he wanted me. That it was as powerful and as ferocious a want as the one singing through my own veins. Before he said another word, I turned toward the bed while I still had the courage. "No," he said, stopping me. "Not yet."

I turned back to him and he wrapped his arms around me, pulling me down with him onto the sofa. I landed in his lap and he was kissing me again—ferociously pressing his mouth to mine, my neck, my throat...and then lower. When he pulled his face away, he looked up at me, his eyes glazed with desire and his features flushed. He lifted a hand to my shoulder, stroking softly along my upper arm.

"Your skin is so soft," he said, his fingers gliding over me as if he'd never touched a woman before.

"Vitamin E," I said lamely when I didn't know what else to say. What does one say when the man who is about to sleep with you lavishes you with compliments? "Thank you" seems kind of stupid.

His eyes didn't leave mine. His hand traveled gently along my collarbone. "Here, too."

I let out a slow breath, excitement jumping into my throat. His touch was igniting new fires I never knew lay dormant in my body—between my legs, all over. My eyes fluttered closed, concentrating on his touch.

His hands stroked lower, dipping into the V between my breasts. "And here," he murmured. And before another moment passed, he pulled me off his lap and sat me beside him on the couch, slipping one strap off my shoulder. I felt the cool air touch my naked breast.

Here we go, I thought. It was not unlike staring over an abyss from atop a rollercoaster that had just paused before plummeting full speed down the hill. My stomach dropped.

I opened my eyes. He was watching me as his hand came up to cup my breast. The breath hissed out between my teeth and his eyes—if it was even possible—seemed to darken.

I'd never exposed myself to a man before. Not like this. Back when I'd dated, there'd been the typical groping in the dark underneath our clothes, parked at the overlook on the Ridge or one of the other places frequented by teenagers. That was as far as it had ever gotten for me before I'd shut it all down and vowed never to date again.

He ran a thumb over the already erect nipple and his breathing quickened. I reached up and grabbed his tie, pulling his mouth to mine. The kiss immediately deepened, his mouth crushing against mine, owning the kiss, like I presumed he owned everything else around him, with confidence, surety.

But his mouth didn't stay on mine for long. Soon he was pushing me back on the couch, so that I lay flat on my back. He hovered over me, hurriedly undoing his tie, unbuttoning the first three buttons of his dress shirt.

With each motion, those black eyes pinned me down—almost dared me to look away. And I couldn't. I was so turned on I could barely breathe, the tightness between my legs knotted so that it was almost painful.

When he settled against me again, his erection pressed against my leg. I almost jumped when I realized what it was. I was under him now—half wondering if he would even bother to move us to the bed for the actual consummation of our deal. I supposed there were worse places one could lose one's virginity than the couch in the penthouse suite of the most luxurious hotel in Amsterdam.

His mouth was on mine, pushing his tongue into mine with urgency, ferocity. He lifted up his body enough to pull the other strap of my dress down, baring me to the waist. I was too delirious with the sensations he was evoking in me to feel embarrassment.

Then his mouth was on my neck, my throat, gliding along my collarbone before it settled on my nipple, licking and sucking tenderly.

White-hot fire blossomed from my breast and I gasped, arching my back. He surged against my leg. If he pushed up my skirt and did it here and now, I would have no complaints. I couldn't wait much longer.

And I'd never even bothered to ask Heath how long this would last once it started.

I wanted it to last forever.

My fingers clutched at the nape of his neck, wanting to drag his gifted tongue and hot mouth to my other breast. The throbbing tension inside me grew impossibly urgent.

"Adam," I whispered. "I want—"

And that's when his cell phone rang.

At first he froze but didn't move, his mouth still pressed to my nipple, his body tensing beneath my hands.

It stopped. After not even ten seconds, it started ringing again. He lifted his head and sat back, fishing it out of his jacket pocket.

When he looked at the caller ID, he exhaled sharply. "Fuck." And then he put the phone to his ear.

"What?" he barked, and I felt sorry for whoever it was on the other end of the line.

I sat up and looped the straps of my dress over my shoulders, my body throbbing from lack of release. Adam looked at me as he listened for a long time on the phone without saying a word. With each passing minute, his face grew grimmer. I reached over and put a reassuring hand on his thigh and he immediately stood up and walked to the window.

"How bad is it?" he finally said, his posture stiff, his shoulders tense.

I grew cold without his body heat near me. I grabbed my wrap off the back of the couch and pulled it around my shoulders.

"Walt, it's fucking midnight here, the team is still at work. They have mandatory overtime in all their contracts. They're putting in late hours tonight."

He turned back to me and shook his head apologetically. I shrugged, giving him a smile. I could be patient. He could deal with this and then come back to me. Strangely, I wasn't tired at all despite the lack of sleep in the previous twenty-four hours.

"No," he said, and it was a sharp, irritated sound. "I'll handle it. That won't—I said I'll fucking handle it, but no one goes home, is that clear? If they do, then they clean their desk and take their shit with them."

He started to pace in front of the window and I sat back, reminded of a puma. His movements were sleek, graceful. I could watch him walk for hours. It would be better if he were only wearing that white towel around his hips, though.

"Give me a minute to get wired in. Yes. Call me in ten."

He set the phone down and turned to me. "I'm sorry. That was my operations manager. We had the servers down today to install a patch. The team found some corrupt code and servers can't come back online until it's fixed—"

"Oh shit, yeah, you don't want a horde of angry gamers pounding at your door. If I wasn't here, I'd be one of them, demanding you get my game up."

In spite of his darkened mood, he smiled. "I'm going to get my notebook so I can see what's going on. Why don't you grab something for yourself out of the bar? I'm sorry."

I cleared my throat. "Will this take long?"

He sighed. "Yeah, probably. I think our night is shot." And despite his obvious irritation and disappointment, he sounded remarkably calm about it.

Me? I was very annoyed. All my hopes fell. So much for the auction. So much for coming to Amsterdam a girl and leaving a woman. So much for—

I turned and left the room. He met me downstairs a few minutes later with a stylish leather laptop case from which he extracted one of the sleekest, most expensive-looking machines I'd ever laid eyes on.

His name was engraved in the stainless steel across the top: *Adam Drake, Draco Multimedia Entertainment*, with the company's logo: a field of stars depicting the constellation Draco. Some girls got excited about jewelry, others about designer bags. Me, I got all hot and bothered over hardware. And while that earlier impression of his *other* hardware had begun to affect me, this bad boy he'd just whipped out of the case made my heart palpitate. That sexy little box was probably ten times faster than mine.

Adam set the notebook on the table, opened it and looked at me. When he noticed the focus of my attention he smiled wryly. If I could only jimmy his password...I wondered how many game secrets that thing carried on it.

"Why don't you go get comfortable? This is going to be intermittent and if you're not tired, I could use the company."

I trundled off to my room where the bellhop had dumped my bag. I shimmied into some clothes I'd brought with me—yoga pants and a tank top. Then I went to the mini bar, pulled out a chilled glass and a Dr. Pepper for myself. After asking what he drank—he took coffee—I fiddled with the automatic coffeemaker and brought it to him, settling on the couch to watch him work.

Once in a while he'd glance up at me. "Why don't you see if something's on TV?" he asked, his hands moving over the keyboard with lightning speed while he spoke. "I'm going to be running a program here in a minute and can come watch with you while I wait."

My mouth quirked. I wondered if they aired reruns of *Friends* 24/7 in Amsterdam.

In the lounge, I flipped through the channels until I found a showing of a famous B movie from the fifties, *Forbidden Planet.* I'd seen it several times before and could have followed it easily had it been dubbed into Dutch. But this late-night version was in the original English with Dutch subtitles.

After two more phone calls and about ten minutes, Adam joined me on the couch. I grimaced, realizing I looked wretched in my yoga pants and tank top—a far cry from the glamorous black dress and glittery heels from earlier.

During the commercial break he told me he'd be right back and climbed the stairs. When he returned, he was wearing dark blue pajama bottoms and a white T-shirt. He again settled on the couch next to me. This time, I leaned against him, nestling into the crook of his arm. He rested his arm on my waist, almost hesitantly at first. As if he was reluctant to touch me.

When I looked up at him, his expression lay somewhere on the spectrum between fear and puzzlement. Had I surprised him with this show of sudden affection? It was nonsexual yet comforting, at least to me. And I had no idea if I could explain why it was so.

After an hour, he was back at the computer and soon I felt my lids growing heavier as Commander John Adams and Altaira, wrapped in each other's embrace, witnessed the explosion of Altair IV from space. I was soon drifting off to sleep.

Sometime afterward, I had the sensation of being carried by strong arms. Was this the moment? Would he lay me across his bed, wake me and have sex with me now?

But it didn't happen and my brief flirtation with consciousness soon evaporated as I sank back into blissful slumber. I dreamt of Adam, of dancing on a cloud with the sound of the orchestra emanating from a bank of computers in the background.

6

WE LEFT AMSTERDAM THE NEXT DAY AFTER A LATE brunch—we'd both slept in until ten o'clock. We checked out at noon and Adam's car took us to the airport. In spite of getting nowhere the previous night, we took our flight home as planned, as Adam hinted that he had to return to work as soon as possible.

I hardly knew what to say to him. We'd talked about everything else under the sun, but never discussed the fact that our deal remained unconsummated. What did this mean? I wouldn't get the money until we'd done the deed. Did he still want to? Or had the near-disaster with the game cooled his ardor?

Adam was on the phone for almost the entire trip to the airport and I pulled out my MCAT test guide but couldn't concentrate. My mind kept drifting to his conversation. He was making plans to visit some investment property the following month in some place called St. Lucia, which I'd never even heard of before.

I shot him a sideways glance, wondering about him. He'd grown up without a father, raised by an alcoholic mother who, it would be presumed, was such an unfit parent that he'd been placed with his uncle two states away as a teenager.

How did that formula add up to an extremely successful and uniquely brilliant man in his field? What drive did he have to pull himself from such a low starting point in life? And what tireless energy kept him going, day after day?

Not long before reaching the airport, I turned to him and he put down his tablet when he noticed me watching him.

"So, what now?" I asked.

His jaw visibly tensed and he turned to face me. "What do you mean?"

His manner was so cold it threw me off and I pursed my lips, irritated. As if he had the right to be brusque with me! It wasn't *my* fault that we hadn't gone through with the deal. I glanced toward the driver and Adam, following my thought, pressed the button to raise the partition before I spoke again.

I began. "Well, we had our night together. That's what the contract called for. I suppose we call it fulfilled and go our separate ways?" I knew what he'd say before the words were even out of my mouth.

He looked askance at me. "And that means, what? We separate in accordance with the points on the contract? No contact? Act as if there's a restraining order between us?"

I shrugged. Wasn't that what we'd both agreed to?

"And then what? You're still a virgin. Does that mean another auction?"

I tilted my head to the side. Hell no, that did not mean another auction. I wasn't going to put myself through that again. And I was one hundred percent sure that Heath would refuse to participate again. Nevertheless, I frowned as if in deep thought. "That's a wonderful idea! I could cash in twice."

But the look in Adam's eyes, when they hardened like black ice, sent a cold streak of premonition down my spine. He stuffed the tablet into the back pocket of the seat in front of him.

"I don't think so."

I crinkled my brow at him. "Wait...what?"

He turned to me as matter-of-factly as if he were discussing the daily weather forecast. "I purchased a product that has not been delivered to me."

I folded my arms. "I am not a product. I am a person. You purchased one night with me and that was it. We had our night together. It was through no fault of mine that I...remain intact."

"I disagree. I purchased your virginity. Therefore it belongs to me. It can't be re-sold."

Now I felt some heat rise to my cheeks. Not from embarrassment, but anger. "This was not a flesh trade transaction, Mr. Drake."

A fist closed over his knee. "What is prostitution *besides* a flesh trade? I own your virginity and I can remove it whenever I wish. Whether it be now or ten years from now, that honor is *mine.*"

I blinked and shook my head, unable to credit my own ears. "Are you saying that I'm beholden to you until you decide to swoop in and collect? I think not."

"Really. So you'll stick with that position. You honestly think our agreement supports your position over mine?"

My mind raced, trying to remember the precise wording of our agreement. My blood began to pump and I cursed that I had relied too heavily on Heath and his buddy to put the wording together to even remember. "It's hardly a legally valid document in the first place."

"Then why draw it up?"

I gritted my teeth. My face heated and muscles tensed. "For protection, to make it clear what the agreement entailed."

"For whose protection? Yours or mine?"

"For *both* of us."

He folded his arms over his chest, sitting back. "Well then, I stand with my position. The auction was for the right to remove your virginity. That didn't happen. I still have that right."

"Not for life. There's the six months limitation that was outlined in the contract."

He nodded. "Right. Then I'll call you in five and a half months?"

I blinked. Mom's mortgage foreclosure came due in two months. "Are you willing to pay me now?"

"Of course not."

I turned to him. "You don't trust me?"

"I make it a policy never to buy what I can't pay for and never to pay for what I can't own immediately. It makes for good business."

I sighed. "Then we should compromise. Because I need that money soon."

He tilted his head to the side, studying me again. "I thought this was about feminist ideals and the 'new paradigm.'"

"I never said it was *only* about those ideals."

He said nothing, just grazed me with that cold stare.

I shook my head. "You aren't allowed to judge me. Not until you've sat where I'm sitting."

He looked annoyed. "What makes you think I haven't?"

I waved significantly at the interior of the expensive town car driving us to the airport. We were sitting as far apart from each other as you could possibly get in the back of that car, but the energy still crackled between us. For some reason I thought that last night had killed that tension between us, but it only seemed to be stronger this morning. I was aware of everything about him, his posture, his movements, the way he tapped his index finger on his knee when his hand rested there. The way his muscular form perfectly filled his clothes. His clean, masculine scent. The way his dark eyes watched me, calculating. Assessing.

"Next week, then."

A week? A rush of heat rose to my features, but this time not from frustration or anger. This heat was one of anticipation. Because despite his annoying talk of "owning" my virginity, the feelings I'd begun to feel last night—the unfulfilled sensations he'd stirred in me—were rearing their heads, screaming to be heard. Last night I'd been sad that this would be over by today. Now I had another week. The mixed feelings swirled and tightened in my chest like a whirlwind about to lift from the ground.

I glanced out the window to cover my reaction. The airport was just ahead. "Will you be in some other glamorous location next week?"

"I'll only be at home. I'm having some guests over for dinner. You could come. Afterward, we'll take the yacht out past the twelve-mile mark."

I turned back to him, my annoyance bleeding through in the sarcasm in my voice. "Because, of course you have a yacht."

He smiled. "Of course."

We didn't speak again through the airport check-in process. Adam was attentive, carrying my bag for me and running it through security, but his manner was brisk, efficient, cool and impersonal. It was as if we were strangers. And in truth, we really were.

When we took our seats next to each other, we started to talk again. We chose neutral, safe territory—the game. He was usually reluctant to discuss it, I'd noticed. He was probably concerned that I'd try to start digging into game secrets again. But I'd waited until after we'd been served a delightful lunch by a lovely blond British Air Hostess who was extremely attentive to all of Adam's needs, complete with her own unsubtle brand of flirting. I began to wonder if he had this kind of effect on every woman in his proximity.

He turned to me over dessert. "So, I know from your blog that you play a Spiritual Enchantress. But you've never mentioned your character's name."

I look askance at him. "Of course not. If my readers knew my character in the game, it might affect the game experience. Gotta keep the trade secrets under the pointed wizard hat."

He smiled. "So what is your character's name?"

I gazed at him suspiciously. "Why do you want to know my character's name?"

He shrugged. "Just curious."

"Are you going to look me up or something?"

"Okay then, what server do you play on?"

"Omni."

He looked pensive. "Hmm. Power gamer."

I shrugged. "Does that surprise you?"

"No. I'm starting to realize you have a thing about power and control."

"Wow, you make me sound so...Dominatrix. Maybe that should be the next class of character you introduce into the game with the next expansion."

He laughed.

I tilted my head at him expectantly. "Do *you* play?" I asked.

"DE?"

"No...World of Warcraft," I snarked. "Of course DE."

"I have a character."

"A *secret* character? Other than your public persona, Lord Sisyphus?"

He looked away with a smirk. "Yeah, I have a secret character."

My mouth dropped. "The truth comes out. You're like King Henry the Fifth."

"What?"

"Oh yeah, you dropped out of geek college so you wouldn't have read up on your Shakespeare. Henry the Fifth dressed up like a common soldier and went around his war camps to see who was talking trash about him."

He barked a laugh. "Shit, if I was worried about who was talking trash about me, I'd have quit this business a long time ago."

"So, how often do you play? Do you group up with other players?"

"Once a week and of course. You know you can't get any of the good stuff done without a large group."

"Why?" I puzzled. "Why would you want to play when you know all the secrets—all of the quest chains, all of the back story? Wouldn't that be boring?"

He shrugged. "I playtest my own product. It's being thorough. I'm always very thorough."

He seemed to be saying something to me, a weighted double entendre, but I didn't get it. "I'll tell you mine if you tell me yours," he said suddenly.

"Character?"

"Yeah, but you can't rat me out on your blog."

I shook my head. "Of course not. I'm under an NDA, am I not? With no expiration date. If you want to know so badly, couldn't you just look me up under my account information? My real name is on that."

"I could. I'd rather you told me."

"Her name is Eloisa."

He nodded. "Okay. Maybe I'll add you to my friends list."

"And you are...?" I raised my brows at him.

He looked at me and hesitated, then cleared his throat. "Magnus."

Of course. Magnificent. And parts of him truly were magnificent. And other parts seemed dark, shrouded, and brooding. I never knew what Adam I was going to get from one moment to the next.

During the latter part of the flight, he'd managed to take a nap and I watched him sleep, utterly fascinated. But it wasn't until we'd landed that I remembered the cell phone he'd given me in Amsterdam. I reached into my jacket pocket and handed it to him.

"Here's your phone back."

"Actually, that's yours. I have my own...an irritating one that tends to ring at the most inopportune times," he said with a grimace.

"But—"

"You said yours wasn't working. I want to be able to get a hold of you, so I arranged for that one and I don't need it. Keep it and keep it charged. I want to be able to reach you."

"Ah, I see. Is this part of that whole thing? You're keeping tabs on me until this transaction is complete?"

He shrugged. "If you want to think of it that way."

I glared at him, tempted to cram the damn thing down his throat until he spoke again. "Besides, you can use the web feature to respond to comments on your blog from wherever you are."

Now *that* I liked. "Hmm. Well, I can keep it until we are...through with each other. But then I'm giving it back."

The expression on his face was enigmatic. "If you must."

When he dropped me off from the airport, he walked me to my door, insisting on carrying my ratty bag. We stood at the door staring at each other for a long, awkward moment.

"So, I guess I'll see you this Friday?" I said.

"Yes. I'll text you."

"Not sure my old car is allowed on the road in Newport Beach amongst all the glittering Bentleys and Beemers. I might get pulled over the minute I cross the city limit."

He laughed. "I'll arrange for a car to come get you."

"Fancy. Don't suppose I can persuade you to turn off your phone that night."

"I might be very tempted." He grinned that boyish grin that made my heart flip.

"Remember, the early dinner will be before. I've invited some friends, so bring your best manners."

I crinkled up my mouth. "I'll try to find some by then."

He took a step closer to me, reached up to brush the hair away from my face. I looked up into his eyes and a jolt of heat shot through me, remembering the feel of his mouth, his hands on my body that brief night in Amsterdam.

Now the magic had followed us home, and swirled around us as we stood on the tattered, rubber mat on my doorstep, likely with my landlady watching through her vertical blinds.

"Until Friday, Emilia," and he dipped his head to drop a chaste kiss on my lips before pulling away, turning to walk down the steps and back to the town car. I watched him the entire way, my mouth slack in surprise. I was at least hoping to get a little tongue.

It was Sunday afternoon and I was exhausted, of course, but I knew I had to call Heath right away—on his strict orders—and let him know how the whole weekend had unrolled. "What?" he shrieked when I got to the part about the phone call, but for a minute I couldn't tell whether it was his concern over the near-crisis with the game patch or that he couldn't believe Adam had delayed the entire thing on account of business.

"He had you on the couch stripped to the waist and playing with your girl parts and he answered the phone? He's gotta be gay."

I laughed. "Wishful thinking, I'm afraid. It was very obvious that he was turned on and very reluctant to answer the phone. Apparently the guy was warned not to call unless it was an emergency."

"Shit. So what's the upshot? He gonna pay you? He had his night."

I cleared my throat, fidgeting from one foot to the other.

"Hello? You still there?"

"Yeah."

"So...?"

"So I think he might have been cool with doing that except I had a big mouth and joked about doubling my money by running another auction."

"There's no fucking way I'm doing another one, doll. Your favor debt to me is epic as it is."

"It was a joke. I was trying to be funny—ha ha. It was awkward, he was acting all cold and distant, not like the night before."

"Okay. So you joked around...and then what?"

"Well, then he gets all weird and starts saying I don't have the right to sleep with anyone else but him until the contract is fulfilled."

"Uhh."

"Is that true? Is he right?"

"Doll, you can do whatever you want...it's not like he can sue you for breach. The money has yet to be transferred into your account."

"What if he's planning to never pay me?"

"Oh, I made sure the agreement states that the NDA goes bye-bye if he doesn't pay you. If he goes through with it and doesn't pay, you sell your story to the press and he's fucked."

I took a deep breath. "But what about the other? That I can't be with someone else until..."

"Were you planning on it?"

"No."

"Does he intend to drag this out for six months and not pay you?"

"That's what I asked him. He made arrangements to get together Friday night and...do the deed in international waters on his yacht."

"Hmm. Okay. That works. Can't help but wonder why he didn't just get 'er done the morning before you left."

I shrugged. Maybe he wanted it to be more romantic? But I couldn't help but wonder at that. The day we were touring around

Amsterdam and Adam had asked me about my dating habits, he'd admitted to me that he didn't do romance. That he'd never been in a relationship before and had little interest. Yet another thing in which we coincided.

"Well," said Heath. "As long as he has a backup plan...but you gotta call me before you leave and when you get back. I don't like the thought of him strangling you out there and dumping you overboard."

I huffed. "Gee, now that's reassuring."

"Mia, I don't think he's a bad person, but he had a pretty shitty childhood."

Now I sat up, interested. "What do you know?"

"I did a background check on him. Mostly public record stuff, really. His mom was an alcoholic and he was placed in the child protective system as a young teen."

"Yeah, that I know. He told me as much."

"Yeah, well, when he got here and started at the new high school he apparently was the victim of one of the most notorious bullying cases in the county."

I tried to picture any suicidal idiot trying to take down six-foot, exquisitely ripped Adam. I'd touched him—he was solid, athletic, strong. My heart bounced at the memory of his body under my shaking hands. Then I remembered what he'd told me when I'd been teasing him about those muscles...that he'd chosen to bulk up as a deterrent to being bullied.

"What happened?"

"Track team. I guess he was a runner—" He was a runner! "One of the better members of the team, but he was the new guy and some of the older kids singled him out. I found several old newspaper clippings at the library from the *OC Register*. A whole group of them beat the crap out of him and then duct-taped his hands, legs and mouth and shoved him in a locker overnight. He was in the hospital in critical condition for over a week. There was a lawsuit filed against the district, the perps were arrested and thrown in juvey. "

The air hissed out of my lungs. "That's horrible."

"Yeah."

"But that doesn't mean he's going to strangle me and throw me into the ocean."

"I know. But I'm just saying. It doesn't matter how rich or powerful a person is, they've all got their demons."

"Do you know who Sabrina is?"

"Huh?"

"He has a tattoo, just above his heart. It says 'Sabrina.' Was that his girlfriend?"

"Nothing I ever saw written up on him ever mentioned a relationship or girlfriend. I have no idea what the tattoo means."

"Maybe it was his dog."

"I took him for a cat person, actually."

We chatted for a few more minutes before I begged off with exhaustion and hopped into the shower. In spite of that, I did manage to cram in about three hours of studying, interrupted briefly by the usual bang at my door.

"Password," I shouted from the couch. She heard me through the open window.

"I aim to misbehave," Alex said and then opened the door and bounced across the room like the Tazmanian Devil on caffeine and landed right beside me with a plop. My old couch groaned down to its wooden frame in protest.

"Studying again?"

I held up my *Gray's Anatomy* by way of answering.

She huffed. "Why don't you just watch the TV show instead of reading that big fat book?"

I feinted throwing it at her and she lurched back, holding up her hands, laughing. "Mom wants to know if you'll come down and eat dinner with us and *I* want to know who is that hot man who dropped you off this morning."

Yep, her mother had definitely been peeking through the blinds.

"Ah, being a *chismosa?*" I said, teasing her with the Spanish word for a gossipmonger.

"Always. So give me the *chisme*," she said, leaning forward and pinning me down with her large, dark eyes.

"He's just some guy I know," I said, shrugging it off and twisting to set the heavy book down on a side table made from a wooden telephone cable spool.

She looked askance. "In a town car with a driver?"

Shit. How was I going to explain *that?* I took a deep breath, deciding to go on the offensive. "Alejandra Carmen Arias. Are you grilling me?"

"If that's what it takes. Are you dating him?"

I sliced a glance at her and then away, shrugging. I was keenly aware that I was the worst liar ever. But better she think we were dating than know what was really going on. Alex went to mass with her mom every week and I was pretty sure she wouldn't approve— feminist ideals or no. "Kind of."

"Mom said he was really good looking."

I suppressed a grin. "I'm glad she approves." Just how long had she been peeking at us through those blinds?

"Come on, Mia! Spill! You are killing me."

I stood up and bushed off my jeans. "Not yet. But soon, okay? I don't want to jinx anything." I hoped that threw her off. Alex had a bit of a superstitious streak in her. Before she could ask me another question I went to the door and motioned her out with me. Who was I to turn down a free, guaranteed delicious dinner? "Can you do my hair for Friday night? I have a date and I want to wear it up."

Mischief sparkled in her dark eyes. "I'll do it if you tell me his name."

I grabbed her hand and shook it. "Deal. Now let's go eat. I'm starving."

7

THE WEEK DRAGGED ON AND I MUDDLED THROUGH HOSPITAL shifts and blog posts and studying a little more grudgingly than I had before. The dream of Amsterdam was a distant memory, like the glitter falling off a cheap knockoff souvenir brought back as a memento of an otherworldly vacation. I'd only been out of the country for forty-eight hours, including travel—but I knew I wanted to go back, and very soon.

I continued taking the birth control pills and bought a few back copies of *Cosmo* to read up on their "great sex" articles, all the while realizing how ridiculous it was to use pop culture as sex education. Until the trip to Holland, I'd never been concerned with having to please a partner. But now, I was determined to make him feel as good as he had made me feel in those few moments when we had been kissing and touching.

Two days before the dinner party, a box arrived from the Netherlands. I opened it up to find all three gowns that were hanging in the wardrobe in my room in Amsterdam. I gasped. The card inside said only, *Wear one of these Friday.*

Since he'd already seen me in the breathtaking black, I chose the long crème-colored one. It had a halter top that looped around my neck and it, too, was backless. This dress, though long, felt like it exposed me more and I couldn't explain why. It was an extremely feminine dress, with a full, creased skirt of gauzy material—the kind that Marilyn Monroe wore when her dress famously blew upward over the air grate in *The Seven Year Itch.*

There were also matching shoes for this dress and the selection of lingerie. Since a bra was again not possible, I selected a tiny pair of lace white panties and left everything else in the box.

My landlady, Lupe, came up with Alex and together they tried to pry my secrets out of me while they worked my hair into an elegant updo.

At one point Alex whispered to me that her sister had seen my mystery guy too, and labeled him "totally yummy."

I agreed with her. I had tasted him. And he was, indeed, delectable. But there was a dark edge that I had no idea how to describe. Like the bitter cocoa powder sprinkled on the outside of a rich chocolate truffle. Perhaps it just brought nuance to his flavor. Or maybe it threatened to ruin an otherwise scrumptious dish.

As the week had worn on, I couldn't stop thinking about that bullying story. For it to have been so severe, so brutal as to merit a lawsuit, multiple arrests and a couple of write-ups in the paper made it serious in the extreme. My heart went out to him. I was unable to even imagine what that must have been like.

Except I could. After my assault, I'd feared the possibility of being bullied if I stood up and spoke out for myself. I'd never found the courage to do it.

I examined myself in the mirror, avoiding my own eyes and that whispered word at the back of my thoughts that sounded a lot like *coward*.

With the dress, the updo and the careful application of makeup, I'd spent more time on my appearance that night than I usually spent getting ready for three days in a row combined. I studied myself in the cracked full-length mirror on the back of my front door for the full effect. I looked like an old-time movie star. I twirled around again and again, watching the skirt spin up around my hips and giggling like a little girl.

I almost fell over when someone knocked. Adam's driver stood at the door. And he walked me to the town car, opening the door. It was four thirty in the afternoon and in spite of that, the 55 freeway was clear going southbound. We sped down the carpool lane and I watched the relentless parade of expensive hotels, billboards and mile-high palm trees speed by. The northbound side of the freeway was, of course another story, as it always was at this time of day. Cars were packed end-to-end and moving inches at a time.

I was grateful that wasn't us, because I didn't want to be late for the big night. I watched carefully as the driver headed straight down the freeway until its very end. So my guess about Adam living in Balboa was right—either on the island itself or the equally impressive peninsula.

A thin finger of land stretching across the harbor, encapsulating the opulent Newport Bay, Balboa housed the county's glitziest homes and their wealthy inhabitants. I wondered why the driver was heading down the peninsula instead of approaching the island from the north, where there was a bridge. From this side, he would have to take the tiny ferry across to Balboa Island and there was often a long line at this time of day.

But blocks before the turn-off for the ferry, the driver hung a left and headed toward the bay. I was now completely perplexed as to where his house was, unless he lived in the middle of the bay.

And then the driver parked on a tiny street near a small walkway that led to what appeared to be the smallest island I had ever seen.

"Where are we?"

"We're going over the bridge to Bay Island, Miss. I'll take you. But we have to park and walk across the bridge. There are no cars allowed on Bay Island."

It was a tiny island, sitting smack dab in the Newport Back Bay. I'd been down in this area many times but had never noticed it. This area was a popular tourist destination in the summer and Mom often drove the two hours down to soak up the sun and ambiance when the heat of Anza grew too much for the both of us.

Who even knew this place was here? There was no more densely populated area in all of Orange County than the Newport Bay, with houses crowded along the shores like soldiers lined up for inspection. Nevertheless, in the middle of it all was a private island.

The briny smell and clean ocean breeze hit me first, when I stepped out of the town car. I glanced toward the late afternoon sun, still hours from setting, my heart pounding faster with each step I took over that bridge.

Bay Island was like no other place I could imagine. About twenty houses ringed the sandy shores, central tennis courts and a private park. The island even had its own caretaker. The driver keyed in at the gate and led me to one of the golf carts waiting nearby. I wondered why we didn't just walk. How far away could his house truly be on this tiny speck of land?

But of course, it was the one furthest from the gate, with its own little corner beach and lawn. And it was one of the biggest homes. As we approached, I mentally sized it up, wondering how many bazillions it must have cost him.

All this for one single guy. I thought about what Heath had learned during his investigations. Adam had had no romantic relationships. Why? It was true he was driven and worked long hours. Perhaps he just didn't make the time for anything else? But why work so hard without having the time to truly enjoy it all? And why not find someone to share it with?

Maybe he saw no need for a relationship or had no desire for it? It couldn't have been for lack of women wanting him. Not only was he ridiculously rich, but he was ridiculously hot. And I had no way to judge, but I imagined he was good in bed—maybe even phenomenal. Or maybe that was just my hope. But then, I had no basis for comparison, so how would I know?

He greeted me at the door, dressed in a camel-colored dinner jacket with skinny black tie and matching black trousers. He was arrestingly handsome, and welcomed me with a kiss on the cheek.

"You look gorgeous," he whispered against my temple as the driver receded with the golf cart to fetch the other guests.

"I didn't want to make a bad impression on your friends, being a north-county bumpkin and all. Best not mention my phone number starts with a 714 area code," I said, instantly knowing how lame that sounded because what did it matter what sort of impression I made on his friends? They'd never see me again after Adam and I went to bed later that night.

A shiver of excitement slithered down my spine and bumps appeared over my arms at just the thought of it. Adam's eyes narrowed as if he noticed, but he did not comment on it. He proceeded to show me around—briefly, because a full tour would have taken at least an hour.

The house was arranged around a wide central hall with rooms opening off to the sides and a mezzanine wrapping around three of the four sides of the floor above. Overhead, a giant skylight let the sun in and the room was bright and airy, emphasized with white furniture. I'd stepped into another dream.

If I lived here, with my own beach and view of the bay, I'd never jump on a plane to Amsterdam or St. Lucia or anywhere else. I'd be grateful for this, my own little cove of paradise, and too scared that it would vanish while I was gone.

Adam watched me with an amused smile as I looked around, commenting on this feature or that. I couldn't get over the private beach and he murmured, for he was standing very close, that maybe we could enjoy it later that evening. Alone.

My pulse raced. "But we'll be on the yacht, by then." And, because I had only just remembered, I glanced down toward the bay and saw an empty slip with a little electric Duffy boat bobbing forlornly beside it.

"Yes, about that," he said, just as the guests were arriving at the front door. "We'll have to postpone our trip in the yacht. I had to put it in for a minor repair."

I opened my mouth, about to question him when he stepped forward and received the other couples—there were six people in all—and welcomed them. One couple was considerably older than

Adam—thirties and forties. One of the men I recognized as Adam's lawyer from our first meeting.

He had the light of recognition in his eyes and he darted a strange look at Adam. Heat crawled up my neck. I knew what was going through his mind. Why'd you bring your prostitute here?

I wondered who Adam usually invited with him to parties. If he hadn't been in long-term relationships, then who was his "plus one"?

Adam stood at my side making introductions. The blond guy, Jordan Fawkes, was Adam's CFO and apparently ignorant of our arrangement or masked his reactions very well. He stood beside a woman who looked like she could be a Victoria's Secret model. She wore makeup from her hairline down to her cleavage and her body was flawless. Her dress was so tight it left little to the imagination. I half expected her to start strutting like she was moving down a cat-walk. She was, however, very kind and greeted me with a smile, complimenting my dress.

One of the other women present was a pretty blonde who looked like she was in her midthirties. Her husband seemed a lot older than her. She smiled widely for Adam, kissing him on both cheeks. Creepily enough, her husband was leering over her shoulder—at me! His eyes scoured me from head to toe and rested on my cleavage, staring at me like I was a steak and he was four weeks into a hunger strike.

I'd gotten those looks before and brushed them aside without much thought. I'd always figured they were some men's way of mak-ing a power play without ever having to say a word or touch a thing. I lifted my chin haughtily and jerked my head away. He wasn't worth another thought.

I also noticed the way his wife attended to Adam's every word and move. She'd been introduced to me as Lindsay Walker, a very old friend. Actually, Adam's exact words were, "We're friends from way back." But the way she kept touching Adam suggested more. She cast a perfunctory—almost dismissive—glance at me when we were introduced and then proceeded to chat him up, reaching out occasionally to touch his shoulder, or his elbow.

In truth, I was bored the entire evening. I had nothing in common with these people and they were all very much a part of the scene here in Newport Beach. And I was very much *not*. I was easily the youngest one there, aside from Ms. Victoria's Secret. I'd guess that Adam was amongst the youngest as well. A few asked what I did and when I told them I was a hospital orderly and a hopeful med student, they made a little more small talk and then drifted away.

I really didn't care about the brush-offs. It was a relief, actually. That way I didn't feel obligated to them to try and entertain them. When we ate—around a beautifully appointed glass table on the covered porch overlooking the harbor—I was at the opposite end from Adam and his "old friend." Lindsay had entered before most of the others and hastily switched dinner cards—I'd watched while she did it, shocked at her audacity—so that she'd be sitting next to Adam. She wasn't old enough to be a cougar, but she was clearly quite a few years older than him. I began to suspect they had a history as I watched them over dinner.

The guy to my right was a financier and he spent the entire meal chatting up the lawyer across from me. I sat in silence and picked at my food, wondering where tonight would lead. Without the yacht, we wouldn't be able to go out to the twelve-mile mark, where, in international waters, we would no longer be subject to the law of the land. We sure as hell wouldn't be making that trip in the Duffy Boat, which was designed for tootling around the harbor.

So, then what? Were we halted again? In irritation, I glanced at Adam, whose head tilted toward Lindsay, listening to something she was saying but looking bored beyond words. He glanced down the table and our gazes met. I froze and he smiled and winked, before looking away.

The guests stayed only an hour after dinner—they were on their way to a concert at the Performing Arts Center in Costa Mesa. Lindsay and her husband were the last to go and again I got that cold once-over from her. It was beyond awkward. Her behavior was possessive. I wanted to tell her not to feel threatened. One fuck and it would be over with Adam. She had nothing to worry about. But curiously, I was having a harder time getting over the irritation I was feeling, both at her presumption with him and his open acceptance of it. Maybe they were friends like I was with Heath. But I just didn't get that sense from them.

She touched him like she had done it a thousand times before. Like she knew him intimately. Like a lover.

And surprisingly that brought my claws out. It was beyond stupid of me to feel that way, but I was like a guard dog with hackles up every time I saw her mouth go near his ear to whisper something funny.

But to my relief, everyone was gone before eight o'clock. Adam asked me if I wanted something to drink and poured some mineral water for himself and a glass of chilled Pinot Grigio for me.

"Let's go down to the beach," he said with a smile.

And how could I resist? There were plush, padded lounge chairs and a cabinet with towels and blankets. He set the glasses on a low table between two lounges and grabbed fleece blankets. He had the complete setup, including a propane heater—the big industrial kind they put out on restaurant patios. It wasn't quite chilly enough that evening to turn it on.

After the yard lights were dimmed, we sat on our lounges. I gazed out over the bay watching the golden lights dance on the water's surface. It was just after sunset and the sky was an otherworldly shade of lavender reflected in the waters of the bay as dusk dropped quickly, like it always did close to the coast. Boats returned from the ocean, their running lights flickering across the water. The distant sounds of a party drifted from one of the neighboring houses on Bay Island.

I glanced over at Adam, who had his phone out, reading e-mail and occasionally replying. I sipped at my wine and burrowed under the blanket watching him. It wasn't freezing but, like every spring night in Southern California, though the days were temperate, the nights got chilly once the sun went down, especially on the beach.

Without looking up from his work he asked, "Warm enough? You want the heater on?"

"No," I said, getting up from the lounge. "I have a better idea to keep warm."

I picked up my blanket walked over to his lounge, and plunked down beside him. With surprise he gazed up at me, then scooted, putting his legs down, one on either side of the lounge and indicated that I should sit between them, which I did, laying back against him.

At first I got that same feeling of weird stiffness—like he didn't know what to do. Clearly Adam wasn't a natural cuddler. But *I* was. I'd grown up in an affectionate family. And I had no idea why I needed to connect to him. Hell, I cuddled with Heath sometimes, when he tolerated it. It was just who I was. But the sense I got from Adam was more hesitant than reluctant, as if he didn't know how to handle it rather than being repulsed by it.

Adam finished his latest text and set his phone aside. I leaned my head back against his shoulder and slowly he hitched his arms around me, pulling me fast against him. We sat in silence for many long moments as the night darkened around us. My blood pounded in my throat, an exquisite tension building at the center of my being. It felt so good, just sitting here.

"How's work? All disasters averted?"

"The old disasters are swept aside by the new ones, as usual," he said.

"One of your guests said something tonight that I found remarkable."

"What was that?"

"I hope he was joking, but he said something about hardly believing you had a chance to enjoy your gorgeous home when you work a hundred-hour week as your norm."

"A hundred hours? That's a bit of an exaggeration." Amusement tinged his voice.

"But not much, I'd wager, because he also said you regularly sleep at your office."

He paused. "I've never pushed any employee harder than I push myself. If they're doing seventy-hour weeks, then I'll do ninety."

I angled my head to look up at him. "But why have all this, then, if you can't enjoy it?"

"Who says I don't? Besides, Miss Doctor, I don't think you'll soon be a stranger to ninety-hour workweeks yourself."

I shrugged. "I guess I've been preparing myself for it. Probably why I've never bothered with a personal life."

"You and I have that in common, then."

I sighed and settled back against him. The phone chirped. Adam picked it up. He typed one-handed while holding me with the other.

"Don't you ever turn that thing off?"

I could almost hear him smile. "Never."

"If I asked you to turn it off now, would you?"

He paused and set down the phone. "If you gave me enough of an incentive."

I smiled. "I'm sure I could think of something."

He brought a hand to my hair. "I like your hair up. But it's much prettier down."

"If you take the pins out now, it will still stay in its same shape, I'm afraid. My landlady did it and she loves a good bottle of hairspray."

"Hairspray or rubber cement?" he laughed.

"Yeah, it's going to hurt like a bitch to brush it out."

He paused for a moment. "I hope you didn't put it up because you thought you had to."

I shrugged, prepared to let him think that was the reason I'd put my hair up—and not because I'd wanted to keep his hands well away from my hair. I did *not* want a repeat of the balcony freak-out in Amsterdam. I took a deep breath. "I know it's silly, but I really did want to impress your friends. I don't think I did."

"On the contrary, I think several of them were quite taken with you."

I couldn't resist. I had to say it. "I don't think Lindsay Walker was."

A pause. "I wouldn't worry about that." But I couldn't tell what that meant—whether he meant I shouldn't bother because I'd soon be out of his life or that Lindsay's opinion wasn't worth worrying about. I decided not to ask.

"So..." I said hesitating. "With no yacht here, I guess that puts a damper on our evening."

His head dipped down, his mouth very close to my neck. "You smell amazing," he said. Urgent need raced through me with those hoarsely uttered words. I turned my face toward his, tilting my head back so I could look him in the eyes out of the corner of mine. His stare pinned me down and I licked my lips. I wanted him to kiss me again.

But he tilted his head away, settling back against the lounge. After a long moment, he kissed my hair, just below my temple, then lowered his mouth to my ear. When he spoke, his breath caressed me, sending frissons of desire down every nerve ending. "We can't be together tonight."

But I wanted it, and judging from the bulge of his arousal pressing into the small of my back, he wanted it too. I angled my head to bare my neck without saying a word. His mouth sank to my nape, kissing me there. I gasped at the shock of pleasure that touch evoked. Every cell on my skin came alive as my body readied itself for him. It wouldn't be tonight, but my body didn't know any better. It wanted what it wanted. And that evening I was right there along with it for the ride.

And the phone chirped again. I tensed. He didn't pull his mouth away from my neck, but damned if he didn't pick that wretched thing up and look at it again. He sent off a quick reply and when he put it down, I locked my hand over his. "Turn it the fuck off," I groaned as he sucked at my neck.

"Are you willing to make it worth my while?" he breathed.

His hands slid down my shoulders, slipping over my dress to cup my breasts, rubbing his palms over the ready nipples again and again until I wanted to scream with pent-up frustration.

I moaned, my eyes squeezing tight, losing myself in the sensation. "Yes," I murmured. His hands glided into my bodice, under my dress, and he rolled my nipples between his thumbs and forefingers. My body glowed hot as if on fire. I arched my back against him. God, his hands were magic on my body.

The fucking chime went off again. I stiffened and he hesitated. Would he pick it up again? It was almost nine o'clock on a Friday night, for God's sake. Couldn't it wait?

He reached for the phone but instead of answering the text, he clicked the red button and the phone obediently powered down.

"Tell me what you want," he said, his voice gruff, husky.

"I want *you*."

That seemed to cause something in him to snap because suddenly he flipped me in his arms and we were facing each other. I straddled him as his mouth pressed to mine in a ferocious kiss. His hand wandered up my skirt. Between kisses, his dark eyes glittered in the low light. "Oh Emilia, I want you, too."

Our mouths came together again in tangled abandon and his hand caressed my inner thigh, higher and higher until it rested atop my panties. When he stroked me there, my mind seemed to unhinge for a moment and everything swirled around me.

"Soaking wet," he said in a hoarse voice and without another word, a finger hooked up over the hip of my underwear and he yanked. The delicate lace shredded and the panties were off. My level of arousal shot through the roof. I suddenly imagined him tearing off my dress in the same manner, laying me down underneath him on the sand—

"Fuck. You are making it impossible to resist you," he said.

He lowered his head and his mouth landed on my nipple, suckling at it through the thin fabric of the dress before pulling it aside with growl and landing on bare skin. I arched into him again. The bulge of his erection pressed against my thigh and his hand was beginning to do wicked things to me.

His thumb stroked softly against the most sensitive parts of my flesh. I couldn't breathe for the longest moment, everything in me tensing.

"Deep breaths, Emilia, enjoy this."

And I did breathe in deeply as he increased the pressure against the bundle of nerves, each touch sending shocks of pure pleasure to every corner of my awareness. My head crushed against his shoulder and I let out a long, low moan. His mouth descended on my neck.

"I'm going to make you come."

"Yes," I agreed. And it wouldn't be long, as far as I could tell.

And he stopped rubbing just long enough to slip a finger inside of me. First tentatively, and then deeper. Then he slid it in and out while I gasped in the rhythm his hand had set.

I was so close. So close. And delirious with pleasure as I was, I hardly had time to realize where his hand was or whether or not I should be embarrassed or self-conscious. "I'm going to come," I finally said.

He did not reply, speeding up the rhythm of his touch. It was just enough to push me up and over the top. I threw my head back and gasped, feeling the convulsions of release wash over me like raindrops in a high desert storm.

But he continued stroking and stroking against my too-sensitive flesh. "I'm going to do it again. And you are going to say my name. And if you don't, I'll keep doing it until you do."

The pleasure was so intense it almost hurt. I tried to push him away. "No, it's too much."

"You're going to come and my name is going to be on your lips," he uttered fiercely against my ear. "Come on, Emilia."

And it was building again and lord, I couldn't believe it but I wanted it so badly—again. I never knew it could happen again so fast.

But I was still resisting him and his hand, my body stiffening. He pressed his mouth to my ear. "Surrender to me," he commanded as he entered me once again, his finger sliding into me—and then there were two fingers and I fell slack against him, deciding, ultimately, to allow myself to go where he would take me.

"You're so tight," he muttered. "So innocent."

And I was close again, biting into his jacket at the shoulder to keep from screaming. "Come for me, Emilia."

And it was so intense—so much more intense. The previous orgasm—as good as it was—was nothing to this one that was approaching like a monstrous wave from far offshore, about to crash down on the rocks. I could barely remember my own name, let alone his, as he pushed me toward a higher climax than I'd ever known.

"Oh God," I said.

"I'm good but I'm not that good."

"Adam—" I panted.

"Better," he whispered. "Say it again."

"Please."

"Again, Emilia."

"Adam. Adam. Adam." And just as I felt the crest of release take hold, he lowered his head and sank his teeth into my earlobe, the pleasure and small, sharp pain clashing with each other.

I fell against his chest, panting. It was several minutes before I remembered where I was or even who I was. There was nothing but an aching, haunting bliss and the feel of his chest rising and falling under me—very quickly with each rushed breath. He was very turned on and I wondered why he'd done this in the first place—why he'd started this when he knew he wouldn't be able to finish it for himself—at least not tonight.

Or maybe he could. I stroked my hand along the rigid line of his erection, easily discernible from base to tip. He stayed my hand, hesitating.

An almost involuntary groan escaped his lips. "No," he breathed. "Tomorrow morning I'll have the boat back. We'll spend the afternoon out, have lunch, go swimming, make a day of it. You can stay the night there."

I looked at him, the question in my eyes. "I can wait, Emilia. You're worth waiting for."

The kindness of those simple words took my breath away. *You're worth waiting for.* It was so opposite of what I'd known from my only serious relationship—if a self-involved high-school boyfriend could even be considered serious. Zack hadn't wanted to wait. Had decided to force the issue when I told him I wasn't ready. That wasn't the answer he'd wanted, so he'd taken what he wanted anyway.

I shivered against Adam and he pulled me to him. "Thank you," I said, voice trembling with an emotion I couldn't fully explain.

When he turned on his phone shortly thereafter, there were four text messages and a missed call. Adam swore under his breath, but took the time to answer each one of them while I sat beside him huddled under the blanket.

His car took me home soon after. Restless yet depleted, I reclined against the leather bench in the backseat, mind wandering over the evening's events. Hopefully things would come to a conclusion tomorrow. But that shard of desire came with a double edge—because it meant that tomorrow night together would be our last. And as much as his hands on me were driving me to new undiscovered countries of pleasure, I suddenly realized how much I would miss him, beyond just his magic hands. His conversation, his boyish smile, his caring consideration, his keen perceptiveness, his clean, ocean smell. I tried my best to ignore the ache at the center of my chest that hadn't gone away since he'd said that simple sentence, *You're worth waiting for.*

But I had to remind myself that a relationship with someone like Adam would be impossible. I would not allow myself to entertain that dream. On the outside, he seemed perfect. But on the inside, he was a man, just like all the rest of them. And they couldn't be trusted.

Once home, I checked my messages. Heath had called, instructing me to call him the minute I got home. Alex had left two, demanding the *chisme* immediately. I glanced at the clock. It was just after midnight so I opted out of calling.

Instead, I wandered the apartment—cleaned a few dishes, picked up my study guide and threw it down just as quickly. Going to bed didn't even cross my thoughts. I knew it would only lead to hours of tossing and turning.

I was too wound up by the thoughts of Adam's hands and the delicious sensations they had awoken in me. Of the memory of his voice commanding me to come to climax, to say his name. Shivers slithered all through me at the memory.

So I did what I always do when I couldn't sleep. I logged on to the game to while away a few hours. Heath had not logged in, nor had my other two game buddies, Persephone or FallenOne. Fallen hadn't been on since the last time we'd played together, three weeks before. An hour later when I was about to log off, my in-game message screen flashed.

Magnus tells you, "Why are you still awake?"

Magnus. The one and only. I ran a command to find out Magnus's class and level. /whois Magnus

The game obediently told me: *Magnus is a level 75 Fire Mage.* Because of course he was a Fire Mage. Fire Mages were the most overtly powerful character class in the game. They had the element of fire at their command, could throw fireballs and command flame to dance on the heads of their enemies, or burn them slowly down with heat damage. I bit my lip, trying not to giggle at the irony—the thought of his hot hands still burned in my memory. How appropriate.

You tell Magnus, "A Fire Mage? Really? No wonder you have magic hands."

Magnus tells you, "At your service."

*You tell Magnus, "It begs the question...what are *you* doing up so late? Working still?"*

*Magnus tells you, "Turn on your headset."

*You tell Magnus, "It doesn't work right. Makes the game lag when I'm on voice."

*Magnus tells you, "How are you playing on that ancient rig of yours?"

*You tell Magnus, "Don't insult my Franken-puter, the trusty little box that could."

*Magnus tells you, "Get some sleep or you are going to be exhausted tomorrow. I want you well rested."

A thrill of anticipation sliced through me. Tomorrow would finally be the night.

*You tell Magnus, "Bossy. I was just about to log off. Enough lag for tonight."

*Magnus tells you, "I'll pick you up at 11 sharp."

I lay down with a nice, dry study book to lull me to sleep, trying hard to get my mind off of all that would happen the next day. It took an hour, but it finally worked.

8

ADAM APPEARED AT MY DOOR AT EXACTLY ELEVEN A.M. Somehow I knew he'd be the type to be ultra-prompt, despite his tardiness at our first meeting. He wore khakis, white deck shoes and a casual button-down, short-sleeved shirt. And, of course, those same sexy designer shades.

He had his ubiquitous cell phone in one hand and a cardboard box under his arm. I jerked open the door. "I'll be right out. Wait here." I said, leaving the door ajar to grab my backpack from my room.

When I got back, he was standing in the middle of my living room, opening up the box. Of course.

"Dude, what are you doing? The place is a mess. I told you to wait outside."

"Is it?" he said, sounding preoccupied. "I hadn't noticed."

I swatted his hard arm with the back of my hand, stunned that it felt like smacking my knuckles against a rock. "Very funny. What the heck are you doing?"

"Your rig is a piece of shit."

"Thank you," I answered acerbically.

"I had this lying around. Figured you could use a loaner."

He pulled out a sleek new laptop that immediately made my heart palpitate with toy-lust. It was ultrathin, made from a matte dark metal.

"What...? What do you mean 'loaner'?"

He spoke slowly, as if to a toddler. "I mean that I lend it to you and you use it for a while and then you give it back to me when you no longer need it."

I made a face at him. As if I'd give that luscious thing back. Like, *ever*. He'd just opened it up and booted it. It was already loaded with everything. The palpitations turned into out-and-out fluttering. My God. It was a work of art. It was a gamer's rig, fully tricked out with all the essentials and a seventeen-inch high-definition screen that was as clear as looking through a window.

"This looks just like the notebook you were using in Holland."

"It's close. Not quite as mighty. It's my backup but I never use it."

Nevertheless, I noticed there was no log-in for him. He'd already reconfigured everything for me, even created an account. "What password did you set?"

He shrugged. "*Magnus rules*. You can change it later, if you must."

I smirked. "Oh, I think I must."

The machine was gorgeous, and easily came with a several-thousand-dollar price tag. I knew I should refuse it. After all, if we were never going to see each other again after tonight, how would I even return it to him?

So I asked him. "How would I get this back to you?"

He paused and I couldn't tell whether he had no answer for the question, didn't wish to answer the question or hadn't even heard the question. His fingers were flying over the sleek backlit keyboard.

I was just about to repeat myself when he said, without looking at me, "Just give it to Bowman. He can bring it down to the complex. I promised him a tour, anyway."

Shit, a tour of Draco Multimedia headquarters? Lucky bastard. "That asshole didn't even tell me," I grumped.

He glanced at me. "You can have one, too."

Our gazes held and my heart pounded. That couldn't be possible. If tonight we were going to—then I shouldn't go anywhere near his workplace after that.

I swallowed. He must have known what I was thinking. I think he was waiting for me to say something, maybe expecting me to back out of tonight. I straightened. I wasn't going to back out. I couldn't. So I just shook my head.

He looked away, features clouded, but I couldn't tell whether he was troubled or just preoccupied. I was starting to feel both— troubled about our inevitable farewell after this evening and preoccupied with how everything would go, finally, tonight.

If things had gone according to plan, this would have been over with a week ago and by now, we'd be strangers once more. And before, I'd felt like that was absolutely the right thing to do, but now...It was weirdly illogical. I wanted to know all about him before we never saw each other again.

Alex showed up just as we were descending the stairs to leave less than an hour later. When she looked up and saw Adam, her jaw dropped and her gaze shot to me, eyes rounding. Subtle she was *not*. I wondered how she'd managed to get over here so fast from her apartment in Fullerton once her mom had called to tell her he was here.

I sighed and made introductions. "Good to meet you," Alex smiled, leaning to shake his hand and bat her big eyes at him. "Mia's told me so much about you!"

My lips pursed. What a little liar. Adam smiled and shot a side-long glance at me. I shrugged, throwing my hands up. "We gotta get going."

Alex watched us go and when I looked back, she waved her hand in front of her face to fan herself—a clear indication that she found him hot. Then she put her hand to her ear, mimicking holding a phone and mouthed an exaggerated *Call me.*

We hit the road and I breathed a sigh of relief. That had been a close call. The more I kept Adam separated from my friends, the fewer awkward questions I'd have to answer later. When I glanced over at him, he had a grin on his face.

"What?" I asked.

"You've told her all about me, huh?"

I looked away, cheeks heating. "She's a hopeless liar," I muttered.

The day was truly beautiful. I was convinced there was no more gorgeous weather on this planet than what we enjoyed in Southern California in May. The smells of the white jasmine bushes that were planted everywhere combined with the blossoms on the orange trees and imbued the air with a honey scent. It was too early for the June Gloom, where mornings were overcast until they burned off into hot afternoons. In May, every day was fresh, crystal clear and sunny.

And in his convertible—a dark blue vintage 1950s Porsche—we zoomed down the freeway in the carpool lane, bypassing Saturday beach traffic.

I'd bundled my long hair as best I could into a ponytail band, making a messy bun. Still errant strands of hair whipped around my face and into my eyes as I squinted through my cheapo drugstore sunglasses, tapping my foot in time with Depeche Mode's "Pleasure Little Treasure" on the stereo. So he liked his music like he liked his cars—classics. I was beginning to realize that Adam was the rock star of computer geeks. And apparently a lot of the tech magazines agreed with me.

Adam parked at a small underground garage a few blocks away from the bridge and we walked the rest of the way—he insisting on carrying my bag, which wasn't heavy at all. I resisted at first, but he practically yanked it out of my hands.

"Your mama raised a very nice boy," I said and then immediately regretted my words when I saw his jaw tighten. How could I have forgotten? I stopped, placing a hand on his rock-hard bicep. "I'm so sorry."

He shook his head. "No worries, Emilia." But those dark brows creased over his sunglass-veiled eyes.

I cleared my throat, still feeling terrible. Taking a deep breath, I started walking again. I decided to ease the awkwardness by talking about a subject I hated as well. "No, I know how it feels whenever someone brings up my dad or asks me about him. I never had a dad. I don't even know his name so I call him the Biological Sperm Donor because that's all he is to me."

He glanced at me sidelong. "You were never curious to meet him?"

I shrugged. "He didn't want me so why would I want him?" And we kept walking, past the park gardens of Bay Island, alive with bright pinks, vivid yellows—all of spring in a flowerbed. "He was

married with a family and he never bothered to reveal that little detail to my mom before he got her pregnant. When she told him she
was going to have a baby, he paid her a big sum of money to shut up
and 'go take care of it.'"

"Ah. A right bastard, then."

"Yep. So I don't give a shit who he is."

He glanced at me again. "But he's well off. You could have, you
know, tried to get the money you need from him."

Now it was my turn to tighten my jaw. "Why ask from him what
I can do for myself?"

And I could tell he wanted to say more but cut himself off with a
slight shake of his head, his grip tightening on my bag. Was he actually angry?

I paused, watching him carefully. This wasn't the first time I'd
gotten the impression he had torn feelings about the auction—this
entire arrangement. I remembered the insults he was slinging
around when we first met—and some of the other offhand comments he had made during our brief time in the Netherlands, always
questioning my judgment and reasons for entering the auction in the
first place.

If he didn't approve, why had he even bid?

Though I wasn't about to question him now. In truth, I was glad
he did bid. But I was getting this weird tight feeling at the pit of my
stomach. It felt like a cold rock sitting there and never moving. It
had something to do with the fact that I was allowing feelings to get
involved. As much as I wanted the money, yes. As much as I wanted
him, yes. I found myself not wanting this to be over yet.

There was too much to find out before that. I wanted to know
what drove him. What his fears were. What his goals were. Had he

already arrived at the ripe age of twenty-six or was he striving for more and if so, how much higher could he go? And what about a personal life? Why was he driven, after being so successful, to still spend ninety hours a week in his office and half his life on airplanes and in hotels?

Then there were the personal details. Had he ever been in love? Who was Sabrina? Why did he have her name permanently inscribed on his heart?

These were things that I would never know, ever, if we slept together tonight.

But there was another voice inside my head, along with the one dying of curiosity to get to know him better. The logical one. The one that said that a man like Adam would only hurt me in the end if I opened up to him. Just like the Biological Sperm Donor had done to my mom. He'd crushed her and she'd never been able to move on. And if I let just one weakness in my fortress show, Adam would do the same to me.

With new resolve, I swore to carry out the original terms of our agreement, no matter what I was feeling inside.

***

The boat was gorgeous, of course, like all of the other things he surrounded himself with. A one-hundred-foot yacht appointed with the most glamorous details, all chrome and marble countertops, wood paneling and recessed lighting. It looked nicer than the nicest home I'd ever been in—besides Adam's. There was a large kitchen, called a "galley" from which Adam's chef/housekeeper worked. She had come along with the captain and they were the only other two aboard besides us, which left us a great deal of room to move about.

Adam told me he often had team parties on the yacht for his employees and used it for other business, about which he was vague. As we talked, I got the impression that his business interests were diversified—he had investments in the hospitality industry and technology hardware beyond just his own company. Draco Multimedia, particularly Dragon Epoch, was his main source of income, but he was beginning to branch out.

We ate a gourmet lunch straight away—poached salmon over a crisp bed of greens. Then Adam showed me the rest of the boat. And I don't know if was by design or by happenstance, but the last room he showed me was his. A room almost as big as my studio, with a lush king-sized bed.

We stared at each other awkwardly in the doorway and he looked almost embarrassed. "I really didn't mean for us to end up here. Not yet, anyway."

I laughed. "I bet you say that to all the girls you bring on your yacht."

"Actually you'd be the first one."

I shot him a teasing look. "New yacht?"

He shrugged, sheepish. "It's not *old*."

"So you never brought Lindsay here?"

He looked at me sharply, "Lindsay? No…no. No."

I laughed at his vehement protest. "It's okay. I realize you two have a history that I know nothing about."

He shifted from one foot to the other, clearly uncomfortable. "Lindsay and I go way back."

I couldn't resist. Not with it dangling out there in front of me like that. "How far back? And was there a bedroom involved?"

He glanced at me out of the corner of his eye and affected nonchalance, putting his hand in his pocket. "We had a history as sexual partners."

"Interesting." I folded my arms, leaning back against the doorjamb. "You don't use the term 'lovers.'"

He snorted. "Love had nothing to do with it."

"Was she married then?"

And Adam's expression grew so horrified that I almost laughed. "God, no. It was like ten years ago." That meant he'd been just a teen.

I wrinkled my nose. I was like a dog with a bone with this, unwilling to give it up. "Dare I ask if she was your first?"

He actually blushed and that's all I needed to answer my question. He gave another one of those fake shrugs. "You can always *ask*."

I ignored the evasion because I already had the answer to my question. Lindsay had popped Adam's cherry. "So, does she always act like that with you?"

He frowned. "Like what?"

"Like you two are still a couple?"

He looked at me like I was an alien. "First of all, we were *never* a couple. We got together and we fucked and that was about it. We didn't date. She was too busy with her career and I didn't really care about relationships. I was too young for that. We're friends now. She's a partner in my uncle's firm."

I was not convinced, wholly, of Adam's cluelessness. He was far too perceptive a person not to have noticed Lindsay's flirtatious behavior. And beyond that I was a little shaken by how strongly I felt about it. Why did I even care who Adam had slept with in his past?

He knew my sexual history—well, most of it, anyway. Shouldn't I have a right to know his?

A grin flickered on his lush mouth. "So why all the questions? You're not jealous, are you?"

I widened my eyes, "Oh, no. No, no. God no." I blathered, flustered. *Now* who was overdoing it? "What's there to be jealous of? You and I have a business deal, nothing more."

But when I talked, my voice was a little too shaky and his handsome face was completely devoid of any emotion. He turned and moved to an inner doorway. "There's the bathroom if you want to change into your swimsuit. I'm going for a swim once we stop."

"Out—in the middle of the ocean?"

He shot me a puzzled stare, as if I'd just spoken Mandarin. "Yeah."

"But aren't you going to freeze your ass off? That water is cold."

He shrugged. "We have a Jacuzzi on board. We get too cold, we get out and hop in the hot water."

I bit my lip. "Maybe I'll just watch from the edge."

He picked up my bag from where it sat on the table and tossed it to me. "Get in your suit."

I grabbed it and went into the bathroom and shimmied into my trusty one-piece. It wasn't the fancy bikini that I'd posed in for the auction, but it was still a nice suit. And it was his favorite color, too. Blue.

When I went to open the door, I heard him moving around out in the bedroom and realized he must be changing out there. Not wanting another awkward repeat of that first afternoon in Amsterdam, I tapped on the door and he told me to come in.

He was shirtless with his trunks—long board shorts—hanging off his hips. I smiled and walked into the room and he ran an appreciative eye down my form, giving a mock wolf whistle. I couldn't help but devour the sight of his body again. He had a narrow waist and solid shoulders, every muscle clearly defined from firm pecs to rockhard abs. He wasn't as tan as I'd expect of an inhabitant of Newport Beach, but of course he spent most of his life under fluorescent lighting in an office in Irvine, so that was understandable. His finely chiseled chest was covered with the slightest dusting of dark hair, with a narrow trail leading down to his navel and beyond.

I looked at the tattoo again. He wasn't attempting to hide it but he didn't say anything when I studied it, either.

"Are you ready to go?" he said.

"As ready as I'll ever be."

He led us on deck to the ladder that took us down to the waterline. He shot me a boyish grin and then dove in headfirst. I hung my feet off the side and dipped my toes in, the shock of cold shooting up my legs. I squealed when he splashed me.

"Come in. Just jump in fast. Get it over with. It feels great after a minute."

"I'm not diving. How do you know there are no sharks out here?"

He laughed, watching me as he treaded water. "I don't. Come on."

And we swam for the next hour or so and it was wonderful fun. Adam pointed out the distant spouts of humpback whales. I saw a pod of dolphins jumping out of the water in the distance. When it grew too cold to stay in the water, my entire body shivering uncontrollably, Adam shot up the ladder first and, still dripping himself, reached into a cabinet where a stack of towels were warming and extracted one, holding it for me to walk into when I climbed the ladder.

It felt wonderful and I thanked him while he stooped to grab one for himself. "Let's go warm up in the Jacuzzi."

On the back of the middle deck, open to the sky, we soaked in the warmth of massaging bubbles while the chef brought us champagne and appetizers. The captain turned the boat around so that we could watch the sunset over the ocean.

We talked and stuffed ourselves on Chef's amazing appetizers: bacon-wrapped scallops, baked brie, and all kinds of great munchies. So much so that our appetites were ruined for dinner. Graciously, Chef told us she would pack a cold picnic for us to take up to the top deck when we were hungry.

And then we were alone watching the sunset paint the sky in deep reds and oranges reflecting out onto the ocean. "So this is what you do in your copious amounts of spare time?"

He smiled. "I'd like to take the boat out at least once a month. Maybe over to Catalina, down to Mexico or just out on the water."

"Taking your work with you, of course."

He kept his gaze on the horizon "Perhaps."

I narrowed my eyes. "Uh huh. With your satellite Internet—I saw that big old office you have belowdecks. It's not for bringing women out here."

"I told you I don't bring women out here."

"You brought me."

He glanced at me. "Yes, but you are an exception."

"Have you ever had a long-term relationship?" I asked.

His dark eyes darted to the ocean once again. "No. I never had the time."

"Ah. So you just have...fuck buddies."

He was amused. "If you want to call them that. And what about you? No fuck buddies obviously, but you don't date, either."

I shook my head. "Nope. Tried it. Didn't like it." I shrugged.

He watched me carefully. "How old were you when you made that decision?"

"Sixteen."

He cursed under his breath.

"Anyway, let's talk about something else!" I said brightly.

He shook his head. "No, I want to talk about this for a few moments longer." I shook my head right back. His gaze hardened. "Don't get like that, Emilia. I think it important that I know if anything painful happened to you. I want to do everything I can to make you comfortable. What happened in Amsterdam—"

"It won't happen again—no need to worry. I did a lot of therapy."

"I disagree. I *should* worry."

I sighed and glanced off to the side. "I had a boyfriend in high school. He was a football star, a senior, and I was a stupid little sophomore with stars in my eyes. He treated me like shit. One night he got drunk and assaulted me. I broke up with him. The end."

Now his face was grim. "He assaulted you...sexually?"

My breathing froze. I had never talked to many people about this. Heath knew it all. So did my therapist. Mom knew some of it but I refused to say any more about it after she started talking about going to the police. It was dropped and she got me the therapist to talk to instead.

I took a deep breath and took a leap. For some reason, those dark eyes compelled me to do so. Sometimes I was a coward—*most* of the time I was. But I could be brave today. Just for today. And speaking of this took pretty much all the courage I had.

"He wanted to have sex and I said no. He got pissed and slammed my head into the steering wheel—we were parked up on the Ridge— up in the foothills. I'd been driving because he was hammered from the party we'd gone to. I got out of the car and took off running. He caught me and—"

My voice trembled and cut off. Adam watched me, his expression grim, but did not move, did not say a thing, waiting patiently for me to collect myself. I took a deep but shaky breath.

"He grabbed me by the hair, pulled me on my knees and made me go down on him." *Eat it, bitch,* he'd slurred while I sobbed. Remembered fear closed my throat. I didn't mention the scars on my scalp, where he had pulled so hard on my hair that he'd torn small chunks of it out. Hair wouldn't grow on those spots for years afterward.

"I hope he got a long time in jail for that," he said and my chest tightened.

I avoided his eyes. Here's where Mia showed herself for the gutless wuss that she was. I swallowed. "He didn't go to jail."

Adam scowled. "*What?*"

I swallowed. "I didn't press charges."

Silence. He said nothing and didn't even move. I knew what he was thinking. Because I thought it of myself every day. *Coward. Mia is a coward.*

"I know you are wondering why..."

He slowly shook his head. "You don't have to tell me."

But I couldn't stop. It was like a valve had swung open on a dam. "I was too scared. He was popular and the quarterback on the football team. Everybody worshipped him. I didn't think anyone would believe me." My voice trailed off and I was disgusted by the whining in my own voice. I straightened.

He glanced away for a moment, as if trying to collect himself. "I understand."

And I knew he did, given his history with being bullied.

I let out the breath I'd been holding. "Thank you for not judging me."

His eyes fixed on mine again, holding my gaze as firmly as a physical grasp. "I don't have the right to judge you."

We sat in silence for a several long, weighted minutes. Then I cleared my throat, gathering courage. "Now will you tell me something?"

He took a deep breath, almost as if he was bracing himself. I had the sudden urge to scoot up next to him. I suppressed it.

"Who is Sabrina?"

He swallowed and looked away. "My sister."

My jaw dropped. That was so not an answer I was expecting. And I couldn't describe the reaction welling up inside of me. Surprise, relief, puzzlement. Who tattoos their sister's name on their chest? "Oh. How cool. I didn't know you have a sister."

"Had," he turned back to me, his face and voice utterly emotionless. "*Had* a sister. She's dead."

I sat back, the wind knocked out of me, shocked both by the news and his expressionless delivery of it. Before I could respond, he leaned forward, readying himself to get out. "Let's go shower off and look at the stars from the top deck. And the view of the shoreline is great now that it's dark."

There was only one shower in the master bathroom and two of us. Adam grabbed two monogrammed terry bathrobes, handing one to me. "I'll go shower in a guest bathroom."

"You don't have to," I said in a shaky voice.

He froze and turned back to me.

"You could shower with me. I saw the place. It's huge."

His eyes lit up but I could tell he thought I was kidding. Likewise, the thought excited me, too. The image of spreading soap across his abs with my bare hands was making my heart pound a little harder.

"Emilia, if I shower with you we will never get up to the top deck."

Instead of replying, I dropped my towel and then shucked off my wet swimsuit in two smooth, quick moves. Then I shot him a grin and backed into the bathroom. "You're going to have to show me how this damn thing works anyway."

A cold thrill thrummed in my throat as his hungry eyes traveled down my naked body. I felt daring, bold, empowered, *desired*.

By the time Adam took off his swim trunks, he was fully aroused. I tried not to look—much—but I have to admit that curiosity got the better of me. His body was beautiful, magnificent and—well, I tried not to let the size of him terrify me.

I backed into the hot spray. The shower had dual heads, one on each side, so we each got our own. And for the first few minutes, we stood on opposite sides of the shower, awkwardly cornering our own spray, warming up while cautiously watching the other.

I lathered my hair before offering the bottle to him. Once he reached for it, I poured shampoo into my own palm and then put it on top of his head, setting aside the bottle to lather his hair. He watched me with a longsuffering, tolerant expression, but his eyes were dark with desire. His slick, hot, naked body was only inches from mine and I shook with anticipation, with the blood pumping through my veins at five times its normal speed.

Moving closer, I swallowed in a tight throat. I stood on my tiptoes to reach the top of his head, and he steadied me by placing hands on my waist. Then he ducked his head for my attention. His hands, where they held me, touched me lightly at first, but as I continued to massage his scalp, his hold on me tightened, fingertips pressing into my flesh. Thrill danced across my skin. I wanted to press my body to his. But I remembered his warning, about not making it to the top deck. Did I want our first time to happen in here?

I pulled away and turned back to my side of the shower to rinse my hair, my eyes closed. But he came up close behind me.

He picked up the bottle of shower gel and poured it into his hand and I twisted to look back at him, ready to feast on the vision of this gorgeous man lathering his abs.

He said, "Stand still. I'll wash your back."

I took a deep breath and did as he told me. His warm hands slicked down from my shoulders, across my deltoids and trapezius muscles to the small of my back. Every inch that he touched sprang alive and I trembled. The soap allowed just the right amount of give and the sensation of his strong hands gliding over my skin set my insides aflame with impossible heat. Then he reached around and smoothed soap across my belly, my hips. His hands skirted my pubic region before slipping up to my breasts—and apparently he must have thought my breasts in extra need of washing because his hands lingered there for quite some time. My nipples were erect and sensitive under his touch, each stroke of his hands piercing my core with lancets of desire.

I was panting, leaning against him. His erection pressed into the small of my back, hot and hard. His head came down to take my ear in his mouth. Shower spray pelted us. "Emilia, if I wasn't a gentleman, I'd pin you to that wall right now and fuck you."

My breath hitched. "Who said you had to be a gentleman?" His mouth was on my neck now but I squirmed out of his arms, pouring some gel in my hands. "That mouth of yours proves that you are a dirty, dirty man..." I said suggestively. He laughed and turned. I started on his shoulders and back and his posture grew rigid. My hands glided over his perfectly defined muscles. My hands sank to his waist, then down to his hard butt.

I turned and filled up on gel again and moved to his front. His body felt exquisite under my hands. A quiet moan escape his mouth as he closed his eyes, savoring my touch. I bent my head to kiss him but stopped myself. Was I ready to start things here, despite what he'd just told me? I stepped away so he could rinse himself off.

I exited the shower, my body still singing with his caresses. I shivered in anticipation of what would happen later tonight, perhaps even on the top deck, under the stars. We toweled off and dressed in casual clothes to go up to the top.

All of OC hugged a south-facing coast that was the curve of Southern California as it twisted its way toward Mexico. At this distance from the coast, the plentiful lights of OC and LA were but a glow along the horizon.

The moon was a tiny sliver of a waxing crescent and so, being just about to set, provided little competition with the stars. The lights from the coastline, however, did prevent maximum viewing.

Still it was far better than trying to stargaze on land. The light pollution over the Los Angeles metropolitan area was considerable and on the best of nights, it was difficult to discern more than a dozen or so stars on any given night. It wasn't like the skies over Anza, which were so dark and clear you could see satellites gliding through the quiet night skies. But out here, you could see almost as much.

Adam had stopped by his office to check his e-mail and I had wandered up to the deck, alone, trying not to be annoyed. It was a wonder, really, that he had ignored it for as long as he did. I couldn't expect a miracle. So I waited for him for almost an hour. He came up carrying two big blankets and—of course—his cell phone tucked into his pocket.

After finding the most recognizable constellations, we lay back on a wide cushioned bench beside each other, gazing up at the black dome above us.

"I still can't believe you were up there."

"Yep. For ten days. And if I get my way, I'll go up again."

"How did you turn off work for that long?"

He shrugged. "I didn't. I worked by satellite for a few hours every day. But I also had to participate in science experiments, too. I enjoyed that a lot."

From here the blackened sea stretched out around us, calm, rocking gently.

I sighed. "It must be so satisfying, to see your wildest dreams come true."

He was silent for a long moment. "What are your dreams, Emilia?"

I shrugged. "You know, I don't have an answer for that besides 'become the best badass doctor ever.'" I frowned, glad for the darkness that cloaked my face. He couldn't see the valley of worry that had etched itself into my forehead. Though I'd finished my premed program, I was still far from that dream. It was a sobering thing, to see the thing I wanted so much in the world just beyond my reach. The one barrier was something I feared more than anything—failure, yet again. It had paralyzed me, prevented me from retaking the test over and over again until I got it right. No, I wouldn't take it again until I'd paid the price with blood, sweat and tears, studying hours and hours a day until I had the material ingrained as a part of the fabric of my brain.

"That's a worthy enough dream," he murmured. "But there's got to be something deep inside—something you've always wished to do or see."

"Thanks to you I think I can cross a couple things off the list I never even knew I had."

He turned his head and looked at me. "That trip to Europe should hardly count. You deserve to go back, to enjoy it like it should be enjoyed."

I sighed. "Maybe I'll do that."

"So what other things have I helped you with?"

"Hmm. Flying first-class. Swimming with dolphins. Spending a day on a gazillion-foot yacht..." I took a deep breath. "Experiencing the most amazing kiss ever."

He was still watching me, and in the dim light I could tell he was smiling. But if he made a sarcastic remark right now, I knew I would die of humiliation. I was still reeling from the fact that I'd even put that out there. He cleared his throat. "What a coincidence," he breathed. "I had that one on my list, too."

I turned my head to look at him. "Had?"

"Yes. But I can cross it off now, too." He rolled onto his side toward me, watching me still. "But that doesn't mean I'm not going to try to do what I always do."

"Oh? And what's that?"

He ran his finger along my jawline before tracing the outline of my lips. His touch burned hot and cold and my lips shivered.

"I always try to top my own personal best," he said quietly.

When he leaned over and kissed me, it was with the force of all the suppressed tension between us the entire day. That talk in the Jacuzzi had brought us closer together and that shower had ensured that both of us had our motors revved and ready to go by the time he first kissed me.

He rolled on top of me, pressing me into the cushion. His hands and mouth were everywhere. And he was going fast, unbuttoning my shirt, and reaching inside. I shivered and he stopped only to reach for one of the blankets to cover us.

He immediately went to my fly and unbuttoned it, reaching inside. I tipped my head back, gasping at the sudden, but not unwelcome, invasion. He knew how hot and wet I was, murmuring heated words about how I was ready. He tugged my jeans off my hips and I lifted them while he pulled them off, tossing them and my panties aside.

"Emilia, you are driving me insane," he said as he pressed his body to mine again. My hands flew up to unbutton his shirt and pull it open. He immediately pressed his bare chest to mine and we both sighed in unison. The feeling was exquisite—his hard, male body pushing against my breasts, the desperate need between my legs.

"Adam, I want you."

And he kissed me, his movements growing more urgent, if that was possible.

His head traveled down to my nipples, suckling each in turn while I arched my back to meet him, my body burning hotter with each passing minute. Then he kissed his way down my belly, across my navel. And lower.

His head was between my legs and he nudged them open as he traced his hot tongue and mouth up the insides of my thighs. Every part of me began to throb in time with my own urgent heartbeat. I knew what was coming next.

Adam was about to go down on me. Suddenly I tensed at the thought of him so close to one of my most intimate places—I didn't think I would have baggage about this, since this had nothing to do with what had happened to me, but my fear of something possibly happening stopped me.

He sensed it immediately and his head came up. "Are you okay?"

I took a deep breath, forced myself to relax. And I let my knees drop fully open. "I'm okay."

He sank his head to my sex, then, his hot breath bathing my inner thighs. I closed my eyes, willing myself to remain calm, to lie back and enjoy what was about to happen, but the anxiety of anticipation was not helping. I felt his finger first, separating me while he kissed my thighs. He pushed it inside me curling it slowly so that it pressed at a certain spot—a place he knew well, apparently—and I immediately gasped, arching.

He pulled his head up. "Bingo. Found it."

And all I could do was laugh. He'd tracked down the elusive g-spot.

"They should give out merit badges for that," he said.

I gasped when the finger moved again. "I'll give you a fucking gold medal if you want, just don't stop."

"Emilia, I haven't even begun," and his mouth sank to my sex, licking along the ready flesh there, before finding the most sensitive spot, my clitoris, and sucking it into his mouth.

The sensation was indescribable. Like his mouth was made of fire and scorching me with the most exquisite pain and pleasure at the same time. I stopped breathing and then let out a little shout that I'm sure every human being within a mile radius must have heard.

I was coming before I even realized what was happening. The spasms came in short, intense bursts and lasted for minutes. Just when I thought they'd stop, he'd press himself harder against me or adjust his head. My back lifted off the bench and I actually—much to my eternal embarrassment—squealed!

I couldn't help it, though. It was just that good.

But even though I felt like a wet rag that had been wrung out, I realized, when he settled next to me again, that he was right. We had only just begun. And now, it was his turn to take pleasure from me.

"You liked that, did you?" he said, appearing immensely proud of himself.

I smiled. "No. Hated every minute of it."

He leaned down and kissed me then. A deep, soulful kiss. It lasted for long moments and with each passing second, I could feel the urgency build within him. I ran my hands over the supple ridges of his chest, around to his back, cupping his shoulder blades, pulling him down on me.

He didn't break the kiss to unbutton his khakis. It was so quiet out here, with only the sounds of the boat and the lapping of the ocean around us. I heard his zipper and an icy thread of fear shot through me. It was niggling—minor—but I tried not to think about what was about to happen. Knew that my fear was silly—unfounded. Knew that afterward, I would be relieved to have it over with.

With a deep breath, I opened my legs so he could settle between them. He was fighting himself to keep his hands out of my hair, I could tell. One hand would approach my hairline and then drop to my shoulder or back. I appreciated it, even though forcing himself to remember probably yanked him out of the moment. I opened my eyes and saw him watching me. When our gazes met, he pulled back and broke the kiss.

He was breathing heavily. "Emilia," he said, and then kissed me again, pulling me closer. His erection nudged against my inner thigh and he groaned, his arms tightening around me. I adjusted my hips underneath him, wondering why he was hesitating.

"Fuck me, Adam," I said, between clenched teeth.

Another groan and he shifted. He was about to enter me. The tip of him brushed against my heat, but then he stiffened, tearing himself out of my arms.

I sat up, watching him in shock as he grabbed his boxer briefs and khakis, pulling them on with a face frozen in something that looked like disgust.

"What the hell?" I said, still completely naked under the blanket.

He shook his head, grabbing his shoes and standing up—his shirt still completely open and exposing his perfect chest.

"This isn't happening," he said in a distant voice. "Get dressed. You can stay in a guest room."

And without waiting for me to reply, he spun and moved down the stairs to the lower deck, leaving me with my mouth hanging open in shock. I watched him go, utterly lost. My whole body shook and my face burned with humiliation. My breath came fast and anger shot a heated streak down through my entrails. How the fuck *dare* he?

With jerky movements I pulled on my clothes, trying to ignore the sinking sensation that made me wish the sea would rise up and swallow me here and now.

Had I done something wrong? Had I not responded to him the way he wanted? In my mind I retraced everything that led up to the moment where he'd stiffened and pulled away. Had I touched him in a place he didn't like or—oh, God—had he been fantasizing about someone else? My hands shook with fury as I dressed.

***

What the hell was that? I couldn't help but wonder. It wasn't even ten o'clock when I checked the clock in my room—the guest room just down from his. His door was open, light off, so I assumed he wasn't in his quarters.

What had made him react so strongly? Why that look of revulsion on his face? Was Adam screwed up about sex? Maybe he'd been abused as a child or teen. The thought turned my stomach but alleviated some of my anger. What if he couldn't help it? But he'd obviously had sexual relationships with other women—at least one of whom I'd met, Lindsay. But maybe it was something about my being a virgin? Of course if that repelled him, why bid on the auction?

I paced in a tight circle for a while before deciding there was no way I could keep still. I slipped on my shorts and running shoes and headed down to the yacht's little gym. Adam had showed it to me on my tour that afternoon—a room with a treadmill, elliptical machine, weights. I could use a nice long run to clear my head.

With my trusty mp3 player and earbuds in, I descended a deck and—after a couple wrong turns—finally found the room I was seeking. I had the light shining from the doorway to thank for being able to find it. So this was where he'd run to.

Undeterred, I queued my music to my running playlist and headed straight for the unoccupied treadmill. I caught a glimpse of him in the corner—in running shorts and a black tank top—at the pull-up bar. So I wasn't the only one who had decided to burn off my sexual frustration with exercise.

His head jerked toward me just as I turned my back on him and mounted the treadmill.

I turned it on and quickly got my pace up, upping the speed probably faster than I should have. I wanted to burn off the energy as quickly as possible. Maybe, exhausted, I could find the courage to talk to him after that.

I was all-out sprinting—Christina Aguilera's "Keeps Getting Better" pounding through my pulse—when he entered my line of vision, standing just in front of me and mouthing something, shaking his head sternly. I shook my head and looked down. He wanted to talk *now?* Hell no. He could wait. Just like I'd waited up on the top deck while he'd checked in on work.

He didn't move when I refused to stop running or look at him. Then he reached out and turned off the treadmill. The safety mechanism kicked in and the slow was gradual. If I turned it on again, I'd only fall, because it would start with a much slower speed than the one at which I was running.

When it came to a stop I yanked out my earbuds. "What the hell was that?"

He scowled at me. "You're going too fast. You didn't even warm up."

"I'll thank you to keep your fucking nose out of my exercise routine."

"I'm not going to sit back and watch you hurt yourself. You can really fuck yourself up that way."

"Well, maybe I'm pissed off and I need a good run."

"Then at least do it properly."

Heath had told me that Adam was once a runner—probably still was—but that didn't give him the right to butt in.

I got off the treadmill and was about to walk off—wishing I had my computer and an Internet connection so I could log on to the game and go hack a few hundred orcs. "Emilia."

I spun on him, face burning. "*What?*"

"You aren't ready."

I knew he wasn't talking about running now. I stiffened. "And who are *you* to determine that? It's *my* decision. My body. I'm twenty-two years old, for chrissakes. I could go out tomorrow with anyone and—"

"No, you can't," he said flatly, hands curling at his sides.

I shook my head. "There's no agreement if *you* refuse to go through with it."

"Oh? So you've just decided to do away with our impending bank transfer?"

I swallowed in a tight throat. I *needed* that money, goddamn it. I shrugged. "Who says you were ever planning to pay me, anyway?"

His jaw bulged. "I never back out of my agreements."

I shook my head. "I can't take this. I opened up to you. You asked me to be honest and I was and now..." I gestured wildly. "It's like you're punishing me because I told you about my past."

He approached me, reaching out to touch my cheek. I closed my eyes and jerked my head away from his hand. "Emilia. Look at me."

I opened my eyes.

"If I didn't care about you as a person, I wouldn't give a shit. I'd just do it. But I'm not convinced that it won't somehow harm you. I'd never forgive myself.

I folded my arms across my chest. "So if not now, when? Never? Adam, I need that money."

He tilted his head, studying me. "You haven't even applied to med school yet."

I glanced away. Could I afford to tell him the real reason? The ranch was literally in trouble. It sounded like a cheesy '80s movie plot, but if my mom lost her ranch and the bed-and-breakfast that went along with it, she'd lose her livelihood. And if that happened, there'd be no more cancer therapy. I'd just opened up to him about my personal life, and he'd taken the decision out of my hands. I couldn't trust him not to do the same if I told him why I really needed the money now.

"I don't have the whole story, I take it. Why do you need the money?"

I stiffened. "Why should I tell you? So you can use it against me?"

Those midnight eyes were hard. Stern. I lifted my chin, staring him down. Did I have any choice but to go along with his decisions? I let out a slow breath.

His gaze didn't waver as he watched me intently. "You thought you were the one in control. Now you're realizing that's no longer the case."

I exhaled suddenly, as if he'd just punched me. "I was never in control, was I? You just let me think I was. I've always considered myself a smart person—smart enough to get a scholarship and get the grades for medical school, but I'm not a prodigy genius and I'm not going to exhaust myself trying to outthink you. Am I just some little toy to play with until you get bored again?"

He blinked, his arms tensed. "No."

"Because that's your problem, you know. You're bored. You're *empty*. All you do is work. You surround yourself with every costly toy imaginable and keep people at a distance. Does anyone love you? Do you love anyone?"

I don't know if it was my imagination, but he seemed to grow a shade paler. He shifted his weight and ran a hand through his dark hair. But I turned and ran back to my room. I didn't want to do this anymore.

He caught me just outside the door to my room, wrapped his hand around my upper arm and pulled me around to face him.

His mouth found mine and though I was still angry, I let him kiss me. His arms came around me and pulled me tight against him. When we came apart, his breath was harsh and his voice was dark, husky. "One more night, Emilia."

I said nothing, looking into his eyes. I put my hands up to push away from him and he tightened his grip on my waist. "Please."

I took a deep breath. "I need something—some kind of—We can't just keep doing this."

He tipped his head down to rest his forehead against mine. His eyes squeezed tight and then opened again. My throat tightened at the determination in his eyes. "One more night. I'll transfer half the money to you on Monday."

I shivered. When I spoke, it was with a shaky voice. "Okay…" I hesitated. "If you still want me."

He slowly released me, stepping back. He took a deep breath, his right hand closing into a fist. "Were you in any doubt until I stopped it?"

I shook my head.

"Then don't allow yourself to think otherwise. I want you. Very much."

My heart thudded in my throat. He wanted me—for one night. And then what? For the first time since entering into this entire sordid scheme, I was beginning to think I'd made a very, very bad decision. With my strict rules, my frenzied grasps at control, I'd boxed myself into an impossible situation, because my feelings for him were starting to grow too big for just one night. Just one more night.

He stepped forward to land a chaste kiss on my cheek. "Good night." Then he turned down the hallway and disappeared into his quarters.

It hurt to breathe. And exhausted, I dropped onto my bed, curled into a ball and slept.

***

The next morning, when I woke, we were safely docked at the slip on Bay Island, nestled against Adam's house. We had a brief, understated breakfast sitting in his kitchen, snacking on fresh fruit and warm crepes prepared by Chef.

He glanced at me several times but I remained mostly quiet, still feeling awkward and completely in the dark about what had happened between us the night before.

"Do you have plans for later?" he finally said.

I shrugged. "Apparently I'm at your disposal."

"No, I mean for dinner. Just dinner."

"Tonight?"

I thought for a moment. I didn't have to be back at work until tomorrow's late shift. I hadn't had a chance to call Heath back, but I could take care of that this afternoon.

"I have to work on my blog posts for the week."

"It's just for a few hours."

I sighed. "Not if I have to spend an hour or two getting ready."

"Oh, no, it's not that kind of dinner. It's a family thing at my uncle's house. Barbecue." I shot a glance at him out of the corners of my eyes. A family thing? Had I heard that right? Suddenly that old beast, curiosity, seized me by the throat and wouldn't let go.

"Okay."

He drove me home and, as always, walked me to the door, carrying my bag. I entered and noticed a sudden movement near my couch. Startled, I screamed.

Adam darted inside past me, pushing me behind him.

"What the—" Heath jerked up from the couch to a standing position. "Fuck. Way to scare the shit out of me."

I breathed a huge sigh of relief and then started laughing. "Heath, what are you doing here?"

"You vanished. I came over here to try to track you down."

Heath and Adam exchanged manly nods of greeting. "Drake."

"Bowman."

Heath turned back to me with the strangest look on his face. "You been gone all weekend?"

I glanced at Adam, "More or less."

"Ah. Okay."

Adam shifted, obviously sensing the awkward moment. "I'll get going, then." He turned and landed a kiss on my cheek, handing me my bag. "See you at six."

Heath stared at the door with narrowed eyes and an open mouth for almost a minute after Adam shut the door.

I began. "I'm sorry I didn't answer your message. When I got in on Friday night it was too late to call and then I totally forgot on Saturday morning because I woke up late and was busy running around getting ready."

Heath, still staring at the door, shook his head and blinked. "Mind telling me what the hell is going on?"

I dropped my bag on a nearby chair and moved over to the fridge in the corner of the studio that served as a teeny tiny kitchen. "Want some water? I think I have a Dr. Pepper."

"I'm fine. I bought a coffee on the way over here. I know better than to come over here and expect anything to be in the fridge."

"Why are you here?"

Heath's face fell. "Because I was fucking *worried.* Your mom keeps calling me because she can't get a hold of you and it's driving me bananas and what the fuck is going on between you and Drake?"

My head spun—all of that had shot out of his mouth in less than ten seconds and I was still trying to process it. "I have a cell phone. I don't have any numbers punched into it." I pulled it out and handed it to him. "Can you put your number in there? And I'll call you so you'll have—"

"Where'd you get this? This is the brand new Galaxy. People are on waiting lists for these."

"Adam gave it to me."

Heath shot me a pointed look, then focused on putting his number into the phone. Then he dialed the number, letting it ring his cell once and hanging up.

"So are you two banging yet or what?"

I took the phone back from him, pressing my lips together. "Or what."

"What's his deal? Can't he get it up? You spent the entire weekend with him and he didn't get busy?"

I took a deep breath. "Friday we couldn't. The boat wasn't there. So we went on an overnight trip last night and..."

"And?"

"And nothing."

"Shit. I *knew* he was gay."

"What? No...no, he's not gay."

"How do you know?"

"I'm not going to go into details. I just know."

"Then what?"

"Things just keep getting in the way and then last night..." I unscrewed the cap from the bottle of water and took a long sip.

"What happened last night?"

"We spent the day together—had a terrific time. And yesterday before dinner we were talking in the Jacuzzi. He asked me about what happened to me in high school."

Heath's frowned. "How much did you tell him?"

I shrugged. "Everything. It was easier to tell him than I thought. It just all came out."

"Okay so what does that have to do with not—" Then his face flushed and he grimaced. "Oh I get it. He doesn't want to touch you now because you're damaged goods?"

"What? No. No. I think it freaked him out for the opposite reason. He said he wasn't sure I was ready. He said he wouldn't forgive himself if I freaked out about it."

"Are you sure he's not just procrastinating? Maybe it's an excuse not to pay you."

I shrugged. "I really don't think that's it. I just don't know."

Heath shook his head. "Are you two dating or something? He's picking you up at six?"

"It's a family barbecue."

Heath cursed.

"What?" I said.

"He's playing you, Mia. This was a deal for one night. Now he's treating you like his own personal call girl."

I shook my head. "That's not true. We haven't—"

"You haven't fucked. But you've done other stuff," Heath said. "You don't even have to tell me that. I know."

I shook my head. "That doesn't make sense. He hasn't even..."

Heath shrugged. "There are all kinds. Maybe he gets off on denying himself."

"Shut up, Heath. Stop trying to make this all sound sick."

"Girl, it started out sick. It's just getting worse."

I plunked down at my kitchen table and Heath's eyes flew to the shiny new laptop. He waved a hand toward it. "New phone. New computer. A fancy overnight stay on a yacht. What's next? A car?

What's he buying with all these expensive gifts? He wants something. He wants more than one night."

I rubbed my forehead. I felt so stupid at this moment, unable to figure out what the simplest things meant. Was Adam using me? For what? I couldn't get the vision of that expression on his face out of my mind—right after he'd stopped himself and pulled away. He'd looked so disgusted.

"*You* picked him out, Heath. *You* said he was the best choice."

"I wasn't lying. He was. But this whole thing started out in bizarro world and took a sharp left turn into fucked-up land fast."

I shook my head, no snarky reply forthcoming. I must have been off my game.

After staring through me for a few tense minutes, Heath finally blew out a breath. "Listen, you are a big girl. I love you, but I can't stand by and watch you get yourself fucked by this guy—in more ways than the intended one."

I couldn't breathe, suddenly close to tears. "Heath, why are you being so hurtful?" Heath's words were only confirming my worst fears. Adam was using me. Adam wanted something from me. Adam would discard me like garbage once he was done with me. Just like the Biological Sperm Donor had done with my mother. Because they were all the same.

"Because I'm worried about you. You aren't actually developing feelings for him, are you? A guy like that will chew you up and spit you out."

I looked into Heath's eyes and shook my head. "I have to take my chances, Heath."

Heath spread his hands out wide. "Fine. You don't have to listen to me. But I'm not fielding your mother's calls anymore. You handle it. Handle it all. I'm out."

And with a disgusted wave of his arm, he turned and left, slamming the door behind him.

I might have laid my head down and cried. I sure felt like it. But I didn't. I logged on to the game instead and took out about two dozen orcs, checking at least a dozen times to see if my friends FallenOne or Persephone were on. Fallen hadn't logged into the game since the day we had chatted, weeks ago. I sent him a quick e-mail, asking how he was and when he was going to come back, then started working on an article for my blog.

Heath's words repeated themselves over and over in my head and I could hardly concentrate on all the things I had to do. Was Adam playing me? For what reason? Was what we were doing truly sick? I couldn't answer. Every time I thought about Adam, strange feelings rose up in my chest and threatened to crowd everything else out. It made it hard to think, hard to breathe.

With a shuddering sigh, I moved around that apartment like a mindless robot, getting the things I needed done before dressing in a pair of white Capris and a pale blue T-shirt for the barbecue.

***

Once again, Adam was prompt when he came to pick me up to take me to his uncle's house. He opened the door for me and I settled into the vintage leather seats of his Porsche.

His uncle lived in the next city over from mine, Tustin, near the rolling hills that swept toward the canyons in OC's backcountry. The homes here were nice. Not mansions like in Newport, but upper-middle-class homes with established but not wealthy inhabitants. And it was in the long white driveway of one of these that Adam parked his car.

We were hardly out of the car before two young boys—no older than six or eight, came racing out of the house. "Adam!" they shouted, clearly excited.

Adam bent and scooped up each one in a muscular arm, pulling them off the ground. "Holy crap!" he said with an exaggerated groan. "You two are getting heavy."

"Put me down!" one of them said. I pegged him to be a few years older than his brother, as he was slightly bigger. Other than that, it was difficult to tell them apart. They had similar features and their hair was the exact same color. "DJ, I get to drive first!"

But the younger one had caught sight of me and tried to squirm out of Adam's hold, his eyes widening and jaw dropping. "Adam brought a *girl,*" he said in clear disbelief.

I laughed—I couldn't help it—especially when Adam rolled his eyes, dropping both the boys and putting his hands on their heads. "These two knuckleheads are Gareth and Dylan—we call him DJ. They're my cousin Britt's kids."

DJ was still staring at me in wonder and approached me while his brother Gareth hopped into Adam's car and started making pretend motor noises while tugging at the steering wheel. "Hi," he said with a cheeky smile. "You're pretty."

"Well, thank you," I said, laughing.

"Are you Adam's girlfriend?"

"Uhh," I said with a glance at Adam, who seemed more amused than embarrassed.

"Stop putting the moves on Emilia, DJ."

DJ turned to his cousin. "Why'd you bring a girl? You never bring girls."

"I'm sorry? Did you forget your cootie spray?" Adam said.

Soon, Adam was ushering me inside, leaving his cousins out in the driveway to pretend-drive the car with the strict instructions that they were not to touch the gearshift or the emergency brake. Clearly he trusted them, and that this was all the supervision they needed. I could hardly believe he'd let those kids fiddle around in that car, which was clearly worth a fortune.

"Don't worry. They get bored with it after about ten minutes," he said.

In quick succession, I was introduced to four more people, all full-sized. The first two were Britt, Adam's cousin, and Rik, her husband—the parents of the two out in the front.

After initial introductions I thanked Britt for teaching Adam how to dance. "He taught me the foxtrot and blamed it on you," I said with a grin and Britt shot an amused look at Adam.

"All that bitching and yet he still remembers all the dances—and is using them to impress the ladies. Why am I not surprised?"

"Hey, I was bitching about the arm twisting—I mean literally." Adam turned to me. "She'd sit on me and twist my arm up behind my back until I agreed to be her partner."

Britt snorted. "Let's just say that I weighed a bit more than Adam back in those days."

I couldn't help giggling at the mental picture.

Next, Adam introduced me to his uncle, Peter Drake, a tall, thin and soft-spoken man. He wore a silly barbecue apron with writing on it that said, "I'm grilling the witness." Adam's Uncle Peter must have been tipped off that I was coming because he showed absolutely no surprise that I was there.

"Welcome," he said. "How do you like your steak?"

"Medium well," I said. And he shuffled out the back door with a plate of raw meat.

Adam was called away to make a phone call—no surprise. He worked even on Sunday during a family dinner. I had no idea how long he would be, so I wandered off to see what kind of trouble I could get into.

I knew Adam had another cousin about his own age but I didn't see him until I ambled down the hall to find the bathroom. On my way back, I saw movement in one of the bedrooms and poked my head in.

"Hi," I said.

A tall man in his midtwenties sat at long L-shaped table that held two nicely tricked-out computers. He was bent over something tiny, holding a paintbrush in one hand. He looked up at me and just as quickly jerked his eyes away. He was a good-looking man—clearly a trait that ran in Adam's family—but he was dressed curiously, with a mismatched sweater vest pulled over a plaid shirt.

"Hi. You're Emilia," he said in a monotone, returning to his detailed brushwork.

I nodded. "Yes. How did you know?"

"Adam told me about you."

I was surprised. He was so matter-of-fact about it. I wondered when Adam had mentioned me to his cousin and in what context.

"What's your name?" I asked, stepping into the room. This looked like his bedroom, but he clearly did not live here. The place was immaculate and there was no bed in it.

"I'm William Drake, Peter Drake's son," he said formally.

"It's nice to meet you," I chirped. Adam had mentioned that he had a cousin on the autism spectrum. For part of my qualifications for medical school, I had volunteered to work with special needs teens and adults—most of whom had Asperger's Syndrome or some other form of autism. I crept up to get a better look at his handiwork.

"May I ask what you are doing?"

"Painting figurines," he said as if it were the most obvious thing ever. My eyes flew up to the shelves above his head, filled to overflowing with painted pewter figurines. They depicted all sorts of fantasy heroes—wizards, thieves, magicians, warriors, elves and dwarves.

"Wow, these are awesome," I said, moving up to get a closer look. The figurines were not more than an inch tall, made of pewter and each painted in great detail, sometimes even with coats of arms on the shields and delicately rendered facial features, which must have required painstaking hours to depict. "You must have hundreds of these here."

"We don't use them anymore. Adam never plays D and D like he used to in high school."

"Oh, these are for Dungeons and Dragons? I've never played."

"We used to play all the time. A big group of us. Adam was the GM." Huh. Adam had been the Game Master. Why didn't it surprise me to find that out? The Game Master was the one who controlled the story and the game environment for the other players, moving their characters within that world. With his penchant for control, I was not surprised that Adam played that role in his group of friends.

"And you painted all the figurines?"

"I paint for my job, too. I work in the art department for Dragon Epoch."

I took a seat across from him, following his delicate movement. He was painting a female sorceress with flowing purple robes covered in golden symbols. "So you must get to see Adam all the time, then, if you work with him."

He glanced at me out of the corner of his eyes but kept working, his head tilted down. "No, hardly ever. I barely see him at all anymore."

I paused, reflecting on that. Especially since this was the first time in our entire conversation that William had shown an emotion—regret. I watched him as he quietly continued his work. He looked sad, lonely. He missed his cousin, who had likely been one of his closest friends—and yet they worked in the same building every day! What did that say about Adam? Why employ a cousin, someone who was once a good friend, and then never spend time with him?

It was true Adam's work kept him immensely busy, but I was certain he could manage thirty minutes to sit with William over lunch once a week.

I decided to change the subject. "I play DE. Did you design anything I know?"

"I'm a colorist. I fill in the color on other peoples' designs."

"So did you work on any designs I'd know?"

"Probably," he said and I couldn't help but smile.

"Don't tell her any game secrets, Liam. She'll try to weasel anything she can out of you," came a dry voice from the doorway and I turned to Adam, who stood watching us.

William didn't even look up when his cousin spoke. He just shrugged. "I don't know any."

Adam came into the room and walked up behind his cousin to look at what he was doing. "Oh, I remember her. Didn't you have her wearing yellow before?"

"Different figure," William grunted.

"So Adam, I heard you used to be a GM for Dungeons and Dragons."

He glanced at the shelf above William's head. "Yeah, a long time ago. Liam likes to keep painting the figurines even though we haven't played in almost a decade."

"He does an awesome job. Maybe you guys should play again sometime." Adam shot me a curious look but said nothing. I could interpret the expression though. It said something along the lines of: *Like I have the time for that?*

We were called to dinner and ate on the back patio around a gorgeous pool. Britt regaled me with more funny stories from Adam's adolescence while he bore the usual brand of family humiliation stoically.

DJ, however, brought up a blush on both of our faces when he asked Adam if he'd kissed me yet. Britt shooed him away before Adam could answer.

I offered to help with the dishes and Adam collected them for me, standing at my shoulder to rinse and dry after I'd washed. We didn't talk much. I was at a loss for what to say. The questions swirled in my mind and knotted at the base of my throat in tight confusion. Why had Adam brought me here? Why risk introducing me to his entire family when he knew damn well I would never be in his life after our contract had been fulfilled? They were a delightful family and I was glad to know he'd had some happiness after the heartbreaks of his childhood.

When we were saying our good-byes, about to walk out the door, William stopped me and placed a small object in my hand. It was one of the figurines I had been admiring earlier. "Adam says you play a Spiritual Enchantress in DE. I thought you might like this," he said, his eyes never meeting mine.

I looked down at the figure in the dim light and sure enough, it was a non-scantily-clad sorceress waving a huge staff above her head while preparing to conjure a spell. She had long black hair and a red cloak that billowed about her. She was intricately rendered, a tiny work of art.

"Thank you, William. It's perfect."

Adam wrapped his hand around mine and we bid everyone good-bye as he pulled me to his car.

Back at my house, after a mostly quiet ride home, he walked me to my door. We stood on the doorstep and he looked into my eyes. "Thanks for coming with me tonight, Emilia," he said.

"I had fun. But..." I shook my head. He tilted his head toward me, asking the question without speaking it, so I responded. "Why would you introduce me to your family? Won't they wonder what happened, when we finally...?"

His eyes fixed on mine, serious, sincere. "Because you asked me and I wanted to show you."

"Asked you what?"

"You asked me who I love. They're who I love."

He bent and kissed my cheek and stood at the doorstep while I let myself in and turned on my lights, then he faded into the darkness. That ache in my base of my throat was rising again. I was simultaneously dreading and anticipating the next time he'd call me. Because I knew between now and then he would never be far from my thoughts. I'd think about him while doing my drudge tasks at work. I'd think about him while writing my blog. I'd think about him while running errands, cleaning the house. And I'd worry. I'd worry about how I'd pick up the pieces when it was all over.

9

ONDAY NIGHT WAS GROUP STUDY NIGHT AT JON'S. Given the weekend I'd had, I was woefully unprepared for this week's subject: acid derivatives. I almost called to claim a sore throat, but I had to go in to work at midnight anyway and figured I might as well use the humiliation of being unprepared as a motivator to study harder for next time. As if failing the entire thing the first time hadn't been mortification enough. Some people are gluttons for punishment. It seemed I was a glutton for humiliation.

When I got there, however, I was in for a surprise. It was only Jon. The other three had canceled for various reasons and he'd decided to go through with it because he really needed to catch up. We cracked our books and got to work.

I should have known that things were going to get weird when Jon opened a bottle of wine and sat a little too close to me on the couch instead of across from me. I was filling out index cards with important vocabulary terms and he seemed fidgety and nervous.

"You getting nervous about the exam?" I asked, without looking up from my cards.

He shrugged. "Nah. I think I have it in the bag."

I took a deep breath and released it, remembering that feeling of utter confidence last year, when I'd gone in to take it for the first time. Since then, I could have taken it a dozen times over to improve the score but I'd kept putting it off, certain I was unprepared and unwilling to face that defeat again if I was right.

I murmured. "I wish I was as confident."

"You'll do great. You're so smart."

I didn't respond. Jon was unaware of my previous failure, as I'd only told people I didn't attend school with—my close real-life friends like Heath, Alex and Jenna, and my BFFs online—Fallen and Persephone. I couldn't think about this tonight. Couldn't dwell on it. I grabbed the glass of wine he had poured and sipped it, distracted.

As always, my thoughts were a jumbled, preoccupied mess. Every time I tried to pull them on track, some fleeting thought of Adam or memory from the weekend would knock them off again.

I also kept dwelling on Heath's words from the day before—his accusations regarding Adam's nefarious purposes. Was Heath right? Was Adam manipulating me? I puzzled over that, wondering what benefit it could possibly be to him. Adam was acting like we were dating but he knew damn well I didn't date—and neither did he. Did he get off on having me under his thumb? Was this his own peculiar brand of kink?

Our deal remained unfulfilled. That first night in Amsterdam hadn't been his fault. His job had interfered. And Friday, the yacht had been out for repairs—or so he'd said.

The more I ruminated, the more wine I drank. And that little creep Jon must have silently been refilling my cup because when I looked up, the bottle was empty. I'd never even asked for a refill. My note cards were now swimming in front of me.

"Whoa...that wasn't a good idea," I said.

"What?" Jon said, looking up from his study manual.

"The wine."

He squinted at the bottle. "Shit, we polished off the second bottle already."

I checked the time on my phone. "Yeah, and now I'm feeling pretty messed up. I'm no good for studying. I have work in three hours."

He set his book aside. "You can't drive home. You should stay here."

"How much did you drink? Can't you take me home? I'll come get my car tomorrow morning."

"I'm not going anywhere for a couple hours. Why don't you just have a nap on the couch? I'll grab a pillow."

There was no way I was staying over here, especially in this condition. Jon seemed like a nice guy, but I didn't know him that well and he'd been after me to go out with him for months. And now, he was tipsy. He seemed nice, but lots of people did until they got a few in them. Even with the wine goggles on, I suspected a convenient setup.

"I think I'm going to go."

He took my hand in his while I was trying to shove index cards into my backpack. "Stay, Mia. Really. It's okay. Call in sick and crash on my couch."

I shook my head. "I'm not comfortable with that." I stuffed the rest of my things into my bag and wobbled to my feet.

My head spun and he took me by the arm as if to hold me back. "Come on, you can't drive."

"I'm gonna call Heath to come get me. I'm fine. Thanks, Jon."

I yanked my arm from his hold and teetered out the door, strode down the sidewalk and got in my car while he watched from the doorway of his apartment.

I fumbled for my cell, opened my contacts and pressed Heath's number, thankful that he'd put in the information the day before. He'd be pissed, of course, but I knew he'd come. That's what best friends were for.

The phone rang twice before he answered. "Heath, I need your help."

"Emilia? Are you all right?" *Adam.* Shit. I'd dialed the wrong number. Two contacts on this phone...two damn contacts and I'd picked the wrong one! I was drunker than I thought.

"Uh. Hi..."

"What's wrong?"

"I thought I was calling Heath and I got you by accident."

A pause. "Are you drunk?"

Shit. "No. Of course not. I was just studying—he had wine and so I drank some and didn't realize I was drinking so much 'cause he kept filling up the glass." Realizing I was blathering, I sat back and sighed. "He's gonna come get me and take me home. Heath, I mean."

"Where are you? I'll come get you."

"No."

"Emilia, tell me where you are."

"I'm in Orange. It's too far for you."

"I have a fast car. Open up the GPS app and send me your location. Can you do that?"

I hadn't used that app yet. "Is it easy to figure out?"

"I'll talk you through it." And he explained how to do it.

"Don't you dare start that car, Mia," he said, clicking off. I frowned, wondering how I'd gotten into this situation, when I heard a loud knock on my window and I jumped.

Jon stood there, gesturing for me to open my door. Instead I rolled down the window. "I'm sorry, Mia. I had no idea you'd drink so much."

I blinked, the world spinning a little bit. "You're the one who kept refilling my glass."

"Come inside. Seriously, you can sleep it off in there."

"Uh uh, sorry." Then I swallowed. "I'm gonna be sick."

"Mia, stop being stupid and come in. I'm sorry. Just come inside."

"I said no, Jon. No means no." I cranked up the window.

He disappeared and then reappeared a few minutes later, trying to talk to me through the window but I ignored him. I tapped my foot and checked the clock on my dashboard, wondering how long it would take Adam and his fast car to get here.

My insides clenched, sending the age-old warning that they were about to rebel. Nausea burned up my esophagus. I wasn't that drunk, but I hadn't eaten much all day and the wine was irritating the hell out of my stomach. I stumbled out of the car and over to the gutter, doubling over. I heaved a couple times but managed to keep the contents of my stomach—although at this point, getting rid of it all might have made me feel better.

As soon as I straightened up, Jon was beside me again. He had a couple books in his hand, holding them out to me. "I'm super sorry,

Mia. I feel bad. You want to borrow a couple of my books to help you catch up?"

I eyed the books. They were expensive study aids that I couldn't afford. They'd be useful. They swam in my unsteady vision and I reached out for them and managed to grab one of them, but he pulled the rest aside. "Let me put them in the car. And then come in and I'll fix you some coffee."

"No—I'm good. I'm getting a ride."

He took me by the arm. "Come on. I don't want you to try to drive home."

I pulled back against his hold. "I'm not going to. Someone's coming to get me. Stop pulling me around or I'll puke on you."

His grip tightened and he bared his teeth, yanking at my arm. "Mia, stop being so stubborn. Just let me take care of you." His grip tightened painfully.

"You're hurting me—let go!" My heartbeat raced in my eardrums and I grew dizzy with a sudden fear. What was this asshole trying to do? What did he want from me?

I swung the book in my hand and cracked it over his head. He spun on me with a hiss. "What the fuck, bitch?" He raised his free hand as if to hit me and I pulled back against his hold with all of my strength, falling on my butt, raising a hand to shield my face. My fall pulled him, still gripping my arm, to loom over me.

Images of that night with Zack up on the Ridge replaced Jon's threat of violence. I'd had blood on my face, but he didn't care. It ran down my chin, into my mouth—that bitter metallic taste mixed with my salty tears. *No!*

I pulled back, trying to get away from him. "Let me the fuck go!"

I turned to run, to scream, call out to the street. Those fuzzy spots were forming at the edge of my vision again and I could tell I'd be panicking a lot more if I wasn't so slowed by the wine. For that I was grateful.

Right at that moment, Adam pulled up to the curb behind my car. His gaze was fixed on me and then on Jon. He'd seen the entire thing.

He was out of his car in a split second and moved so fast he was a blur. I could see the former track star in all his glory. In seconds, he was between us.

"Back off and let her go!" Adam ordered.

"I'm helping her. She's going to drive off drunk," Jon slurred. I yanked against his hold. It was as tight as ever.

Adam grabbed Jon's free arm and twisted it up behind his back. Jon doubled over, yelping in pain. "I said. Let. Her. Go."

"Who the fuck are you?" Jon screeched, yanking his hand away from my arm as if he'd burned himself. I fell back against the ground, rubbing where he'd grabbed me.

"You all right?" Adam called to me. I didn't say anything, rocking, holding myself, trying to get the panic to subside. "Emilia—"

"I'm okay." I finally said, looking up at him. His gaze on me grew intent and he shifted his hold on Jon.

"Apologize to her, fucktard."

"What the—agh!" he yelped in pain when Adam tightened his grip on the arm. "I'm sorry—I'm sorry!"

Adam let Jon go and stepped back. Jon spun, widening his stance as if he wanted to start something. Adam stood his ground, eyes locked on Jon—giving him a "mad dog" stare, as we'd called it in school.

"What the hell were you doing, trying to get her drunk?" he growled through clenched teeth.

"Dude, I was just refilling her cup."

"Adam, let's go," I said, now worried that he wasn't going to stand down.

Adam's hands curled into fists at his sides. He had at least four inches and about thirty pounds on Jon. "You pull that shit again, I'm gonna fuck you up."

True fear crossed Jon's features. He wavered, looking unsure.

Adam took a step forward. "Don't *ever* touch her again, got it?"

Jon's face flushed a violent shade of red. He shifted to a more threatening stance. "What are you, her fuckin' boyfriend? She doesn't *like* men, you know."

Adam failed to look intimidated by the show. He moved up to Jon and got in his face. "She likes *men* just fine. Maybe she doesn't like *you* because you're an asshole."

Jon took a swing at Adam. But Adam shoved him away before his fist could connect. And that idiot landed on his back, staring up at Adam with open-mouthed shock.

Adam took a step forward. "And a bully. And I really hate bullies," he said, his eyes glittering dangerously.

I pushed to my feet, managing to grab his arm. "Adam, please let's go."

He didn't respond, his arm stiff with rage. He pulled me forward with him. "Adam," I said, moving in front of him. The look on his face—that chill glint in his eyes actually made me go cold inside, made me wonder what he could be capable of. I pushed against his chest. "Please, it's over."

But he surged forward again and as I stepped backward, I stumbled. He caught me, wrapping his arms around me. Jon scurried up from the ground, taking advantage of Adam's distraction to hightail it to his door, slamming it shut and latching it loudly.

Adam stared at the door as if deciding what to do. "Adam, please. It's over. Thank you for helping me." I went up on my tiptoes and kissed him on the cheek—after bracing my hands to balance on his strong shoulders.

His arms relaxed and he finally looked down at me, troubled. "He hurt you," he said.

"Not much. It's fine."

He shook his head. "It's *not* fine."

"Well, you scared him so badly I'm sure he'll shit his pants the next time he sees me."

"He won't be seeing you again because you won't be going anywhere near him," he said through clenched teeth.

I took a step backward deciding not to mention the regular study group. It was true, I'd never be coming over to Jon's again. I resolved to talk the others in the study group into finding another location for our sessions.

Adam cursed when I trembled in his arms. "You're not okay, Emilia." He guided me toward his car. I could tell by the way he held me that he was tense, a fist still clenched tightly at his side.

"I'm sorry you had to come all the way up here from Newport," I said as a means to change the subject, lest he get an idea in his head to pound down Jon's door and finish the job.

"I was just in Irvine."

"It's after nine. Why am I not surprised that you were still at work?"

He helped me to the car. "You okay? You feel sick?"

"No. I think I'll be okay."

"Because if you puke on my interior, I'm gonna make you clean it with a Q-tip."

I snorted.

"You need me to grab anything out of your car?"

"Yes. My backpack and my books, please? I'm so behind on my studying." I handed him my keys so he could lock up my car.

Inside his car, I fell back against the headrest, grateful that the top was down and I could swallow gulps of fresh night air. It helped stave off the nausea.

"You haven't retaken this test yet?" he muttered when he set the books on the floor beside my feet. "If you keep putting it off you'll never get it done." I shot him a sharp glance, wondering how he knew that the MCAT was a retake for me. No one knew that besides my inner circle—not even my mom! Had Heath let it slip? I let my head loll back against the headrest, my thoughts swimming. I vowed to rip Heath a new one for that slip the next time I saw him.

Adam was quiet the entire way home. We listened to Alison Moyet of Yaz begging her lover not to walk away from love. I suddenly felt a wave of melancholy wash over me as the golden lights of Orange's antique streetlamps passed us by. I didn't like to be saved. I usually saved myself, but here I was, letting Adam swoop in and take care of things. And the worst part? I found myself enjoying it.

When he parked, the thunderous booms of the nightly Disneyland fireworks sounded in the distance, heralding the time as shortly after nine-thirty. Adam helped me out of the car, taking my bag and things in his other hand. "I can walk by myself just fine."

He guided me up the steps nevertheless and when we got into the apartment, the first thing I saw was the clock—almost ten, and I had to be at work at midnight.

I sighed and sat down, putting my head in my hands. "What's wrong?" he asked.

"I have work in two hours."

"You can't go."

"I'll make some coffee. I'll be fine."

"You're not going. Call in sick."

I shook my head. "I can't blow off a shift—I need the money."

He walked over to my phone and picked it up, flipping through my list of important numbers. It wasn't hard to find—it was labeled "work," after all. He dialed the number without another word. "Yes, hello, this is Adam Drake, a friend of Mia's. I wanted to let you know that she isn't feeling well this evening and can't make her shift. Yes. Yes I will. Thank you."

He hung up and turned to me. "See? Simple."

"I'm sure *you* call in sick to *your* work without going into withdrawal convulsions."

He shrugged. "That's a little different."

I rubbed my temples. My head was really starting to throb. "Yeah, easy for you to say with your fat bank account."

"If everything went through like it should have, your bank account is quite a bit weightier, too."

I looked up at him though it hurt my eyeballs to do it. "You sent me money?"

"I told you I would."

I frowned. "But I haven't even—we haven't even."

"I said I never go back on my agreements. Now—where's your coffee?"

I thought for a moment. "Oh, crap, I used the last of it on Friday and never bought any more."

"Water, then? And aspirin? Or you're going to feel like shit."

"When did you become the expert on hangovers? I thought you didn't drink."

"I've had a hangover or two in my life. Not fun."

I put my hands to my eyes, my mind jumping to the subject it had been stuck on since my argument with Heath the day before. "Adam, are you using me?"

He had my cupboard doors open, peering in with narrowed eyes, clearly disapproving of what he saw—which was probably old packets of rice mix and a herd of dust bunnies, if memory served me correctly. And with this much wine addling my brain, I doubted that it *would* serve me correctly.

"Using you? What do you mean?"

"Heath said you are manipulating me. He thinks you're putting this whole thing off on purpose."

Adam froze—just for a split instant, but even in my hazy state, I noticed it.

"Are you?" I repeated.

"Here's a bottle of water—and your aspirin's in the bathroom?"

I glowered at his back as he disappeared into the bathroom. I took my aspirin and drank the water. Then I stood and walked toward him. "We can always take care of this whole thing now."

He pressed his lips together. "You're drunk, Emilia."

"So... that was the original plan, anyway. Drink a lot of wine and then lie back and think of medical school." I snorted, though at the back of my mind I was vaguely aware that I shouldn't have said that. I probably shouldn't have snorted, either.

His dark eyes glinted in the low light. "Do what, now? Lie back and think of medical school? Was that your idea of how this would go down?"

I shrugged and took another step forward, until we were touching, chest to chest. "Maybe. You plan on showing me it could be different?"

He didn't move, just stared at me. "When the time comes, you'll see it's very different."

I tilted my head up toward him flirtatiously. "Show me." And I pressed my lips to his in an open-mouthed kiss. He returned the kiss, sliding his tongue into my mouth before pulling back.

"I will show you—just not when you are smelling like Ernest and Julio Gallo's wine cellar."

I threw my arms around his neck with wild abandon. "Come on. My bed is right over there."

"You're right. Let's go then." He bent and scooped me up and I let out a little squeal of surprise. He carried me over to my little twin-sized bed and laid me down on it.

"Time for sleep, Emilia."

I lay there, squinting in the light. "Why are you putting this off?" I asked quietly.

He smoothed my hair back from my face, sitting beside me on the edge of the bed and didn't speak for a long time.

"Let's talk about it when you are feeling better."

My eyes fluttered closed. I had to admit that my head was throbbing and all I could think about was how tired I was. "I'm sorry," I finally whispered.

"For what?"

Sleep was reaching up to take me. "For saying you were empty."

And I don't remember much after that—except for the vague impression, minutes later, of him leaning down to kiss my cheek and murmuring against my skin. "You were right."

10

I WOKE UP FAIRLY EARLY—AROUND SEVEN—AND IT TOOK ME A few minutes to clear the cobwebs out of my mind, but thankfully I had no headache. I remembered everything that had happened the night before with a sudden rush. Cursing my own stupidity for having drunk so much wine at a study date, I crawled out of bed, working the kinks from my neck and back, and took care of my brief morning routine. Shower, dressing, breakfast.

I opened up the computer and went to the webpage for my Cayman bank account to check the balance. It wasn't that I didn't trust him, but I was curious. And it was just as he'd said. Transferred from his account into mine, dated the day before. First thing Monday morning. I shook my head, trying to figure out what the hell was going on and strangely feeling like I was digging myself deeper and deeper into a hole that I had no idea whether I liked or not.

I had half the money. Shouldn't I be happy? But for some unsettling reason, I wasn't. This payoff represented a barrier between us—like a wall, half-built. The balance of our transaction would only complete that barricade, blocking us from each other forever. After his kindness the night before, I had to admit to the regret—even if I just allowed myself to wallow in it for a few moments before solidifying my resolve that things had to be this way. That it was for his protection as well as mine. We had the power to hurt each other. With this safeguard in place, it could never happen. We both knew it would end and exactly *when* it would end. Or so I hoped. There was still that niggling matter of why he kept putting this off.

I bent my head, resting my forehead in my palm for a long moment, and when I opened my eyes, I saw the key sitting on the table next to the computer. It wasn't mine. There was a sticky note attached to it with neat, even printing that I did not recognize. It was an address—somewhere very close, near the Old Towne area at the center of the city of Orange. I stared at it, puzzled, starting to understand Heath's description of where we were: *Bizarro world with a sharp left turn into fucked-up land.* When I inhaled, my chest felt tight, my heartbeat thumping. Was this a key to his house? Why the Orange address?

Just then the phone rang. I checked caller ID, blew out a breath and picked up the phone. "Hi, Mom!"

"Mia, where have you been all weekend? I was worried sick."

I paused, clearing my throat. "I'm sorry. I got super busy. Extra shifts."

"I called your work," her voice trembled when she said it.

Fuck. Silence. Caught lying to her. I never lied to her. I squeezed my eyes shut, shaking. "I'm sorry."

"What's going on? Why are you lying to me?"

I gulped. "I—I'm fine. Okay? You don't need to worry—"

"I'm a mother. I worry. If I can't get hold of you, then I try to find out what the hell is going on. Heath—"

"Mom, please don't call Heath anymore. We are kind of not on the greatest terms right now."

"Okay, now I'm *really* worried. Can I come down there?"

I took a shaky breath. "I'm sorry, Mom. I just. I'm not ready to talk about it."

"Are you—are you seeing someone? Is that it?"

I bit my lip. "Um."

"Mia, do you have a boyfriend?"

"No."

"Then what?"

"There's someone. But I'm not ready to talk about it, okay?" And by the time I was ready to talk about it, he'd be long gone out of my life, so it didn't matter anyway.

A long pause. "Is it serious?"

I cleared my throat. "No. Not even serious enough to mention, which is why I haven't. I'm sorry I lied to you."

"Mia, this is a good thing. I'm glad you're dating."

Dating. A ball of sickness bunched in my stomach, but whether it was because of the thought of actually dating or of lying to my mom about dating, I couldn't tell.

"Mom, I promise that if there is anything to talk about, I will. Just...just you've got to let me go about this my own way, okay? Please?"

"Only on one condition. That you let me know where you are."

"Of course. I have a new phone. I'll text you the number, okay?"

We said good-bye soon after. She still had that distant, hurt tone to her voice and I felt like the biggest jerk for causing it. But the news that I was "dating" was probably a big enough shock in and of itself. She'd been bugging me for years, even though she never seemed to follow her own advice.

After dressing, I set aside the key and went back to the computer. With this unexpected free time—normally I'd just be returning from my shift about now and collapsing into bed, exhausted—I decided to while away a few hours in the game.

Katya, our fourth group member who was our regular healer, sent me an in-game message.

Persephone tells you, "Hey Mia."

You tell Persephone, "Kat! Let's go kill stuff."

Persephone tells you, "Can't. I'm just logging off. Had to babysit my mainframes on the graveyard shift."

You tell Persephone, "Where have you been? I was getting worried that you'd vanished like FallenOne."

Persephone tells you, "What's up with Fallen, anyway? Haven't you chatted with him lately?"

You tell Persephone, "No. He's gone kinda weird. I think it had to do with my auction."

Persephone tells you, "Well, yeah...duh. He's probably jealous as hell."

You tell Persephone, "Really?"

Persephone tells you, "Duh, Mia. He totally likes you. He's always giving you equipment and magic items. You guys chat and have in-jokes that I just don't even get. Since you're so hell-bent on punching your v-card, he's probably crushed that you didn't invite him to fly out and get the job done."

I sat back with a sigh, a heavy weight collecting in my chest. I liked Fallen. A lot. And yeah, once in a while, I'd felt a twinge of a crush on him but there was no possible future with him. He was just a friend. And really, I knew so little about him. He could be fifty years old, married, a grandfather, for all I could tell. I realized that I liked the idea of what Fallen could be to me rather than the actual person, since I knew so little about him.

Men as friends were much safer. A force of nature in the guise of a man who threatened to tear my ideologies apart by the foundations, was not an option. I shoved that thought of Adam aside and replied to Katya.

You tell Persephone, "Did he tell you that?"

Persephone tells you, "He refuses to talk about the auction whenever I bring it up. Which, for the record, is not often. But you go, girl. More power to you. I hope you get lots of $$$."

You tell Persephone, "Hey, on another topic, you know how I asked you to guest post on my blog about Dragon Epoch? I'm going to need that first column by Friday. Can you do that?"

Persephone tells you, "Yeah. Sure thing. Hey, I'm going to send you my quest notes on stuff I got done this morning. I think I might be close to finding another clue about the Golden Mountains quest chain."

I snorted, suppressing a laugh, speaking aloud instead of typing, so she couldn't see my snarky response. "Yeah, good luck with that one, Kat." According to Adam, the task was nearly impossible.

After she logged off, I played, but I couldn't concentrate and my character kept getting killed. I logged off and checked my blog, responding to comments. There were complaints about the fact that I hadn't done my weekly DE update for two weeks now.

A little while later, my phone chimed with a new text message. It was Adam.

Good morning. How are you feeling?

Not bad. You?

Did you find the key and address?

I keyed back, *Yes. What is it for?*

Meet me at that address at noon? We can grab a quick lunch afterward.

I still have to go get my car.

Look out your window.

So I did. And there, parked at the curb in its usual spot was my little beat-up 1993 light green Honda Civic. He'd walked back to Jon's house the night before and driven my car back here?

OMG, I can't believe you did that.

Would rather you didn't have to deal with that d-bag again.

Thank you.

Meet me at noon, k?

Ok.

The address, when I checked it out, was actually within walking distance of my little studio—and right smack dab in the middle of the historic Old Towne district, which served as an attraction for just about the entire county. Movies had been filmed there and the entire place was like a time capsule—a glimpse into the early twentieth century, complete with Watson's, a 1950s-style drugstore and café, which hadn't changed in over sixty years.

The town centered around the Plaza, one of the last traffic circles in California, with a circular park at the center replete with fountains and centuries-old trees.

Above all the curio shops and trendy eateries, the old red brick buildings housed vintage apartments. And I was standing in a narrow alley at the base of the stairs that would lead me up to one of them.

I was confused. Obviously the key was to the apartment, but what on earth did he mean by giving it to me and telling me to meet him there? Maybe it was his other residence? But I could hardly imagine him having another one, especially one only twelve miles from his home in Newport, where he hardly spent any time.

I climbed the steps and unlocked the door. Since I was a tiny bit late, of course he was already inside, standing by the window with his cell phone to his ear. By the sound of the conversation, it was his administrative assistant. He turned and smiled.

As always, that smile snatched my breath away. He had on suit trousers, a crisp white dress shirt and a thin dark blue tie. Clearly he'd pulled himself away from meetings or something important at work to be here. I exhaled sharply and returned his smile. I wanted nothing more than to launch myself into his arms and press that exquisite mouth to mine. It was like I was addicted to the taste and smell of him.

But I restrained myself—barely.

Adam rattled off a few more orders and clicked the phone off. "How do you feel this morning?" he asked.

"Good. Okay. No hangover, thank God."

"I'm glad."

"Thank you. I really didn't mean to call you last night."

His expression grew serious. "I'm glad you did anyway."

"Thanks, too, for getting the car." He only smiled in reply.

I stepped into the room, glancing around. The outer shell of the building might have been vintage, from the 1920s, but the inside was all modern—stainless steel kitchen appliances with dark granite counters and recessed lighting. Gorgeous crown molding. Beyond the main kitchen and sitting room, a doorway opened into what looked like a sizeable bedroom. It was, however, completely vacant.

His phone chimed. He checked it but tucked it back into his pocket. I quirked a brow at him. "Shouldn't you be ensconced in your office behind your desk, muttering the twelve steps for workaholics anonymous, right now?"

He grinned. "Even workaholics take a lunch break once every blue moon."

I moved up beside him and shared his view out the window. "Nice place," I said. "Yours?"

"Yeah." Because *of course* it was. "Recent acquisition. Investment property."

"And the apartment is vacant because...?"

"It's between renters." He tossed a glance at me and then out the window with a casual shrug. "I have a management company handle my properties for me. But I have someone in mind for this location."

He turned back to me, shooting me a meaningful look, implying that I was the "someone in mind." His implication hit me like a balled fist. I took a shaky breath and turned away from him so he wouldn't see the look on my face.

But I couldn't hide my reaction for long because Adam was as sharp as a razor.

"What's wrong, Emilia?"

My jaw set but I didn't turn back to him. "I hope you don't mean me."

He paused. "And if I did?"

I turned around and faced him. "I can't afford the rent you must be asking."

"You can now."

I breathed in deeply and exhaled slowly. A tiny voice in the back of my head—the voice of calm rationality—told me that he was doing a kind deed. He was helping me out. He was—

No. *Just no.*

My spine stiffened and sudden tension arced between us. "Is this the part where you hand me a roll of hundreds and tell me to go out and buy something pretty?"

His features tightened, almost imperceptibly. "I was going to offer it to you at the rent you're currently paying for your studio. This place is safer than your neighborhood. It would put my mind at ease."

"That's impossible. You'd take a huge loss on it."

He looked away. "I don't care about the profit right now." His phone chimed again. He reached for his pocket and froze when he saw the look on my face. His expression was grim when he snatched the damned thing and looked at it. This time, he took the time to reply by text.

I folded my arms over my chest and started to pace.

"Emilia—just consider—"

I turned on him, my shoulders and back so stiff I almost wrenched them with the motion. "I can't live here. You know it as well as I do."

"I do?"

"I can't live in your apartment because of what happens after we..." and my voice died out as our gazes clashed. His features chilled. He jammed a fist into his pocket and his eyes flew to the window again.

I couldn't help but hear Heath's words spoken to me a few days before. *What is he buying with all of these expensive gifts? He wants more than one night...*

"Adam, what are you doing?"

"What do you think I'm doing?"

"I'd say I suspect you're trying to set me up in a fuck pad but we aren't fucking. So that's out."

"And if I said I wanted to help you out, would you believe me or would you twist it into something it isn't?"

I shook my head, my fists clenched. "I don't need to be saved. I can save myself."

"Oh, that's right," he said quietly, walking toward me, watching me with stony eyes. "That's what this whole auction was about. You 'saving' yourself."

I stared into his face as he came to a stop inches from me. I could smell him. That warm, male body of his that smelled of ocean breezes. I swallowed, wishing I could clamp my own nostrils shut. Even when I was annoyed with him, he still affected me like no one else ever had.

"If indeed you ever intend to take the auction seriously—"

He shook his head. "And that three hundred and seventy-five thousand in your bank account means, what? I've been paying for the pleasure of your company these past three weeks?"

I shrugged. "I have no idea. Only you know the answer to that. And you don't seem to be sharing."

Now he looked supremely annoyed. "So should we just drop on the floor and fuck right now?"

I brought my chin up and looked him straight in the eyes. "Sure, let's have at it. Get this over with."

"Is that what you want? For it to be over with?"

My mouth opened to shoot the sharp retort on my tongue but nothing came out. I clamped my lips shut. My shoulders shook so I grabbed my arms, crossing them over my chest. My hesitation confused me. Why not just say "yes?" I blinked. Because I didn't want it to be over. Not yet.

"Why are you drawing this out?" I finally asked, my voice hardly more than a whisper. I was aware that I wanted a certain answer from him. I didn't know precisely what that answer was. But would he tell me what was going on inside that ultra intelligent brain of his? Or would he pull back into his cold façade again?

"I don't have to share my reasons with you. I'm the wallet in this deal, remember?"

Yeah. That wasn't the response I was looking for. Definitely not. Heat crawled up my neck to infuse my cheeks.

"I'm not a call girl. I'm not your mistress. So stop trying to treat me like one."

"See, you're doing it again. You're twisting it into something it isn't."

I clenched my teeth. "I'm not moving into your fucking apartment."

His expression did not change and he didn't even move. "Tell me why not."

"I don't have to share my reasons with you," I mimicked his words back to him.

"Because you think it means I'm treating you like a mistress?"

I tensed, thinking of my mother's story. One with a sad ending for someone I loved most in the world. She was young, fresh and naïve. She thought she'd found the man of her dreams. Turned out he'd only used her and then discarded her, leaving her to fend for herself and a baby besides. My hands squeezed my upper arms and I blinked.

"The Biological Sperm Donor did the exact same thing. And that's exactly what it meant when he did. To make sure my mother was always under his thumb until he was done with her."

His expression changed, just slightly, as if understanding dawned. Then he shook his head. "I'm not him."

"I know."

"No, I really don't think you do." Then he lifted his hand to my face, touching my cheek, then back to my ear, until he trailed a finger down my neck to my collarbone. His touch was ice and flame. Thrilling. I trembled under his hand.

He felt it, his eyes darkening. He bent his head until our faces were inches from each other. "I'm never going to give up, you know."

I tilted my head toward his, our lips less than an inch apart. I peered into his eyes. "Neither am I." Then I grabbed his tie and pulled his mouth to mine.

When our lips met, it was explosive, a clash of wills, of unrealized anticipation. His hands moved to my shoulders and he pushed me toward the nearest wall, pinning me between it and his hard body, never removing his mouth from mine.

His lips, his tongue devoured me. His body, every delicious, solid contour of it, imprisoned me. His hands slipped from my shoulders, moved down my arms to encircle my wrists. With this hold he pinned my hands against the wall to either side of my head.

I pressed against the resistance—not struggling to break free, but to test the strength of his hold. His hands pushed against mine, then he laced his fingers through mine, fusing our palms flat against each other and holding my hands, like he held my body, against the wall. His tongue explored my mouth, his head moving against mine.

When our lips finally parted, our breath came in short, needy gulps. He pulled back just far enough to pin me down with his stare. "*I'm* in control, Emilia. Don't forget it," he said in a voice like steel.

I was about to reply when he cut me off, sealing his mouth on mine again. I halfheartedly tried to free my hands and he held them fast, his fingers tightening around mine. Like a wildfire catching on dry grass after a hot California summer, scorching heat raced through me.

He pulled away again. "*I* say when this is through. And I don't have to tell you my reasons."

"You asked for one more night. I'll give it to you. But after that—" He cut me off again, kissing me forcefully. Arousal glowed red-hot deep inside me and his stirred to life against my abdomen.

With an abrupt jerk, he retreated, loosening his hold on my hands. I could free them easily if I wanted to, but I didn't. I didn't want to talk. I didn't want to think. I wanted to surrender to the feelings inside me—the ones screaming for control. But like he'd insisted—*he* was in control, if only for this moment, by pulling himself away. By depriving me of more of his succulent mouth.

He swallowed. "Next week I'm going to the Caribbean on business. I want you to come with me."

I finally remembered to breathe again. "For some chaste sightseeing, amusing dinner conversation and coitus interruptus?"

The dark eyes glittered, but whether with annoyance or suppressed amusement, I couldn't tell. "You've promised me one more night."

I knew he had something up his sleeve. He was maneuvering something. My heartbeat buffeted every pulse point in my body.

"That's more than one night," I whispered.

His eyes darted a challenge into mine. "Yes."

"And what happens afterward?" I barely managed to get out.

A long pause while he looked at me. He released my hands but did not move. I slowly lowered them. "I guess we'll see." And then he waited, running a hand through his hair, taking a step back.

As usual, he had completely flipped the dynamic between us. I'd walked into that confrontation thinking I had all the power. And I did. Until he had decided it was enough and wrested it from me as if I was a toddler with a toy she shouldn't have been holding.

We watched each other for long moments. "You can't keep doing this," I said.

"Actually, I can. Say you'll come, Emilia."

Oh, I knew Heath would freak when he heard this—if I agreed to go, be gone practically a week. My mom...what would I tell her? She'd call and want to know why I wasn't getting back to her. And the blog. And my hospital job.

But this would be our last time together. He couldn't drag it out any longer. And the feelings he was stirring inside me, quite frankly, terrified me. The sooner we were through with this and I was back to my safe, normal life, the better.

My answer came out in a breathy sigh. "I'll go."

"Now tell me you are going to move in here," he said in a deadpan voice.

"No fucking way," I breathed.

The right corner of his mouth tugged up in a smile. "I figured I'd give it a shot."

I stuck out my tongue and he laughed.

He checked his watch and backed away suddenly. "We gotta go grab some lunch downstairs. You like Cuban?"

"Floriano's? Sure." Heath treated me to Floriano Café when he had the urge for Cuban. I didn't know whether it had anything to do with his ongoing crush on one of the waiters or his constant craving for a plate of Pork al Habañera.

I followed Adam down the narrow antique stairway, through the glass door and into the alley. He held the door for me and, walking beside me, placed a hand at the small of my back. Every muscle there pulled taut in response to his touch.

We shuffled down the narrow alleyway and past the cigar shop, where old men sat outside blowing sickly sweet smoke into the Plaza, and settled in to one of the metal tables on the sidewalk.

"So tell me, whose idea was it to dress the female characters in Dragon Epoch in armored lingerie?" I said, finally broaching a subject I'd avoided until now—my teasing commentary of his game on my blog.

He glanced at me sidelong from his study of the menu. "I came up with the story concept and the game architecture. I didn't design the women's clothes."

"But you had final approval. Why not throw the poor things in something that will cover up their bare midriffs? How would that armor even help them, anyway?"

"I bow to the overwhelming research provided by my marketing people and the game devs who push the issue constantly. Were it up to me, those poor elf maidens would be covered from head to toe."

I smirked. "And would they be as busty as they are now? Who makes bras in Yondareth, anyway?" I said, referring to the fictional world in which Dragon Epoch was situated.

He suppressed a laugh. "You wouldn't believe me if I told you."

Suddenly the flash of a memory popped up in my mind. All those figurines that William had been painting—most of them had been women! "Shut up—not your cousin!" My mouth dropped in shock.

"Yep. Blame Liam. I'm totally innocent."

I peered at him. "I could call you many things but 'innocent' is not one of them."

As we talked, a group of people came out of the nearby Starbucks on the corner and one of them stopped when she saw us at our small table.

"Adam?" she said. We looked up. It was Lindsay, of all people, and when her eyes landed on me, they widened.

"Linds," he said mildly. "How's the coffee break?"

Without being invited to do so, she grabbed a chair from another table and plunked down in front of us. I glanced at Adam, who looked uncomfortable—probably because I knew their history now. Oh, I could turn this into a thing of beauty. Make Adam suffer a little bit and stick it to this lady with her sneers at my faded jeans and T-shirt.

I scooted my chair closer to Adam's until they were flush up against each other. Adam cleared his throat. "Lindsay, you remember my friend Emilia?"

"Everyone calls me Mia, actually," I said, leaning forward to shake her hand with the fakest damn smile I'd ever faked. "Adam was just talking to me about you!" I said sweetly.

Lindsay turned to Adam with a small smile. "All good, I hope."

He shifted in his seat and I laid my hand on his upper thigh, curling around the inside—like I'd seen couples who were obvious lovers do so many times. I rubbed him there, affectionately, and leaned into his shoulder.

"Oh, *of course* good! He thinks the *world* of you," I said, shooting a worshipful smile at Adam. My hand crept northward.

Adam clamped his hand on top of mine under the guise of holding it, prying it off his leg and lacing his fingers around mine. He brought my hand to his lips and kissed it. The shock of it raced down my arm. "You're so patient with me, sweetie."

Lindsay's eyes almost popped out of her head watching Adam's display—although faked, as I knew. I surmised that Adam, who acted awkward and stiff whenever I leaned up against him in private, was not prone to open affection like this. Given Lindsay's openmouthed reaction, this was completely out of character for him. Maybe we could really put on a show and have him jumping all over the chairs like Tom Cruise on the Oprah Winfrey show.

Just then, the waiter came to take our order. "I'll have whatever he's having," I cooed dreamily, hoping he didn't order something vile. He ordered the Floriano combo plate—way too much food for me. But, hey, I never complained about leftovers.

"What are you doing up this way, Adam?" Lindsay asked.

He looked at me and then back at Lindsay as if to say, *Isn't it obvious?* And suddenly I got the spark of an idea that this meeting wasn't coincidental. I shot a sidelong glance at Adam, who still had my hand clamped inside his.

After only a few more minutes of empty conversation, Lindsay pushed her chair away from the table. "Sorry, didn't mean to interrupt and I have to get back. You are coming to the party on Friday, Adam?"

He smiled. "Yes. We'll definitely be there. Emilia's my 'plus one.' Thanks for the invitation." I scowled. What was this? A party? A Newport Beach party thrown by Lindsay? Ugh. No, thank you.

Lindsay's shoulders visibly slumped and she turned away, adjusting her designer sunglasses and walking off toward one of the business buildings in the plaza.

"Well, that was lucky," he said. I noted that he still hadn't let go of my hand, but I didn't say anything.

"No, it wasn't," I said. "You planned that."

Adam reached into his pocket with his free hand and pulled out his sunglasses. "Maybe I did."

I studied him. "Why?" He hesitated and I added, "If you say you don't have to tell me your reasons, I'm going to kick you where it counts."

"So violent," he grimaced, shooting me a sidelong glance. "She came down to the complex the other day for lunch. Told me she'd filed for divorce from Jerome."

I grinned at him. "Did she put the moves on you?"

He shot another look at me and then away, clearly embarrassed.

"She did, didn't she? I knew it. She wants you."

Adam's mouth quirked. "Lindsay is a friend. Nothing more. That's not going to change."

"Why not just tell her that instead of throwing me in her face?"

His hand tightened around mine. "Is that what you think I was doing? You're twisting again."

"Kissing my hand and calling me 'sweetie' is not your typical behavior."

I couldn't read his face, veiled behind the sunglasses. "Perhaps not."

Our food arrived then and he released my hand so we could eat. We dug in, silent over our meal for a few minutes. I shot him a few speculative looks, which he pretended not to notice. So I was his decoy. That explained a lot, actually. He was keeping me around to deflect Lindsay—or maybe others—from getting any ideas. With Lindsay beginning a divorce, she'd be vulnerable, on the prowl. Perhaps this was Adam's way of letting her down easy. Or avoiding her during this period where she might have a wrong idea, because even if *he* pretended not to notice it, it was clear to me that Lindsay wanted Adam.

"Can't avoid it forever, you know," I said, picking at my *maduros*.

He swallowed a forkful of Spanish rice. "What's that?"

"Marriage. Someday you aren't going to have a shield to hide behind."

He seemed to intuit my meaning immediately. In response, he only shrugged.

I pressed the matter because I'd forgotten how he tended to turn my position of control back on me. Even when it came to conversations. "No desire to find the right person, settle down, make little baby prodigy geniuses?"

He snorted. "Maybe I'll think about that when I'm forty." He ate for a moment in silence before he looked at me. "And you? What's your plan?"

I chewed a mouthful of chicken and bell pepper. It was spicy, flavorful and tender. I shrugged. "I told you, I don't date. If I don't date, I'm never going to meet that special guy—especially since I don't believe he exists in the first place. I'm going to live a life devotedly single and on my own terms. It was good enough for my mom."

"But your mom had you."

I thought about that for a moment. "Sure. We got along, mostly. Sometimes more like sisters than like mother and daughter. If I ever have the desire to become a mother, there are options for that, too, that don't require a man."

He didn't say anything in reply and we finished our lunch soon thereafter. He took a phone call that came in, handling some new crisis during the length of our walk back to my place. I walked beside him, silent but for the squeaking of the Styrofoam box that carried my leftovers.

At my doorstep, he ended the call, shoving the phone in his pocket. "Emilia, will you come to the party with me on Friday?"

I raised a brow. "I've been wondering when you were going to ask me, seeing as you already volunteered me to be your 'plus one.'"

"I'm asking you now."

I took in a deep breath, knowing that I probably shouldn't. "I don't think—"

"I've been waiting to see you in the red one." He meant the red dress—the one I hadn't worn yet. I'd kind of been wondering what it would look like as well.

Maybe I could get away with this by not telling Heath. I knew what he'd say. He'd say the exact same thing that tiny whisper of rationality at the back of my head was saying. *Tell him no. You're already giving him more than one night.*

I took a deep breath. "Okay." Geez. Sometimes I just seemed determined to go against everything in my better judgment. And lately, every one of those decisions somehow involved this man.

"I'll see you Friday," he said stepping away as if afraid I'd change my mind if he lingered on my doorstep.

I watched him go, headed back into Old Towne to get his car. A knot twisted in my chest. This was dangerous. I was in too deep. And he was in control, just as he'd said. Instead of one more night, as I'd promised him, it was now a cocktail party and a week in the Caribbean. Soon it would be more. And I found it increasingly difficult to tell him no.

My head wanted me to resist, but my heart wouldn't allow it.

11

AFTER WORK THE NEXT DAY, I MET HEATH AT HIS PLACE. I brought the fixings for a Caesar salad and he'd bought the ground beef and stuff for hamburgers.

Things were awkward at first. I could tell Heath was studiously avoiding the entire subject of Adam and the auction. He was done, it seemed.

But when we were about halfway through our hamburgers, I asked him the question that had been burning on my mind. "How do you do a hand job?"

Heath choked on his burger, his eyes widening. "Damn. At least give me warning to clear my mouth before you pop that shit on me."

I giggled. "I'm sorry. It's just that I was reading this *Cosmo* article and it confused me because—"

"Stop right there. If you get your sex education from *Cosmo* then you are in for a world of hurt—or he is. Those articles are insane."

"Okay. So would you be embarrassed if I asked you to explain to me how it works?"

He laughed. "Embarrassed? Doll, I'm gay. Penises are like my favorite subject—shit, that'd probably be the case if I was straight, too, with boobies a close second."

Over dessert—I'd picked up fresh strawberries at a local stand and served them over cheap angel food cake for strawberry shortcake—he used a banana to demonstrate the art of pleasuring a man with your hand. I might have had radiation burns on my face from all the blushing after that, but I did follow his advice and dump those back magazine issues into the recycling bin when I got home.

***

Lindsay's cocktail party was an absolute dud. When she saw us arrive together, she widened her eyes in exaggerated surprise—or mock horror, I couldn't tell which. She then pretended to be called away on some very important errand. I think she had planned on being Adam's "plus one." For the rest of the night, she pretended I didn't exist. The other guests might have done the same but for the fact that Adam stuck to my side like Velcro the entire time.

I wore the red dress. It was modest at the top with a sweetheart neckline, short-sleeved but formfitting and rather short to showcase my legs, which were, in all, not bad legs. And I'd taken extra special care shaving so I wouldn't have any cuts or scrapes to hide. I wore the glittery black shoes I'd worn in Amsterdam with the black dress. I didn't even try with my jewelry. Anything I wore would look fake compared to all the shiny *real* jewels I was bound to see at the party. I chose the only real gems I owned—cultured pearl earrings. And that's it—no ring, necklace or bracelet.

We kept up our affectionate routine. Adam held my hand the entire time and was very attentive. He stood close and when he spoke for me alone, he whispered in my ear, hooking an arm around my waist. I could tell we were the talk of the party because we got a lot of speculative looks. Adam was not seen in public acting affectionate with women, it seemed. Was this act solely to discourage Lindsay and her designs or to set others on alert as well—an elaborate plan to keep people at a distance? If anyone was capable of elaborate plans, it was Adam.

Afterward, he took me back to his place, which was only a few miles from where Lindsay lived in Laguna Beach. I wondered what he had in mind for the rest of the evening. Another trip out on the yacht?

To my utter surprise, his plan was to sit in his movie viewing room, watch *The Lord of the Rings* and eat popcorn. I loved popcorn and Tolkien, so I was perfectly happy with that. However, at one point he disappeared and came back wearing pajama pants and a T-shirt.

I muttered something about it not being fair that I had to stay in my dress and he vanished again, returning with a T-shirt. I went into the bathroom and put it on. As it was one of his, it went down past my panties and left my legs bare. When I came back into the room, his eyes followed me to where I sat in my recliner just next to him. We had our own little theater to ourselves with a high-definition widescreen and top notch sound system—like I said, hardware got me giddy. And we could attend this nice little private theater in our pajamas.

When the first movie was over, he was about to key in the command for the second. By then it was after ten and I mentioned that I should probably be getting home. "Why don't you stay? I have half a dozen guest rooms you can choose from. And two more movies." So here it was, his next request for more.

I hesitated. "Wouldn't that count as one more night?" I said.

His eyes shot a challenge into mine but his smile didn't fade. "Nope."

"What makes you think I'm inclined to give you a freebie?"

He held up his remote. "Come on...you know you want to..."

I sighed. "If I can get another batch of popcorn and a toothbrush—and you turn off your phone until the movies are over—then I might consider it."

"Done, done and..." he gave an exaggerated sigh, pulling his phone out of the drink caddy where he had rested it. "Oh, what the hell. Done."

He turned the phone on twice to check it during the slow parts— Arwen's dream and that silly scene where Aragorn gets knocked over the cliff by a warg.

After the second time, I hopped into his recliner, grabbed the phone and stuck it down my shirt. We watched the remainder of the movie pressed against each other, our legs intertwined, his strong arms wrapped around my waist.

During the prologue to the third movie, we started kissing. And from there we pretty much ignored *The Return of the King*. His hands were all over me—though I suspect that partly might have been an effort to locate his phone. My hands feasted on him as well.

We spent the entire two and a half hours making out like teenagers in the back of their parents' borrowed minivan. And I don't think I'd ever been so turned on in my life. Which, of course, wasn't saying much, since my three weeks in this man's company comprised about 98.5 percent of my sexual arousal experience. It was stunning, the feelings that were stirring in me—like parts of my body I hadn't known existed previously were coming alive.

After Aragorn was crowned king and the credits rolled, we were in the dark and still going. He'd had his hands on my breasts for the previous hour, driving me insane with the continuous stimulation, teasing them to points, putting his hot mouth on them. Because, yeah, my T-shirt (or, rather, his T-shirt) had hit the floor long before—along with the phone—and was quickly joined by the one he was wearing.

Then I reached down and started stroking him through his pajama pants and he uttered a harsh groan. Oh, he liked that very much. We wouldn't be having sex tonight, but it was about time he had some fun. After all, he'd been so attentive to me before. And I had to admit that Heath's accusation of Adam having a weird little self-denial fetish was at the back of my mind, too. *Maybe he gets off from denying himself.*

But once my hand slipped inside his pajamas, he wasn't protesting. I wrapped my hand around him and stroked softly up and down just like Heath had instructed. His organ was hard—long and thick. I loved the feel of the soft skin gliding under my hands, the rigidity, the sound of his husky groans as he surrendered to my stroking.

I moved my hand faster and his arms around me grew tighter. He sank his teeth into my neck, sucking, and I knew I was probably going to be covered in hickies for the next few days. But I didn't stop, because it was really turning me on to have this power over his body. I lowered my head and kissed his hard, muscular chest, licking and sucking his nipples, as he had done to me.

Then my mouth went to his ear, "I'm going to make you come."

His hoarse reply, "Yes, you are."

"I want you inside me, Adam. I want to know what you feel like in me." I said those words and I meant them. It was time. I was tired of waiting. It wouldn't happen tonight, but it had to be soon or I thought I'd explode from the tension of it all.

I stroked faster and faster until his body went rigid and I could feel the contractions of his orgasm. Hot semen dripped across his flat abs and my hand and when finally he came down from wherever I had taken him, he glanced down, carefully removing my hand from his now too-sensitive flesh. "Look at the mess you've made, naughty girl."

My lips found his and we kissed, long and languorously. "I might need to be punished later."

"Yes, you might."

There was a full bathroom near the theater and we moved in there for a shower. Another warm, sexy shower together. After he had cleaned himself off, he moved to me with the soap and insisted on lathering me from head to toe. From behind, he massaged my shoulders and again displayed that interesting habit of paying special attention to soaping my breasts.

"I *am* going to be inside you, Emilia," he breathed against my ear when he was done.

Then his hand was between my legs. I leaned my back against him.

"I'm going to slide it in slowly. I'm going to watch your face when you take it in. I'm going to fuck you until you scream. And then I'm going to make you beg for it again. And again."

His fingers glided over my yearning, sensitive flesh while he pinched my nipple in his other hand. In hardly any time at all, he returned the favor I had just done him. My orgasm came fast and intense. I stiffened in his arms and he held me against him. His hoarse breath scorched the back of my neck. He pressed against me, hard once more.

Even given that conversation I'd had with Heath, I didn't know a man could be ready again that quickly. Of course we hadn't actually had sex, so that might have had something to do with it. As much as I tried to educate myself, it was thoughts like these that showed me how little I really knew about these things. Adam had been a patient and thorough teacher thus far. He'd been too patient for my tastes. I was ready for the next lesson and he withheld it like an obdurate schoolmaster.

Maybe it was time for the student to rebel.

***

It must have been two or three in the morning by then but neither of us was tired.

He grabbed a change of clothes, and a new shirt for me—this one a rugby jersey that came down a little longer on my legs but also had sleeves that ran well past my hands. I ended by rolling them past my wrists. We went to the kitchen and snacked on cold cuts and cheese, both of us famished.

I tried to take advantage of his orgasmic afterglow by prying out his closely held secrets, but no luck. "Okay, what about the tiniest fraction of a microscopic hint?"

His mouth creased with suppressed amusement. I'd been at this for over ten minutes. "I don't do hints."

"What about bribes? I could bribe you."

He laughed now. "With what?"

I leered at him suggestively.

"Okay, one hint."

"Oh goody!"

"Yellow."

I glared at him. "Wait, what?"

He shrugged, "That's my hint. Take it or leave it."

"I'm leaving it right where I'm going to leave all the naughty things I was about to do to you in return for a good hint."

"You're a little late on your bribery. You should have been throwing out that offer while we were watching the movie."

"Oh, I think a good bribe might get you going again."

His gaze slid down my bare legs again. "I think you might be right." He said. "Are you tired? I need to check on a few things, but I think I could stand to get a few winks before the sun comes up."

He gave me my promised toothbrush and showed me to a guestroom not far from his. But after I brushed my teeth, I made my way to his bedroom. Wherever it was he'd wandered off to do his work, it wasn't here. I used the time to inspect his room, struck by how impersonal it seemed. It was exquisitely decorated to look like a beach cabana, with canted ceilings lined with bamboo and dark beams. Voluminous buff-colored linen drapes hung over floor-to-ceiling windows and the smooth floor was inlaid in different colors of wood in intricately patterned parquet.

But there were few personal touches that gave any clue about who he was, except for the desk. I moved to it, my eyes sliding over its shiny surface. There were pictures of his Uncle Peter with an arm around both of his cousins, Britt with her two adorable boys. There was a picture of Adam and the kids at Disneyland standing beside

Mickey Mouse. I smiled at each photo, relieved to have found even small clues to the person underneath the persona that he showed the world, even me. I noticed no pictures of his parents and given what I knew of his situation growing up, I wasn't surprised. But the last picture in the row gave me pause. It was a snapshot in a 4 x 6 frame and I picked it up, studying the two children in it.

The color was faded but the younger child, a dark-haired boy, was obviously Adam. He had teeth missing but was grinning wildly nevertheless. He had his arm around the neck of an older girl, this one honey-blond with green eyes. She looked to be in her preteen years. She glanced at the camera sidelong, as if irritated at having her picture taken, but her arm was wrapped tightly around Adam. She was lovely and I guessed that this must be Sabrina, his sister.

While I studied the photo, I felt a presence behind me before I even heard a thing. I spun and faced Adam. When he saw the picture I was holding, his expression sobered.

"She was a pretty girl," I said lamely.

He threw a furtive glance at me, then laid the laptop hooked under his arm onto the desk, avoiding my gaze. I had guessed right. "Yes," was all he said.

"You don't look very much alike."

"We had different fathers."

I looked down at the picture again and replaced it gently. "I'm sorry for your loss. You loved her a lot."

He took a deep breath, still staring at the picture. "Yes. I loved her more than anyone else on the planet."

I approached him and wrapped my arms around his torso. "She was very lucky, then. To have your love."

Adam didn't move, didn't respond to my show of affection. I glanced up and he was still staring fixedly at that faded photograph. "That's the only picture I have of her and yet in my memory, I can't remember what she looked like then. Or later, before she died."

"How old was she?"

"Twenty."

"And you were...?"

"Thirteen. Happened just around the time I came back to California."

Despite the fact that he had neglected to respond to me, I released one of my hands to caress his back. "I would have loved to have had a sister, even if for a short time."

His mouth set and he seemed to finally grow aware of me, looking down. "I would have rather not had a sister than to have had one and watch her die the way she did."

I pulled away from him and sat down on the edge of the bed. He watched me for a moment, his face all tense planes and rigid angles. I patted the space beside me.

He glanced at it but didn't move.

So I asked him the unasked question. Because I sensed that despite his reluctant demeanor, he wanted to talk about it.

"How did she die?"

His eyes fluttered closed and open again. "Overdose."

Addiction. There was that family theme again. He'd once mentioned to me that he feared it more than anything else, that he firmly believed in the genetics of addiction. It seemed his beliefs had ample basis in the personal lives of the people closest to him.

"I'm sorry," I said, completely at a loss to say anything else.

"Don't be. It's been thirteen years. I tried to save her once and she refused to let me," he shrugged but it was an affectation rather than a show of indifference. He was pretending a nonchalance that he didn't feel.

"No matter how hard we try, some things will always remain out of our control," I said.

"I can't accept that."

Of course he couldn't. That was a huge part of what made him *him*. But maybe that was the crux of his problem, too.

"Maybe you should."

He ran a hand through his hair and looked at me. "Emilia, it's getting late."

I took a deep breath, aware that he was trying to blow me off. It *was* late, but I wasn't going to let him off that easily.

"You're right. It's too late to work."

He quirked a sad smile. "It's never too late—"

I shot a significant look at the laptop sitting on the desk. "If I leave, you are taking that to bed with you. So which is it, that or me?"

He watched me with hooded eyes but remained silent. He was actually considering choosing the laptop over me! Heat rose in my face. "Okay. I see how it is." I was getting too close. I was making him uncomfortable, so now he was getting rid of me to work on his computer. I wondered if he took that damn thing to bed with him every night. Maybe he habitually kicked whatever fuck buddy he had at the time to the curb after sex and ran back to his laptop.

I turned to leave.

"Emilia," he said, reaching for my arm and closing his strong hand around my wrist. "Stay."

I clenched my teeth. "Only if that thing stays on the desk."

He gave a long, resigned sigh. "It's late—early. Let's get some sleep."

Without another word, I went to the top of the bed, pulled back the covers and slipped in. He watched me, his handsome face impassive, but the light of something in his eyes said he was not unmoved by the gesture. I rolled over on my side, my back to his side of the bed.

He went around to the other side, turned off the light and after a moment, I felt the weight of the bed shift. We were still some distance apart, as the bed was a massive king-size. Another long pause before he reached out, hooked an arm around my waist and pulled me back flush against him. His legs curled under mine. We were spooning. I never took Adam for the type of guy who would spoon. And here, this display of affection was for me alone. There was no potential girlfriend or ex here to deflect. This was just him and me. *Us.* Curled together.

In this safe environment in the darkest hour before dawn, I turned my head toward him. "Do you want to talk about it?"

He didn't answer for so long that I thought he wouldn't. Or that maybe he had fallen off to sleep when I hadn't noticed. "She was all I had. She was a sister and she was a mother when our mother was incapacitated, which was most of the time."

His hand slipped under my shirt to rest atop my belly. Despite my fatigue, a curl of excitement tightened there in response to his touch. I put my own hand on top of his, lacing our fingers together. He curled his fingers inward, locking them in a tight embrace.

"But things between her and my mother got bad, really bad. My mother couldn't stand the sight of her and drove her out of the house when she was fifteen. We were homeless shortly thereafter—bouncing around from shelter to shelter."

"Shit, that's horrible."

"It's worse. She ran away, hit the streets—the same old cliché. She was soon addicted to drugs and selling herself to support the habit."

My breathing froze and I went cold inside. That hung in the air between us for a few moments before he drew in a deep breath, the cool air rushing past my neck. His sister had sold herself for money, drugs, to her ultimate destruction. Intuition told me he had drawn a parallel. I'd sold myself, too, for money. An ominous feeling covered me like a shroud. Was this the reason Adam had been putting things off between us?

He spoke again, his voice quiet and a little groggy. "Last time I saw her, I hopped a bus when I was twelve and went down to Seattle to find her. She looked horrible. I begged her to come back with me but she wouldn't. Threw me back on the bus and yelled at me to get the hell out of the city. I never saw her again."

I turned around in his arms so that I was facing him. The watery light of predawn was just starting to seep into the room. I couldn't see his eyes, but stared into them anyway, his face inches from mine.

"There's nothing you could have done otherwise."

He was silent.

"Adam..." I said and on impulse, laid a hand on his whisker-roughened cheek. My courage died out along with my voice. I was going to tell him that my feelings for him were now growing to an inappropriate level. But to say those words was to believe that these feelings were true and right and I just couldn't trust them. I could never let myself be vulnerable again. Every time I had in the past, I'd been stomped down. This was *business.* My heart thudded at the base of my throat.

"What?" he said, his voice thick with emotion, his warm breath scurried over my cheeks.

"I'm so sorry about what happened to her. It's a terrible, tragic thing. You can't blame yourself."

"I don't."

I took a deep breath. It hurt to inhale. "Good. And I also think you shouldn't compare her situation to mine."

A long pause. "How could I not? The moment I sleep with you, you become a prostitute and I become your john."

I shook inside. "Is this the reason, then? Why we haven't—why you keep stopping it?"

He didn't answer. Even now, he wouldn't answer. But hadn't we crossed into this forbidden territory already—whether or not we ever slept together?

"So we won't do this. Really. I'm okay with it. We can end this here."

He went still, even holding his breath. "It's not your decision to make, Emilia. You're in too deep for that."

"But why—" He cut me off softly pressing a finger to my lips.

"Remember who's in control," he said, his voice edged with exhaustion. And I knew that now was not the time to argue this. Not with him having just laid himself bare to me.

So I didn't. Instead, I curled in close to him, nestling against his hard chest. He wrapped his arms around me, rested his chin on my head and he slept.

But I couldn't. Despite the fact that I was utterly exhausted, my mind raced through the ramifications of what had just occurred—of the knowledge I'd just gained. Adam and I would never have sex, because he believed that the minute we did, he'd become like the men who had destroyed his sister.

But could I go through with this after hearing Sabrina's story? After hearing of the innocent who'd been forced to allow herself to be used? Used and thrown away, like trash. I had refused to think that what I was doing was the same thing as prostitution, but Heath, and then Adam, had rightly corrected me of that notion. And now the implications were finally sinking in.

12

WE SLEPT IN ALMOST UNTIL NOON AND HAD A QUICK brunch at the breakfast bar in his kitchen. Then he dropped me off at home so I could get some work done on my poor neglected blog.

"Come to family dinner tomorrow night," he said on my doorstep.

I clenched my jaw. "Are we just going to keep ignoring this?"

His eyes flicked out to the road and then back to me. "Yes or no, Emilia?" And with that evasion, he answered my question: *Yes, we are going to keep ignoring this.*

I swallowed in a tight throat. "I'll come." Because this was almost over and part of me didn't want it to be. I knew it must be, but I was willing to grab at the few moments that remained.

"Pick you up at six." As always, he kissed me on the cheek and took the steps two at a time down to his car.

I shut the door and leaned back against it, trying to ignore the aching emptiness I felt whenever he left.

Checking my messages, I saw that both my mom and Heath had tried to reach me. I dialed my mom first and noted right away that she sounded unusually cheery.

"Mia! How are you?"

Still feeling guilty about the way our last phone call had gone, when I'd lied to her, I was buoyed by her high spirits. Was she in love? It sure sounded like something major had happened. Would she tell me, or was this an act to cover for the money situation?

"Hey Mom. I'm doing fine."

"How are things with your boyfriend?"

I blew out a breath. "He's not my boyfriend."

"I can be optimistic, can't I?"

I shifted uncomfortably, twirling a lock of my hair around my forefinger. "I suppose, but that means I can do the same for you. You don't have someone special in your life, do you?"

"Who am I going to meet up here in crusty old Anza? There are no available men up here who are still in their right mind."

Good point there. "It's about time you did find someone. I've been out of the house for almost four years."

"Don't you worry about me, sweet pea. I'm just fine and feeling better than I have in a long time. Worry about yourself."

I contemplated that. Either she was putting up a marvelously good front or something *had* happened. How could this be, if the ranch was about to go into foreclosure? Guessing wasn't going to get me answers, so I decided it was time to end the silence on this subject. "Mom, can I ask you something?"

"Sure, as long as it isn't about my dating," she said.

I took a deep breath and dove in. "When I was up there in January, I saw some of your mail..."

A long pause. "Uh-huh."

"I saw the mortgage notices." I cleared my throat and continued. "They said foreclosure by July. I've been waiting for you to inform me yourself, but for some reason you must not think I can handle it."

"First of all, this is not your problem, okay? I didn't tell you because I was handling it. And I didn't want to worry you with your big test coming up and all that you had on your plate. You're about to graduate from college! It should be a happy time for you. And thank God it can be."

I shifted where I stood, putting a hand on my hip. "What do you mean?"

"I mean that it's taken care of. I can't give you details yet, but I will when you come up in June. But it's handled. The ranch is just fine and even better, I'm starting to work on getting it ready to take in guests again. I'm hoping by July I can get a little summer business rustled up."

I shook my head. "What—really? You aren't lying so I won't worry or some other bullshit like that?"

"Language, Mia. I hope you don't talk like that around your boyfriend."

I sighed. "Mom."

"Okay, okay. He's not your boyfriend. Maybe I'll get to meet him at your graduation?"

I gritted my teeth. "Mom, we were talking about your mortgage."

"Yes. And now the subject is closed. It's taken care of and I'm telling you the God's honest truth. Okay? So stop worrying and stop trying to take care of me. I'm not a wilting chemo patient anymore. I feel better than I have in a long time. For a lot of reasons."

I took a deep breath and decided to believe her. "Okay. Thank God. I'm so glad."

"You've been fretting over this since January?"

Fretting. That was an understatement I was willing to let her live with. "Yeah. Kinda."

"Well, don't. I can't wait to see you in a few weeks, my little graduate! You are going to look amazing in that cap and gown."

"Yeah. Until then I'm turning off my landline for the next week and hitting the studying hard. If you need me, send me an e-mail or text me, okay?" Okay, so Mom had just come clean to me and now I shamelessly lied to her—again! Or at least, I didn't tell her the whole truth—that my phone was turned off because I'd be out of the country.

She sighed heavily. "Okay. But if you don't get back to me in a timely manner, I'll be forced to harass Heath and you know how much he loves that."

"Love you, Mom. Talk to you soon." And I clicked off, sitting back and feeling like a fifty-pound weight had just been removed from my chest.

Her mortgage was taken care of. She didn't have to give up the ranch. She was even preparing to take on new guests! Had she gotten a loan? A grant? It all seemed so improbable but there was no mistaking that she was telling the truth. My mom wasn't as good a liar as I apparently was becoming. My eyes wandered up to the ceiling and I couldn't stop grinning. I wasn't even annoyed at the thought of probably being enlisted as a free ranch hand over the summer.

Then, of course, my mind wandered to the auction. To the conundrum I found myself in. To the fact that Adam would never fulfill the terms of the auction. I thought about the almost four hundred thousand dollars sitting in my Cayman Islands bank account—money I'd never properly earn.

And I came to a decision. Minutes after I'd told Heath about the trip to St. Lucia, I dropped the second bomb on him. He was so blown away that I had to repeat myself.

"I said I want you to refuse the bank transfer."

"What? Why are you sending money back to him? I thought terms had been fulfilled, so to speak?"

"No."

"I don't get it. *Still?*"

"It's a really long story."

"Maybe you need to fill me in."

"I'm calling it off. I can't do this."

"Damn, that's a fucking relief. Drake took it okay?"

I pinched the bridge of my nose with a thumb and forefinger and prepared to tell yet more lies. "Yeah, he thinks it's a good idea, too." And truthfully, that is what he could have meant last night. He'd hardly said two words to me this morning. Whether it was because of fatigue or regret for having revealed so much about himself to me, I couldn't tell. I'd tried my best to pretend everything was the same between us, even though everything had been turned on a ninety-degree axis and we were in uncharted territories now.

"And what about your money issues? What about med school?"

Half of the money issues no longer existed. "I'll find another way," I sighed. Maybe I could learn to pole dance. I coughed. "Loans or something."

"Fuck, I can't follow you two. You make my head spin."

"Please, Heath. I promise I'll tell you everything when I can. But, you know...the NDA." I threw that out there as the dumbest excuse, hoping he'd swallow it.

He didn't. "Yeah. Whatever. Listen, I've told you now and I'll tell you again, I don't like what all this has done to you. I still think he's yanking you around and I don't like it. Now he's got you thinking you're his girlfriend instead of his call girl."

My chest tightened and I cleared my throat. "Not at all. We aren't dating and there's been no discussion about boyfriends or girlfriends or whatever. And I've already decided that once I get back from the Caribbean we aren't going to see each other again." Some unknown force coiled itself around my chest and tightened when I finally gave voice to the thoughts that had preoccupied me for the previous few hours.

Heath paused. "And he knows that?"

I squeezed my eyes closed and uttered the lie in a completely normal tone of voice. "Yeah, sure. He agrees with me."

"And you aren't going to sleep with him?"

"No."

"So you aren't going to see him again. You aren't going to sleep with him. Why are you even going on the trip?"

I cleared my throat. "Because I promised I would."

"I still don't get it. But if you do end up letting him sleep with you, just remember the old saying about buying the milk when you can get the cow for free."

"Shut the hell up. I'm not a cow." I laughed, but the laugh had a manic quality about it, like I was on the edge of some weird kind of panic.

***

For Sunday evening family dinner, we made it to Adam's uncle's house early. Britt and her family had not yet arrived. Uncle Peter had the fixings for beef and chicken kabobs lined up to barbecue and I helped him spear them onto the sticks in preparation for cooking. Within minutes Adam pulled himself away to deal with a "quick issue at work" over the computer.

I was concentrating on pushing slimy pieces of raw chicken onto the wooden stakes without gagging. Raw chicken always grossed me out.

"So how's the studying for your MCAT coming along?" Peter surprised me by breaking his usual silence to make conversation.

"Oh. Not so good. I keep getting distracted."

"You need to tell him to leave you alone so you can study."

I smiled, popping a cherry tomato onto my stick. "Oh, I can't blame it *all* on him."

"Adam's a wonderful boy and I love him like he's my son. He *is* my son in many ways. But he can be overbearing sometimes."

That was an understatement. I picked up a chunk of sweet onion and kept going. "I'm not going to argue with you about that."

"He's strong willed. Always has been. It's how he's gotten where he is. But you are going to have to get tough with him when he gets like that with you. He'll respect you for it."

I suppressed a smile. My standing up to him aggravated him more than it engendered any respect, as far as I could tell.

"I hope you stick it out," said Peter after a long pause. "He's happier than I've seen him in a long time."

My face burned, and I suddenly wished he'd change the subject. "That's good to know," I said quietly. "So, how many of these chicken kabobs am I making?"

And with relief, the subject was ditched. A good thing, too, because the doorbell rang and Adam called that he would get it. A few minutes later, he entered the kitchen with Lindsay and some younger man I'd never met.

I hadn't known that Peter had invited his work colleague or I would have prepared myself for the casual gutting with the eyes she usually tossed my way. I took a deep breath and pasted on a fake smile. Lindsay didn't bother, but moved up beside Peter, gave him a kiss and handed him a bottle of wine. "Thanks for having us over. It's been ages."

As usual, she was put together impeccably. Flawless makeup, beautiful clothes. She wore spiky heels and a designer dress—for a family barbecue. She was poised, elegant. I felt awkward and tomboyish next to her. And though she'd never been openly hostile to me, I also felt defensive around her—and downright aggressive whenever she went within three feet of Adam. Which, unfortunately, was often. And that wretched habit she had of touching him. It made my blood pressure soar.

After our kabobs by the pool, Adam quickly excused himself to take yet another phone call. Inside the house, I wandered down the hall to look at William's figurines again. He wasn't in the room but I hoped he wouldn't mind my getting a closer look.

I wasn't alone long, however, because Lindsay tucked her head inside the room and froze when I turned to meet her gaze. To my astonishment, instead of leaving, she entered.

"Hey," I said awkwardly.

Lindsay looked around the room. "This is Liam's room, you know, not Adam's."

I nodded. "Yeah, I knew that. I was coming to get another look at the figurines."

"Oh yeah, his little statues. He's spent hours on those for years. Poor guy."

I looked at her in surprise. "He seems quite happy."

Lindsay shrugged. I'd noticed little interaction between her and William. In fact, it seemed like William had studiously avoided her.

"I've known this family for a long, long time," she said, giving her little factoid dump a nonchalant air but saying something completely different with her meaning. As if her having known Adam longer gave her some kind of weird seniority over me. I didn't reply, replacing a tiny huntress on the shelf and picking up a musketeer.

Lindsay cleared her throat. "So how long have you and Adam been together?" she asked in that same blasé tone as she moved toward a bookcase that held some trophies. I squinted. They looked like track trophies but I couldn't see the name on them. They must have been Adam's.

And I had no idea at all how to answer her question. "Not very long." I said.

"Really," she said and I wondered when she'd spring her previous relationship with Adam on me. I almost yawned. How very predictable.

Surprisingly, she didn't.

"Has he stood you up for work yet?"

I shrugged. "Once or twice," I lied, wondering what she would do with that.

Lindsay looked taken aback. "It's still new. You don't have to worry much yet."

"Worry? What about?"

"Adam's a married man," Lindsay said as she took out a trophy from the bookcase, studying it. The light reflected off the metal plate and I could easily see Adam's name and his event—the Hundred-Yard Dash. First place. 2002.

My stomach dropped at her words. Adam? *A married man?* "*What?*"

She turned to me with an enigmatic, almost condescending smile. "He's married to his first love: work. I'm afraid no woman could compete and will always come a distant second."

What a shitty thing to say to someone whom she thought her "friend" was dating. Did she mean to scare me away?

"I'm always up for a good challenge."

We were interrupted when Adam appeared in the doorway. Lindsay replaced the trophy and turned toward him with a smile. Adam looked at me. "We have to get going. Something came up at work. I gotta run in for a little while."

I wished I hadn't looked at Lindsay after he said it. The knowing smile she shot me made my blood boil. Adam had just confirmed every crappy thing she had just said.

He waited for me at the doorway, then took my hand and turned and bid Lindsay good-bye.

Okay, she was annoying but she wasn't terrible. In fact, she could have been a lot worse. She had said some things that were blunt but nothing that was untrue. Anyone who knew Adam for any amount of time—and in my case, only a month—would have to be an idiot to not figure out he had a serious problem with work.

But it didn't matter to me. It *couldn't* matter. It was some other woman's problem. Some distant woman in the future, maybe when he was forty, like he'd said. As we drove home and as those thoughts raced through my head, I felt twinges collecting in my chest, making it hard to breathe deeply.

My fists closed in determination. There was no future for us. There could never be. Our lives were speeding in completely different directions and our beginning had almost predestined one certain ending.

But I couldn't commit to it with everything in me. Something was holding me back. Something deep inside didn't want to see the end. When he pulled up at the curb, I didn't move to get out of the car.

He turned and looked at me expectantly. "What's up?" he asked.

I turned to him. "Why did you bid on the auction?"

He expelled a long breath, ran a hand through his hair and looked out the windshield ahead of him. The question had clearly taken him by surprise.

When he didn't respond, I continued. "I know, now, how you must feel about this situation—because of what—because of your sister. And I totally understand that. But what I don't understand is why you chose to participate in the first place."

He shrugged and sent me a sidelong glance. "Do you have to? The point is that I did."

I shook my head. "Adam—"

He pointedly looked at his watch. "You've got an early shift tomorrow if I remember correctly. And I have to get to the complex." He opened his door, slammed it and came around to mine. I slowly exited, glowering up at him, but he studiously avoided my gaze.

At the doorstep when he bent to kiss me, I turned my face away. I wasn't ready to give up yet. "This is a game for you, isn't it?" I whispered, my teeth clenching.

He frowned. "You're twisting things again."

"Why am I going with you to the Caribbean?"

"Because I want you to," he said without hesitation.

"But why? We aren't—" He bent and cut me off when his mouth landed on mine. His large hand wrapped around my jaw, holding me in place while he explored my mouth with his. When he pulled away, his eyes held mine in a mesmerizing stare. I could see the reflection of myself in there—like staring into two tiny dark mirrors.

"I'm not going to discuss this with you now."

"Will you discuss it with me later?"

His face took on a pensive expression. "Yes. Definitely. After the trip."

I opened my mouth to protest. We weren't going to see each other after the trip. But I remembered at the last minute that I hadn't explicitly told him that. It was my sole decision. And I hadn't told him about that or returning the money. So I clamped my mouth shut and said good-bye.

He had secrets, yes. But so did I.

13

The Perks of Being a Hot Chick...Posted on the blog of Girl Geek on May 31, 2013

*A*CCORDING TO STATISTICS, THE PLAYERS OF MMORPGS SKEW much higher toward the male population than the female. But have you ever wondered why, in spite of that fact, there are so many bikini-clad females running around the plains of Yondareth in search of adventure?

There is a young man in my guild who will only play female characters. Every time he is asked why in guild chat, he gives a different answer. Sometimes it's because he wanted to play in-game with a friend (a female) who had a jealous boyfriend and he didn't want her to get in trouble. Sometimes he says it's because if he has to stare at his avatar all day, he'd rather be staring at a lithe, sexy tree elf in a chainmail teddy than at some idiot, doofy dude with a tin can on his head for armor.

But, dear readers, I think I've gotten to the bottom of the real reason why he plays girls instead of guys. I have conducted a "scientific experiment" and the results are conclusive. Chicks get more free stuff as beginning characters than their male counterparts.

Case in point: Borrowing my friend's laptop, I created two different toons on the same server, both exactly the same but for one tiny detail. One was a sexy, scantily-clad underdark elf named SmokinHawt, and the other was a gangly almost adolescent-looking tree elf male who carries a branch as a shield, named Poindexter. In the same newbie area, chopping away at bats, spiders and skeletons, I ran them both around, asking for free stuff.

"Buff pls?" I'd ask the high-level healers for their blessings. Nine times out of ten, SmokinHawt received their beneficence. Seven times out of ten, poor Poindexter was ignored.

"Got any free stuff?" I'd ask while gesturing with submissive actions, bowing, scraping and saluting. SmokinHawt was fully clad in level-appropriate armor within the first hour. Poindexter was given a rusty sword and a dented shield after a few hours of begging.

It didn't stop there. SmokinHawt got gold, quest items and general pats on the back—along with flirtatious gestures and in-game messages. Poindexter was neglected and died approximately thirteen times.

Thus, after having conducted this thoroughly-unscientific double-blind study, I have come to the conclusion that the young men who prefer playing female toons do so for purely mercenary reasons. Because their bank accounts fill up much faster that way!

Gold diggers of Yondareth, beware: I am on to you!

**

We flew first class to St. Lucia a few days later. And I was thankful for that because it was a long trip. From LAX to Miami alone was almost six hours with a layover and then another eight hours on to the Hewanorra International Airport in St. Lucia.

As our plane approached the lush Caribbean island, the first thing I noticed was the gorgeous colors of the water—brilliant blues and bright greens—and then the jagged, pointed mountains, called pitons, all covered in green. And finally the rooftops, each one a different color—turquoise, orange, copper green, red. I sat up with excitement, gazing out the window, my mouth hanging open. I'd always dreamed of seeing the Caribbean. And here I was, stepping into the dream once again.

Adam noticed my excitement, watching me with my face pressed up against the window like a puppy on his first car ride. "Excited?"

"Yes! I even bought a new swimsuit."

"Good."

I'd also brought all three of the fancy dresses he'd given me and the adorable sundress that Heath had picked out for me at Harrods.

"Wait till you see where we are staying."

I turned to him, grinning. "It's going to be hard to top that place in Amsterdam."

He smiled. "I agree it would be hard, but this place does. Of course, I may be a little biased because I am a part owner, but it's a pretty amazing luxury resort. I'll let you form your own opinion about it."

Luxury resort.

And he wasn't kidding about that. Emerald Sky, it was called, and it climbed one of the verdant green hills I had seen from the air, designed to look as if it had sprung from the mountain itself.

Each room was more than a room—it was an entire luxury suite in itself with three walls. The side overlooking the bay was completely open. With warm weather all year round, it wasn't necessary to enclose them though I did notice brackets for retractable walls in case of storms. Stacked on top of each other and climbing the hill, the suites were also completely private. And the most amazing feature of all: each suite had its own indoor infinity pool.

As an owner, Adam was given one of the two Universe rooms, which, I learned, were the best rooms in the hotel. When we were shown in, I walked around with my mouth wide open. The infinity pool, tiled in glass jewel-tones, hung on the edge of the fourth wall and it was bigger than my kitchen. Beside it, there was a table for dining and a seating area. Behind and tucked off into the corner was a king size bed with pale white netting tied to the four dark wood posts. There was a kitchenette to the rear of the suite and every luxury. Even given the gorgeous blue waters and white sand beaches that looked like they were made out of talcum powder, I wasn't sure I ever wanted to leave the suite.

"This—this is—amazing," I finally said after Adam had watched me with open amusement as I tripped around the large space, inspecting everything.

"Are you tired? Do you want a nap?"

"I want a swim!" I said.

And he smiled. "We have a reception with the manager of the hotel for dinner, but I'm free until then. And then I'm in meetings most of the day tomorrow, so I made some arrangements with our majordomo for you to have a tour of the area, maybe a little snorkeling if that's something that interests you."

I looked down at the rainbow tones of the glass tiles underneath shimmering blue water. "I want to try out this pool."

He shot me an arresting smile. "Now that I can get interested in."

I found the bathroom—back behind the bed and a few steps up. It, too was open to the outside but still quite private, even from someone who was standing below. I quickly changed into my black and white bikini—it was gorgeous and made me feel sexy and it hadn't been overly expensive. And thanks to another splurge—leg waxing, ouch—and a manicure and pedicure, I felt resplendent, glamorous, full of energy and excitement and not my usual scruffy self. I had stepped into the princess dream again.

I was already in the pool and of course he'd pulled out the dreaded laptop to check on work—lest the world had fallen in while he was on his flight. I was irritated at first but also relieved that it didn't take much taunting to entice him into the pool. He changed and got in with me. We swam, talked, flirted.

We talked about the game, of course. He was still clam-mouthed about the clues I wanted, though he wasn't above throwing more red herrings out with a playful gleam in his eye.

I asked him about his past. "So how did it all start? When did you find out you had a gift with programming?"

He squinted out over the bay, arms hooked over the edge. "We weren't well off, after my dad died. And we moved around a lot. Somewhere along the line I acquired this secondhand Gameboy." He smiled. "That thing was my prized possession, but I only had a few games for it. And I got bored with them after a while. So I hacked into it and started writing my own games."

My brows shot up. "That's amazing. How old were you?"

He grimaced. "I'm not going to tell you because then you'll call me an even bigger nerd."

I shook my head, laughing. "Not possible. Your nerdness is pretty huge as it is." And then I blushed, realizing my words could be interpreted another way.

He laughed. "Thank you."

I splashed him. He splashed back.

"So how old *were* you?" I asked again.

"I think around ten or so," he said simply, with no attempt at bragging. Still, that answer blew me away. He responded to my obvious shock. "But I had little else to do. I missed a lot of school in those days because—well, because of the home situation. I had hours and hours to work on it. And I was pretty determined."

"Ah, so it started young, then."

"What was that?"

"Your incessant need to always be working."

He made a face. "It's not *that* bad."

I watched him with open skepticism. "Really? So your family never complains that they don't see you—that the two times I've been with you to family dinner were the first times they'd seen you in months even though you live nearby. Your hundred-hour workweeks all come at a price. You just don't see it."

He sobered. "I've been better lately. Last few weeks I've only clocked in around sixty or so."

I shook my head in mock wonder. "Only sixty. Such a slacker." My words were serious but I wanted to lighten the mood so I splashed him again. He sputtered in surprise and then grinned, ducking under the water, shooting straight for my legs. I tried to dart to the side but he grabbed one of them and jerked me back toward him. When we came up for air, we were both laughing and he pressed me to his chest.

When we stopped laughing, he kept me there and my heart slammed against my sternum. No matter how much time we spent together, no matter how much we fooled around, he still had the same effect on me as that first day we'd met. A surge of excitement glided through me, washing over me like a warm tropical rain. Something sparked in his dark eyes and he pulled me to him, bending his head. His mouth met mine in a steamy kiss and I laced my fingers around the back of his neck, returning the passion.

We kissed for long minutes and my hands slipped down his wet chest. He held my upper arms and his body hardened under his trunks. I pulled away. "So we can't skip dinner, right?"

He shook his head, but he did look regretful.

"Well then, we should probably get ready."

He smiled. "Good call."

***

The reception was a quiet but glamorous event, with select hotel guests, staff and other owners present. It was a black-tie affair, so I got to see Adam in a tuxedo for the first time ever. And he was stunning. I wanted to grab him by his thin satin lapels and pull his mouth to mine.

We had this night and the next two nights together. And I intended to enjoy them. If I could manage to pry him away from work as easily as I had this afternoon, I might just be able to.

Earlier, I'd come out with my updo—a hairstylist had come in to help me with that—along with my makeup, my glamorous high heels and that gorgeous backless black dress. His appreciative eyes had taken me in and it made me tingle from head to toe.

"Emilia, you take my breath away."

We spent a few hours at the reception. Adam introduced me to many people I would never see again so I didn't bother trying to remember their names.

Then he left me, to talk business with several of the other owners. Other men tried to approach me but I was good at rebuffing them. If the years of social self-exile on a hip college campus had taught me nothing else, they'd taught me the cool art of the brush-off.

When we returned to the suite, candles were lit, the mosquito netting around the bed had been let down and the covers had been turned back. We gave each other an awkward look. The unresolved sexual tension hung heavy about us and stuck to our skin like the balmy tropical air. Fortunately, we were both exhausted. But what about the days to come? I doubted either one of us had considered the consequences of sharing a bed when it couldn't lead to anything more.

For bed, I changed into a T-shirt and my underwear and he peeled off everything but his boxer briefs. There were fans in our suite, going night and day, and a slight breeze coming up from the bay, but it was a warm night and we would be sleeping without covers.

Uneasily, we settled on the bed—strangely—on the same sides we had taken that one night we had spent together in his bed. We stayed apart for a long time, but despite our exhaustion, it took awhile to fall asleep.

Hours later, I woke up in his arms and he was kissing my neck. I rolled over and in the dim light saw his eyes widen. "Hi."

"Hi. I didn't mean to wake you up. I just couldn't resist a little taste."

I smiled. "A little taste sounds nice," I said as I lowered my head and kissed his bare chest. He kissed my hair and I turned my head, looking out over the bay. The light was a steel gray—maybe an hour or two before dawn and everything was still and quiet.

"I'm sorry. I was wide awake," he whispered

"Are you bored?"

He sighed. "I don't get it. It's only two a.m. at home. I can't sleep."

"What are you thinking about? Work?"

His dark eyes were enigmatic. "No. I was wondering what happens when we get home."

I hesitated. Did he know that I'd planned to end it after this? Or had he come to the same decision I had? My heart sped up a beat. "You mean with us?"

"Yes."

I cleared my throat. I didn't want him to know that I had returned the money until we got home. I didn't want him to know I'd decided this wasn't good for either of us. That it would be easier for us to go back to our former lives. That I'd find another way to go to med school.

"Let's not think about it now. There's plenty of time later."

"I can't not think about it."

"Think about something else—like... how good it feels when I kiss you all over your yummy chest." And I did just that, mouth gliding over his hard muscles, tasting him everywhere.

He let out a long breath, clearly enjoying it and I paid great attention to every nuanced detail, every taut hill and creased valley. He cleared his throat. "That *is* something very nice to think about."

He tried to sit up, attempting to gain control of the situation, but I pushed him back down again and he grinned. "About to ravish me, are you?"

I kissed my way down his abdomen, over his perfect six-pack. "Can you ravish the willing?"

"Good point," he said with a hoarse laugh.

His briefs were tenting with his arousal and I rubbed the taut ridge before reaching into his underwear.

"We seem to have a big problem here."

His lips were on my breast when he started laughing.

I rubbed again. "Yes. A very, very big problem."

"What does the doctor prescribe?"

"Friction. Lots of friction will reduce this swelling."

His eyes darkened. "I can get behind that treatment."

I laughed. "I'm sure you can." I tugged on his briefs and he took a moment to shuck them.

"Yours come off, too," he said.

I sat up, pulling off my T-shirt and panties. His hands grasped my hips, then traveled up my waist, heading right for his favorite place.

I pulled his hands away. "I believe I was in the middle of pre-scribing treatment."

He smiled and lay back. "As the doctor commands."

I leaned forward again and kissed him over his chest—quickly this time and then down, over his flat, muscular stomach. And, then, gathering my courage, I traveled even lower.

My hand encircled the base of his shaft and quickly, furtively, I touched my mouth to the soft skin.

He sucked in an entire chestful of air and sat up immediately. I didn't pull away.

"Don't do this."

Defiantly, I lowered my mouth, taking the entire tip of his erection between my lips.

"Emilia—" he said shakily. "You don't have to do this."

I pulled my head away. "I know I don't have to. I *want* to. Just...whatever you do please don't put your hands in my hair."

He didn't move for a moment and I still held him in a tight grip at his base. Slowly he relaxed and lay back. I said, "Just enjoy."

"Oh, you really don't have to tell me to do *that*," he breathed.

And tentatively, I lowered my mouth again, trying to ignore the quick rush of my heartbeat. This fear was a barrier, a hurdle that I needed to overcome. I needed to lose myself in the moment and dispel the past, realize that I was giving pleasure to someone I cared about and I need not be afraid.

But the cold dread was there when bits from that past scene flashed into my memory—memories of gagging and sobbing. I closed my eyes, blacked them out, concentrated, breathed through the panic that threatened to rise up at the very back of my conscious. My therapist had taught me some techniques and I rarely had to use them anymore, except for in triggering situations. And this could be one.

Fear was a hurdle—an obstacle whose greatest power was in keeping me locked in to one place, one moment in time. I focused on the positives of this particular situation, of the throaty gasps of my partner, who was obviously enjoying himself. Of the rush of power, knowing I was making him feel this way. That I was on top and I was controlling the situation. I could pull myself away whenever I wanted.

Soon my mouth sank lower, taking more of him in, my tongue running along his length. His hands grasped at the bed sheets, his legs tensed. My hand tightened around him. I hesitated, wondering what the culmination would be—would he give me warning? Would I be able to pull away in time—or would I want to? I hadn't even decided yet.

Instead of worrying about answering those questions, I concentrated on the now, losing myself in that moment so that I had no awareness of the passage of time, of how long it had taken to bring him to this point. All I knew was that his deep breaths and hoarse murmurings of my name tore currents of desire through me, each one of them a pebble dropped into deep waters, my soul rippling from their centers.

I moved my mouth up and down until suddenly he tensed, sitting up. He moved my head away and grasped himself. He came on my breasts and stomach instead of in my mouth. His protectiveness warmed my heart. And I thought back over his behavior since the beginning, from that strange moment on the terrace of the penthouse in Amsterdam. He'd been like this from the start—even when he didn't know me very well.

A few minutes later, in the shower, I told him. "You are a very special man, Adam Drake."

He looked at me for a moment, hesitating as he washed his hair. "What did I do wrong now?"

I laughed. "No. I mean—just—thank you for being you. I know that sounds corny, but that's exactly what I wanted to say." I moved up to him and kissed him soundly and then backed away. He resumed washing his hair, watching me, a smile on his sexy lips.

We kissed each other good-bye—I in my beach cover-up and bathing suit, ready for my day tour, and he in his business suit, sans the jacket. Before he walked out the door, I blotted some perspiration off his forehead.

"Thanks, dear," he muttered in parody and kissed me as he left.

And I enjoyed my day, taking in the snow-white beaches and even doing a little snorkeling. My guide took me to the beautiful Diamond Falls, a gorgeous cataract that fell down multicolored rocks and shimmered in the early afternoon sun. I savored the stunning scenery of this pristine Caribbean island, even though the heat was considerable.

I made it back to the suite by about four o'clock. Knowing that Adam would be returning to dress for dinner, I wanted to be ready. I put on the cute little sundress from London and the matching shoes, brushed out my hair and pulled it back and applied a little makeup to go with my brand new tan from the afternoon.

I was in the bathroom finishing up when he entered. I hurried with the finishing touch of my lip gloss and skipped down the stairs to greet him.

The first thing that clued me in that something was wrong was the stiffness in his shoulders, his jerky movements as he set down his laptop case on the nearby desk, unbuttoned his vest and undid his tie. I hesitated behind him, certain he'd heard me. But he made no acknowledgment.

I took a deep breath. "Hard day?"

He didn't look at me but his hand stopped for a moment before resuming. "It was a pleasant and easy set of meetings. It's been a very good day, actually." But the tone of his voice belied him. It did not match his words. "Things were going well, until I checked my e-mail."

I puzzled at that. "Bad news from home?"

He continued to avoid my gaze, rolling his tie so it wouldn't crease and then laying it aside with care. "It was an e-mail from Heath Bowman, actually."

I swallowed in a tight throat, heart thumping with sudden worry. "Is he okay? Was he trying to get hold of me?" Adam unbuttoned the first few buttons on his shirt. When he turned to me, his face was stern—and he looked very much like the asshat I'd first met at that hotel in Costa Mesa over a month ago.

"He's just fine. But he had a *lot* to say to me—ranting about shit that I had no idea was going on. And I'm not a person that takes kindly to being left in the dark."

I tried to think of what Heath could have written to piss Adam off so badly. Then, with a sinking feeling, I remembered my last conversation with Heath—where I'd asked him to refuse the money. God damn it, Heath. His timing sucked.

I folded my arms defensively across my chest. "What did he say that has you so pissed off?"

He shrugged stiffly. "You tell me. *You* seem to know a lot more about what's going on here between us than I do."

A dark feeling of foreboding fell on me like a blanket. I shifted my stance. "Yeah, there's… probably more than one thing you could be pissed about."

His gaze sharpened. "Thanks, Emilia," he said tightly before walking off and disappearing into the bathroom.

Shit. I ran to my bag and fished out my phone, frantic to pull up my e-mails before he came back. Maybe Heath had cc'd me on the message he'd sent to Adam or at least deigned to tell me what he meant to accomplish by e-mailing Adam. This was the first time since arriving that I'd even looked at the damn phone. But the reception on this side of the hotel was crappy and my little loading symbol spun and spun without ever updating. When I heard him behind me I jumped and dropped the phone onto the nearby chair.

I turned, tucking a strand of errant hair behind my ear. His vest was off and the glimpse of his strong neck and chest where his shirt opened drew my eyes. I swallowed. I didn't want this confrontation. Not now. Goddamn it. I didn't want it *ever*, actually. I'd just wanted to fade back into the woodwork—let my fairy tale dissipate and go back to my normal life without ever having to deal with this unpleasantness.

I cleared my throat. "Okay, first, about the money…"

He looked at me expectantly but he said nothing, waiting for me to continue.

"After our conversation the night I stayed over at your house, I decided—I mean, I figured we wouldn't go through with this, right? So—so I thought it was best to have the money sent back to your account. I asked Heath to do it. No—no services rendered, no payment. And this—this whole fucked-up thing can just fade away and we won't have to—"

His jaw clenched. "I don't want that money back."

A fist closed at my side. His eyes darted to it. "Well tough shit. You're getting it back."

He sighed and looked away, out over the bay. "It's not prostitution if we don't sleep together."

I shook my head. "Um, no. Wrong. You sent me money. We've been fooling around. It *is* prostitution. I obviously don't have the same problem with it that you do, so don't turn this around on me. I'm doing you a favor by calling this off."

He blinked. "The auction was for your virginity."

"That's a clear-cut argument, if you're splitting hairs." I raised my hand and jutted a finger toward his solid chest. "You keep saying that you're the one in control of this situation and yet you have been losing control all along and *that's* the real reason you're pissed."

His jaw set but he stood absolutely still. A fist of foreboding closed over my chest. He wore that strangely calculating expression—the one that meant he was thinking about ten other things alongside the conversation he was currently having.

When he spoke, it was with a quiet, even voice despite the anger in his eyes. "If you sent the money back, there is no deal now."

I shifted my stance, feeling like a dragonfly about to be lured into a spider's web. "That's right. The deal is canceled."

His eyes met mine, hard as flint. "So what about this bullshit about not seeing each other again when we return home?"

I exhaled. "That was always part of the agreement—"

He made a chopping gesture with his hand. "But you just said there is no agreement."

I shook my head. "There's no future for us. I mean, given how we first met and the arrangement and how everything has turned out. Heath said it best and I ignored him for so long. It's sick. This is sick."

The flush crept up from his jaw into his chiseled cheeks. "And what the hell does Heath know about us? I mean about what's *really* going on here. He doesn't. So why are you letting his opinions influence you? Why are you listening to him and not to me?"

I lowered my face, put my hand to my forehead. I couldn't say the words that were almost on my lips. *Because I can't trust you.* Now it was my turn to remain silent. Because honestly, I had no words and I could feel his agitation mounting no matter how much he fought to appear calm.

"So everything that's gone down between us is *sick?* What happened in that bed this morning was *sick?*" He spoke in an even voice that was taut, edgy. A vein at his temple throbbed.

I shook my head. "No."

"Then what is this all about? Do you want to end this?"

"I don't even know what 'this' is! What is there to end?" I finally said. Then I cleared my throat, my arms stiffening with indignation. "This was you...bidding on an auction for some unknown reason—an auction that you fundamentally cannot believe in. And then prolonging the outcome for as long as you can. You've manipulated this all along and now you are asking me to trust you? To listen to you? You should have let me go at the beginning so I could go through with this with someone else."

He swallowed. "It's not too late," he finally said. It sounded like the words had been torn from him.

My chin came up and I folded my arms across my chest, his words stinging me like a shower of sharp pebbles. "You're right. It isn't."

But my chest felt heavy. Because I wanted *him,* now. I wanted the experience to be with *him* and I couldn't name why. The thought of going out and finding someone else—maybe Mr. New York or some Arab sheik or something—actually left me with a sick feeling.

If I couldn't use him for the money, then maybe I could use him for the experience my body had been craving since he first touched me.

He moved up to me then, with hard eyes and stiff posture, a hand working at his side. He looked into my eyes, first one and then the other.

"Emilia," he breathed. My eyes fluttered closed. "Look at me."

I opened my eyes and tilted my face to him. I wanted him to kiss me. I wanted this tension between us to ease. And the fierce ache rising up from the center of my being told me I wanted his hands, his body on mine. No more talking. No more arguing. No more discussion of a "deal."

As if he read my thoughts, his mouth sank to mine, his hand steadying me at the back of my neck, curving around my bare flesh there. Goose bumps prickled down my arms and legs.

His kiss was so overpowering, it sucked me into him—like I was caught inside a raging hurricane, wrapped inside this force of nature called Adam and could not find my way out. When he pulled away, we were both panting. "There," he said in a hoarse voice. "Would you mind telling me what was 'sick' about that?"

I fought for breath and he pulled me to him again, another powerful, consuming kiss. I shivered in his arms and his hands went to my shoulders. With two swift movements, he pushed my sundress off my shoulders and it slid to the floor. His mouth was on my neck, running his tongue and lips along the sensitive skin. The touch struck molten sparks through my body. I wrapped my arms around his neck. One of his arms locked around my waist. The other went around to the back of my bra, unfastening it easily.

"I need you," he said.

My eyes closed and my body heeded his call. "We shouldn't," but my voice was weak, faltering, because I could not put the full force of my belief behind it. His mouth, hands and tongue were too convincing otherwise.

His head came up, taking my ear between his lips, running his tongue over the lobe. Heat shot through my body. "Can you deny this?" he said in a harsh whisper. "Can you just walk away from whatever this is between us?"

And then he backed toward the bed, pulling me along with him. I stepped out of my shoes. My nerves pulled taut like harp strings. His eyes were flame and frost from one moment to the next—anger, passion, pure lust.

"I'm going to show you what we can be like together."

He pulled me to him again and we kissed and my body responded to the sensual promise in those words. I trembled. "You'll hate yourself if you do this."

"I'll hate myself more if I don't," he said between clenched teeth.

He turned and laid me gently on the bed. Wearing nothing but panties, I looked up at him, feeling vulnerable as his burning eyes raked over me. They scorched me like errant embers from a bonfire and he made quick work of unbuttoning his shirt and losing it, along with his pants.

He freed his erection from his underwear and he was naked. My breathing slowed. He was beautiful—every developed crease, every curve of firm, packed muscle. His ready shaft, a potent reminder of his maleness.

"Take off your underwear," he said. And slowly, my eyes locked on his, I did. Somewhere in the back of my mind I doubted where this was appearing to go. We had been here before—several times—

and he had always pulled away, always stopped himself with an iron grip on his self-control. It would happen again, despite that ragged wildness I saw deep in his black eyes. He'd fight for control and he'd win. And he'd do nothing he'd regret.

Under his scrutiny, my nipples came to hard points and damp heat pooled between my legs. Slowly, he lowered himself to sit at the edge of the bed, running an almost reverential hand over my breasts, my belly, my thighs, my sex. "So beautiful. Emilia. You are so damn beautiful."

I closed my eyes. I'd just been thinking the same about him. "Thank you."

He took a deep breath and spoke the words haltingly, as if some part of him still fought and struggled to keep them inside. "If you tell me right now you don't want it, we won't do this."

My gaze fixed on his, unwavering. It was time to tell the truth. The consequences be damned. "I want this, Adam. Not because of money, and not because anyone is making me. I want it because *I* want it."

He moved so fast it was almost a blur. He was on top of me in seconds holding my arms against the mattress as his body pressed me down with his. His mouth was on mine again, but at that moment, I realized it wasn't going to be long. He wouldn't spend another second on foreplay because we'd been engaging in the most frustrating game of foreplay for a month.

He nudged my knees apart and I spread them for him. He stared into my eyes, just like he'd said he would. *I'm going to watch your face when you take it in.* And in one, sure, confident move, without any more hesitation, he pushed himself inside me and there was nothing slow about it. His body was so hot, as if he was on fire.

I tried not to stiffen from the sharp pain I felt as he penetrated me. He saw my face, my widening eyes. He felt me tense underneath him, but he didn't pull back. He pushed in without letting up, as if once having decided to travel down this path, he wouldn't turn away from it.

Soon he'd eased himself all the way in and he paused, still watching me closely. "You all right?"

I didn't speak, just nodded. His hands gripped mine, and our fingers entwined. His mouth connected with mine, our tongues twisting around each other. And he began to move. I'll admit, there was more than a little pain. He felt very big inside me as my body stretched around him. But as he maintained his gentle rhythm, there was something else there. A deep, fulfilling pleasure. A feeling of ultimate connection. Not just at the juncture of our bodies but our hands, our mouths. I'd never felt physically a part of someone else as much as I did at this moment.

And the erotic slide of him deep inside me, with each thrust, spoke of possession and belonging. He possessed me and belonged to me. I did the same.

Soon his movements came faster, more urgently, his eyes closed in concentration. He released my hands, rising up on his elbows, watching me again. The changed angle relieved some of the pressure and sharp, breath-stealing pleasure shot through me, erasing the discomfort.

I found myself urging Adam to continue doing what he was doing, telling him how good it felt. When I moaned his name, it seemed to put him over the edge. He plunged into me, pushing his hips flush against mine, penetrating deeper than before. I caught my breath, somewhere on the threshold of pleasure and pain. He stopped, his breath coming so fast it was difficult for him to speak. "I'm not coming until you do."

He reared up so that he was on his knees and continued. I gasped. His strokes came fast and steady, as he recognized that I was close. I squeezed my eyes closed, concentrating on that wave of ecstasy rising up inside me. The only thing in my awareness at that moment was the feel of Adam's shaft sliding inside me.

My back arched off the bed and I was coming in air-stealing, body-convulsing waves of sheer gratification. Only a few more strokes and Adam was coming too, pushing himself as deep as he could go. His orgasm tore through me as if it was my own.

He lay on me for a minute or two after it was done. I wrapped my legs around him, now cherishing the feel of him inside me. When his eyes finally opened, he looked into mine and lowered his mouth to mine, kissing me again.

We lay in each other's embrace for long, quiet moments before I finally cleared my throat. "I think I should get up and shower."

He nodded, scooting aside to allow me to rise. When we left the bed, I noticed he'd stopped to stare at the bedspread. Looking back, I saw a small bloodstain there. A strange look crossed his face and he ran a hand through his hair, then reached out and yanked the counterpane off the bed, tossing it into the corner. Minutes later, he joined me in the shower. He was still strangely quiet and we both had receded into our own worlds. No fun scrubbing each other this time.

We'd crossed a threshold we could never uncross. We'd taken a step that could never be untaken—that small evidence of a permanent change in my body was also evidence of a change in us. In who we were, both to ourselves and to each other.

Adam washed quickly and got out, wrapping a towel around his waist and leaving the bathroom. But I lingered, soaping myself slowly, focusing on the soreness between my legs, examining my own feelings. I was different now. It was just a bit of skin, like I'd always imagined. But when I'd imagined how it would be, I'd always thought nothing would change. Feelings wouldn't change.

But this was different. These growing feelings for Adam were the biggest reason. *No, Mia.* Stupid girl. I swallowed a sob in the shower as that realization rose up in me. I could love Adam. But I wouldn't allow it because it went against everything I'd stood for—for so long. I was Mia, the girl who stayed single by choice. The woman who would always take care of herself, because I didn't need anyone to save me. I saved myself.

The thought of never seeing him after this weekend cut a deep and painful trench into me. But I knew it had to happen—and it had to happen before these feelings made me dependent on him. A wave of sudden pain lanced through me like a lightning bolt. The feelings would pass. They were fleeting, I reminded myself. I would stand firm to my decision.

And after all, what the hell were we doing here? He didn't want this any more than I did! There was no reason for me to feel guilty. He was an empty, loveless workaholic who got his needs seen to by fuck buddies. My heart was racing again. I left the shower on shaky legs—and only because my fingers and toes were starting to shrivel.

You aren't going to sleep with him in St. Lucia, are you? Heath's words came back to me like a sharp slap. I froze, placing my own addendum to Heath's admonition—*because that would be a big mistake.* I shook my head—it was too late for self-recriminations.

But I still had a choice. We could enjoy our last day and a half here and call it quits after. I was no longer getting paid for the job but I had enjoyed it nonetheless. There was nothing wrong with enjoying another day of it.

When I dressed and went out to the main room, almost dreading to see him again, I could tell by his quiet demeanor that similar thoughts had run through his head. He was dressed in khakis and a red T-shirt bearing a *Star Trek* logo and the word "expendable" printed across his chest. His feet were bare and he sat in front of the open laptop, typing away at that maddening pace, the glow of the screen falling across his handsome features.

Without looking up, he asked, "You hungry? I was going to order room service."

I didn't answer, but walked over to the menu to look it over. Nothing looked appetizing but I knew—I *knew*—that if I didn't order, he'd think I was pining or regretful or whatever. The key was to act natural. Act like nothing had happened.

Fuck. As if.

"It all looks froufrou." I said by way of excuse.

He looked up. Maybe he felt insulted. He was an owner here, after all. "You can order whatever you want. It doesn't have to be on the menu. You want a steak or something? That's probably what I'm going to order. I'm famished."

I shrugged. "Sure." But the thought of a heavy steak in my stomach right now made it twist with disgust.

He went back to typing. "I'll send the order in right now through the web page."

I hesitated, hit with a wave of irritation. "Are you working?"

He didn't look up. "Yup. Just thought I'd peek in at what's going on with the progress of our European launch."

I frowned. Work hadn't been on the schedule for this evening. Yet he'd logged in the first chance he could get after we'd—after...

What was this heavy feeling in my chest? I shot a glare at him. He was pulling away from me, and he was using work to do it. Just like he had with everyone else in his life—his friends, his beloved family members. Why did I think I would be immune from this treatment?

His behavior stung. He went back to typing, clicking away on his keys, never pulling his head away from his work, giving his complete attention to it. I wasn't the type of person who needed someone's undivided attention all the time. In fact, since I'd never desired a relationship, I was pretty low-maintenance when it came to that.

But given what had just happened between us for the first time, and my first time *ever*, I would have thought he'd be more attentive. Or at least, that's what I would have liked. Instead, I got a wall of silence. He was a tortoise retreating into the hard, impenetrable protection that was work.

The worst came minutes later, however, when dinner arrived. The majordomo laid it out at our table just at the edge of the patio overlooking the bay. Adam ignored both of us as he continued to work. I busied myself by trying to get my e-mail to finally download on my phone. Nothing from Heath at all.

When the majordomo left, I sat down at the table and looked at Adam. "Your food's getting cold."

He typed for just a minute more and then approached the table. "I'm starving," he muttered. Then he picked up the plate and his utensils and took them back to his desk, leaving me there to eat alone.

My jaw dropped but he didn't notice because he cut a piece of steak, popped it into his mouth and returned to his work. From my angle, all I could see on his screen was a bunch of incomprehensible symbols and commands. He was working on some kind of program.

My gut burned. I tried to examine the reasons behind my anger. I felt brushed aside, used. He'd gotten what he'd wanted and moved on. I was a nonperson now. Couldn't I at least be a friend? Why shower all this attention on me and then the minute we were intimate, ignore me? It made me wonder if that's what it had been like with my mom and the Biological Sperm Donor. He'd used her, too. And then he'd set her aside like she'd never existed when he had no further use for her.

With a jolt of fury, I stood up from my nearly untouched plate, unwilling to mull any of this over in silence and watch his weird way of brooding. I went to the bathroom and grabbed my swimsuit.

When I came back, he glanced up from the screen questioningly but said nothing. I pretended not to notice.

I waded into the pool, which really was too short for laps, but I couldn't think of any other way to work out this restless energy short of leaving the room. If I did that I'd be sending him a signal. That I resented or regretted what had happened between us. And I didn't. But I *did* resent his current behavior. If he wanted to ignore me, fine. I could do the exact same thing.

I pondered all of this, as I continued my short lapping—four strokes, turn, catch breath, four strokes turn. Lather, rinse, repeat. It was starting to make me dizzy and I had no idea how long I'd been at it when I felt a strong hand wrap around my upper arm, pulling me to a halt. I came up sputtering. He was standing beside me in the pool.

"What the hell?" I said.

"I kept calling you and you wouldn't stop. How long do you plan to keep at this?"

I shrugged. "I don't know. How long do you plan to blow me off?"

He shot me a sharp look. "I'm blowing you off? Why do you think that?"

I wiped the water out of my face. "Maybe because you wired in the first chance you could get and you're eating dinner over your keyboard. You might do that all the time when you're alone, but in company, it's pretty bad manners. And because you're not talking and I have no idea what is going through your head."

He looked away but not before I noticed irritation on his face.

I continued. "Please don't tell me you treated your other fuck buddies that way."

"You're *not* a fuck buddy."

I pulled my arm free, turned and pushed over to the edge of the infinity pool, looking out over the dark bay. The distant crash of the ocean and smell of salt rose up on the breeze. From behind me he sighed. "I'm sorry you thought I was blowing you off."

My face flushed hot with anger. "Not an apology. Don't bother wasting your breath with that bullshit. Do you have any idea how it makes me feel that you would just ignore me like that after we—after what happened between us? Like yesterday's forgotten trash."

He came up beside me, hooking his muscular arms over the edge, careful not to touch me. He looked into my face, I kept staring out over the bay. "I'm sorry," he said after some long, tense moments. "I wasn't ignoring you on purpose. It's something I do when—when I'm thinking."

I took a deep breath, the tight anger only easing a tiny increment. I looked at him then. He'd shucked his shirt and pants and it looked like he'd jumped into the water in his underwear. "Then talk to me. Tell me what you are thinking about."

He paused. "I was thinking about how I never intended for it to go this far."

A band tightened around my chest. "So you *are* feeling regretful. Guilty that it happened."

"No," he said, turning to me. "I'm feeling regretful and guilty that I enjoyed it so much I want to do it again."

A new tension thickened between us. I struggled for breath, because I felt the exact same way. "But you won't?"

He looked out over the bay. "It was never supposed to go this far," he repeated.

Though I hated how he dealt with his inner conflict by shutting me out, I found that inner conflict utterly a reflection of his goodness. He wasn't using me. He was *afraid* of using me. He wasn't disregarding me. He was holding my feelings in such regard that he was denying his own. How could I be angry with that?

"But it did. And there's nothing to regret in that. There was no 'deal.' There were no principles violated. The money—"

"To hell with the money, Emilia. I don't give a shit about the money."

I turned to him, clearing my throat. "Here's the deal, Adam. You are acting like you did something wrong, like you 'took' something from me or somehow despoiled me. You know what? It's our culture that leads men to think like that...that purity in a woman is the ultimate prize."

He grimaced. "You sound like your Manifesto, now."

I shook my head. "I didn't just write those words for the hell of it. I believed them. My purity was worth no more than yours or anyone else's. I just happened to be a lot older than most when I finally—"

"Gave it up?"

"Gave it *away.* And it means nothing more than that. You did me a favor."

He gritted his teeth so that the muscles in his jaw bulged.

I continued. "I enjoyed myself. You said you enjoyed yourself. What is there to regret or feel guilty over?"

"What comes next," he stated flatly. "It's the way I think. I'm a programmer before I'm anything else. Everything in programming is cause and effect. What are the possibilities that spring from each and every line of code? What will spring from this?"

"Stop thinking fifty steps ahead of this one. Just think about the one thing that comes next. What do you think that is?"

His eyes roamed my face. "If I had my way? It would be me fucking you again." His eyes lowered to my lips.

I stopped breathing, heart rushing with excitement. We stared at each other in silence for a long moment before I spoke. "I think that sounds like a pretty good step."

He hooked his arm around my waist, jerked me flush against him. My body came alive with the feel of his hardness. We held each other for long moments. Then he slowly, sensuously began to kiss my neck.

"Damn it, Emilia," he breathed. "How did you strip me bare so quickly?"

I reached up, holding his rough face in my hands and we kissed

He kissed me long, tenderly. Our tongues slowly played against each other. Desire arced through me like lightning across a mountain sky. The touch was jagged, searing. His hands were on my back, untying my bikini top, sliding to my breasts.

"How is it possible that I want you more now than I did this afternoon?" he growled against my neck.

I pulled myself up, hooking my legs around his waist and we continued to kiss. The tightly packed muscles in his back roiled under my hands.

"We were *both* very eager."

He pulled back to look at me. "I'm not sure how eager you were," he breathed, a smile quivering on his lips. "I got the sense that you were lying back and thinking of medical school."

I laughed. "Hardly."

"I had to fight with myself not to start again the minute it finished. I wanted you so much that I knew once wouldn't be enough."

His words stole the air right out of my lungs. My body was responding with scorching fire, tightening tension.

"I'm going to do it again, Emilia. And again."

His hands were on my hips and I freed my legs so he could yank down my swimsuit bottoms. Would we even bother to leave the pool? His fingers rubbed my sex as he sucked my nipples. I fell slack in his arms, focused on the searing pleasure commanding all my senses. The taste of his wet skin, the feel of his taut muscles, the smell of him. He continued to rub and I began the inevitable climb toward orgasm. My hands clamped on his shoulders and I threw my head back, calling his name.

He stopped. I suppressed a yelp of frustration. He said, "Turn around and put your hands on the edge."

I stepped back and looked into his face. An animal hunger—something I hadn't seen in his eyes before—glowed there.

"Do it."

The thrill of anticipation jacked up several notches with his command. I turned and placed my hands on the edge of the pool, feeling very exposed. I was naked, looking out over emptiness. No one could see us. We were in total privacy. Adam bent and kissed the nape of my neck, my ears, my back, his hands coming up to cup my breasts and knead them gently, rolling the nipples over in his hands. I gasped and arched against him, reaching behind me to hook my arms around his neck.

"Back on the edge, Emilia. Keep them there."

Slowly. Very slowly. I obeyed. He grabbed my hips and pulled them against him. He was naked, now, and his erection pressed against me. I gasped.

But when I thought he would enter me, he didn't. He slid his shaft along the seam of my sex, reaching around my front with one hand to press down on my swollen flesh, now fully aroused. And he began to rub against me both from the front and from behind.

The feeling was exquisite and soon the quick build of tension between my legs increased, bunching in my belly, heating my insides. I was about to come—the orgasm just beyond my reach.

He stopped again. "Adam!" I cried.

"What?" he whispered hoarsely in my ear.

"Stop playing around, for fuck's sake," I growled.

"Tell me what you want. Exactly what you want." He punctuated the command by pressing down on my clitoris again, as if I needed reminding that it was there. I stiffened against him.

"I want your cock. I want it inside of me."

"And then what?"

"I want you to slide it in and out until I come," I panted.

I stopped breathing when I felt the tip of him at my entrance. "Ask me nicely."

"Fuck me."

"Nicely, Emilia."

"Fuck me, *please.*"

Without another word he slid into me—pushing in so quickly that my entire body froze. The water lapped up and over the edge of the pool with the force of his movement and I gasped. His chest pushed against me until I was bent forward and he began to move, his chin resting against the top of my head.

He grabbed one of my hands and pressed it, under his, against my sex. "Touch yourself here."

And I did, and the combination of these two sensations—of him sliding inside of me from behind, and the pressure on that bundle of nerves in the front soon had me panting.

I was still sore from the last time but that did not detract from the incredible pleasure building inside me. It built more quickly, more intensely than before. I let out a shout. He slammed into me from behind, faster and faster, the water splashing all around us.

And I was coming. And this time in hot, urgent pulses that temporarily kept me from breathing. He pushed himself in deep and let out a hoarse groan and he was coming, too.

When he withdrew, I was bent against the edge of the pool, gasping for breath. He pulled me up against him, holding me to him from behind. "You swallow some water?"

I shot him a glare of mock-annoyance. "I guess I didn't need to walk for a few days, anyway."

His chest rumbled against my back. "I can just carry you everywhere."

And with that he picked me up and carried me out of the pool. We dripped everywhere, as he swerved around the bed and right toward the bathroom.

This was a dream. And I never wanted to wake up. His arms were a haven around me, soothing me, giving me a sense that I was safe within them. But my heart couldn't help but rebel—reject the new home it was being offered. It had lived imprisoned inside its own fortress for too long. I had thrown away the key to that lock years ago. Even if I wanted to, I doubted I could muster the ability to find it.

Later, I gnawed on my cold steak. I couldn't get it down fast enough, I was so hungry.

"You know, they can heat that up for you or fire you a new one," he said, approaching in a white terry robe, his magnificent chest peeking from its opening.

"I just made a cold steak sandwich with my roll." I held it up for his inspection and he took a bite, nodding his head after a minute.

"That's not bad."

"Get your own."

"I'm not hungry anymore. For food, anyway." He shot me a meaningful look.

"If you are hungry for anything else, it's going to be a while before I can recharge."

He glanced at the clock. "It's not too late to go out. Do you want to go up on the patio for dessert or a glass of wine?"

I eyed the bed longingly. "I'm worn out. I'm going to go to bed, I think. You go ahead, if you want."

He looked at me then. "I'm going to clear my schedule tomorrow."

I smiled. Had I gotten through to him? "Thank you."

"I'm not familiar with many of the local sights as I don't usually play tourist when I come. But I know there are many good places to visit."

"From the little I saw today, there are. It will be great to finally spend some time with you." Though whether it was in bed or out and about, I wasn't sure I cared, at this point.

He grimaced as if in regret. "Yeah, I'm sorry. But this was a business trip and I only get down here once a year at most."

Maybe I hadn't gotten through to him after all. I struggled to hide my disappointment. "Sure," I said, nodding overenthusiastically. "I get it." Work always came first. That was his indirect message and I thought of Lindsay's question, *Has he stood you up for work, yet?* As if any woman in Adam's life would have to accept that in order to have him. Well, not me.

"I think I'll take a short walk." He changed into his clothes and I pulled on my T-shirt and brushed my teeth, collapsing into bed. I knew damn well that he wasn't strolling the deck. He'd grabbed a flash drive and stuck it in his pocket when he thought I wasn't looking. He was headed to the resort's business center to log in from there. If I were a gambling person, I would have bet on it.

Hours later, I was vaguely aware of him coming to bed. After a moment, I felt his warm breath near my neck. He planted a kiss on my cheek before rolling over to sleep.

14

S T. LUCIA WAS EVEN MORE BEAUTIFUL THE NEXT DAY, AS I toured it alongside Adam. We were able to spend time at a secret beach known only to the locals. And I suggested we go back to Diamond Falls so he could see it, too.

He'd told me we should go somewhere different because I'd already seen the falls the day before. But I had insisted. And in the end, as we watched the gorgeous white waters of the cataract tumble over the colored yellow, blue and taupe rocks of the cliff, he wrapped an arm around my waist and kissed me on the cheek, thanking me for bringing him.

The coastal water was a shade of brilliant turquoise against baby-powder white sand. And it was so warm, unlike the water off the coast of California, which was really only tolerable—and even then still chilly—during the height of summer.

We returned to the hotel in the late afternoon and I immediately went to the bathroom to wash off the beach. I took my time, leisurely letting the warm water sluice over my body, reinvigorating me after a full day of sun and sightseeing. I had my eyes closed, rinsing my hair, when I felt a rush of air near me.

The shower was open to the rest of the bathroom, tucked in a corner of colorful bright blue tile. I felt his presence behind me long before he actually touched me—to nudge me out of the way of the water spray!

"That's enough water hogging," he said with laughter in his voice. I stepped aside but didn't leave the shower, watching while he scrubbed himself down, washed his hair and rinsed himself of sand, salt and soap. The masculine hardness of his body was beautiful to behold. I wanted to reach out and touch it, map the valleys and hills of the firm muscles under his skin. I didn't think I could ever get enough.

When I looked up into his face, I saw him watching me watching him. He smiled and held my gaze, lowering his hands from where he rinsed his hair, reaching for me and pulling me against him.

"You better watch out." I murmured against his lips as I pressed my hands to his hard chest. "You might accidentally get a tan while you are here."

He laughed. "Are you mocking me, Ms. Strong?"

"If you got a tan, you'd *definitely* lose your geek card."

He pressed his mouth to mine and we kissed as the warm water coursed over us from the rain showerhead—like a tepid tropical downpour. I kissed the raindrops from his jaw and the small curl of a rumble rose in his chest.

"This is the fourth time I've showered with you and every single time I've wanted to pin you to the wall and fuck you," he growled.

"And this time?" I said breathlessly.

He kissed me again, this time forcing my mouth open to accept his invading tongue. His hands went to my hips and he moved us to the corner of the shower. When he pulled his mouth away, my breath faltered.

"This time I'm going to finally do it," he said in a hoarse voice.

He lifted me several inches off the ground and sandwiched my body between his and the cold, smooth tile of the shower. He kissed me again and nudged his knee between my legs, cueing me to open them for him. I locked them around his hips and he gasped against my mouth. "I don't think I'll ever get enough of you," he murmured.

My arms tightened around his neck as he maneuvered the lower halves of our bodies to line up properly. "Likewise," I said.

He entered me in one swift push and I gasped. The fit was tight and things were still tender from the newness of this intimate contact. I braced my hands against his shoulders and with a groan, he began to move against me.

Our wet bodies slid together in sensual abandon as he drove himself in, again and again. His mouth pressed against my temple and he rocked his pelvis against mine, the pleasure scorching me.

"I don't know how I kept my hands off you all this time," he groaned against my hair without once missing a beat in his rhythm.

"Adam," I whispered. "You feel so good inside me. Make me come."

He pulled my right leg away from his waist so I could leverage myself, tip-toed on the floor. My left leg remained hooked around his hips. He drove into me with longer, fiercer strokes. "You're so tight. So goddamn tight. You feel so good. Like you were made to fit only me." He kissed me along my brow and the rise to climax threatened as he continued.

And with a few more fierce pushes, I was coming, gasping his name. But he didn't stop, didn't wait for me to catch my breath. His movements grew more urgent, more rushed until with a long growl, he climaxed, stiffening, his pelvis grinding against mine.

After several long, silent moments, his body went lax, his face buried into my neck. "Fuck," he breathed, his fingers pressing into my hips. "That was incredible."

His mouth found mine and we kissed, his arms latching around my waist, cinching me against him. I pulled my mouth away laughing. "I think we just wasted about fifty gallons of water."

He gave me a lopsided grin. "It's your fault for being so fucking irresistible." He kissed me again—a dizzying caress of his lips on mine that made me want him again as ferociously as before. I pulled away, knowing that if this didn't end now, we'd never get to dinner.

I took the brief time away from him to contemplate us in silence. Every time I was in his presence, that rushing force of nature tore at me, made me want to release my convictions and be blown away by him, whisked away into the unknown by gale force winds from the grounding bedrock to which I clung.

There were things I needed to do. A person I needed to become—that vision of myself in surgical scrubs, which had been so important to me for most of my youth. I was the one who was going to save others, save myself. I couldn't get carried away by someone else's will. My past failures notwithstanding—I closed my eyes and my fists in conviction—I *had* to hold on to that vision and not allow it to slip away.

On our last night together in St. Lucia, we ate at the Place, the resort restaurant that featured flavorful Caribbean-inspired cuisine. Adam dressed in a black suit and I wore the crème-colored gown from the night of Adam's house party, feeling again like Cinderella about to dine with her handsome prince.

His eyes slipped over me appreciatively as we sat down. I shook my head, laughing. "You are unbelievable."

He smiled. "What? I was about to tell you how gorgeous you are."

"And how you can't wait to get me out of this dress."

"I was going to save that for a little later, but since you took the words out of my mouth...Let's just say that dessert isn't on the menu. The last time you wore that dress, I tore off your panties. I can't be completely responsible for my actions later tonight." He grinned wickedly.

"Unbelievable," I repeated. "Making up for lost time." And my eyes darted away. I tried not to think about the horrible letdown that would follow when we got off that plane in LA. Something tightened in my chest and—contrary to everything my head had been telling me, my heart began to wonder if I could bargain my way out of the decision to end things after tonight.

What if we agreed to get together occasionally for sex—and maybe dinner once in a while? Would he even want it? I glanced at him as he cut into his pecan-encrusted snapper.

He was so damn handsome in that suit—or who was I kidding—in just about anything he wore, and even better naked. And he was kind most of the time—the times that he chose to act like a human instead of a robot.

I was ready to make a tradeoff for more time with him, on my terms.

We lingered over our crème brulée dessert, which apparently *was* on the menu. He darted a pointed look at me from where his head was bent, scraping out the last of the custard with his spoon. I set aside my barely-touched dish, folded and refolded my hands on the table. It was time to stop being a coward.

I took a deep breath. "I don't think I could've picked a more perfect night for our last night together."

He didn't look up but his features chilled. Setting down his empty dish, he stared at it for a long moment. "It doesn't have to be," he said in an even, quiet voice.

Maybe he'd been thinking the same thing I had. Maybe he was ready to bargain for a little more time, too. He looked up and fixed me with that intent, dark stare. The air pressure thickened between us, making the barometer soar as I struggled to find my breath, to find my will. That I wanted to be with him again so much scared me. If it happened, it needed to be on *my* terms, not his. "It needs to be," I said, my voice faltering.

His brows lowered just a fraction over those piercing eyes. He took no other action but to enfold one of my hands inside his, running a thumb across my wrist in a sensual, possessive move. I swallowed, struggling to ignore the desperate thumping of my pulse.

He seemed to be wrestling with himself, coming to some unknown decision. I braced for the myriad of possibilities of what it could be. Of them all, I could never have predicted in a million years what would next come out of his mouth.

"We are more to each other than you realize, you know," he said.

My wrist trembled inside his hand, feeling so vulnerable, so delicate, so trapped. Cold fear clamped at the base of my throat. Was he about to admit to feelings for me? It was time to push him away. Far away. "Adam, we've had a lot of fun together and I've had an amazing time. But we hardly know each other. It's only been a month—"

"No." He swallowed. "It hasn't."

I clamped my mouth shut and waited expectantly for him to explain himself. He gave a short nod as if reassuring himself and then glanced away for a split second, his hand still wrapped around my wrist. "You once asked me why I bid on the auction. I never answered you, but I assume you still want to know."

I nodded.

"I can tell you the exact moment I knew I would win that auction. *Win* it, not just bid on it. You'd sent me the rough draft of your Manifesto to read and we'd been up discussing it in game chat past two a.m. I'd spent most of that time trying to talk you out of the whole thing, but you wouldn't budge and when you started to get upset, I dropped the subject. That was the moment I knew I'd prevent it in another way because I *could*."

I grew cold inside and dizzy with disorientation. What the hell was he talking about? I never had that conversation with him. That was months before we'd even met! I'd stayed up talking that night with...My jaw dropped. I shook my head.

"What—?" I gasped.

He watched me intently, like a child might watch a firecracker after lighting the fuse and waiting for it to explode.

I shook my head again. "That wasn't you. It was—" Fuck. No. *No.* This couldn't be happening.

I remembered that conversation. He'd been so adamantly against the auction. He'd tried to pick apart every single argument I'd made in the Manifesto and it had hurt my feelings. We'd sent in-game messages back and forth for hours, my wrists growing sore from all the furious typing.

And my mind flew to the times before. When I'd poured my heart out to him about my mom and how sick she was. About how helpless I felt being too far away to care for her, to drive her to all her appointments. He'd consoled me then. Had told me I was making her proud by staying in school. That I was so close and that he believed in me.

I was shaking and pale and static crackled behind my ears, the only other sensation where his fingers tightened over my wrist. I struggled for a breath as if I'd been underwater a hundred years. "You're FallenOne."

And, almost imperceptibly, he nodded, his obsidian eyes never leaving mine. I couldn't breathe. My eyes fluttered closed. I pulled my arm back and felt only the tiniest resistance from his hold before he relinquished it.

I stared at the tabletop between us, my mind racing over all the things he knew. Every experience we'd shared. Our regular gaming group of four had always had a great time playing together, but Fallen and I had spent hours and hours just alone in each other's company. Online text chat, doing personal quests in the game, sharing quest notes and items. In some ways, I felt as close a friendship to him as I did to Heath.

To Fallen—to *Adam*—I corrected myself. "This doesn't make sense. Fallen lives on the east coast—he's a student—" I said, my voice shaking, still unable to look at him.

He shifted in his chair. "Some of that was to mislead you. Some of it was stuff I never actually said but you led yourself to believe. Sometimes I was on the east coast for work when I logged on."

He knew so much about me and I knew practically nothing in comparison. On the day my mom had told me about her diagnosis,

I'd turned to him because Heath was on a camping trip with his then-boyfriend. Fallen and I had chatted all night long and logged off at six in the morning. I'd cried to him. *Sobbed* over the very real possibility of losing her. I struggled to breathe. "How—how did this happen? Why didn't you tell me?"

He glanced away and folded his hands on the table in front of him. "I've told you that I go into the game and play from time to time. I playtest my own product—I wasn't lying about that. I get into groups and help people finish quests and get the rewards that they needed. It's fun to see them enjoying the game so much." He hesitated and cleared his throat but didn't look at me.

"One night I grouped with this Barbarian Mercenary and Spiritual Enchantress and their friend, Persephone. I could listen to your voice chat even though I was in text. I think we were working on one of the newbie quests that night. That last piece of quest armor for Fragged—I mean Heath. I've had fun in other groups but never like that night. I laughed so hard at all the witty jokes that were flying around as we went through that annoying dungeon. And then Heath told me about your blog, said I should go read it. So I did."

He shot a tentative look my way, but I was staring into my own little happy place somewhere on the tabletop. "I loved the blog and—well, I broke my own rule about not grouping with the same people more than once. That night after work when I logged in, I went looking for your group again. I seldom left the office that week. I actually looked forward to logging on with you guys every night. That probably sounds pathetic—"

I still couldn't look at him. "No more pathetic than my looking forward to logging on to group with you all weekend."

He paused, fidgeted with his laced hands for a moment. "Between reading your blog and gaming with you and then spending all that time in game just getting to know each other over in-game messages as much as we did. I got to know you. I got...attached."

Some invisible vise clamped around my chest and my eyes and throat stung. That same cold fear was back and this time I was numb with it. I blinked, worked my hands on the table in front of me, tried to tune out the irritating sounds of dinnerware and chatter from nearby tables. My eyes drifted to the candle flame gleaming inside a hurricane lamp on the table. What did this all mean? We *were* more to each other than I'd realized—but it had never been more than *he'd* realized. We'd been on unequal footing all along. He'd known everything and had willingly kept me in the dark. And now, he said he was attached.

I drew in a sobbing breath. I was attached, too. But now, I was determined that there would be no tomorrow for us. It was too life-altering. That cut would slice me twice as deeply. Tomorrow I'd be losing both Adam and FallenOne with the same severing blow.

I pushed back from the table and out of my chair. "We should go," I said quietly.

His eyes widened and he stood. We faced each other across that table for a long moment. The swirl of chaos inside me told me I had hours—probably more like days or weeks—of thinking to sort all this out and figure out what it was. But I didn't need him to speak to me of being attached. I didn't need his confusing tempest-like sway ripping my control from me.

I didn't say another thing as I turned to leave and he followed closely behind. We twisted down long walkways and up two flights of stairs to make it to our suite. After several long minutes of silence,

Adam rested a light hand on the small of my back, walking beside me in the darkness as the balmy Caribbean air swirled around us. As my dress was backless, I was all too aware of that hand and the heated imprint it left on my skin, the way his thumb moved across it with the tiniest caress. I was so focused on that touch that I nearly tripped and fell in my heels, making a huge fool out of myself.

Back in the suite, things felt tense, awkward. I looked around the room, with the candles lit and the bed turned back, the white mosquito netting loosed and dancing in the breeze like an errant bridal veil. My heart started to race. How could I avoid the conversation, the declarations that were certain to come, that were hanging in the air like dark clouds threatening to drop a torrent of rain at any moment?

He'd moved to the dresser and, after having doffed his coat, was now undoing his tie. He looked at me, his face unreadable, but he didn't say anything.

I went to fetch my T-shirt, which was in the dresser beside where he stood. I thought to change for bed because I couldn't think of anything else to do. I wasn't terribly tired and I knew I'd have no ability to concentrate on a study guide.

I pulled the shirt from the middle drawer on the dresser while he watched me with unreadable eyes. He had unbuttoned his shirt and I was feeling weird and tense and shy. I kept my eyes averted.

I moved to the bed, stepping out of my heels and letting the gauzy material of my skirts float around my legs. Of the three, this was the dress that most made me feel like a fairy princess. Only thing was, midnight was about to strike and I could feel it in every tense look we shared, the silence hanging over our room.

And my handsome prince—well, he wasn't who I thought he was, either. I reflected on that. He knew so much about me and yet he'd always kept himself a mystery from me. He was hiding still, behind the persona, behind this entire arrangement. Heated anger stirred in my chest. I was most angry with myself, for not knowing, for not realizing. While I'd mostly found Adam remarkably easy and fun to be with, I'd never once associated him with FallenOne. How could I have been so blind?

I almost went to change in the bathroom, but that seemed silly after we had seen so much of each other. I laid the shirt on the bed and tried not to focus on where he was in the room—or the fact that he'd removed his shirt and undershirt and now wore only his suit pants and socks. I wouldn't look. Nope, I wouldn't. Confusion or no, my body still wanted his. Hungrily so. Probably more now than before we'd started sleeping together.

I reached around and unhooked my skirt before loosening the halter at my neck and lowering it, feeling the cool bay breeze hit my breasts, bringing my nipples immediately to hardened points. I unzipped the skirt and stepped out of it.

Suddenly his hands cupped my hips. He'd come up behind me while I was concentrating on trying not to notice him. I froze and he slowly pulled me back against him.

"Hello, beautiful," he whispered against my hair.

I closed my eyes, shivers cascading down my spine in a waterfall of quick succession. Just a couple whispered words and the lightest touch from this man and I was in pieces, ready to surrender to him.

I didn't say anything, just let him hold me for a long moment, the feel of his warm, muscular chest pressed against my back stirring my desire to life.

"Emilia, I'm sorry I didn't tell you sooner."

I held my breath. His hands cupped my shoulders, traveled down my arms. I didn't want to talk. I wanted our bodies pressed together, sticky with sweat and passion. I wanted one last memory before I said good-bye.

I turned around in his arms and pressed myself to him. "I want you. Right now."

He hesitated, looking into my eyes for a long time before bending to kiss me. I wanted the storm. I welcomed it. I wanted him to fly over me and overwhelm me, to suck me in so I wouldn't think or feel anything else but his hands, his mouth, his body.

I threw myself into that kiss, opening for him, hooking my arms around his neck to pull him to me. This would be our last time together. A tiny sliver of me lightened with relief. At the back of my mind, the greater part of me protested.

His eyes darkened and his hands were on my breasts, softly caressing the peaked nipples, sending sparks of pleasure through me. He nudged me toward the bed and I acquiesced, swept up in him.

"Emilia—" he said.

"Shh." I put my hand on his mouth. "No talking."

He pulled my hand away, grabbing both my wrists, leaning against me to push me down on the bed with him. He held my arms above my head, cinching my wrists together in the grip of one hand to secure them there.

He then proceeded to kiss me senseless. His other hand floated across my breasts, my stomach, to rest at the apex of my thighs.

His head came up and he looked me in the eyes, a multitude of questions unasked. I wouldn't let him give them voice. I couldn't. I squirmed against his hold, pushing my chest toward him.

"Stop it," he said. I stilled, looked at him with the question that he didn't wait for me to ask. "You're using sex to avoid talking about this."

I closed my eyes and pushed against his hold. His grip tightened in response and my pulse leapt. I ached for him everywhere. "Please, Adam. I want you inside me."

His hand returned to rest atop my underwear and he began a firm but languorous stroke. My gaze flew to his and he had that calculating stare that had taught me to be wary. "You want this?" he asked, sinking his mouth to my nipple, taking it between his lips, his teeth.

I gasped, throwing my head back, arching myself into him. "Yes. Now. I want you now."

He tore his mouth away almost violently, eliciting another cry from me. The pressure of his hand on my sex increased. "What about tomorrow? Do you want me tomorrow, too?"

I froze and looked away. Now I understood him. If I was using sex as avoidance, he was using sex to force the conversation. His hand stilled, then slipped inside my underwear. His touch was light but I shivered everywhere, needing more. "Don't talk about tomorrow," I whispered, my eyes closing tight.

His fingers slid inside me and stopped again. "*I* want to talk about tomorrow. And the next day. And the one after that—"

I struggled against his grip on my hands. My eyes shot open and I fixed him with a ferocious stare. "*No.*"

He moved his fingers again, stroking in and out, and my eyes rolled back, an intoxicating dizziness overtaking me. Trying to concentrate on anything else was like downing three shots of whiskey in quick succession and then walking a tightrope.

"Fuck me," I whispered.

His hand didn't stop its tortuous slide inside me. The tension tightened in my belly. I moaned.

"I don't want to," he said, his posture stiffening. "Not if I can't have you tomorrow, too. And the day after. Not if this would be the last time."

Despite my aggravation with him, his hands were working a spell on me. I was so close, and he knew it. He withdrew his hand, then rolled his hips on top of mine, pinning me down. "Will this be the last time, Emilia?" he asked, his voice husky. His erection pressed against my sex.

Here was my moment of leverage. I'd dictate my terms. He'd have no choice but to abide by them. I couldn't have planned it better. "I'll have sex with you again." I gasped when he moved over me, fitting himself between my legs. "I can be your fuck buddy."

He thrust against me again, his hand still clamped around my wrists. "But I don't want a fuck buddy."

I hesitated, frowning. Wouldn't most guys be overjoyed about that type of arrangement? He seemed more annoyed than anything else. Confusion swirled inside me. It threatened to rise up and drown out these other, more pleasant feelings. "We could hook up—"

His expression went blank, his voice flat and even. "I want more than a cheap, quick fuck."

My jaw clenched and eyes narrowed, irritation contending with arousal, threatening to supplant it. "Then you can fucking buy me dinner once in a while," I ground out between clenched teeth.

Our gazes collided in silent struggle. He released my wrists and I immediately put my hands on his solid shoulders and shoved. He didn't budge.

"I know what I want," he said in that firm, charged voice that held an angry undercurrent. "And when I put my mind to something I tend to get it."

Heat flushed my face and I looked away from his dark, penetrating stare. "I hate to disappoint you, but in this case, you aren't going to," I replied.

He studied me for a long moment and I couldn't take his scrutiny a minute longer. I pushed on his shoulders again and he slid off, unburdening me of his weight. I sat up and ran a hand through my hair while he rolled on his side and watched me.

"What are you afraid of?"

I clenched my teeth. "Who said I was afraid?"

"*I'm* saying it."

Stiffening, I bent to snatch up my T-shirt and pull it over my head, turning my back to him in the process. "There are two of us talking here and only one of us is a proven liar. I'd stop talking if I were you."

I jerked to my feet and began pacing in front of the bed. Adam watched me with enigmatic eyes the color of midnight. "Actually there's only one of us really talking. Me."

I smirked, gesturing at him sharply. "The proven liar. That's just great."

He shrugged. The movement was stiff, like he was faking it. "You're the one who's lying now."

I halted, turning to him with arms crossed over my chest. "Oh? And what am I lying about?"

"Your feelings. About the fact that this doesn't bother you. You don't want to talk because you're afraid of what this is going to start."

Hot anger pooled, settled into my joints, stiffening them. "I'm pissed at you for not telling me the truth. How's that? I may have been preparing myself to lose you tomorrow, but not Fallen."

"You don't have to lose either one of us," he said quietly.

I put my hands to my forehead. The whole concept made my brain ache. "You are still two separate people in my head. I haven't even had a chance to absorb any of this and you demand to know my feelings? *I* don't even know what the fuck they are."

He stood and walked toward me slowly, as if I were a scared rabbit that might hop away from any sudden movement. The ambient light gleamed on his muscular torso, his pants slung low on his hips. He was so damn sexy he took my breath away, even when he was irritating the hell out of me. He stood very close but didn't touch me.

"Then allow yourself the time to figure it out. Give *us* the time."

I sighed and looked away, off to the side, anywhere but at him. "No."

His hands came up to take my shoulders in a gentle hold. When he spoke, his voice had a desperate edge to it. "Emilia—"

"No!" I gritted out between clenched teeth, finally meeting his gaze. "Explain to me about this fairy tale you are proposing. About how something like this is supposed to even work—even beyond the trust issues, which are monumental at this point. With my two jobs and preparing for medical school and your hundred-hour work-week, how would something like that work? Neither of us even date."

"It's not a fairy tale. It's a real life, honest, grown-up relationship where two adults work out their differences once they decide they want to be together—"

I pulled back against his hold on my shoulders and he dropped his arms. I continued to back away. "Is all this because you feel guilty about us sleeping together even though you never planned for it to go this far?"

He shook his head, running a hand through his hair. "No." His fist knotted.

"I think it *is*."

His head darted up to pin me down with an angry glare. "Well, you're *wrong*. You have no fucking idea what is going through my mind, so stop twisting things to support your cynical and warped view on the world."

I stood still, stunned. I'd never seen an angry outburst from him. I put up a hand in surrender. "Fine. I'm sorry for doing that. I hate it when people do it to me."

He fixed his unwavering gaze on me. "Why aren't you willing to give it a chance?"

I took a deep breath. "Because I don't want a relationship. Not with you. Not with anyone."

"Why?"

Frustration crawled up my spine, tightening that knot between my shoulders. I put my hands to my temples, closing my eyes. "You are making me crazy, Adam."

"Because I'm forcing this conversation when you want to avoid it? It's been the elephant in the room for days—weeks, now—and I'm not going to shove it aside any longer, no matter how uncomfortable it makes you. When we get back to California, I want to know where we stand. *Exactly* where we stand."

My mouth set, irritation burning like hot lava. "You'll be standing in your office somewhere in Irvine and I'll be standing in my apartment in Orange."

He folded his arms across his chest and angled his head, studying me. "I'm not amused."

"Quit trying to save me. I don't need you to save me."

He blinked. "Emilia, I'm telling you I want you in my life. I want a relationship with you—as equals—and you somehow twist me into your knight protector coming to a meek maiden's rescue?"

I sighed, suddenly feeling exhausted. "Isn't that what it is?"

He shook his head. "That bastard really fucked you up good. He's screwed you because in every decision you make for the rest of your life, you'll never even consider trusting someone enough to allow them in."

I tensed. "I did my therapy. I'm fine. That little shithead has no part in what decisions I make—"

He exhaled in exasperation. "I was talking about your father."

Those words hit me like a blow, knocking my breath away. I held up a hand to ward off any more words he might consider hurling my way. Because they stung, like darts sinking into my skin.

I fought for breath. Memories of taunts on the playground from my erstwhile friends—*Mia doesn't have a daddy. She's never had a daddy.* At least their daddies came to see them on the weekends, or took them on fancy vacations once in a while. Mine just wished I'd never existed, if he ever thought of me at all.

I wasn't the only child from a broken home. Well, that would imply that our home had ever been in one piece to begin with—but at least they knew their fathers, their paternal grandparents, their siblings, their heritage. Their *names*. Late at night sometimes I'd hear my mom crying. She'd rifle through a box of letters that I knew were from him. A box of letters that I wished I could burn when she wasn't around.

She'd tried to tell me, once, who he was. She'd wanted desperately to talk to me about him—upset that I'd only heard the negatives from her and from my grandmother as I grew up. But I'd screamed at her. I'd thrown a vase against the wall and shouted that I never wanted to hear her speak a word about that scumbag. And I'd stormed out of the house.

He hadn't cared about me. Why would I care about him? I tried to breathe, instantly aware of the truth behind Adam's accusation. It burned me like the raging wildfires that screamed through the dry hills in autumn.

"Don't even—" I said, baring my teeth.

He didn't flinch, didn't even move. "Hit a nerve, did I?"

"Fuck you," I whispered, struggling to dam the tears. They clogged in my throat. I hadn't cried in the longest time. I was a tough woman. But Adam had shredded my defenses in less than five minutes. He knew too much. I stepped back and gestured stiffly at him. "You don't know shit about my father."

His expression was grim, gaze focused on me like two laser beams. "I know he turned you into a coward. I know that every single man you look at for the rest of your life is tainted by him. And I know that you are running scared—not just about this but about your entire future. How many times did I tell you to go out and retake that goddamn test? You could've taken it a dozen times by now but you still haven't. You keep studying and studying, hoping for that perfect moment when you'll know *everything* because you're afraid to fail. In your education, in your *life*. So you protect yourself in this little isolated cocoon you've built. You're a *coward*," he sneered.

"What—are you a fucking shrink now?" And I hated how my voice sounded, that strangled sob that escaped my lips on that last word. He heard it because his face changed immediately, softening for the slightest fraction of a second before I got in his face. I strode up to him and shoved against his chest. What I really wanted to do was throw my best right hook at his perfect jaw but, like my attempt at pushing him, it would have done nothing.

He caught my wrists and wouldn't let go when I flailed them. His grip tightened, holding them still easily. I spoke between clenched teeth. "Get out of my head! You have no right to throw your amateur theories in my face because I make a decision you don't agree with. Especially when you are so fucked up yourself!"

A warning gleamed in those coal-black eyes. "*I'm* fucked up?"

I nodded. Fury built inside of me like a pressure valve ready to blow. I wanted to hurt him like he had hurt me. Lash out. Cut him deep. And I knew enough about him to do the damage.

"I *know* you are." I took a deep breath. "You bought into the auction because you were trying to save me from myself. You say you aren't my knight protector but you want to be. I'm not *her*, Adam. I'm not Sabrina and you can't save her by saving me. It's too late."

His eyes fluttered closed, then open and his grip around my wrists tightened just slightly. "You think I don't know that?"

I shook my head. "You're just as big of an addict as she was—and your mother. You won't touch hard liquor or drugs but you'll numb yourself to exhaustion every day with work."

He opened his mouth to protest but I rode over him, raising my voice. "Because you're clever. You chose an addiction that was socially acceptable. In our culture, it's a good thing to be a hard worker. People won't suspect the real reason you do it, if you're successful." He paled but I couldn't stop myself. I'd plunged that knife in, now I had to twist it.

"Admit it. Work fills the exact same need as drugs or booze or food. It numbs you, it keeps you at a distance from life. It shuts out everyone who loves you. Your uncle, your cousins. Your friends."

He released my hands and stepped back as if I had burned him. I pressed forward, unwilling to cede my advantage. I gestured at him with a pointed finger. "I know exactly what would happen if we were in a relationship. Maybe I'd become a diversion for you for a little while, until you got bored or until the next time you had to get your junky fix. Which wouldn't be long, I'm sure. Just like I know you went up to the business center last night after we had sex in the pool." He blinked as if I'd slapped him. I gritted my teeth and delivered the last few words with all the venom I felt, still wounded from his accusations. "You have no heart of your own and yet you are trying to convince me to open up mine to you? No, Adam. No way."

The cords on his neck pulled taught and his hands clenched into fists. He shook his head at me. "Unbelievable," he whispered. We watched each other for long, tense moments, my fingernails clawing at my palms. I was flushed. He was pale. I was full of rumbling rage. He was simmering with quiet fury. We made an odd contrast in opposites.

His mouth tightened, and he shook his head. He turned from me and went to find his shirt where he'd hung it across the back of the chair by the desk. With short, jerky movements, he pulled it on and buttoned it.

I was anchored in my spot, unable to move, unable to speak. All I could do was feel—feel this pounding wave of agony washing over me as he withdrew, those hurtful words still saturating the air between us.

He grabbed his shoes, sat down and slipped them on. I watched, mute and helpless. Those words were like the threshold we'd crossed together earlier—something to hang between us forever, to link us together and push us apart. They could never be unspoken.

"Adam," I whispered, suddenly fearing what he wouldn't say more than what he would.

He looked at me, his eyes blank, cold. "You were right. What was I thinking? I'd finally decided I wanted a *woman* in my life. You're just a sad, scared little girl." He stood and spun, heading for the bathroom. And I was rooted, unable to move, breathe, think. Unable to focus on anything beside the pain blossoming inside me.

Minutes later, he reentered. I had gone to the couch, holding my knees to my chest, my mind racing with what to do, what to say. He walked to the door and turned back to me just before leaving. "I'm moving to another room for the night. I suddenly lost my desire to sleep here."

I tipped my forehead onto my knees and he waited just a minute before jerking the door open and slamming it closed. I was cold inside. I could cry if I allowed myself, but the tears didn't come. I squeezed my knees tighter to me, wondering what this meant. What would the plane ride home be like, sitting next to him, silent, seething?

And after that, after he dropped me off, then what? Never see each other again? That had been my clever safety mechanism, clearly delineated and structured from the start. But there was no deal to conclude. So what would be our conclusion? Complete and total estrangement—as if the fairy tale had never existed at all?

A tiny shard of glass pierced the center of my chest and my soul was bleeding. I didn't want to think about it. Somewhere along the line, I moved to the bed and curled into a tight ball and fell into a restive, dreamless sleep.

15

I SHOULDN'T HAVE WORRIED ABOUT THE PLANE RIDE HOME because he didn't go home with me. In the morning, the major-domo brought me a note with my breakfast. It was a hurriedly scrawled and impersonal card, signed by Adam, saying he had business that would keep him in the region for another week and that he'd seen to all the arrangements to get me home safely.

Furiously, I shredded it, frustrated at his lack of willingness to compromise. It was all or nothing with him. So we would become strangers again because *he* had decided we should be strangers. My chest seized again in memory of our confrontation the night before. We'd hurled hurtful words like daggers and the wounds were still fresh, stinging. They might never heal.

Every time I looked at the empty seat next to me on the way home, something twisted in my heart. Already the space where he'd occupied my thoughts and musings felt like an empty, echoing room.

And then there was the annoying fact that every time I shifted in my seat, the twinge I felt was a reminder of all that had gone on between us and I relived every touch, every heated whisper, every kiss. I ached from the inside out.

***

Under normal circumstances, I would have gone to Heath's house, probably by way of a supermarket, fetching myself a pint of mint chocolate chip ice cream, and commiserated with him. But I was still angry with him about the e-mail he'd sent to Adam—the one that had sent us spiraling down this crazy path in the first place.

Instead, when I got home, I showered, closed all the curtains and slept the remainder of the day and into the next day. I didn't bother to turn the phone on until I woke up at noon.

And of course, there was a message from my mom instructing me to call her as soon as the weekend was over. As it was Monday morning, I complied, riddled with guilt that I'd been ignoring her so much since the whole thing with this auction had begun.

I tried to ignore that hollow, aching feeling in my chest whenever I thought about Adam. I tried not to think about him as much as possible. I didn't succeed very often. My mind seemed drawn to him, like white blood cells swarming on an infection. I laughed at that simile. How very appropriate. My obsession with Adam, this persistent soreness, was not unlike an infection.

"How was your study retreat?" my mom asked when I finally got around to calling her back.

"Oh, it was good. Got a lot done." Too bad none of it was actual studying, but it had been a lot more fun.

"Am I bringing you back home with me after graduation?"

I sighed. Shit. Graduation was at the end of the week. I'd had the semester off but I was walking with my class and I had done next to nothing to prepare for commencement. "I'd rather follow you up. I want my own car while I'm there." I tried to figure out how I could get out of staying the full week. I'd already taken off way too much time from my job and was in danger of losing it.

"I've got some surprises for you when you get home. I can't wait." I gritted my teeth, but the thought of fleeing all this for a few days and retreating to the comfort of my quiet high desert hometown was oddly comforting.

After the phone call was over, I boxed up everything that Adam had "loaned" or gifted to me. The four dresses and accessories, the smart phone and the laptop. I trashed the underwear, not wanting the reminder that it served.

And with every jerky movement, I could hear the voice at the back of my mind. *Sick. Sick. Sick.* Despite my reluctance to admit it, Heath was right. The whole thing between Adam and me had been sick. Nothing good could have come from our beginnings. The entire interaction between us had been forever tainted by the now-notorious auction.

I was numb when I went to work early the next morning. My supervisor called me into her office, berating me for missing so much work and putting me on formal warning. In different circumstances, I would have cared a great deal. To lose that job would mean I could no longer afford to live on my own, to say nothing of its value on my résumé. But I was frozen inside. Dead. And nothing seemed to get through but that distant, constant pain. That feeling that something vital was missing.

When I got home from work, Heath was parked at the curb of my apartment complex, playing a game on his iPad. I walked right by his car, pretending not to see him, my grip tightening on my back-pack strap.

I continued on when I heard the car door open and slam, when I heard his hurried footsteps behind me. I climbed the stairs and didn't turn until I'd fished out my key to unlock the door.

"Hey Mia," Heath said. His tone sounded like he was forcing him-self to be casual. I turned and glanced up at him before snapping the door open and walking inside, not bothering to close it behind me.

"Mia..." he began and I dropped my backpack on the kitchen chair and turned to him, arms folded. "I guess this means he told you about the e-mail, huh?"

I tilted my head at him. "What do you want, Heath?"

He blinked at my abrupt manner. "I—I wanted to see if you were okay."

"You mean you wanted to see if I survived the blast of that bombshell you decided to drop right in the middle of our trip?"

His face crumpled with concern. "Mia...I'm sorry, okay? I thought I was acting for the best."

"For whose best? Mine? Or your conscience?"

He paused and changed stance from one leg to the other. "I take it he was pissed. He never replied to me."

I clenched my teeth and walked over to the box I'd packed up earlier. Grabbing a roll of packing tape out of my backpack, I began to seal it up. "Yep. He was pissed. But it doesn't matter now. It's over."

Heath watched me for a long moment and I grabbed a marker and wrote Adam's name on the side of the box.

"I'm sorry, Mia," he repeated, folding his hands over his chest.

I shook my head. "Don't be. It's how I'd planned it all along."

"What happened over there?"

I clenched my teeth. "Don't want to talk about it."

"Okay." He shot a wary look at me before nodding to the package. "You want me to drop that off for you?"

"He's still out of town. You won't get your tour of the place."

His face clouded. "He sent you home alone?"

I shrugged. "He still had business in the Caribbean. I had to get back to work."

"I don't give a shit about a tour. You aren't all right, Mia."

I jerked a hand at him and his eyes widened. "I'm. *Fine.*"

He held up a hand in surrender. "Okay. Okay. You're fine. But I'd still like to drop that off for you, or at least drive you over?"

I sighed. I could use the moral support to go into the building, even if I knew Adam wasn't there. I hadn't even had the courage to log on to the game since I'd been home.

Heath told me I should unseal the box or it would never make it past security, so I grabbed a kitchen knife and slit it open again. It was early afternoon when we hit the road, our truce unspoken. I hadn't accepted his apology but ultimately I knew—even if he didn't—that the differences between Adam and me had not been Heath's doing.

Heath asked me about the details of the commencement ceremony, and told me he'd make plans to be there and sit with my mom. As we drove, my frosted heart that wanted to cling to the resentment began to thaw.

Fifteen minutes later, we exited the 405 freeway and drove down one of the broad, perfectly planned streets that the city of Irvine was known for. Heath turned in to an industrial park that housed the campus of Draco Multimedia Entertainment.

We approached the central building in the complex. It was designed like a modern day castle with intricate turrets of mirrored glass lined in steel. The mirrors caught the early afternoon sunlight and the entire building gleamed as if it were the fabled seat of Camelot. So, the knight protector spent his brooding days inside a castle. Why did that not surprise me?

We entered a huge lobby with a circular information desk. Everything inside was chrome and granite and bright as the daylight outside, thanks to all the windows. Heath and I gaped in awe. There were displays and artwork from the various games produced by the company everywhere and I couldn't decide where to look first.

In fact, I was so gap-jawed looking at an exact one-quarter replica of "The Mistress's Lair"—a three-dimensional model of an ice palace—that I forgot to address the guy at security.

"Oh! I'm dropping off a package for Mr. Drake." The security dude looked unimpressed.

I opened the flap and he made a quick search of the contents, then wrote my name on a temporary badge and instructed me to drop the package off at his assistant's desk. Then he called back to the desk to let the assistant know that I was coming.

I nodded and shrugged. "Okay."

Heath was still gazing out over the mezzanine at even more elaborate game displays downstairs. "Oh for God's sake, go down and look, then. I'm sorry you didn't get your tour."

"You okay to walk back there?"

I shrugged. "It's not that far away and it's just one of his assistants. He's still out of the country. I'll just dump it and be right back."

Heath wasn't looking at me. A certain display had caught his eye.

I cleared my throat. "Wow, is that an alien coming up behind you to assault you with an anal probe?"

No reaction.

I laughed and he walked off with a wave of his hand. With my box in hand, I followed the security officer's directions through a big set of double doors, past glassed-in offices that consisted of open desk configurations—no cubicles, it seemed, at Draco Multimedia. People were working on sleek desktop computers, collaborating over tablets and generally focused on work. It was a hive of organized chaos. Down the central hallway, I continued past a glassed-in atrium and patio with grass and planters and artfully arranged tables, now empty because it was just after lunchtime.

I finally made it into Adam's neck of the woods. The security officer had made it seem much closer in his directions than it actually was. Adam's office—and that of the other company officers, for their names were all on the doors—was preceded by a large atrium complete with receptionist and several busy-looking assistants.

I moved to the nearest one. "I'm leaving a package for Mr. Drake. Security said to bring it here?"

The receptionist pointed to an assistant at a desk a little further back. The assistant, a bespectacled college-age looking kid in dress shirt and tie, glanced our way, standing up as I approached. "Ms. Strong?"

"Yes. They told you about this package I was bringing up?"

He shot a curious glance at me and then to the box. "Yes. I'll need to inspect the contents before I can take it off your hands."

"Yes, of course. There are just some...personal effects."

He nodded. "He asked me to tell you he'll be out in just a moment."

I frowned, looking up from his work. "Who?"

The assistant looked puzzled. "Mr. Drake."

"*What?* But—but he's still out of town."

The assistant shot me a concerned look. "No, he came back yesterday. He's here."

My eyes rose from his inspection to a set of heavy double doors that led toward the inner sanctum—likely the offices—all lined in glitzy chrome. At that moment, they swung open.

I jumped back from the assistant. "I have to go," I choked. But I was nailed to my spot when I saw a man and a woman emerge. The man was dressed in an impeccable suit, deadly handsome. My chest tightened as if caught in a constricting band. Adam.

If there had been any chance of my seeing him here, I would never, ever have come. He bent to speak to a woman at the desk nearest to the doors—giving her some instructions, it looked like. The woman said something to Adam and then, horrifyingly, glanced in my direction.

Before I could step back, before I could turn and bolt like a coward, my eyes flew to his companion. I knew her too. Her platinum blond hair was artfully arranged around a gorgeous, glamorous face. Lindsay. They stood so close together, they looked like a couple.

I was so dumbstruck that I couldn't move, even when Adam straightened and his eyes immediately flew straight to mine. Every muscle in my body turned to jelly and I could hardly breathe. The assistant continued digging around in the box, oblivious to my distress. He extracted the laptop and laid it on the table in front of him. Adam saw it and his features hardened.

He looked away then, and, to my increased astonishment (was that even possible?), he slipped an arm around Lindsay's waist, bent and whispered something in her ear. Something that made her laugh and sway against him.

I didn't stay to watch any more. I ran. The assistant called after me but I didn't stop. I ran as fast and as far as I could. Because now the tears were coming at last. They blinded me. And I could hear his voice in my head. It was all I could hear. *I've decided I wanted a woman in my life. You're just a sad, scared little girl.*

A sad. Scared. Little. Girl. And compared to me Lindsay was all woman...successful, mature, sexually experienced, and very much into Adam.

I dashed through hallways and out into the parking lot, gasping for breath. And then I ran some more. I ran until I couldn't breathe any more. Then I leaned up against the nearest car, doubled over.

Five minutes later, someone stood beside me. I almost jumped out of my skin until he spoke. "Mia, what the—?" Heath said. "You shot out of that door like a bat out of hell. What the fuck? Are you *crying?*"

By this time, I'd been gulping for air, tears and snot all over my face and, what's worse, I had the hiccups.

"Heath, just get me the fuck out of here, please."

Without another word, he slipped an arm around my shoulders and guided me toward the car. I kept my eyes away from the building. I didn't want to chance seeing them again. Every time I thought about that hard look on his face, new tears seeped out and by the time we made it off the complex property I was a bubbling, oozing mess.

Heath's face was grim. "I take it you saw him in there? What about staying on for business for another week?"

My face was in my hands, and thus my voice was muffled. "He must have been lying." He just hadn't wanted to fly home beside me.

Heath was very worried about me. I could tell. He insisted on ordering takeout after we got home and he sat across from me at my broken down little table while I picked at my mandarin chicken.

"Maybe it might do you some good to get away for a bit."

"I just got back."

"No, I mean spend a little longer with your mom. Maybe stay with her for the summer. She could use the help, now that she's getting the place ready for guests again. I could pack up your place here and throw the stuff in storage. Other than your miserable little orderly job, you really don't have a reason to be out here for the next year or so. Why not save the money you'd be spending on rent and expenses?"

I sighed. "Because going back to Anza is going backward."

"Just think about it. Maybe just get away for a week or two? It would make your mom happy and get her off my back for once."

"If I take any more time off my job, they are going to fire me."

"Good riddance, then. There are other jobs you can get. Or you could put more time into the blog and make more money out of it. I've got a new template design that allows for more ad space. You could sell more ads that way. Or we could go after a company endorsement. I know you've been reluctant, but—"

My chin was on my chest now and I was sniveling miserably. "I'll think about it."

And I did. I thought about it all night. Not necessarily the part about going back to Anza, but the whole bizarre sequence with Adam. The calculated action with which he, knowing that I was watching, had slipped his arm around Lindsay's waist, obviously letting me know that the *woman* whom he'd selected to replace the scared little girl was Lindsay.

After crying out all the tears I thought I had, there was only numbness left. I had to be at work at noon the next day, but I didn't put on my greens. Instead went down to my supervisor's office in my jeans and resigned on the spot. She wasn't nice about it. But she could tell by my swollen eyes and dark circles that I wasn't happy to begin with. She made sure to tell me that I'd been a good worker up until the previous month and I agreed with her. Things had been great until they fell apart. Until Adam. Now I had no job. No money in the bank and about a thimbleful of self-respect left to my name.

***

The day before commencement, Alex and Jenna dropped in to give me a graduation gift and beg me to spend the summer in OC with them. They had *such plans!* And they had tickets to San Diego Comic-Con! And...they had costumes for cosplay and needed another "hot chick" to complete their look for "Steampunk Sherlock's Angels." Alex's mom was sewing the costumes for them.

They also wanted to know if I could get Heath to dress as Sherlock Holmes because he was tall, but he'd have to dye his hair dark.

"Come on, Mia, it would be *so fun!* Picture it—brass-plated corsets, fishnet stockings and kick-ass boots," Alex said breathlessly. "If Heath won't do it, maybe you could get your yummy man to—he already has dark hair and he's plenty tall enough."

Jenna perked up, upon hearing this. "Yeah, when do I get to meet this tasty man, anyway? I'm sick of hearing Alejandra gibber about him and I've only seen that long-distance shot she got with her phone—"

"What?" I slapped Alex on her arm. "You took a picture of him?"

Alex shrugged. "What else is a hopeless *chismosa* to do when you won't give me anything to work with?"

I sighed heavily. "I'm not seeing him anymore and I'd rather not talk about it."

Alex's forehead buckled. "This isn't because of that test, is it? You didn't break up with him because you want to study or something dumb like that?"

I shot her a heated glare, but Jenna was the one who spoke up, watching me closely. "Alejandra! Don't be rude."

"No, it wasn't because of the test." My chest tightened. Something about her assumption bothered me. It reminded me of how I'd chosen to give stupid excuses about not going out, not socializing at parties. Throughout my four years of college, I'd huddled inside my comfort zone, spending any spare time that wasn't consumed by study or work or blog to log on to games and lose myself in them. Because it was safe, known. Because there would be few surprises and anything that could happen, I would be ready for.

I dropped my head against the back of the ripped couch, gazing at the ceiling. Adam was right. I really was a coward.

16

WHEN THE GOING GETS TOUGH, THE TOUGH GO
running home to Mommy. And after commencement, I did just that. I packed up what I could and I
hit the road for Anza—a two-hour drive down some of the most
remote stretch of highway through the Inland Empire and beyond.
My car twisted along the road upward into the Cahuilla Mountains
that overlooked the much more famous Californian resort town of
Palm Springs.

And as I wound up that narrow two-lane highway into the hills,
a measure of calm settled over me. I grew assured that things would
be all right in the end. That this pain was temporary and like the
dying sunlight of that day, would fade away to nothing. Someday.
Sometime.

But it didn't feel temporary. I felt changed, somehow, as if my
life, my heart would never be the same. They say life's experiences
change you—that your brain grows new neural pathways in response
to trauma and new lessons learned. I wondered how many pathways
I was going to get from this. If I was ever going to learn my way

around it. And in this moment, I felt more resolved than ever to protect myself—keep myself dependent on only myself. Because I was the only person in this world I could be sure of. I could be sure of Heath, until he met someone new and could hardly be prevailed upon to fix my eternal string of scrapes. I could depend on my mom, but as the experiences of the previous few years had shown me, she might not always be around. Her near-death had shaken me to my core and showed me that nothing was permanent.

But one thing was permanent. Me. My ambition. My drive. The fortress wall I'd built around my heart and kept vigilant watch over. And I'd spend this time reinforcing, repairing the weak spots that had allowed Adam inside to do his damage.

I had no idea how much Heath had told Mom while they'd sat together at commencement. I know she had no knowledge of the auction, but Heath could have couched his description of my time with Adam as a relationship without mentioning all the ways it was sick and twisted between us. Mom had known I was seeing someone, but she had no details, like the fact that her daughter had willfully sought a way to prostitute herself.

Our little ranch sat on fifteen acres of high desert scrubland. The main house, which my mother called the homestead, had many guest rooms on the top floor. There were also three matching little cabins that shouldered up to the homestead for guests who wanted more privacy. The main dining room in the home was huge, to accommodate the Bed and Breakfast crowd. Until her illness, Mom had run a fairly successful business, with many regular repeat guests coming up to spend time away from civilization, go hiking or ride our horses. My mood relaxed, as I looked down over our spread in the pale light of early evening under a golden high desert moon.

Mom didn't question me too closely when I got home. She snatched me up in a big hug and made my favorite dinner—kabobs and hummus and baklava for dessert. Mom instructed me to get an early night's sleep and warned me that we had a lot to discuss in the morning. Relieved, I fell into my bed, exhausted.

The next morning, I was out in the stables saying hello to my favorite four-legged friends. My horse, Snowball, greeted me with an excited whicker. He'd been my best friend since the fourth grade and his muzzle was aging and gray now, but he still snapped up the carrots I offered him with all due enthusiasm.

At lunch, I munched my garden-fresh cucumber and tomato sandwich on rustic bread as my mom tossed furtive glances my way. I knew she was dying to ask me about my relationship status with the mystery guy and trying to find ways to bring it up, so I decided to head her off.

"So you said you had some surprises for me. Do they have anything to do with the restoration of the cabins?"

Mom gave me an expectant look. "So you noticed?"

"I'd have to be blind not to. Did you win the lottery and not tell me?"

She laughed. "Kind of. If getting cancer could be considered a lottery."

I sobered, suddenly my heart raced with fear and I could feel the blood drain from my face. "What? Is it back?"

Mom's mouth dropped and she reached across the table to put her hand over mine. "Oh no. No, sweet pea. I'm sorry. That's not what I meant."

She got up and went over to the desk where she kept her mail and business papers and pulled out a manila file folder from its stand.

She placed it on the table next to my lunch plate. "Early this year, I got this in the mail. I didn't say anything because I wasn't sure what to make of it. It sounded too good to be true.

I opened the folder and quickly read the letter, which was printed on generic letterhead. It was from a charity institution that helped out adult cancer patients who had fallen on hard times because of the disease. It *did* sound too good to be true—like a "Make a Wish" foundation for adults. Generously, the institution—called "The Golden Shield Group"—had offered to foot half the balance of my mom's mortgage and fund the other half as an interest-free loan to be paid back over the next twenty years.

I couldn't believe my eyes, scouring the letter and flipping it over to read the papers beneath it. "This is—"

"Incredible, I know. I didn't believe it either. But I checked them out online and went to Pohlman's Law Office here in town and had him work with their attorneys. He assured me it was all legitimate."

"Damn, Mom. This is better than the freakin' lottery."

She smiled. "Yep, see? Here's the paperwork from my attorney. It gets better, though. One of the entrepreneurs behind the group, finding out about my setup, offered to front me some money as a silent partner. We've come up with a joint business plan and profit sharing—"

I took the papers from her. "Holy crap! So this is what you are using to pay for the renovation?"

"It's almost done. And I've already been working with Heath to get the website redesigned and updated. He's coming up next weekend to take new pictures. Isn't it exciting?"

I sat back, marveling at how luminous and animated my mother was. She hadn't been like this for years, since before the cancer.

There was color in her cheeks and she had put on some weight and she actually, for the first time since she'd begun chemo, looked *healthy*.

My mom noticed me staring. Her smile faded. "What?"

I shook my head. "You're doing awesome, Mom. I'm so glad." I smiled, happy for her, still trying to ignore that ache at the back of all conscious thought. Trying to erase the image of Adam with his arm around Lindsay's waist. A sharp pang pierced me whenever I thought of it—which was, it seemed, all the time.

Mom, keen as ever, picked up on it immediately. She collected the papers from the table and filed them again. "Now let's talk about what's going on with *you*."

I shook my head. "There's nothing to talk about."

She shot me a curious glance and she rubbed her index finger along her bottom lip like she always did when she was hesitating. "You were dating someone."

I glanced away, fidgeting in my seat. I'd allow five more minutes of prodding and then I'd excuse myself. "I was. It was nothing. It's over." All the truth. Just not the whole truth. But I couldn't find it in my heart to tell her that so much had changed along the way. That I'd lost something—a vital piece of me that felt like a gaping hole right at the center of my being. And that it might take a while to learn how to fill that up.

"What happened?" she asked in a quiet voice as if she might startle me out of my uncharacteristic forthrightness by speaking any louder.

I shrugged. "I had to study and my jobs. He had to work. There was no time."

"Do you want to talk about him?"

I leaned forward, rubbing my forehead with my hand. "No. Not really."

She sat silent for several minutes and I closed my eyes, preparing to make an excuse to go. She surprised me by dropping the subject and reaching for my half-empty plate, standing to take it to the sink.

"Mom—" I stopped her when she would have walked away. She halted, looking at me expectantly. "The Biological Sperm Donor..." I began shakily. "I think I'm ready to find out more about him."

My mother sank back to the chair across from me, setting the plates down. I studied her for a moment. She was a lovely woman. She had the olive skin and dark coloring of her Greek ancestors and had been quite the stunning woman in her youth—had taken a turn at modeling as a teen. In her early forties, she was still striking, and before the cancer, she'd looked at least a decade younger than her actual age, with hardly a line marring her skin. But that harrowing ordeal had etched lines at her mouth and a few into her forehead.

We held each other's gaze for a long, silent moment. She straightened, squaring her shoulders. "Okay." She nodded. "What do you want to know?"

"What's his name? Who is he?"

And so she told me. Patiently, evenly, she answered all of my questions. I kept my inquiries away from the private details of her life with him. I already knew he'd completely won her over at first before casting her aside like garbage. I didn't need to know anything more about that. But he had a name, now. He was a person. Not just some anonymous figure upon which I could focus all my hatred. His name was Gerard Dempsey. He was of Irish and English descent. He was a successful real estate entrepreneur and had gained his millions that way. He had one sister, no brothers and three other children, all much older than me.

I also learned that he had never contacted my mom after I was born. Never written her a letter or made a phone call, though he knew exactly where we lived. She told me I had her eyes and hair color, but that my skin, jaw and nose were his.

She offered to show me a picture—the one picture she had of him—of them together, but I declined. I didn't want to see them together, happy. Her young face full of bright ideals, unaware that he was stacking lie upon lie on top of their relationship like a house of cards.

"Did you love him?" I finally asked.

Her eyes drifted away to focus off into the distance. They took on a dreamy quality. "I did. Or rather...I loved who I thought he was, when I thought I knew everything about him."

I breathed in slowly. "Love is dangerous. Deceptive." I shook my head. "No offense, but I think it's for fools."

When she returned her gaze to me, her eyes were hard. "Mia, you are far too young to be talking like that. You sound like a bitter and lonely old lady."

I clenched my teeth. Maybe I was, on the inside. Older than my years, wasn't that what they called it?

Mom spoke again. "There are nice men out there. Lots of them. Most of them. Don't waste your life being bitter and angry about the one dud your mom screwed up on."

I froze for a moment, strangely reminded of Adam's words in the echo of my mother's. *Every single man you look at for the rest of your life is tainted by him.* I shook my head to clear it. "Why didn't you ever date again?"

She shrugged. "You were the most important thing in my life and I didn't trust my judgment enough to bring a potential loser into your life again. So I just didn't."

"And now? I've been out of the house for four years."

She nodded. "Yeah. I've been working on it," she said cryptically and then stood, gathering the plates and scooting off to the kitchen while I gazed after her thoughtfully.

I took over for Mom with the horse care and she was able to move on to fixing up the house and preparing to reopen the B and B. After a week, I'd called Heath to let him know I was staying in Anza for a while. He packed up my apartment for me. He was the best friend ever—but I also suspect that part of it had been done out of guilt for his part in what had happened between Adam and me.

My days fell into a mundane but comforting routine of waking up early, feeding the horses and cleaning out stalls, doing all the outside work, turning them out and exercising them during the cool hours of the morning.

Then, after a shower, I worked on the blog for several hours. Even with the crappy Internet connection on the ranch and my old box barely squeaking by, I still managed to put up some content every day.

But I was guarded in my posts. Much more guarded than before. I'd always been careful not to reveal geographical or personal information about myself but even so, whenever I sat down to write, I had the specter of Adam peering over my shoulder. I knew he was reading. Or maybe he no longer cared. Maybe he was too busy embarking on his new fulfilling relationship with "real woman" Lindsay.

Daily, my mom and I would congregate for lunch and swap stories, share news, both local and national, and grow closer than we'd been in a long time.

The hottest hours of the afternoon were for sitting next to the swamp cooler in the kitchen with my medical books around me, studying.

Yep. That was my exciting life in Anza, but I found myself, as the weeks passed and the date of my big test approached, feeling stronger, more self-sufficient and discovering new things about myself that I'd never explored before. I also found myself Googling alternatives for people with premed majors who didn't go to medical school. They weren't all bad—research, nursing, consulting—but they weren't my dream. And I knew I was going to have to dig in deep to find the courage to take that damn test again and face another possible failure, or else say good-bye to my dream forever.

The most surprising thing was, out of the blue one night, I wrote a letter to the Biological Sperm Donor—Gerard, I corrected myself. From now on, I was going to refer to him by his name. I knew I'd never mail it. But I'd researched and found out more about him from the information that my mom had given me. I also tried to find anything I could about my three half siblings that were almost two decades older than me. I had one half-brother, Glen, who was thirteen years older than me and two half-sisters in their late thirties.

I wrote this letter to Gerard, my father, and in it I poured out all my grief at the loss of a parent I never knew. I resented him but I also wanted to know him. And at last I let myself admit that. I wanted it, but not enough. I wanted my hatred for him to melt away so I would be free. Because my entire life I'd seen those feelings as a fortress protecting me from potential hurts and damages. Instead of a fortress, they had been a cage, holding me back.

And maybe someday, somewhere along the line, I'd finally be able to open my heart to someone, once it had healed.

Heath came up the following weekend and stayed in his old room. He'd lived with us during the last three years of high school when his own parents had thrown him out after he came out to them.

We went out at certain times of the day to catch the light just right for his photos. It was during his sunset shoot that he broached the forbidden subject.

"You heard from Drake?" he asked casually as he pivoted his camera on its tripod to get a better angle of the homestead house and the three cabins all lined up nicely alongside it.

I shook my head, following his vantage point down the long slope of our drive.

"You haven't logged in to the game in weeks. I keep looking for you. You going to quit?"

I shrugged. "There're lots of games out there. I can play something he didn't design."

"It sucks that you are going to let him drive you away from a game that you love and all your online friends. I've gotten messages from both Persephone and FallenOne saying they were worried about you."

My insides tightened and I swallowed. "Oh really? Fallen asked about me?"

"Yeah, couple nights ago. Said he was worried. Told him you were at your mom's."

"Shit," I said, squeezing my eyes closed and turning away from him to rest my arms on the ranch fence that surrounded our property. "That's all he told you? He didn't tell you his name or anything like that?"

Heath hesitated. "Why would he? He's never told us his real name."

I clenched my teeth, staring toward the dying sun. "Yeah, he had a reason for that."

"What—that he's a chick or something? Or someone famous? Remember when we all used to try to think up what movie star or famous athlete he was?"

I drew in a breath and held it. I wanted to make my voice sound as calm as I could when I told him. It wouldn't tremble or break—it would be strong, clear. "FallenOne is Adam." Shit. It had quavered. The moment I'd said his name, I'd heard a slight tremor right at the end of the second syllable.

There was a long stretch of silence. "No shit?" he said, his voice dark.

I nodded. I wished it was all just a joke.

"Well—fuck—that explains a lot, I guess."

"Like what?"

"Drake always seemed kind of familiar to me. He didn't to you?"

He'd overwhelmed me. Completely. Like the storm I often likened him to, he'd obliterated everything else around him. I shrugged.

Heath shot me a concerned look. "It really didn't end well between you two, did it?"

"I'm not going to talk about it."

He sighed. "Mia, I'm just worried. You don't look well. Your mom says you aren't eating much and you work yourself exhausted every day."

"It's good for me."

"Holding on to anger and resentment isn't."

I sighed. "You've been hanging around my mom too long."

"What did he do to you?"

I blinked and looked away. "Nothing I didn't want him to do."

His brow trembled. "Ah." Then he cleared his throat. "That's not what I meant. I mean why are you like this? I've known you for ten years and I've never *ever* seen you cry like you did that day in Irvine. You aren't eating, aren't acting normal. Are you at least going to retake your MCAT, still?"

I looked away. "The jury's still out on that decision."

He scowled. "I hope you don't give up on your dreams because some dickwad played you."

"If I don't, it's not because of him." I ground out.

"Okay. please don't kick my ass when I ask you this..."

I darted a warning glare at him. "If you have to start it out like that then maybe you shouldn't ask."

"Mia... did you fall in love with him?"

"No," I snapped, folding my arms tightly in front of me. "And even if I had, it wouldn't matter, okay? He's the one who walked out on me."

He looked pissed off. "I see."

I held up a finger and pushed it at his face. "No more talking about this shit, okay? It's over. It's the past. I have a life to get on with. No more bringing it up."

He stared at me for a long moment before he simply nodded and pulled his attention back to his camera, adjusting the tripod.

After Heath went home, falling into my normal routine again comforted me. And a week later, my mom announced gleefully over lunch, "My first Internet reservations are coming in!"

I was pleasantly surprised. Heath had just rebuilt her website the week before but there hadn't been much traffic on it.

"Yep, some people coming in for the regular rooms starting next week and the week after next, someone booked the best room in the house—Roy Rogers." The biggest separate cabin, the "luxury suite" of our ranch. Every room we had was named after a famous cowboy or cowgirl. I'd secretly named my bedroom Annie Oakley because there just weren't enough awesome cowgirls on our list.

As much as I'd shucked my cowgirl identity when I'd gone off to college, I started to feel the comfort my younger self took in being with our animals. It was a healing experience. I didn't have to worry about lies or bullshit from animals. I didn't have to worry about being double-crossed. As long as they got their food and their exercise and the occasional bit of human affection, they were happy.

A week later, Mom and I hurriedly made the finishing touches for our new guests and welcomed them in. We'd gone down to nearby Temecula and shopped at the home stores for new bedding and sheets to match our theme for the cabins.

In the Roy Rogers room, the paint smell had faded, mostly because we kept it open and aired morning and night and dusted daily—because on a ranch, there is no shortage of dust. It wasn't the penthouse suite of the Amstel Amsterdam, or the VIP suite in the Emerald Sky Luxury resort, but it was something.

Because I'd been helping my mom get our first guests checked out, I didn't get to work with the horses until mid afternoon. I'd decided to give them the day off because making them work during the sweat of the day—and July in Anza was no joke at all—would have been too cruel. But there was still work to be done. Like poop. Because hot or cold, rain or shine, horses made poop. And I had to clean it.

I was out in the stalls and then in the barn, battling flies and bored horse—Snowball, who was not interested in having poop taken out but was very interested in love from his favorite person. And who was I to resist? But after twenty minutes of this, I was getting impatient, shoving him aside to get at the poop in the sawdust.

I was hot, sweaty, bedraggled, smelling of horse crap and covered with sawdust shavings. So of course this was the moment when Mom decided to pass through the barns with our new suite guest— who had apparently just checked in—on a tour of the facility.

"Snowball, move your fat ass," I growled at the horse, giving him a good-natured slap on the bum.

"Mia, are you in here?"

"No," I answered between gritted teeth. What the hell? She had just heard me yelling at the horse.

"Our new guest is here. Come on, I just want to introduce you."

I sighed. Snowball was going to have to live with the remaining bits of poop for another day. I huffed out of the stall, placing the rake against the door but not removing my giant gardening gloves. I'd make this quick, give him a smile, a few words of welcome and a nod and be about my work. I approached my mom standing beside a tall man. As they were backlit by the afternoon sunlight, I didn't get a good look until I was too close to turn away.

But when I did finally see his face, my feet grew instant roots into the ground and I almost flopped on my face from the momentum. Because towering over my mom, a subdued smile on his face, stood Adam.

He had on jeans, tennis shoes, a casual button-down shirt and he was as gorgeous as ever. I hadn't spoken to him in over a month. Since that last heated night in St. Lucia. I'd thought I'd never see him again. Yet here he was, looking down at me with benign eyes that missed nothing. Not even the snowfall of sawdust in my hair.

My heart began to thump at the base of my throat and I swallowed, suddenly finding it difficult to breathe. What the hell was he doing here? Was he posing as my mom's newest guest? Cold panic rose up from my tight stomach. How on earth could I hide this reaction from my mom? The blood was draining from my face—I knew that much. Was he here to torment me with regret for the things I had said to him? Was he here to try and make amends?

I didn't know what to feel. So many emotions swirled inside me. I was loath to admit that one of them was a complete heart-charging thrill at seeing him again. Another was a dread, a fear. Would he expose me to my mom? Tell her about the auction—about what a terrible, bitter, child-person I was?

Mom's voice cut through my buzzing thoughts. "Here she is—this is my daughter, Mia."

Adam's gaze shot to mine like a bolt of lightning and I suddenly felt myself starting to sweat. A heat built inside me so quickly, it felt like I would combust from the inside out.

"Hi, Mia," Adam said. And I was at least thankful he didn't carry out a ruse that we didn't know each other. No false "nice to meet you." I jerked my eyes from his, which speared me, and dropped them to the ground in front of my feet.

Mom continued, completely oblivious to the tension thickening the air. "This is Mr. Drake. He'll be with us for the next week. He's preparing to hike a segment of the Pacific Crest Trail from here to Yosemite. Sometime soon."

The Pacific Crest Trail stretched from the Mexican border to Canada, tracing the crests of all the mountain ranges of the three states in between: California, Oregon and Washington. The hearty people who hiked it were either "thru-hikers," doing the entire run in seven or so months straight, or "segment-hikers" who pieced up the trail into bits and did it a little at a time, sometimes over the span of many years.

So this was the story that Adam had given my mother. He was going to do a segment hike of the PCT? What a load of bullshit. My eyes flicked back to Adam, whose smile had faded but whose face bore a certain grim self-satisfaction.

The breath I'd just drawn flew right out of me again. I shifted, putting my hands on my hips because I had no idea what else to do with them.

"Hey, Mr. Drake," I croaked out. "Welcome." My mom frowned. She'd finally noticed my weird reaction and there would be questions later, no doubt. But I feared being alone with her much less than being alone with him so I resolved to stick near my mom's side all night—and probably find lots of excuses to drive into Anza proper or even down the mountain for the next few days.

"Dinner is in two hours and I've asked Mr. Drake to join us," Mom said, throwing a pointed look at my grubby clothes.

I only nodded. I had no other words. I didn't look at Adam again—didn't have the courage for it. And as he followed my mom out of the barn, he darted one last glance my way before turning out of my view.

As soon as he was out of sight, I fell against the nearest stall door, my back sliding against it until I sat on the ground. My heart hammered like I'd run a marathon and I shook—a deep-freeze hardening my soul. The nearest horse, Whiskey, poked his head out and nudged against me. I was utterly floored by this new development.

I had just begun to move past this whole thing—or so I'd thought. But now I felt just as shivery and vulnerable as the girl who'd rushed out of the Draco Multimedia complex while sobbing the month before.

A splinter of pain passed through me as I remembered the circumstances behind that last time I'd seen him, with his arm wrapped around his former lover. Maybe Lindsay was going to come up to meet him here? Maybe he'd arranged this on purpose so he could flaunt her in my face, because that day at his office wasn't enough? Would I be able to suffer though seeing them here, together?

If it weren't for the fact that mom needed my help so much for this next week, I might have been tempted to call Heath and ask him if I could go crash on his couch until Adam left. It was inevitable that we'd have to interact with one another, but I resolved that I would try my hardest to avoid the confrontation he sought. With this tangle of unwanted emotion inside of me, I went on the rest of my poop hunt with a vengeance.

17

I T TOOK ME AN HOUR TO RECOVER FROM THE SHOCK OF SEEING him again so suddenly—and *here* of all places. It was obvious he was here to see me, and, after checking the reservation book my mom kept at her desk, I was reassured that he would be here alone. The only reason he'd leave his girlfriend behind to come up here would be to confront me. But why? What more was there to say between us that hadn't already been said?

Adam didn't seem the type to want to rub salt into the wounds. Or at least I would have thought so before that display at his office. He'd been rubbing plenty of salt then. I burned with anger at the pretense under which he was here. Whatever it took, I'd keep my mom from getting involved. With any luck, he'd leave and she'd never know that there was a history between us.

I didn't want to talk to him and resolved that I wouldn't, except to exchange shallow pleasantries for my mom's sake. I had no desire to find out what his current dating status was or if he was sleeping with Lindsay again. The very thought of it hurt like a bitch.

After showering and doing my hair, I helped Mom put the finishing touches on dinner by tossing the organic, handpicked salad. She was an excellent cook—part of the entire picture of her livelihood. She made breakfasts for her guests every day, creatively concocting new and special repasts. Breakfast was her specialty, but her dinners were damn good, too. When I was little, she'd gone to culinary school during my summer vacations to get better at it.

Dinner was beyond awkward. The only one not affected by the silent uneasiness was my mom. Adam and I did not talk to each other. The entire conversation was conducted through my mother.

"Mia's a medical student."

"Not yet," I corrected her.

"Well, she will be once she aces this big test that's coming up."

At least Adam didn't ask me sham questions that he already knew the answers to—like he had the first few times we'd met. He did mention that UCI had a good medical school and that I should consider applying to it. It was already on my list. Though the thought of attending school in the same city where his company was located had greatly lowered it in ranking on my list of top schools. UC Davis, in northern California, was starting to look better and better.

"I understand you have some wonderful back country around here, even off the PCT," Adam said to Mom.

"Yes, great for hiking or riding. Do you ride, Mr. Drake?" Mom asked.

He laughed. "No, not at all. I think I can count on one hand the number of times I've been on horseback."

If he was angling to get a guided ride from me, I'd have to be quick on my feet to deflect the request. My mind raced with excuses

I could come up with. Sore throat? I had to study? A horse had stepped on my foot?

Mom said, "If you're interested, we have some great horses for beginners and Mia used to take guests on sunset rides. Maybe I can coax her to do one for you if that sounds like something you'd like to do." Shit, shit, shit. Shut *up,* Mom.

Adam fixed his dark gaze on me for a moment and my eyes stayed glued to my plate, shoveling in my food as fast as I possibly could. "That sounds like a wonderful idea, but how about a hike this evening, Mia? Do you hike?"

I took a long time to answer, my mind running through at least a half a dozen more excuses—all lame—before I spit out probably the lamest one of them all. "I'm a runner."

"Perfect, so am I."

Fuck. I should have known he would say that. As always, he'd thought a few steps ahead of me and had been ready.

"I would only slow you down on a run," I said, anxious to evade this.

Adam smiled, gazing into my eyes knowingly. "It would be fun. Do you know of any great views?"

Mom, of course, had to put her two cents in. "Why don't you take him up to that vista spot you love so much?"

Sometimes I wish I could tell her to shut the hell up. I gritted my teeth and darted Adam a murderous look. He looked supremely satisfied, like a bear that had just dug into a picnic basket.

An hour later, I was in my room changing into my running gear when my mom knocked on the door and came in. "Did I put you on the spot back there? Are you okay with taking him out for a run?"

I hesitated. Here was my chance to back out. Maybe I could tell her I thought Adam looked suspicious, like I didn't feel comfortable being alone with him. That second half, at least, was true. But it might make Mom suspect something and I'd really prefer she not find out the truth. Beyond that, Adam would know why I'd bowed out and he'd already called me a coward once. My pride was on the line. And lastly, that curiosity beast was nipping at my thoughts, asking endless questions. Likely I'd be able to get some answers when we were alone. I shrugged noncommittally. "Sure."

"Mia, I don't know what's been up with you lately, but can I ask you to put in a little extra effort with this guest? He's a CEO for a company down in Orange County and he's mentioned possibly doing some retreats up here for his employees. I know you don't schmooze, but just...you know, turn on your sunny personality. I know it's in there somewhere."

"Yeah, sure," I grunted, already preoccupied with what this run was going to entail.

There was no way I was going to outrun him. I'd seen him move, after all, and he was like a human cheetah. Maybe I could lose him on one of the upper trails, but Mom might get pissed at having her first cabin guest after the renovation dying of dehydration while wandering the barren hills of the Cahuilla Mountains in search of an oasis. Maybe I could get away with just pushing him into a cactus patch.

I resigned myself to the fact that I was stuck with him for the run, but that didn't mean I had to be nice to him.

We set off along the edge of our property into the long shadows of early evening in midsummer. I had a snakebite kit strapped in a fanny pack around my waist and a six-foot, two-hundred-pound shadow clipping closely at my heels. I scooted over to the far right on the trail, hoping he'd go around and ahead. His legs were longer and his stride much bigger than mine so he'd be free to open up if he were in front.

However, having to stare at his muscular back and rear, his gorgeously cut legs in his running shorts was not my first choice either. I just needed him off my heels.

After a few beats, he moved to go around me but then matched his pace with mine. I was going at a good clip, which ended up being an easy jog for him. He wasn't even breaking a sweat.

As soon as we were out of view of the house, I stopped, bent, and put my hands on my knees. He stopped, too, and of course he wasn't even winded. Asshole.

"What's wrong?" he said.

And I straightened, shooting him a death glare. "What's wrong? How about you being here in the first place?"

He handed me his water bottle, which I waved away and his eyes took on that mischievous, calculated look of his. "I don't suppose you'd believe it was a coincidence?"

I shook my head. "Why are you here?"

He took a long swig from his water bottle. "Can't we at least walk while we talk?"

I dramatically swept my arms toward the path in front of us as if to sarcastically say, "After you."

He started to walk and he again matched his pace to mine so that we walked shoulder to shoulder.

"I talked to Heath last week," he said in answer to my question.

My fists tightened at my sides. "He needs to mind his own fucking business."

Adam shot me a look and then focused again on the trail. We were gaining some elevation now, moving to a higher vantage point where we would be able to look down on the little valley that contained my mom's ranch and the neighboring properties. At sunset, the sky was incomparably beautiful, all magentas and purples against the ruddy desert sand. I came up here often at this time of day to calm myself, to try and ease my troubled thoughts of the day. I'd been doing it for years. And now I was taking Adam to my special spot. The flame of irritation singed me.

"Maybe he was being a good friend. A concerned friend."

"What has him so concerned? If he told you that I was shriveling into nothingness up here while pining away for you, then he's a damn liar," I said with a bit more heat and vehemence than I would have liked.

He walked for a few beats but didn't look at me. "Not at all."

"So what did he say to you?"

"He said that you had moved away. That you were thinking of backing out of your exam."

I bit the inside of my cheek. Fucking Heath. He had forced this confrontation, preying on Adam's conscience. Adam wouldn't even have shown up if he didn't feel responsible. "And why do you care whether or not I take the test? I thought you were through with me."

He hesitated. "Maybe I feel responsible for your plans not going through."

I shot him a sharp look. "Well, don't. It's my life, my decision."

"So you *are* going to take the test?"

I hesitated, bought time by coughing into my fist. "Of course. I already paid for the damn thing and it wasn't cheap." It was true, after all. I'd kept pushing it off but finally decided to commit myself by sending in the registration. The date was getting closer and I still didn't know if I'd make the trip to show up.

"Good," he said quietly.

My chin came up. "Yeah, so now that your guilt is alleviated, you can get back to your life down there." He was quiet, but I just couldn't shut up. Man, I wish I had shut up. "I mean, your show of contrition is touching and all, but I've got other things to take care of around here rather than babysit a fake guest and get my mom's hopes up that people are actually interested in staying here again."

He stopped walking and turned to me, clearly insulted. "I was honestly interested in staying here and I *am* planning a segment hike."

I shook my head. "*You* are taking a month away from work and your computer to do that?"

He shrugged. "Maybe I'm taking longer."

I laughed in disbelief. "And maybe I'm the Queen of England."

He shot me a heated glare and we walked in silence until he hit the summit of the trail—a ledge that overlooked the valley below us. We weren't really high up, but high enough to get a nice view of the sunset, the high desert landscape all bathed in angry reds and oranges.

Adam stood, squinting over the canyon. I glanced up at him, memorizing his handsome face. A dry desert wind blew up here, stirring our clothing and hair. He spoke in a quiet, almost reverent voice. "So since we are going to be on the same premises together for the next few days, and for your mom's sake, can we call a truce?"

I folded my arms. "I'll be perfectly nice to you. Just stop trying to get me alone because we really don't have anything to say to each other."

"Really. Nothing at all?" he said mildly.

I shifted, hating how petty I sounded. I cleared my throat and looked down. "Except that I honestly hope that you and your family are well."

He glanced at me and returned to admiring the view. "Thank you. They are."

I took a deep breath and let it go. "And...I hope you do find happiness. I—I never said that before but I've wanted to. I hope..." and my voice died out. I wasn't going to wish him happy with Lindsay because, let's face it, I wasn't Mother Teresa. I couldn't go that far.

He turned to me, waiting for me to say more and when I didn't, he spoke. "Maybe I'm already happy."

Pain seized me. I couldn't look at him. "Then great," I said in a tiny voice.

He turned and watched me closely. "And you?"

I shrugged. "I'm getting there." Another long pause, then I cleared my throat. "We'd better get going. It will be dark soon."

I turned to leave but was brought up short when he reached out for my arm to stay me. His touched burned my skin and I flinched. I turned back to him and he said, "I was serious. I took a leave of absence from the company."

To say I was shocked was an understatement. I opened my mouth and then closed it. "For how long?"

He shrugged. "As long as it takes to prove to myself that I can do it."

"And how is that working out for you? Any withdrawal symptoms yet?"

He did not look amused and I realized the inappropriateness of my joke. I looked away. "There you go again, Mia," I said. "Putting your foot in it as usual."

He ran a hand through his hair and looked at me. The boyish vulnerability I saw there almost ripped my heart, still beating, right out of my chest.

"I'm glad you did it," I finally said. "And I'm glad you're happy. And..." Deep breath, curled fists. "I'm glad you've found someone."

And with that, I turned and started my run. Maybe if I caught him off guard—and while running downhill, I could get far enough ahead of him that I could avoid him for the rest of the night. I soon heard his feet behind me, hitting with regular steps that matched mine.

When we finally hit the bottom of the hill and flat land, he stopped me again. We were both breathing heavily. "Are you?"

"What?"

"Are you really glad I've found someone?"

Hell no. I shrugged. There was no way I could answer that question in any way that would preserve my dignity.

"Emilia, I'm not with anyone."

My breath stuttered. "Excuse me?"

"There hasn't been anyone since you. I'm *not* with Lindsay."

My head spun. "But—"

"I know it's hard to believe because of what you saw. But I was pissed off, okay? Lindsay had come down to the complex to have lunch, but when my assistant said you were there, I was getting rid of her. I thought you'd come to talk. When I saw that package on the table, well, I wasn't thinking straight. I did that to Lindsay to purposefully hurt you."

My breathing hitched. "Mission accomplished, then," I said in a falsely bright voice. But I was dizzy with the wave of relief that washed over me at that news. I almost toppled. Relief came first, then crackling anger. How many times had I replayed that scene in my mind? How many times had I pictured them together as lovers—each time sinking a knife deeper into my heart? I fought for breath, feeling close to tears again, to my utter humiliation.

"I'm sorry," he breathed, his brow creasing at my reaction.

I didn't reply. I doubt I could have even if I'd wanted to.

"Emilia—"

And he would have reached for my arm, but I stepped away and ran all the way back to the house with him close behind. I laid it out flat—ran as fast as I could and he stayed on my heels easily.

When we stopped, I didn't run for the door. Mia the coward would have done something like that. Instead I lingered at the front porch, glancing at the glow coming from behind the blinds in the window. It wasn't yet dark enough for Mom to turn on the porch light so we were masked in the violet darkness of dusk.

I didn't say anything but I didn't move from my spot, either, still breathing heavily. In spite of the churning emotions, I liked having him here with me. It beat the hell out of that distant, empty ache. This pain was sharper, more acute, but he was *here*. Standing close enough that I could feel the heat radiating off of him in his sweat-soaked shirt.

He took a hesitant step toward me. God, I wanted him to touch me. I wanted to touch him. I turned my face to the side, unwilling to look into his intent eyes. "Hurting you wasn't the only reason I did it," he finally said in a hoarse voice.

Pain radiated in my chest whenever I breathed. "Oh?"

"I wanted to prove to myself—and you—that you cared." He moved a step closer, reached up to run his thumb along my jaw and tilt my head toward him. I backed away and he followed until I came up against the pole that held up the overhang of the front porch. His face was inches from mine and my heart beat on every micrometer of my skin. "You do care, don't you, Emilia?"

I closed my eyes and swallowed, trying to summon up every ounce of anger and annoyance I felt for this man. But his thumb— that tiny touch along my jaw, shifted to glide over my lips, making me crazy, awakening that deep hunger inside. I cared. Of course I fucking cared. I hadn't been able to rip my mind away from him in the month we'd been apart from each other. He was the first thing I thought of every morning, the last every night and he slipped effortlessly into most waking thoughts during the moments between.

"I never said I didn't care," I finally said, lamely.

"You never said you did, either."

My eyes found his, I shivered and he pulled his hand away. "I care," I whispered.

His head closed the distance on mine and he pushed my head back with the force of the contact. Our mouths met, eagerly tasting each other. My body rose up to meet his, my hands clamping around his neck to hold him to me. With a low groan, he plunged his tongue into my mouth and together our tongues danced. Desire pervaded me, right to the deepest center. I wanted the touch of his mouth, his hands, his body. I wanted the words to go along with them. I wanted to know *he* cared.

When he reached for my waist, I pulled my head away though everything in me screamed in protest. I put my hands on his damp, hard chest. I wasn't ready for more. Not yet. Maybe not ever. I needed time to think. Time to breathe.

He was breathing heavily again and his arousal pressed against me. I trembled. My body wanted to answer that siren's call. Before, I'd only imagined what it could be like between us. But now, I knew exactly what kind of pleasure I could expect in his arms, his bed. It took every ounce of willpower to resist. "You only came because you felt guilty about my not taking the test," I said.

He hesitated. "No. But it did give me the excuse."

"Since when have you needed an excuse?"

He shook his head. "I've never done this before."

My eyes held his. "I can tell."

"Emilia—I owe you an apology for what happened at my office. It was an asshole thing to do and I knew it the minute I did it. And I am so damn sorry."

I drew in a shivery breath. I was so confused. As usual, Hurricane Adam was stirring up this swirling force of nature around me, catching me up in high-speed winds and dangerous tidal currents. I needed to think about what he was telling me. I needed a quiet place, to be alone. I shook and his arms tightened around me when he felt it. "Good night, Adam," I said in the quickening darkness.

He paused, then released me, stepped back with clear reluctance. "Good night," he said in the faintest hint of a whisper.

I fumbled in through the front door on shaky legs, avoiding my mom's inquiries about the run with a few grunts and "It went great's." Then I was off to curl up with a study book on my bed under a bright white reading lamp. I didn't even pretend to study. There was no way. I immediately tossed the book to the floor and pressed the heels of my hands to my eyes, unable to get Adam's words out of my mind.

I *did* care. It was true. And he knew damn well the truth of that. But how *much* did I care? And how much did *he* care? What was this? Could it be...? *No.* No, it couldn't be because I had refused to allow it. He'd hurt me. That stunt with Lindsay had gutted me and that was what scared me most of all. I'd given him the power to do it to me. Loving someone meant giving them the power to crush you—putting the tenderest, most delicate part of yourself in the palm of someone else's hand.

I dammed the unshed tears under my lids, berating myself for the wimpy crybaby I'd become since this had all started. He had no right to come barreling in to wreak havoc on my emotions like this. Just when I thought I might be able to sort things out. Just when I'd been trying to pull things together, become a stronger person.

He appeared to be doing the same thing with his life—forcing himself to walk away from work must have been painful. It was hard for me to imagine him without his cell phone or laptop. Why had he taken that step? Had he been as affected by our time together as I had? Were these changes in response to what I'd said to him?

I shut my eyes tight, hating this chaos swirling inside me, groping to find some semblance of order. He had no right at all to do this to me. And how was I supposed to withstand the next six days with him around?

The solution, I decided, would come in being cordial but distant. Keeping him at a distance would protect me. I'd let him get too close tonight but I wouldn't make that mistake again. I could never allow anyone to have that kind of power over me ever again.

My resolve strengthened and with a sigh, I turned off my light, rolled to my side and lay there for the next three hours, far from sleep.

18

AFTER BREAKFAST—DURING WHICH, MERCIFULLY, WE DID not speak much—Adam got into his new hybrid electric car and sped off toward Anza proper, saying he wanted to explore the town.

In all honesty, I didn't know what could possibly keep him longer than an hour or so. Anza was a small community perched on the edge of the Cahuilla Indian Reservation. Other than rugged outdoors and the Pacific Crest Trail, which bisected town, Anza had little more to offer the casual tourist. Perhaps I'd get Mom to suggest a visit to the Anza-Borrego State Park tomorrow. That would keep him out of my hair for the entire day if he set out after breakfast.

I helped Mom clean up the breakfast dishes and she had a strange smile on her face. I asked her what was up. "Mr. Drake is a really good-looking man," she said in answer.

I shot a wary look at her. Had she seen what had happened on the porch the night before? "Yeah, I guess so."

"You guess so? What, are you blind? He's, what, almost thirty or so? If he were a few years older…"

Eww. Mom had the hots for Adam? That was gross. "Mom…"

"I'm just saying. If a guy like that doesn't get your motor running, then maybe you should go back and talk to Dr. Marbrow for a few sessions, find out what's going on with your natural urges."

I blew out a breath of disgust. "I refuse to talk about 'natural urges' with you. And don't you dare decide to go all cougar on me, please!"

She shrugged and laughed at me. Shaking my head, I left the kitchen for the stables, ready to throw myself into my work for the day.

He was gone most of the morning and did not return until after lunch. Not like I was keeping track or anything. Though, I might have glanced down the road a few thousand times while I was working with the horses in the arena.

On his way back in, at around two o'clock, he took the long way to his cabin, walking near the arena where I was lunging Tate. I had on my jeans, boots and my old hat.

He smiled and waved. "Howdy, cowgirl."

I waved in return.

A few hours later, my mom told me that she had seen him take off on a trail and asked me to run some clean towels over to the cabin. Mom usually did this job and I really, *really* wished she would do it today. The thought of going into his cabin—of possibly being seen entering his bedroom…

So I ran over as quickly as I could with the stack, knocked on the door, waited and knocked again. When no answer was forthcoming, I used the master key with some relief, and entered.

I left the fresh towels on the counter in the bathroom while I gathered up a few of the used ones and draped them over my arm.

I collected some empty water bottles on the desk to put in the recycling, figuring I'd better take the opportunity to tidy up a little. As I grabbed one of the bottles, I inadvertently knocked over a stack of papers that fell to the floor. Cursing, I threw the towels and bottles just outside the front door and then went back inside to pick up the papers.

I gathered them and then reordered them, forcing myself not to violate his privacy by looking. Many of them were trail guides and local information, some flyers and menus from the few diners in town.

But I started when I saw the unfolded sheaf of papers with letterhead from Pohlman's Law Office —a lawyer whose name I recognized. Not long ago, I'd looked over similar paperwork handed to me by my mother. The letterhead of my mom's lawyer.

This was the same lawyer—one of only two in town—who had officiated the paperwork for my mom's anonymous benefactor. The one who had invested in the ranch as a silent partner, taking a mere twenty percent of any profits accrued, if and when we ever stood to make a profit.

My hands shook. Because now I had to find out why Adam had my mom's paperwork. But as I read on, I discovered that it wasn't Mom's paperwork. It was Adam's. Because Adam was Mom's benefactor. And at the bottom of the page, his signature said so, and the date, showing he'd signed those papers today.

My heart thumped so hard it was painful. The deal had been initiated before the auction. Weeks before we'd ever met in person. I felt like the coyote in that old cartoon who'd had the floor sawed out from under him. He stood there waiting—waiting for the fall. And the room spun from my disorientation and my hands shook.

I dropped the paperwork onto the desk and scurried out of that room as fast as I possibly could, stooping to pick up the towels and bottles. But I wasn't fast enough because Adam stepped onto the porch at that moment and I jumped so hard I dropped everything. Towels went flying and bottles went bouncing.

"Here, let me get those," he said.

"No!" I shrieked, still shaking. "No. I've got it." And I bustled around like a freak trying to pick up every last thing while he watched me with the most obvious puzzlement I'd ever seen on his face.

"Emilia, what's wrong?"

"Mia—" My mom showed up right behind me. "I'll get the towels." And with a huff of frustration, and still shaking as if it was forty below outside instead of a toasty ninety-five, I shoved them into my mom's arms and walked away.

"I gotta...I need to be alone for a while," I gasped and then headed out toward the front of the house. What I really wanted to do was get in my car and screech the hell out of the driveway, but I wasn't about to stop everything, go inside and start searching for my car keys. So I set foot to the highway instead.

I walked for about ten minutes before I noticed a long shadow moving up behind me. The way it moved, the way it gained on me even when I stepped up my pace, I knew exactly who it was.

I stopped so abruptly that he almost ran into me. We were standing on the roadside along an empty lot. I ducked through the ranch-style fence into the field. Of course, he followed me.

"What has you so freaked, Emilia?"

I kept walking, this time, not trying to outpace him but the words were rolling around in my head so that I could hardly round them up to form a coherent sentence.

Then I turned on him. "*You* tell *me*," I ground out.

He shook his head, utterly confused.

"Why do you have paperwork in there declaring yourself as my mother's secret investor?"

His mouth set. "You went through my papers?"

"I knocked them on the floor because I'm a fucking clumsy housekeeper. If you didn't want me to find them, you shouldn't have left them sitting out there like that. It's not like they were locked in a document safe."

He shifted his stance, looking away. I could tell he was pissed. So the fuck what if his secret was out? It was just another one in his long string of secrets. "I set them down there because I just got them today, in town, from the lawyer. I had no idea you'd be going into the room." He looked back at me with narrowed eyes. "You were never supposed to see those."

I tried to breathe while gesturing wildly with my hands. "I don't get—Why did you—how could you have known—when—?"

And I would have continued on like that if he hadn't put his hands on my shoulders, pulling me to face him. "Take a deep breath and calm down. You are shaking like you saw your own ghost."

And I was. And no matter how hard I tried, I couldn't control it.

"Emilia," he said again, this time quietly and I looked in his eyes.

And then I scowled and smacked his chest with the back of my hand. "You tell me everything now, Adam Drake, or... or I'll beat the shit out of you."

He caught my hands and held them inside his easily. And then, he pulled one of my curled fists to his mouth and kissed it.

I yanked away from him, tears immediately springing from my eyes.

"I'll tell you everything," he said in an even voice. "If you promise me you won't flip your shit when I do."

My voice was as shaky as the rest of me. I grabbed the insides of my elbows. "I can't promise you that."

He swallowed and looked away, actually looking afraid. Definitely an emotion I had never seen cross his face. Sighing, he ran a hand through his hair.

"Even though we only physically met two months ago, I've known you for over a year. I told you in St. Lucia that—that you meant something to me. I read your blog all the time. I liked your articles, your insights. You're very witty, and I looked forward to my blog feed updating with your articles, even when you were mocking my game or lauding the competition."

He shook his head, remembering some past frustration. "Sometimes you really pissed me the fuck off and other times I laughed so hard my sides felt like they'd split open. But—beyond that, I really felt I knew you. Especially when we started spending so much time together in game. I looked forward to those times. It was like a bright spot during a dark day smothered in work and responsibilities. I couldn't wait to log in and share laughs with the group. I enjoyed them all, but with you—" He took in a deep breath and exhaled. "It was different."

He shot me a look. "But then you wrote the Manifesto. You already know how much I hated it because I argued every single point of it with you for hours. The whole idea of the auction offended the hell out of me. You know the reasons why I feel the way I do about women resorting to selling their bodies."

I looked away and he hesitated. He released my hands and cleared his throat. "And I just had to know, you know? What would drive you to do this? I had this image of you in my mind as this self-possessed, funny, mature, very intelligent, modern woman and then you put up the Manifesto and I just...." He blew out a breath, shaking his head.

"In my gut I knew it had to be something else—that you were desperate for a reason even though you never told me that there were financial issues behind it beyond the cost of medical school." His gaze sharpened. "So I had you investigated."

Those words hit me like a blow. "What do you mean, 'investigated'? You mean like a PI walking around with my picture asking questions about my past?"

He looked long and hard at me. "No. I just had a buddy run some financial history on you. And your mom. And I figured it out. So I set the wheels in motion for a charity organization I'm associated with, Golden Shield Group, to help her out in a way that would have absolutely nothing to do with the auction."

Thoughts were writhing inside my head. My interior had transformed into a howling gale that threatened to tear at my soul. I swallowed a sob, turned from him and began walking.

For two steps, he let me go, then he followed. "Emilia—"

I stopped, putting my head in my hands, and began to pace in front of him. "How many more secrets are there, Adam? It's like you're a fucking onion with layer upon layer of lie. First you win the auction, but you don't bother to tell me you never want to have sex with me and so you drag it out between us, leading me to believe it would happen even though you had no intention of it ever happening. Then I find out that we've actually known each other way longer than I thought and now *this.*" I could hardly get it out. The betrayal threatened to suffocate me.

Adam followed my movements, his eyes dark with worry. "This is it. You know everything now."

I shook my head. "Why did you bother with this entire charade?"

He rubbed his jaw. "Because I couldn't help it. I never wanted you to go through with this. I told you—I never intended for it to go so far. But—" He hesitated and took a step toward me, but I could tell he really didn't want to say any more.

"But what?"

He steeled himself and when he spoke, his voice was quiet. "But I lost control. I couldn't help it." He closed his eyes. "I'm not proud of that fact. But whatever this is between us got a lot bigger than me very quickly. I couldn't stop thinking about you from one time to the next and I kept telling myself that I'd cut things off the next time and the next time never came because every time I was with you I discovered I wanted you more. And not just in my bed, Emilia, though that part was driving me crazy."

I stopped pacing, my arms folded in front of my chest. I listened to him but could not look at him. He spoke again. "I wanted *more* and I've never wanted that from any other woman *ever.* I wanted to spend all night watching movies with you or taunting you with irrelevant hints about the game or arguing over which version of the first *Star Wars* trilogy is better or having you taunt me about how my taste in music is exactly like your mother's."

He paused and I finally looked at him. I wish I hadn't. Emotion was written on every feature. His eyes pinned mine down, dared me to look away. "Every minute I spent with you made me want a hundred minutes more."

I extricated my gaze from his. My eyes stung and emotions threatened to bubble up from my chest. I couldn't catch my breath. He moved to stand in front of me and, slowly, carefully, he placed his hands on my shoulders. "I'm going to say something right now that I know is going to scare the shit out of you because it scares the shit out of me. But I have to say it." He paused, waiting for me to look at him. But I knew what he was going to say. And I didn't want to hear it. Finally my eyes met his.

"Please, don't," I whispered.

He closed his eyes, clearly disappointed. When he spoke, his voice was shaky. "I love you, Emilia. I love you so goddamned much that I can't breathe when I don't know where you are or how you are doing. This last month has been torture. I wonder if it's possible to have room in my heart for anything else but these feelings."

I couldn't respond, just shook my head. I wanted him to stop talking and I wanted him to never stop.

He cleared his throat and continued. "If this past month without you has taught me nothing else, it's shown me what I want. I want—I need— you in my life. If I have to, I'll wait as long as it takes to get that."

I put a hand to my forehead, tears coating my cheeks now. I'd never cried in front of him before, but now my barriers were so brittle, so fragile that I seemed near tears at every moment.

Anger burned at my cheeks, the base of my throat. I was so pissed at what he was doing to me. With those words he'd seized control again—like he always did—declaring what my future would be. He'd wait as long as it took but that meant that, ultimately, he'd get what he wanted. And he was a man who didn't settle for anything less.

I stepped back from his hold, my fists balled. "Fuck you, Adam Drake," I hissed. "I never asked for you to come into my life and arrange things. I never needed you to save me!"

His head tilted in that way he had of studying me, his eyes calculating. This outburst had not been a surprise to him. He swallowed, squared his shoulders.

"No. Probably you didn't," he said so quietly I could barely hear him over the raging, wild twister of emotions swirling inside of me. "But I sure needed you to save me."

And with that, he turned and walked away. And every part of me wanted to throw myself after him, wanted to wrap my arms around him with all of my strength and pull his body against mine.

Instead I doubled over and sobbed, pain wracking me from forehead to ankle. I sobbed so hard that my head felt like it would split open. I sobbed so hard that I could barely catch my breath, gasping like a diver on an empty tank. The hurt was too much, too intense.

Those words. Those words every woman dreamed of hearing from a wonderful man like Adam had made me sob instead. Because I doubted I had what it took to ever live up to them. To ever be able to return those sentiments. Because Adam wasn't the one who was empty inside. *I* was.

***

By the time I made it back to the house, it was well after dark. Adam's car was still in the driveway. Mom had made and served dinner—to which she had apparently invited him, because they sat at the table over their empty plates, talking and sipping wine.

I tried to file past the dining room unnoticed but Mom stopped me. "Mia, I made you a plate. Come eat!"

I stood in the doorway, aware that I looked like complete shit. I had dust and tear tracks all down my cheeks, swollen eyes and nose and dried snot all down the front of my shirt. I refused to look at Adam, who was apparently fascinated by his own empty plate.

"I'm just gonna go take a shower and hit the hay."

Mom frowned. "Are you—?"

"Yeah, I'm fine." I cut her off with a significant glance at Adam's bowed head.

She didn't look convinced. "Oh, okay. Well, Mr. Drake let me know that he had some business come up. He's going to have to check out early in the morning."

My eyes shot to Adam's and we held each other's gaze for a long moment. My heartbeat came with increasingly sharp, stabbing twinges.

My voice was barely above a whisper. "I'm sorry to hear that." I cleared my throat. "Excuse me." And I withdrew, heading straight for the shower.

I turned the water temperature up as high as I could tolerate it. I needed it to wash away the numbness, the painful emptiness inside me. Tomorrow he'd be gone and this time I'd likely never see him again. By rejecting him, by allowing him to go, he'd know that I wanted him to get on with his life. Without me.

I thought about his accusations, about the reasons why I couldn't let him in. I knew it was because I was certain he'd hurt me. He'd leave me. All men leave. And he would too. Just like the Bio—Just like Gerard. *Every single man you look at for the rest of your life is tainted by him.* I was agonizingly aware of the truth in his words. Adam was not Gerard. Adam was not married, was not using me. Adam wanted more. Had just told me he was in love with me and, for all that meant, I honestly felt he believed it.

Adam was not Gerard. And there were many men in the world who weren't. And I had to stop believing, in my childish way, that because one didn't want me—because Gerard had rejected me before I was even born—that everyone else would, too. I had to find the courage to believe it and follow a path to happiness according to that new belief.

I stayed under that pulsing hot spray until it ran tepid and Mom banged on the door in protest because there was no hot water for the dishes.

"Mia," she said when I got out, wrapping my robe around my dripping body.

"I'll be fine, Mom."

"Our guest...Mr. Drake—"

I panicked, heart racing. "Did he leave already?" I grabbed her arm with my urgent need to know.

Mom wrested it free from my grip and frowned. "No. I told you—tomorrow morning. You two already knew each other, didn't you?"

I pulled back, turned and walked into my room. Of course, she followed me. "Mia, is he the guy you've been seeing?"

I stopped, that same old muscle knotting between my shoulder blades. I sighed. "Yes."

"You know I'm a shitty judge of character, so you shouldn't trust me as far as you can throw me, but—"

I turned. "Stop blaming yourself, Mom. Stop doubting yourself. You made one mistake and you shouldn't beat yourself up for it for the rest of your life."

Her face set into grim lines. "Wise words that *you* should live by. You shouldn't be basing your entire life on my mistake, either."

I slumped onto my bed and looked at her. I took in a shaky breath. "I'm scared."

She sank onto the bed next to me and put her arms around my shoulders. "Growing up is a scary thing. I think I know why he came up here and I think I know what decision you are scared of making. And the only thing I can tell you is that the decision is yours and yours alone to make. But consider me. I've been alone for a long time by choice and I'd rather you found someone who makes you happy. Mia, if you love him, don't choose to be alone."

*If you love him...*I rested my head against her shoulder and closed my eyes, that pain throbbing deep inside me again. I sighed, knowing the truth of her words.

***

In nothing more than my nightshirt and underwear, I stood on his doorstep in the cool desert night, shaking but not from the chill. In the distance, I could hear a pack of coyotes calling to each other, and the ubiquitous chirps of crickets.

There was no light coming from under his door and as it wasn't very late, I was concerned. As far as I knew from the nights we'd spent together, he was not one to retire early. But maybe he was tired tonight.

Well, tough shit, I'd wake him up, then. This couldn't wait. I reached up and knocked loudly on the door, listening carefully for footsteps to approach on the other side. But there was complete silence.

I glanced at the window. The curtains had not been completely pulled to cover it so I pressed my face against it, cupping my hands to look inside. And I couldn't see a damned thing because it was so dark.

"Adam?" I called through the window giving it a bang with my fist and then waited. Nothing.

For long moments I refused to let myself believe that he wasn't on the other side of that door. I knocked again. Called again. My stomach twisted until it threatened nausea. Oh God—Oh God! He'd left. I gasped for breath. He'd packed up his stuff and gone even though he told Mom he wouldn't be leaving until the morning. He'd driven away while I was in the shower. *Fuck.*

I had to go after him. There was no other way. I could chase him down to OC tomorrow but who knew where he'd be or how I could find him? I didn't have his number because it was in the contacts of that damned phone I'd given back to him. I had his e-mail, but he'd just told me he was going without e-mail contact during his break from work.

I knew where he lived and could go to his house, but if he was planning a leave of absence from work, who knew where he'd be tomorrow—maybe on a plane to somewhere far away?

Tears threatened at the realization that he was gone. The tiniest of voices in the back of my head asked what if I never saw him again? What if I never heard his voice? Or felt his arms tighten around me? What if I never knew love like this ever again?

Nearly paralyzed with grief I spun and pressed my spine flat against his door, my mind racing to come up with a plan. I'd run and grab a pair of jeans and my keys. I'd get myself down the mountain *tonight.* He was two hours away. I'd bang on his door at one in the morning if I had to.

Shit. I struggled to breathe, tears coating my cheeks now. How could this be happening? My back slid along the door until I sat at his doorstep. I pressed my face to my knees, helpless with the loss. I'd only just managed to acknowledge that I could have these feelings—that the world would not implode if I allowed myself to love a man.

This man. This wonderful man. He was gone and I'd paid dearly for my stubbornness. This love had cost me more than three-quarters of a million dollars. It had cost me my heart.

And there was no buying it back—at any price. It belonged to him. *Forever.*

If he still wanted it after I'd shoved him away. Fool, Mia. *Coward.*

I sobbed into my hands, unable to find the strength to follow through with my plan. The will was draining out of me and threatened to leave me in a pool of misery right here on the porch of this little cabin. My shoulders shook and I was thankful that there was no one out here to hear me wailing like a baby.

And God only knows how long I would have allowed myself to sit there, a pathetic, weeping mess, if I hadn't heard the scuff of shoes stepping across the porch, coming to a stop right beside me. I looked down at a pair of big feet in sneakers—the same ones Adam had worn when we'd gone running a couple nights before.

I froze but I kept my face covered. He didn't move for a moment and then sank onto a knee to look into my face.

"Don't you think you've done enough of that for one day?"

My breath was painful in my chest and my head bounced back against the door behind me. I looked at him through swollen eyes as, humiliatingly, I hiccupped. "I thought you left."

He frowned. "Tomorrow. I was feeling restless tonight. Went for a little walk."

I stared at him dumbly, unable to find the words to match this jumble of feelings inside me. They were tangled, like spiderwebs all sticky and matted inside my chest.

We stared at each other for a long, tense moment and I found that I was barely breathing. My chest would rise just enough to catch a mouthful of air before it blew back out again. His gaze intensified.

"Do you want to come in or would you rather sit out here?"

Without a word, I snuffled and struggled to my feet. Adam rose and opened the door, which, I only then realized, was unlocked. He flipped on a light and held the door for me, as if unwilling to turn his back on me for fear that I might bolt out into the night again.

And yeah, I might have been inclined in that direction, but he blocked my easy escape, so I inched into the cabin.

I threw a glance around the room, saw the stack of books on his nightstand, one opened and facedown on the bed, *Segment Hiker's Guide to the Pacific Crest Trail.* My eyes darted back to where he waited, just inside the closed door.

My entire body started to shake—like an unattractive shivery kind of shake. He watched me from the doorway, attentive to my every move but standing stiffly, unmoving.

Those dark eyes gave nothing of his feelings away. He was waiting for me to do the talking. *I* was the one who'd been blubbering like an idiot on his porch, after all.

I still had no idea what I was going to say. I took a deep breath and asked him a question instead. "Why? Why did you come into my life and completely wreck everything I knew? I thought I was happy. I thought I didn't need anyone..." My voice faded.

His lips turned up in a humorless smile. "I could ask you the exact same thing."

I mopped at my cheeks with the back of my hand. "I've done more crying today than I have in the past ten years combined. I'm not this much of a sniveling idiot—I swear I'm not." I put my hands over my face. "I just—I don't know what to do."

He paused, shifted his weight so that he leaned a sturdy shoulder against the door. "Yes, you do."

I dropped my hands and shook my head mutely.

"Come here, Emilia."

And I did. I walked straight into his arms. And he pulled me to him and the tears came again. He kissed my hair, his arms tightening.

My head fell against his shoulder and my arms slid around his waist. And I breathed him in, feelings of desire and belonging coursing through me. His arms felt so good around me, so solid, so real.

My voice trembled as I took a deep breath and finally spoke. "I need you," I said. His mouth moved to my neck and he kissed me there, bolts of electricity shooting down every nerve connected with that spot. It had taken everything in me to admit it...because I'd led my entire life until that very second firmly believing that I didn't need anyone—not a goddamn soul. That Mia Strong was an island, a fortress.

But I needed Adam Drake. I needed him as much as I needed to breathe, eat or drink. And finally my brain allowed my heart to admit it.

"I need you so much," I repeated. "I love you."

He took my face between his hands, holding it still. He raised his head so he could look me in the eyes. "I can't promise that things will be perfect, Emilia. But I can promise you that I will never give this up. Because I don't think I knew how to live before you came into my life."

He pushed the hair back from my face but never took his eyes from mine. I sniffled, the tears still coming, and I shook in his hold. "I'd be lying if I said I wasn't so scared I could pee myself. But I'll never deny it again. I've loved you for longer than I even know. I fought the good fight but I can't fight anymore. I won't fight it. I love you, Adam."

And we kissed. And it was like that first time... that connection swelling between us, strengthening. In his embrace, I found comfort, closeness. And when the kiss grew more intense, presaged something more to come, I knew, too, that I was ready for that as well. Adam nudged us toward the bed and I went with him...and whether it was to make love or to just lie beside him while we talked all night, I knew that whatever happened, it would be all right. Because *this* was so right.

ABOUT THE AUTHOR

Brenna Aubrey is an author of New Adult contemporary romance stories that center on geek culture. She has always sought comfort in good books and the long, involved stories she weaves in her head.

Brenna is a city girl with a nature-lover's heart. She therefore finds herself out in green open spaces any chance she can get. A mommy to two little kids and teacher to many more older kids, she juggles schedules to find time to pursue her love of storycrafting.

She currently resides on the west coast with her husband, two children, two adorable golden retriever pups, two birds and some fish.

Printed in Great Britain
by Amazon.co.uk, Ltd.,
Marston Gate.